Nautical

Delights

By

S.L. Gape

2018

Nautical Delights © 2018 S.L. Gape
Triplicity Publishing, LLC

ISBN-13: 978-0999737033
ISBN-10: 0999737031

Printed in the United States of America

First Edition – 2018
Cover Design: Triplicity Publishing, LLC
Interior Design: Triplicity Publishing, LLC
Editor: Miranda Campbell - Triplicity Publishing, LLC

Acknowledgement

Thanks once again to all the team at Triplicity Publishing who have worked tirelessly once again, and helped me to achieve a number one bestseller in Worlds Apart. Here's hoping the additional work that Miranda has put it will get Nautical Delights to number one too. Thank you all.

I'd also like to thank Sarah and Lisa, for once again proofing for me; you're amazing, ladies, and I genuinely can't thank you both enough. Love you both.

Dedication

For everyone out there who loves a 'love story'. For those of you who don't, laters haters, this ain't for you ha!

My 'goatesses' - you humour me through procrastination, and make me LOL when I'm trying to 'adult' XOXO

Chapter One

"So, what do I call them? Is it Lord and Lady?"

"No, why the hell would it be?"

"I don't know. They *are* a Lord and Lady."

"Well that's just, 'up their own asses,' pretentiousness in itself!" the check in agent slammed.

"What then?" her colleague whispered, noticing the family head towards them. "They're coming back now," she snapped through clenched teeth, noticing her colleague bend her head down lower.

"*Why*? Why do you need to call them anything? Thank you, *sir*. Have a good day, *sir*. Here are your family's seats, *SIR*."

"Of *course*," she whispered. "Hi sir, all sorted now?" the check-in agent said with her very best 'please don't bark at me for *not* calling you your highness, or your lordship, or something.'

"Yes, I trust the seating is correct for all seven of us?" He eyed cautiously.

"Why of course, sir." She smiled through gritted teeth at the difficulty of the family.

*

"Madam, champagne, kir royale, or mimosa?"

Elizabeth looked up to the beautifully preened, and evidently gay air steward. "Hmm...."

"Darling, your father has ensured we have some Moët, so you may as well just have champagne. At least we know it's *semi* admissible," her mother insisted, throwing a darting glare to the young man.

"Champagne, please." Elizabeth gave in defeatedly with a small grimace at the manner at which her mother acknowledged people.

"Of course, madam." He addressed her with a sense of civility and despondency before offering a conventional, ever-faint sadness in his eyes that Lizzie had witnessed her entire life.

*

"We're going up to the bar, Libs. Are you joining us?"

"Hmm, no thank you. Just in the middle of some research." She smiled curtly to her siblings and their respective partners.

Elizabeth, or Lizzie, as she preferred, reminisced back to the summer's day in her teenage years where she'd started to feel a distance forming between her family, and chose to take control. Finding the strength, she decided to take ownership of her life and act. *She'd advise them that from that day forward she'd be referred to as Lizzie.* She recalled the day, striding confidently through the grounds, her confidence and strength growing insurmountable the closer she got to her parent's study. Not that it was really a study, it was more of an... an adults room. The place that Elizabeth, Vivian, and Annabella were never allowed. She recalled getting there, the fear as she knocked. The strength was all but lost at the prospect of demanding a family meeting to take her life back. Take control. *Her choice, her name, her life...* she thought, remembering the day she realized she wasn't anything like her family. *Nor did she wish to be.*

"Oh, do come, Libby. What are you going to do instead? We're on holiday; you need to relax at some point," Vivian said.

"I know, but we have a long journey and I don't want to dehydrate myself," she murmured, looking up and noticing eyes on her. "I will finish this last part and then join you," she said defeatedly.

"Don't work too hard, Libs; we're on holiday after all," Ollie called back to her, ushering his wife upstairs to the bar area of the aircraft.

"She's just like her father, aren't you sweetie?" her father said, placing his hand on her shoulder. "Nothing wrong with pushing yourself to get the best life for you and your family," he bellowed proudly.

Yes, a family I'll never have because I work so damn hard, she thought, watching her family disappear.

"Want another?" a whisper came from behind her, and Lizzie turned to see the crew attendant smiling softly.

"I'd love a coffee, if that's at all possible." She smiled.

"Of course," he said, taking the champagne flute from her table.

"Actually..." She grabbed his wrist before he could get it. "You should probably leave that." She smiled sadly. "I will... hmm, I'll have some more soon." She sighed, deciding not to tell him it'd be more difficult than it was worth, not having the evidence of Moët for her family to see.

"Yes, of course. I'll get your coffee ASAP for you." He smiled, rushing off out of sight.

Lizzie put down the medical journal, feeling a sense of relief at the information she'd retrieved. *She'd email her*

3

medical director when she landed to tender the information.
She grabbed her purse from her bag and pushed herself to
join her family on the upper level.

*

"Oh, you made it, darling. What would you like? Moet?"
her mother said, more as a statement than a
question. Elizabeth smiled slightly, and sat in the seat her
brother in law, Hugo offered her.

"Cute purse, very last season though," Annabella said to
her sister.

Lizzie smiled slightly, sipping the champagne the
attendant passed her, choosing to ignore the comment.
Lizzie almost always chose not to react to anything her
family said. She was different, always had been. Annabella
and Vivian didn't work. They were both like their parents—
very aristocratic—whereas, Lizzie was not. Her father's
career as a chief surgeon, then up to medical CEO, meant
that his first born would follow in his footsteps. Lizzie's
place at Oxford was guaranteed prior to her mother having
even reached her third trimester. Of course Lizzie was set
on her way for a career in medicine. Her father was on the
board, he contributed economically and now, despite no
longer practicing, he was still heavily invested in it. Unlike
her sisters, Lizzie was happy to work. She didn't have any
issue working hard and had zero interest in becoming a
socialite. Or a *kept* woman. Bella and Vivvi had grown up
with and like their mother. It was ever so cliché, but they
spent every weekend at the golf club—each woman
sporting the newest fashion trend—or in their New York
penthouse, rubbing shoulders with "anybody who was
anybody." Weeks were spent on yachts in St. Tropez and

Cannes, at annual film festivals, and of course, bi-annually, their sojourn to Milan. Fashion week was a necessity in vying for the notoriety the family name imparted upon them. Unlike Bella, Vivvi, and their mother, Lizzie spent her weekends studying to ensure that she was top of her class. That, the family name, and her father's status, which had afforded her place at Oxford, were never called into question.

Elizabeth was chosen specifically to attend a placement residency at Harvard and offered prime posts all over the world. It had nothing to do with letting the Barrington name down; it was the opportunity of deviating from her family with the least amount of bother from them. And it worked. She'd spent time in the states at school, as well as 18 months in Singapore as a medical trainer, and she was certain she would do it again.

Elizabeth didn't doubt that her family liked her, or even loved her. That had never been disputed, but her father felt no shame in highlighting the favoritism he gave to his eldest child. Much to her dismay, she knew it was solely based on her medical career. Her mother on the other hand, like her father, was born into money and ascendancy with no desire or intention to work. *Her* job, as with her sisters, was merely an aristocrat. It was to be *seen* at the established events and, well, not much else truth be known. Their nine bedroom home was managed with varying personnel and that allowed the women to concentrate on other things.

"Darling!" her mother snapped. "Please listen when I talk to you. It's ever so ungraceful when you don't."

"Sorry, Mother, I was just enjoying the Moët." She smiled widely, knowing her mother would not notice the sarcasm. "I managed to bring some pink Dom also." She smiled.

"Oh, wonderful. Hopefully, the flight hasn't impacted the fizz. Anyway, darling, I was just asking if you could attend fashion week this autumn? You really do need to come, it's such fun," she said expectantly.

Lizzie knew it was a while off yet, and couldn't deal with her mother's austere ways, certainly not at the beginning of a two week vacation. It was best while contained with the family that she just go along with it. "Mother, I told you. I've booked the time off, so unless anything untoward happens, I'll be there. It's been a while and—"

"—and you could most definitely use a little inspiration and... updating," Bella said simply, pointing her finger up and down Lizzie's body.

"Well, this is true," she responded softly, trying to defy her eyes which desperately wanted to check the outfit she'd specifically researched. Her low-cut Stella McCartney white jeans and off the shoulder silk Chloe vest were even featured in a magazine last week.

"Well, that's because our beautiful big sister here doesn't have the time to keep up to date with us fashionistas with all the work she does," Vivvi said, in what Elizabeth knew to be a compliment.

Elizabeth smiled slightly, knowing that Vivvi was trying to be diplomatic, but like the rest of her family, even a compliment, which was rarely given, was something you could call into question. Yes, she was the outcast in her family, and even at 34 years old that recognition was becoming more prominent with each family event. Had it not been for the fact that Lizzie, like Vivvi and Bella, had inherited her father's slim, tall frame, and green eyes, *and* their mother's dirty blonde hair, you might've assumed that she was switched at birth. Unfortunately, Bella, the youngest of the sisters—and to her absolute dismay—was virtually identical to Elizabeth. Many a time had the siblings been asked if they were twins, allowing Lizzie some satisfaction in her life.

Chapter Two

"Excuse me... excuse me!" Lizzie heard a shrill from behind her, refusing to look back at her mother. She had literally, only moments earlier, been thinking about how their flight to Miami was far less cumbersome than she'd anticipated. "Darling, when you pay over 100,000 pounds for a holiday, you do not need to pull your own cases," her mother said. Lizzie squirmed, knowing already that the look and acts of disgust on her mother's face would make her family the talk of the airport. And not in the way most of them had hoped.

Elizabeth upped her pace. Partially, so nobody could affix her to her family, and so she could escape the embarrassment. Her mother admonished people as though they were her personal "workers."

Lizzie stepped onto the air-conditioned bus, taking the ice-cold water from the straight faced dreadlocked man before her. She thanked him for his assistance as she maneuvered herself to the back. Wanting to put her ear buds in for the journey, she considered her options, knowing full well it would generate further affliction. Opting for the quiet life, she discreetly seated herself out of the way. The journey wouldn't be too long, and then the countdown until the two week holiday was over could commence!

*

Elizabeth removed herself from the bus, noticing the long, wooden walkway to their yacht—the private charter for their annual family holiday, and home for the upcoming two weeks. The situation wasn't new for her. Year after year, they "holiday-ed" on a private charter around the Caribbean and would ordinarily spend enough money on the charter that, if needed, it could house at least five individual families. Lizzie walked toward her luggage, but her mother's glare stopped her in her tracks. She turned to face the wooden walkway out to their yacht. A couple of men rushed past her and assisted the driver with the luggage as a tall, dark, salt and pepper haired man walked towards them. He was confident in his stride, clearly the crew manager of their yacht.

"Lord and Lady Barrington, welcome to Miami and your home for the next two weeks." He stopped, pointing to the 250-ft. luxury yacht. "It really is a pleasure to have you and your beautiful family aboard. I'm Jose Luis, and I'll be your crew manager for your vacation..."

Lizzie tuned out his words in favor of his strong, Latino accent. Eventually, Lizzie sloped off from Jose Luis's introductions and directed her attention to two, young men and a woman counting their cases. She wasn't sure why they counted the cases, but she continued to watch the men jump up and down like spoiled children, the dreadlocked driver hiding his head in his hands, and shaking it heavily. The only woman with them grinned, holding her hand out and taking money for what Lizzie could only assume was some form of bet.

"Elizabeth, would you please pay attention? I'm not spending two weeks with you drifting in and out of attention!" her mother snapped. Coming back to the here and now, Elizabeth stood up straight, following her family and Jose Luis toward the boat.

As they got closer, Lizzie could see some of the crew standing in a straight line, ready to welcome her family. The crew—in their trademark, pristine uniform of beige chino shorts and navy polo neatly tucked in, each sporting identical, tan boat shoes—were elegantly put together. It was a perfect pairing for the undeniable elegance and expense of the Iconica yacht before them.

Jose Luis said something in Spanish to his crew, and the young men gathered the luggage, moving aside to follow the family aboard. "We have a full team of 16 crew members serving you and your family. This is my second in command, Darcie," he said, pointing to the woman to his left.

Darcie must have been around Elizabeth's height. Maybe 5'9 or 5'10. Her honey blonde hair looked a little longer than shoulder length, but it was difficult to tell in the high ponytail she'd currently pulled it back into. She was deeply tanned, as the deck crew always were, and it left her hairline completely white with beautiful light shades, resembling highlights, throughout. Elizabeth looked down to Darcie's leg, cringing at the prospect of her mother's disapproval upon seeing the deep turquoise color artwork around Darcie's left ankle and calf. *She knew her mother would have some comment or other to make about the Rastafarian man and tattooed woman.* Lizzie noticed the sunglasses the woman wore were pointed towards her. She said something in Spanish to Jose Luis, and then left without a second glance. *She was Spanish, but she didn't look Spanish. What did Spanish look like?* she thought. *Dark... tall, dark, and handsome, like Jose Luis. Maybe he was her father.* Although, she hadn't seen her eyes *or* crow lines, if she had any; she'd been hiding them behind the glasses. Elizabeth thought she was likely around 30. She loved her Spanish accent; it sounded so beautiful. It literally fell from her lips like the most beautiful opera singer. *It was like the perfect music.*

"So, there is a... there is three master bedrooms, but all the rooms have en suite..." He paused, interrupted by Annabella.

"We will need the masters. Libby doesn't need a master as she has nobody to share with," she said harshly. Jose Luis looked back at the lone woman, giving her a slight smile and shoulder shrug to match.

"Okay then. Si, perfecto." These were the very few words she knew in Spanish. Why had she never learned this language? *It was beautiful, and pretty sexy.*

Jose Luis spoke in Spanish and Lizzie watched the young men scatter off with their cases. Jose Luis directed each of them to their rooms before being left solely with Elizabeth. "Last by no least." He smiled and unlocked the door for her. "Lady Barrington, I no say, but though this is not master, this is only room with private balconette." He smiled to her softly in his broken English.

"Thank you, Jose Luis," she said shyly. "And please, call me Libby," she added softly. "That's what all my family call me." She smiled.

"Of course, madam. You need anything, you call us on the telephone," he replied and left the room for her to get settled.

Chapter Three

Lizzie looked at the time, knowing she had to make a move, and felt rubbish at the façade she'd have to put on of the perfect family, the pretence of them over dinner each night. On the plus side, the sooner she got ready, the closer she was to another day down of vacation and ending this horrible nightmare. She looked at herself with complete uncertainty once again as she assessed her light grey linen pants and lemon Stella McCartney vest.

Making her way downstairs, she walked out to the pool and jacuzzi area, captivated by the breath-taking sunset. She was always taken aback by the beautiful scenes when she came on these holidays, hoping someday she could share it with someone special.

*

Lizzie was the last to arrive at the outdoor seating area. It was stunning. A 14-seater marble table on the outer deck with LED lights surrounding it. The view was picturesque. A simple black backdrop with the most incredible white moon and the faintest palm tree shadows in the distance.

"Darling, we've been waiting for you," her mother said disparagingly.

"Sorry, Mother." It was all she could muster up as she distantly regarded the beautiful scene that no one else appeared to notice.

*

Darcie noticed the beautiful woman the moment they arrived. Her exceptional "togetherness," her long legs, the beautiful, long, golden locks perfectly assembled in slight waves, like she'd spent a million dollars having it styled. What she hadn't reckoned was that someone could look so sad. She saw her look of disgust after noticing her tattoo earlier, knowing full well that she questioned how and why a company like hers would allow not only a crew member, but a deputy, with full visible art.

Darcie had met women like Libby before. *Like her? Sheesh, even like her sisters and mother. They loved a bit of "rough stuff."* To them, Darcie was the typical low-class lesbian that they all wanted to have a little "experiment" with. Not that the one she assumed to be the youngest daughter of the Barrington family had showed such interest. In fact, she was disgusted with the artwork on her leg earlier today, but she could easily see... *Hmm, what was her name again? Arabella? No, Annabella.* She could see from the way Annabella eyed her that she would totally be up for it.

Darcie had done the job for 10 years now; she knew when someone was interested. She spent all day, every day, and all week, every week with beautiful and perfectly preened millionaires. They flirted in and out and offered the world, unaware of her own financial circumstances. Immediately, she noticed that at the first moment Lady Annabella Barrington's husband was out of the way, she'd be all over Darcie like a fly to poop!

*

13

"Darling, is the food not acceptable?" her mother inquired, noticing the immediate attention of the staff around them, which left Lizzie feeling incredibly embarrassed and awkward.

"Yes, Mother, I just feel.... I just feel somewhat sickly after the flight today," she said glumly, pushing her food around the plate. They had lobster thermidor, not unusual for the first night's dinner. Elegant, upper class, and more importantly, *statement making.*

"Well, it could be jet lag," her father stepped in. "Maybe you should go to bed and start afresh tomorrow?"

"Darling, she's barely spent any time with the family," her mother put to him.

"Yes, dear, I know. But it's no good if she is too tired. She may as well get an early night this evening and then she will be on form for the remainder of the two weeks," he said.

"Mother, Father," she addressed. "I'm fine, I'll be perfectly well—"

"No, your father's correct, you need to go to bed now, and you'll feel significantly improved tomorrow," she confirmed, returning to her meal.

Lizzie knew not to try and question the decision her parents made, and instead opted to do as she'd been told and go to bed. *As a plus, it was one day of this dastardly holiday out of the way.* She stood from her place at the table. "Yes, of course, good night. I shall see you all in the morning." She smiled slightly, feeling the glare of the Rasta man, Jose Luis, and the blonde woman, all of whom hurriedly busied themselves after she caught their eyes.

*

Darcie had never before experienced anything like this evening. *The woman must've been around 28, 29. Being told to go to bed at 8 pm? Sheesh, this was gonna be a long ass two weeks.* The woman had barely touched her food, literally just moving it about on the dish, but that didn't mean she should've been sent to bed hungry. She couldn't seem to get the scenario out of her mind.

*

Elizabeth felt mortified the crew had witnessed that debacle. More so, that the beautiful blonde had seen it. *Jesus, 34 years old and being sent to bed with no dinner?* She felt disgraced. Lizzie got up and locked the door to her room. She removed the hidden case under her bed and checked the door before opening it slightly. She rummaged around within it and pulled out a galaxy ripple chocolate bar and a pack of cheese and onion crisps. She quickly locked it, hid it back under the bed, and made her way over to the balcony. *God, she could murder a Costa right now.* She opened the door and immediately felt humidity and sea air hit her. She was tremendously impressed with the balcony, which she'd only just found time to investigate thus far. It was large, slightly rounded with the curve of the boat, and housed a rattan sun lounger and a table with two chairs over at the far end. She moved toward the table and chairs and sat down, taking in the cool sea air. Lizzie opened the chocolate bar, hearing the grumbles of her tummy as she stood and took in the surroundings. The boat was beautifully lit and she could hear the laughter of her family from the open plan dining area at the back of the boat. There were spotlights all the way around the base of the boat which beautifully illuminated it, giving prominence to the specifically highlighted individual turquoise waters hidden by the mysteriously dark waters. Lizzie happily sighed, taking another bite of her bar. She noticed the room to her right, and more importantly, the woman and man who sat looking up at her. It must have been a crew room of some form as she'd recognized Jose Luis and the blonde. *What was her name again? It was unusually elegant,* she thought, trying to recall the name tag. Darcie, that was it. *Spanish Darcie.* Who'd just seen her eating a chocolate bar. A 34-year-old woman being sent to bed without dinner and eating a chocolate bar instead. She felt humiliated once more. Elizabeth threw the crisps onto the side table as she switched off the balcony light and returned to her room, no longer feeling it necessary to enjoy the tranquillity of her private balcony.

Chapter Four

Lizzie turned, wondering if that was a light knock she'd heard at the door. It was so faint, she questioned if she'd heard it at all. She listened quietly at the door, hearing no sounds at all. Carefully unlocking it, she pulled it ajar ever so slightly, and noticed a silver platter tray on the floor. She checked the area and didn't see anybody around. Taking the tray back inside, she lifted the lid, and saw a freshly made ham and cheese baguette, coffee with milk, a bottle of sparkling water, and a note. *A note?* She opened the paper.

Something more substantial than candy.

She re-read the words again. *Candy? Her family would never use that terminology. More importantly, her family wouldn't give her a second thought.* They were all far too self-obsessed to think of anyone but themselves.

She stopped, stroking the note softly. *Was it Darcie? She saw her eating her ripple. Could it have been her?* She smiled inwardly. "Don't be so ridiculous," she said aloud. The woman was Spanish, well, Latino of some form. She could be Mexican, Argentinian, Puerto Rican, Portuguese— any number of things. God, she wished she knew how to speak Spanish. "Stop it." She grimaced at the thoughts in her head. She was acting like a child. *Of course it hadn't been her and if it was her, it wouldn't have been of her own accord. It was likely Jose Luis, who'd also seen her, and probably asked one of the young men to do it.*

Though just a tiny part of her would hold onto the fact that it was Darcie. It was stupid, and she of course knew fine well it was, but truth be known, this was how she got through her family holidays. Had for years. Someone within the staff would catch her eye and with that, she'd spend her time fantasizing. *No—that was a bit weird—daydreaming that something could develop.* Not necessarily romantically. Okay, well, quite often it would be romantically, but most certainly on a friendship level. Someone who could whisk her away from the nightmare that she was confined to each year.

Nothing ever happened, obviously. These people were light years away from her family, and when your family constantly illustrates that, making it all the clearer that everyone else is classes below, it's hardly surprising that they avoid her at all costs. Albeit, that wasn't strictly true. Over the years, she'd seen looks between staff and Annabella. There was one year she was convinced that she'd seen a look between a woman and her, but she talked herself out of it. Obviously, there was no way it was true. But ultimately, year after year, this was how she got through the annual family holiday, and this year would be no different.

Chapter Five

Lizzie checked her phone, trying to adjust her eyes as she slowly came around. 5:40 am. The time difference usually played havoc the first few days. For her though, this was her favorite time. Family breakfast was at eight am, which meant that before her family got up, she could spend some time alone.

She took a quick shower and got into her Chloe bikini, which was also no doubt, so "last season." If it was up to her, she'd happily just wear one from Next, but god forbid she arrived without having gone to Harrods for the latest designer beachwear. She grabbed her phone and wrapped the sarong around herself as she made her way down to the lobby.

*

Lizzie found a coffee machine and switched it on as she went outside and opened up one of the towels. She placed it over a sun lounger by the pool and appreciated dawn. It wasn't fully light yet, but the yacht softly swayed, and she pulled the chair in the direction of the sun slowly starting to peek through.

She made her way back into the kitchen, surprised to see Jose Luis at the coffee maker filling the cup and the room with the strong aroma. "Oh, good morning. I hope I didn't wake you," she said, concerned for the gentleman before her.

"Not of course. How you take it?" Jose Luis asked.

"It's fine, I can do it," she offered.

"No, it's fine. Cream and sugar?" he said in his deep Spanish accent.

"Erm, just milk please." She sighed, turning to see the 'Rasta man' and Darcie. She picked up a medical journal and gripped it tightly to her chest.

"You sleep okay?" Jose Luis asked, handing her the coffee.

Smiling, she thanked him, taking a sip before responding. "Mmm, lovely. Yes, very well, how about yourself?" She noticed each of the employees faces stop and turn toward her with a look of surprise.

"Yes... very well. Thank you."

"Great. I... um, is it quite alright that I go watch the sunrise? If I'm in the way, I can go to my room? This is the time I usually enjoy some quiet and have a snorkel before the family awakes," she said softly.

"That's fine, mon," the Rasta man said. "I, Deacon, but you can call me Deek. And if ya want some company on that snorkeling, you just holla. That's no problem."

Elizabeth wondered if her mother had spoken to Deacon yet. She could only imagine the look of disgust as he was not the typically well-spoken staff they were used to. She liked him though. *He was fun.* She wondered if the daydreams may pan out to something more this year. "Thanks, Deek. I'm Elizabeth, but you can call me Liz..." She stopped. "Libby. I'll be just out here," she said, pointing to her towel. "Thanks again, Jose Luis." She held the coffee cup up and nodded as she turned on her heel and passed Darcie, noticing the slight nod returned. Jose Luis said something to the others in Spanish, which she'd hoped wasn't about her, before hearing the female voice say "claro." Again, it sounded as beautiful as a song from her lips. She needed to find out the meaning, making a mental note to at least learn some basic Spanish pleasantries at some point today.

*

Lizzie spent the past 40 minutes silently watching the sun rise on the ocean. There hadn't been a cloud in sight, and she was disappointed that she'd left her camera in her room and had to utilize her iPhone instead. She considered returning for it in case she didn't get another sunrise as good, but didn't want to run the risk of waking up the family. She wanted to appreciate it alone. It was just after 6:30, and she knew she wouldn't have long before everyone was up and about.

"You want some more coffee?" Jose Luis asked. The staff looked up from their papers when she walked back in.

"No, I'm good, thanks. I was just wondering if I could possibly get some snorkel equipment?" she asked politely.

"Sure, girl. I'll get it. What fin size you want?" Deek said in his strong Jamaican accent. He was a lovely looking man. His plaits were just past his shoulder, pulled back into a hairband with one sole plait braided in green, yellow, and black threads. Colors she knew to be the Jamaican flag. With a chiseled jaw line, and a beautiful smile, he must've been around his mid to late 20's.

She smiled, realizing she was ignoring him and just staring. "Um, I'm sorry, a seven please." She made her way back to her towel where her phone and book were. She removed the kimono and stood with her hands on her hips, taking in the sight of the Caribbean before her. She sighed, allowing comfort to flow through her veins.

*

"That's some smooth body, girl." Deek laughed into Darcie's ear.

"Shut up, man." She nudged him, embarrassed he'd caught her watching one of the Barrington women remove the cover up as she took in her toned body. Her attire hadn't allowed visibility to see her definition other than being slender, but the girl was perfectly trim and tall. She could imagine the lack of proteins, fats, and sugars in her diet and assumed she predominantly opted for lettuce leaves. *But she'd seen Elizabeth eating candy last night after her parents had all but sent her to bed.*

"Shame she's more into you then, huh, buddy?" She smirked at her young Jamaican friend.

"S'ok, Darcie. It's definitely the other sister that's got eyes for you." He winked and jogged on over to the leggy blonde in a simple black suit with only one shoulder to it. Lizzie's highlighted, perfect waves gently swayed in the early morning breeze. Darcie watched on amusedly at the sight of Deek as he worked his magic, and watched the woman's smile grow. She touched his arm thoughtfully, *maybe seductively*, she thought, and turned away from her colleague and his potential new conquest.

*

Lizzie had been snorkeling in the reefs, surrounding the boat for what felt like 10 minutes. Her watch told her it'd been 45. She desperately wanted to stay here, but knew that her family would be getting up any minute. She needed to get ready for breakfast and the day ahead.

"Good spotting?" said a familiar Jamaican twang as she walked back inside, drying off her hair.

"Sure was." She gleamed, looking over at Darcie watching her. *God she'd love to see what was behind those glasses.* She noticed the woman's lips open, as if she was about to say something. A clicking sound came from above, notifying that her family was on their way down. Lizzie looked at them in despair, and darted off, leaving nothing but remnants of water behind her as they all stood in confusion.

*

Lizzie got back into her room before any of her family saw her. It wasn't that she wasn't allowed to be there without them. It's just that if they knew each morning of her holiday was spent happy and without burden—her pre-family breakfast—they would try to get involved. Perhaps make breakfast earlier, which essentially meant spending more time together. She was disappointed that she didn't get to hear Darcie's voice once more. She wondered what her voice sounded like in broken English. Jose Luis' was beautiful, so she could only imagine that the beautiful Spanish lady's voice was far greater. She shook herself from the thoughts as she jumped into the shower and got herself ready for the day. She lay out the wet swimsuit on the sun lounger on her balcony, and quickly redressed in a cream suit this time.

Chapter Six

"Ah, at last!" Vivvi spoke loudly. "We thought you may have fallen into a deep coma."

"Vivvi, it's one minute past. Hardly late, is it? Clearly, I needed it. Or maybe the wonderful dreams." She mused, looking at her family all watching her. *Jesus, how the hell had she ended up in this family? Which DNA had gotten switched along the way?*

"Darling, do sit up straight. Are you hungry? You didn't really eat last night," her mother stated. "Mind, the calories from the nuts will have kept you full, I'm sure."

Lizzie kept her head down, and accepted the coffee from Deek, who leaned over her and placed it down, giving a gentle squeeze to her shoulder as he did. Lizzie looked around the table, wondering if anybody had noticed, and smiled slightly at him.

"So, Daddy, what's the plan for today?" Vivian smiled widely.

"I do believe we shall shortly make our way out to the Caribbean." He smiled. "While Key West is pretty, I've never been a fan, so we shall head out to the more prestigious places." He nodded and returned to his breakfast, leaving Lizzie once more feeling sunken and subdued at the crassness of her family.

*

"Nice suit, Libby," Bella said with a peer over her glasses.

God, she was showing off in front of the crew. Lizzie rolled her eyes, lying back down. "Thanks Bella, it was 90% off at Harrods." She giggled and lifted her magazine again, discreetly eyeing her sister's disgust.

"Darling, I do wish you wouldn't ridicule your sister. It isn't funny making jokes such of that aloud," their mother scolded Elizabeth. "You do not realize you bring the family's name into disrepute with such vile comments."

Lizzie refrained from the comment she wanted to make about their surroundings, the lack of their golf club cronies being able to hear the comments.

"Well, I for one, didn't take to the discount section. Mother, this was an exceptional choice, don't you think?" Bella said, sporting the smallest possible amount of material that barely covered her. The suit was hot pink, an open V trailing all the way down to her belly button with cut out sides and thin crosses. Completely inappropriate to wear around anybody other than her husband, least of whom her parents.

"Certainly, darling. Having the time to spend as much as you do in the gym is very deserving for such a piece." She smiled.

Was that a dig at herself? Lizzie thought as she slowly looked to her mother. She worked exceptionally hard both at work and in her spare time to have the body she did, and in her opinion, it wasn't too bad. Granted, she was 34 now, so maybe not as young and firm as her younger sister Bella. Lizzie eyed her mother suspiciously, and noticed Darcie's glasses looking towards her. *Sheesh, why couldn't she take those blasted glasses off, so she could see where she was looking?* She suddenly saw Bella make a bee line for the beautiful, Spanish blonde.

"Hi, would you join me in a photo?" Bella smiled widely. *A smile that would melt most hearts,* Lizzie thought. She couldn't hear the conversation between the two women, but she could see that Darcie stood facing the camera. Bella turned into her side and pushed her barely covered breast against the other woman's. Lizzie sighed quietly, once more deflated by the situation. She turned over on her sun lounger and leaned forward to continue reading her magazine and ignore the situation that surrounded her.

*

"What do you mean you're feeling poorly, darling? You simply must come to dinner. It's Nobu in the Atlantis!" her mother said stunned.

"I know Mummy, but I really do think I've had too much sun. That, and the pink Dom have made me feel incredibly queasy. Plus, Daddy said we are here for a couple of days."

"If you're absolutely sure, darling?"

"Yes, Mummy," Bella said angelically.

*

Lizzie was tired and unbelievably unimpressed with the evening's events. *On a scale of 1 to 10 it was a very clear 11 of shitness.* The biggest sadness of all was that at 34 years old, she still didn't have a single friend that she could call upon.

"How's the food, darling?" her mother asked simply. Lizzie looked up, disappointed that she now needed to engage in communication with her mother and respond.

"Extraordinary, Mother. And yours? Father, how about yours?" she asked courteously.

"Exceptional, darling. See and they say money can't buy you happiness." He smiled widely, dabbing his mouth with the napkin provided.

Lizzie smiled softly and continued moving the salmon around her plate as discreetly as she could.

"Please, Libby Lou? Come on, you work so hard. A night in a club in the best hotel in the world will of course make you feel better," Vivvi said pleadingly.

"Go on, darling. You need some release, doing the job we do," her father added.

She had absolutely no desire or inclination to do this, but the alternative was having to listen to everyone go on and on if she didn't. *At least this way, maybe a few more bottles of Dom would mean she could forget about the day's events and mark another day off the calendar,* she thought positively.

*

"You okay?" Oliver asked.

"Yes, fine, why?"

"Libby, I know you're not a fan of mine, but I have been part of your sister's and family's life for an incredibly long time. I can see when you aren't yourself," he said simply.

Lizzie was stunned. How did you respond to that? She had possibly exchanged 10 sentences with Oliver in the eight years that he and Annabella had been together and married. "Of course, silly. I'm just so very tired," she said, knowing her brother-in-law was as self-obsessed as the rest of the family, and would accept what she said.

Oliver smiled softly to her. "Come on, how about I take you home and leave Vivvi and Hugo to it? I should probably check on my wife," he asked quietly.

Lizzie smiled to him and squeezed his forearm. "I'd love that," she said, before getting another bottle of Dom for her sister and brother-in-law. "Come on." She smiled to Ollie as they left the club.

"So, are you going to tell me what's really going on?" he asked, clearly intoxicated.

"I have no idea what you mean," she stated factually.

"Of course not," he mumbled, returning to the view out of the window.

*

Having made their way to bed, Lizzie quickly showered and got into her oversized Harvard t-shirt. It was her comfort clothing, reminding her of happier times. *Some of the best times of her life, in fact.* She pulled the silk bedding over her, paying attention to the moon that illuminated her cabin, and slowly awaited sleep to take her.

Lizzie tried desperately to think of something happy to help relax her enough for sleep to take over. It was already after four a.m. and she still couldn't sleep. Each time her eyes closed, she saw her sister. Her *straight, married* sister breast to breast with Darcie. Beautiful, Spanish Darcie, who she'd spotted from the moment they arrived. Darcie, who seemed to be making bets with the rest of the crew, about her family. *Were they betting on who would sleep with one of the Barrington's? Why was she doing this to herself?* Annabella was gorgeous, young, and confident. Why would one of these people not jump at the chance to sleep with a beautiful woman? No less, a beautiful, half-naked woman, who'd *pretended* to be sick to stay in and flirt with the most beautiful woman on the planet.

Lizzie, sad, dishevelled, and beaten, sighed. *How could she ever compete? She had one day down, one of which would probably be her favorite day of the entire year.* She allowed the day to ease her mind and eventually fell asleep.

*

Lizzie woke a mere two and a half hours later. She probably wasn't far off an ordinary night of sleep at home. She debated going downstairs, or waiting until family breakfast, but decided on the former. She decided to make the most of her time. This was her vacation too, and she lived for the mornings out here.

She walked over to the coffee machine and switched it on, turning swiftly upon hearing the footsteps behind her.

"I need to give you a job with me, you keep coming and doing coffee before me, no?" Jose Luis smiled softly as he acknowledged her.

"If only," she said sadly, and walked off to the same spot she'd taken yesterday. The clouds were more prominent today, and the sunrise far less distinguishable than yesterday's, but in normal fashion, it was quiet, calm, and perfect for her. Lizzie enjoyed the time alone, peacefully processing her life. She felt dejected after yesterday, and needed to forget about it as quickly as possible. As typical, the sunrise was nowhere near as good now that she had her camera with her, but it was still there, and still beautiful. It was magnetizing all the same.

Lizzie had always felt far less superior to her sisters. No, to *every* other woman, in fact, though she didn't believe she was all bad. Ignoring her insecurities, she built up the confidence and removed her kimono before walking back inside to the coffee. She semi confidently walked up to where Jose Luis, Deek, and Darcie were, bravely asking if she could pinch some more snorkeling equipment, and suddenly felt a little less confident than she'd hoped.

"Girrllll... Dang, you looking good," Deek whistled, playfully bumping her hip.

"Erm, thanks," she said shyly, making her way back outside, leaving them without the opportunity to respond. She put the snorkeling equipment on, and made her way into the water for her second day of snorkeling in the Bahamas. This was one of her favorite places to snorkel; here, and St Bart's. The boat would go to various snorkelling places today for the whole family, but right now she just wanted to forget about yesterday, and enjoy some time alone with the ocean. *Her favorite place.*

The water was perfect. At seven am, she could already feel the heat beating down on her back, and the sea life was incredible. She loved the moment, forgetting about everything that surrounded her, all the negativity. Checking the time on her camera, she felt a distaste rise in her mouth, and realized she needed to leave.

Making her way back on the boat, she quickly showered the salt water off and walked back over to a lone Darcie. "Thank you," she replied curtly, putting the equipment down in front of her.

Chapter Seven

Lizzie sat at the table suddenly very hungry, thankful when Jose Luis placed a cup of coffee down in front of her. "Thank you," she said quietly, grabbing a croissant.

"You are aware of how many calories are in those aren't you, Libby?"

"Yes, it just means I'll have to work harder at the gym when I return," she responded without thinking. She never spoke back to her mother. Annabella always had, but as the baby of the family, she never could do anything wrong. "What is the matter, darling?" her mother spoke with an edge to her voice.

Lizzie luckily hadn't gotten a chance to answer as Bella and Ollie walked into the room. "*Good morning all!*" Bella announced, loud and happy, which meant she was clearly feeling better today.

"Oh, darling, glad to see you are feeling better. I was worried," her mother said graciously as she gently touched her arm.

"Thank you, Mother. Clearly, an early night was all that was required," she said, throwing a smirk to the gorgeous Darcie, making Lizzie feel sick to her stomach.

"Miraculous recovery it seems. What exactly were the symptoms, Annabella? You have two of the best medical practitioners in the U.K. at the table." She tried her best to hide her snark behind the question she posed.

"Yes, but you and Father are surgeons, sweetie. Isn't that what you always tell us, Daddy?" she questioned; and in true Bella style had managed to nicely avoid Lizzie's question.

"Correct, darling. Anybody can be a doctor, but to be a truly great surgeon like Elizabeth and I is far more formidable." He nodded directly to his eldest daughter who was thankful of the distraction of her phone starting to vibrate.

"No phones at the table," her mother said distastefully.

"Father, it's work," she confirmed.

"You may be excused, Elizabeth," he said, overruling his wife, and favoring the work he and his daughter undertook.

*

Lizzie tried to stay on the phone for as long as she could, until her manager became acutely aware of her desire to continuously redirect the line of questioning in a bid to extend the call. His parting words: "Go have fun, you're on holiday." He was completely unaware that she would rather resit her medical exams than be here right now.

She sighed heavily before returning to her family. On the plus side, at least he was happy with her recommendations for the research she'd done on the flight over.

"Everything okay, Elizabeth?" her father questioned.

"Yes, Father. I sent a few emails following some research I've been considering. It was regarding that. It's looking positive, so we'll discuss it when I return home."

Her father was just about to speak when Annabella stepped in. "Ohhh, Doctor Barrington saves the day once again." She giggled, knowing the sarcasm was lost on her family.

"Well, some of us need to work, darling. And we'll make a difference." She quipped back, equally hiding the intended sarcasm.

Bella turned to face her sister with venom before gracefully smiling at her parents. "Sweetie, you're hardly saving the world. If you weren't doing it somebody else would be." She smiled. "Right, who's up for jet ski's!?" she sang, before Lizzie or anyone else had the opportunity to respond.

Her family removed themselves from the table without any acknowledgement of their breakfast to the staff while Lizzie quietly began clearing up after herself. "Thank you ever so much for the breakfast, guys," she said somberly.

"You're more than welcome," Jose Luis said in his strong Spanish accent, looking at the sadness in the young woman's eyes. "Oh, and miss Libby?"

"Yes?" she inquired thoughtfully.

"I think you make a very big distance." He smiled politely.

"Excuse me?"

"*Difference*, you mean, mon. And me too, girl." Deek laughed and playfully punched his boss.

"Sorry, I mean difference. You make a difference." He rolled his eyes and Lizzie noticed the laughter from Darcie. *She had a beautiful smile, and laugh. No! Stop those thoughts,* she admonished herself.

"Thank you." Lizzie smiled slightly and made her way back outside.

*

Darcie couldn't work out the dynamics of this family. Sure, the guests always came and treated them like crap.

They were rude, and obnoxious. *But this girl was different; she didn't act like her family, nor like any other family.*

The constant sadness in her eyes was harrowing, and who could blame her with the way her family spoke to her. Especially Annabella. Having family members throw themselves at the crew was not unusual. Whether it be her, Deek, Jose Luis, or any of the crew. Nor was it unusual for a straight woman to throw herself at Darcie. While she didn't feel she gave off any signs of being gay, they seemed drawn to her for whatever reason, and this time was no different. She'd noticed Annabella eyeing her seductively when they arrived. When she gave her a winning smirk, she knew Bella was out on a mission. She'd flirted with her all day yesterday with little innuendos every time Darcie was alone. And then of course, she used the age old, "I'm too sick to come out this evening." It wasn't new to her, or the crew. They'd even gone out on the island to allow Darcie some alone time. Some folk thought it was a bit trashy, and maybe it was, especially knowing Bella was a married woman, but that wasn't her issue. *If chicks wanna have some fun, then why the hell not?* She buried the edge of guilt she felt.

*

The best thing about being moored was that her family couldn't force them to do stuff together. She could enjoy snorkeling around the stunning Bahamas with the sun heating up her neck and shoulders as she pretended that she was on holiday alone. The fulfillment from a day snorkeling around some of the most stunning coral reefs in the Bahamas really did make it bearable. She got out of the water, already feeling the premature sting of the evening's shower from too much sun. She animatedly reached into her bag, ecstatically happy from her finds, and tried her best to run the lotion wherever she could reach. She looked around disappointedly, noticing Hugo, Vivvi, Ollie, and Bella on the jet skis and her parents out on a pedalo. She was a surgeon, so of course she was never going to run the risk of skin cancer, but she was desperately eager to jump back in.

"You need a hand?" Deacon appeared from nowhere and nodded towards the sun cream she tried mercilessly to extend to her back.

"Erm... " she pondered uncertainly, feeling it somewhat intrusive, and noticed a smirking Darcie behind him. "Would you mind, awfully?"

Deacon made a clicky sound with his lips and tutted. "Girl, why would I mind rubbing sunscreen into a beautiful woman?"

"Well, I wouldn't go quite that far, but thank you." She turned around and handed him the bottle.

"Well, I'll be damned," Lizzie heard, immediately freezing in her spot from the gentle squeeze of Deek. "Well, well, Mother and Father will be thrilled that after 20 years you've turned to the opposite sex." Bella smiled, her already tanned arm holding onto the step ladder she climbed. She smirked, lifting her sunglasses to eye her sister and the Jamaican man.

"Grow up, Bella!" Lizzie shouted, rushing to the back of the boat and hurriedly diving back into the ocean. She quickly dismissed the thoughts, that the crew might now be talking about her, to the back of her mind.

*

"Nice *snorkel*," Deek said to Lizzie as she got back on the boat, 25 minutes after her parents had warned her that she must not be late for dinner. She enjoyed the thrill of the ocean in solitude, and knew when she finally got back on the boat—having left it long enough—they'd have all gone back to their rooms to get ready.

"Exceptional." She smiled widely to Deek, thankful he hadn't distanced himself now that he knew he wouldn't get anywhere with her.

"Glad to hear it. You need a little drink?" He laughed, holding up the rum and nodding towards Jose Luis and Darcie sitting quietly at the table. Suddenly, Jose Luis's demeanor changed and he instantly sat up, unsure of the direction Deek's question would go.

"Rum? You mean to say, you need to drink to put up with my family and I?" Lizzie raised an eyebrow, looking at the faces before her. Well, I sure as hell do. It best be Appleton." She winked and checked her silver Cartier watch embedded with diamonds. It wasn't her thing really, but as her 30th birthday gift from her parents a few years ago, she ensured it was suitably 'en wrist' when in their presence. "God, that's good. Look, I apologize for my sister's words earlier. I hope she didn't embarrass you. If it's any consolation, she would've only been looking to embarrass myself," she confirmed sadly.

"What happened earlier?" Jose Luis asked seriously, now half standing as Darcie placed a hand on his forearm and pushed him back down again.

"Nada Jefe," Deek advised in his Jamaican Spanish, and smiled to her softly. "Don't you worry, girl. I got yo back." He winked and poured another small amount in her teacup.

"Is this the norm?" she asked, confused at the drinking utensil.

"Aye, only when we tryin a be discreet mon." He laughed.

Lizzie noticed the manager sit up straight again. *Was he confused and uncertain on how to manage the situation before him? She liked it. She liked him. Them. Well, maybe not Darcie, the hoe,* she thought, chastising herself for thinking that way.

"Great, I'll ensure each afternoon when I return that I ask for a tea instead of champagne," she said, laughing. "Thanks, guys." She walked off before turning back to them. "Oh, and Deek, for the record, my sister normally wants *everything* I have, so you may be in luck. You may climb that scoreboard after all." She finished the rum, leaving all three of them open mouthed.

"Well, it's a decent job. I got taste then, huh? And I'd rather be friends with the lesbian," he said, saluting her and laughing while his superiors still sat open mouthed.

*

Lizzie lay on her bed, smiling up to the ceiling as she recollected the past hour. Bella, in usual style, tried to belittle her, "out" her, and… well, was just plain awful, really. But it backfired. She'd stepped up and the guys had been... nice. *Normal.*

It may not have been the daydream she'd hoped for. There may not have been romance or anything, but Deek and Jose Luis were great. Even the deputy captain was starting to relax a little around her. It was going to be a fun time. She could just feel it in her bones.

*

Lizzie got up early and was in her swim suit at super speed. She'd spent some time on the balcony this morning, and the ocean looked incredibly still. Better still, they were maybe only a kilometer away from land. She quietly made her way up to the main deck, and grinned as she saw Jose Luis holding her a steaming cup of coffee alongside Deek and Darcie. "Wow, service with a smile or what!" she smiled blowing and sipping a little.

"That tan coming on just fine, Doctor B." Deek finally smiled and whistled a low, long tune.

"Why, thank you. Courtesy of course, to the beautiful Bahamas." She winked.

"Yeah, mon. One day you gotta let us come out and play wit you."

"Free ocean, buddy. It's a free ocean. I'm on countdown." She winked and set her coffee on the side. Rushing to the back of the boat, Lizzie splashed loudly into the water in what her mother would only deem as disgraceful and unladylike.

*

Lizzie spent what felt like a lifetime, living free, and exploring the ocean. Knowing she'd have to go inside soon, she explored further, ignoring the requirement to live the "Barrington life" and deal with her family's admonishment. She felt a nudge to her left shoulder, and turned around rapidly, feeling the mouth piece release as her mouth filled with sea water. The next thing Lizzie remembered was what she could only assume drowning might feel like. She was dying, and the world was sending her Darcie angels. *Wow, Darcie angels had the most stunningly blue, turquoise eyes.* Her head suddenly rose above water as tight arms wrapped around her. Lizzie choked on the water she'd swallowed, spitting it back out into the beautiful, blue eyes, and coughed. She was still holding on tightly to Darcie, her legs wrapped around her waist, her arms around her neck. They were millimeters from each other. Darcie saved her and now she was in her arms, unable to pull away from those eyes. *The color, they were... perfect. Beyond perfect.* They were quite literally as turquoise as the water they bobbed up and down in.

Darcie shifted her arm a little, looking flushed as the realization hit them both. In a bid to prevent her from drowning, Lizzie's strong legs wrapped firmly around Darcie's waist, and Darcie's arm locked securely around her, her hand placed on Lizzie's bottom. Darcie quickly blushed, and pointed at her watch before taking a little *too* long to remove her hand from the other woman's firm ass. Lizzie checked the time. "*Shit!*" she shouted, jumping out of Darcie's arms. She grabbed the snorkel gear she'd lost in her fright, and hurriedly swam back to the boat before her family caught her.

Darcie watched the woman rush off, still reliving the beautiful feeling of Libby's firm butt against her hand, and her legs wrapped tightly around her waist. *God she'd felt good,* she thought. *She couldn't believe she'd wasted time on her sister when she could have had the beautiful, and apparently gay, Libby.*

Chapter Eight

The day had been long since leaving the Bahamas and traveling to their next destination. Unfortunately, that meant Lizzie spent the entirety of it in her family's presence, leaving her agitated and short tempered. The only thing that kept her going was the recollection of earlier that morning when she finally caught sight of Darcie's eyes. They were far prettier than anything she'd ever seen. Her hand had rested on her bottom, and now she considered if Darcie grazed over her cheek. In all the commotion, she couldn't be sure, or whether it was a little bit of wishful thinking. The thoughts were bittersweet. On the one hand, she didn't want to relive this beautiful memory with this beautiful woman who had seemingly slept with her sister, her *straight* and married sister no less. But it afforded her a far less stressful day having something nice to focus on. Either way, tomorrow would be a fabulous day. She only had the night to get through, which would of course be all about executing the histrionics. Conducive to her plans, Lizzie smiled a little as she considered having some fun with Darcie *and* her sister. She pulled out one of her favorite Burberry dresses—a metallic sequin, light-material dress. It hung low on the shoulder with an oversized neckline, which meant that it allowed a great deal of visibility of her back and one bare shoulder. The asymmetrical base revealed much of her now tanned thighs. She checked her reflection in the mirror, smiling as she felt the faint increase in confidence. She looked good, she couldn't deny that. She'd lightly curled her hair, so there was a gentle wave to the long, honey blonde locks. Streaks of sun-kissed blonde snuck in, and her glowing, golden brown skin was prominent. The outfit would've been paired with heels if she were at home, or of course, if it was Vivvi or Bella, but she didn't want to overdo it. It was simply met with her black Louboutin gladiator sandals.

Lizzie confidently made her way to the dining area at the front of the yacht. It was perfectly lit by candles and the moonlight, brazenly glowing in all its glory. She lightly strode towards her family, who she could already hear whining about something as she passed her three favorite crew members. Lizzie immediately noticed Darcie's jaw drop, her eyes examining her as she walked past. She felt a sudden boost of confidence. *Mission accomplished.* She curled her smile as she acknowledged a flustered looking Darcie, before quickly turning to busy herself. Lizzie hadn't seen Darcie without her sunglasses before the incident this morning, but this evening, those beautiful eyes were on full show. *Had she noticed how taken Lizzie had been when she was face to face with her? Is that why she wasn't wearing them? Was she trying to play her at her own game?* She was brought around by a low whistle from Deek. "Damn girl, who you are trying impress?" he whispered.

"Nobody. I just thought I would try to make myself feel a little better," she said, squeezing his muscled arm a little. "Good evening, all." She smiled, wishing she'd individually greeted them just so she could hear that Spanish voice once more. Snapping herself out of it again, she continued the elegant stride to her family, which she knew Darcie would watch now that she had her attention.

"Good evening, family." She smiled and took her seat next to her brother-in-law purposely, which allowed full view of Darcie, who didn't seem to look impressed each time Lizzie looked at her with a slight smirk. *Oh, she liked this. This must be what Bella feels like given the confidence levels she holds. Well, arrogance was probably more fitting.* Vivvi was similar, albeit hers was far more confidence than arrogance. Her arrogance was merely the family trait of superiority. Vivvi, being the middle child, didn't have the petulance and brattishness their younger sibling had. She was more reserved and well... mature.

"So, what are the plans for tomorrow?" their mother asked as the first course was served.

Darcie, to Lizzie's right, placed a dish in front of Hugo as Deek placed one in front of her. She moved slightly out of Deek's way, allowing her arm to gently graze Darcie's thigh. She looked down at Lizzie, eyeing the woman cautiously. "I'm sorry." She smiled politely and turned to continue with her conversation. *Oh, she loved this.* It'd been a while since she'd flirted, and not that she would go anywhere near the woman who'd slept with her sister, but equally, two weeks was a considerable length when you were trapped on a boat with people who persistently galled you.

*

She totally did that on purpose, Darcie thought. She could see the glint in her eye. Was she flirting with her or just fucking with her? Either way, the girl's confidence appeared to be growing. Especially in that outfit tonight. *Two can play that game.*

She grabbed the jug of water and started at the head of the family. Lord Barrington just so happened to be perfectly placed opposite Libby. The woman talked to the husband of the wife she'd slept with a few days ago, a hook-up she was already regretting. Darcie noticed Libby take a strand of her hair and slowly twirl it around in her fingers. She was mesmerized by the action. *Given she was sexy as hell, and a surgeon, she would be very good indeed with those fingers.* She bit her bottom lip before slowly looking up at the slight smirk on Lizzie's face. *Dammit, she did it again. This was not right, nor good; she was always the one in control.* She continued to fill their glasses, each time getting a little closer to the doctor.

Darcie reached Hugo and could already smell the airy, floral scent of Libby's perfume. She could tell it was expensive. It was one of the luxuries she still afforded herself. *She would enjoy this.* She shifted slightly, leaning over Libby's shoulder, and purposely brushed her bare thigh against her arm just as Libby had done a moment ago. She poured the water into her glass, and repeated the action, realizing Libby caught on; she knew it was intentional. Darcie moved back up and this time, gripping the back of the chair, she very faintly brushed her fingertips over Lizzie's bare back. She noticed her posture catapult, which left Darcie grinning like a kid in a candy store. *Game, set, match,* she thought amusedly. *Well, this was fun.*

*

Lizzie froze at the light brush of Darcie's soft fingers. She'd seemingly taken control back from her and now cockily stood smirking at her. "Bugger," she muttered under her breath. Lizzie was quiet for the remainder of the meal. Partially due to the response from Darcie, partially due to it having been an incredibly long day of pretence, and because it would add to impending theatrics. *God, she hoped this worked.*

"You're very quiet this evening, Elizabeth. You aren't really contributing to the meal," her mother questioned conspiratorially as the after-meal coffees were distributed.

"Hmm, I think I got too much sun. I'm not feeling so good," she said, feigning illness.

Bella eyed her suspiciously. "Maybe you have caught what I had?" she questioned, throwing a look to a somewhat embarrassed Darcie.

"My understanding was you had a diarrhea type bug, *sister*," she questioned, raising an eyebrow to her. "So, I don't believe so."

"Elizabeth, please watch your manners at the dining table. We do not need to hear such vulgarities," her mother said sharply.

"Sorry mother, it wasn't meant as a vulgarity. It was merely a professional opinion given I have no such symptoms likened to what Annabella had." She took a sip of the coffee and made a sour face before placing it back on the saucer and moving it away from her. "Please excuse me, I'm a little chilly and require an outer layer," she shivered, knowing that her father would recognize the symptoms to be of heat stroke. It was a game, always had been. Well, at least until her sister decided this year to bed the only good-looking employee, and tarnish her plans. She sighed heavily as she walked past the crew.

"You want some agua?" Jose Luis kindly offered her a large bottle of water.

He was such a lovely guy. He and Deek both were, and she had to admit it; even Darcie was this morning, coming to let her know it was time for her to get out. She hated lying, well, except to her parents. From the grand old age of eleven, it'd become easier and easier as she consistently convinced herself it was for good reason. It was to allow her to live a life of simplicity and infinitesimal contentment.

Lizzie lay on her bed and read a few pages of her book, allowing sufficient time to set the scene to them. She enjoyed the wine this evening. *It was a beautiful full-bodied red, and now she was going to have to discontinue the party,* she thought glumly. She really should try and sneak something to drink into her room, so she could enjoy a glass on her balcony. She wondered if she could get Deek's attention down in their little hideaway to send some of the Appleton up.

It'd been nearly 10 minutes now. She got up and grabbed the black shawl she brought along. It was amusing. Her family was *that* self-obsessed that they'd never registered how year after year she set the exact same scene with the exact same attire. She splashed a little water on her face and turned the air conditioning back on as the heat grabbed her, leaving the room with a glum look plastered back on.

"How are you feeling, Miss Lizzie?" Jose Luis asked concernedly, to which she offered a shy smile and a gentle nod.

"Darling? How are we? I was going to come and find you," her father eyed her, looking at her face. "You looked flushed. And drops of perspiration?" He put the back of his hand to her forehead. "You have a discomforting temperature. You should know better than to get sunstroke, Elizabeth," he said.

"It must've been when I fell asleep," she murmured, ignoring his disappointment, and happy to get the theatrics out of the way.

"Well, you need a cool shower and plenty of liquid. Do you have rehydration salts with you?"

"Yes, Father."

"Good, no more alcohol for you. It will heighten the symptoms," he nodded, taking the glass she was nursing. She hoped she could have smuggled some back to her room.

"Yes, good point. Well, I guess I'll see you tomorrow, then."

"No, you should stay on the boat and out of the sun. Being in the sun all day will simply cause further issues," he reminded her.

"Oh…" she said sadly, looking around at her family who now all watched her.

"We are not able to get an enclosed car tomorrow, plus it defeats the purpose of the adventure. There's always next year," he nodded, turning his back to her. "Jose Luis, another bottle if you may?" he called out, leaving Lizzie to turn on her heel and leave her family and their celebrations.

And that, as they say, is how you do it…

*

"So, what do you think's going on there?" Deek asked as they cleaned up out of earshot of the family.

"Who knows." She rolled her eyes. "But that's the second time they've sent her to bed in so many days," Darcie spat.

"Maybe it's a ploy. Wouldn't be the first time one of this family's member's fell for da charm of Darcie." He grinned.

"Doubtful," she said contemplatively. Surely not; she wasn't like the others. *She was different. She was... herself.*

Darcie couldn't help but think about the situation. She was potentially going to be alone on deck with this woman, a woman who may or may not be ill. *God, why did she fuck about with her hoity toity sister? She was such a dumbass.*

*

Lizzie heard a faint knock again. She rushed to her balcony and leaned over. "*Hmm,*" she whispered thoughtfully, noticing that Darcie and Deek were in their little snug, talking and laughing. She walked over to the door and opened it, immediately looking down at the floor and seeing a bottle of red and a crystal glass alongside it. Leaning down, Lizzie contemplated thoughtfully again. *Who the hell was doing this?* She immediately grabbed the bottle and snuck it back inside, allowing herself to once again relive the taste of the beautiful, full-bodied red.

*

Lizzie woke as early as normal, and though she was disappointed at the prospect of not being able to snorkel, she couldn't possibly run the risk of running into her family. She took her book over to the sun lounger on her balcony, and basked in the serene beauty at her fingertips, happy to enjoy it until her family left.

Pulling herself up, she rested her head on her forearms as she looked around her. *How could she be in one of the most beautiful settings in the world and feel like... shit? Yup, that pretty much summed it up.* She wished she could celebrate this in all its glory with someone that meant something to her. Someone she was in love with. But how could she? She could never put another person through her family, least not someone she cared for. She sighed deeply as she turned, noticing her Spanish bombshell staring at her. Lizzie smirked as she watched Darcie fall backwards, realizing she'd been caught.

"Fuck!" Darcie yelled, annoyed with herself for letting her mind run away with her. The woman was beautiful, but she'd screwed up any chance of getting near Lizzie, given that she'd already fooled around with her sister. *She didn't look ill. She looked... relaxed. At ease. And surely if she had heat stroke, she wouldn't be in the sun. Was she just faking? No, she couldn't be. She wasn't like the rest of her family, or any of the other families she crewed for.* It was wishful thinking, most definitely on Darcie's part.

Chapter Nine

Darcie finished cleaning up the deck, unsure what to do next. The guys left a while back on the assumption that the beautiful woman who hadn't left her room, *not* even for snorkelling, had feigned illness for Darcie. Albeit, she now doubted that conclusion. She'd taken her towel and swimwear down to the small beach section at the end of yacht dock, and chilled with her book, ignoring the uncertain thoughts of whether to go check on the lone woman. *She couldn't do that.* She must be sick. If she wasn't, she would be all up in her business like her sister was a few days back.

Darcie briefly caught sight of something out of the corner of her eye. "What the fuck?" She sat up rapidly. Pulling her glasses down to aid a better view, she looked incredulously at the woman. "What the actual hell?" she said again, watching Libby, dressed in denim cut-offs and a tank, drag a Louis Vuitton case down the walkway. "*What the...*" Darcie said a third time, rushing behind her plastic chair so she could assess the crazy woman's intentions.

Chapter Ten

Bugger, every sodding, buggery year. Lizzie never computed the difficulty of wheeling a suitcase over sand. Even if it *was* only a small one. She continued to drag it between the shops, and onto the main streets before finding a taxi to get away for a while.

*

"Fuck... fuck, fuck!" Darcie cried out to the air as she followed the woman. "Follow that taxi!" she shouted as she jumped into a cab, and pointed to the one in front of them. *Fuck, she will get herself killed.* She felt a rapidly growing fear as she'd played back the rich woman struggling around in a third world country with the Louis Vuitton baggage.

The cab pulled up behind them as she watched Libby get out in the middle of nowhere. Nothing but a green and brown painted hut with two missing windows. One had wood and tape across it, the other was bare. "*Seriously?!*" she spat, acknowledging that in all her years of this job, she'd never experienced any guest to be as dumb. "Here!" She threw the bill at the driver and jumped out of the cab. Darcie rushed over to the woman, who struggled to pull the Louis Vuitton bag across the grass.

"Lady Barrington? *Lady Barrington!?*" she shouted, wondering why she wouldn't acknowledge her. She quickened her pace to a jog, fearing for the woman as she chased after her. "*Libby!*" she screamed again in one last attempt.

The woman slowly turned to face her with a look of shock and surprise. Darcie finally caught up with her, her hands on her knees, and tried to catch her breath. "What the hell are you doing!?" she spat.

"You're English?" Lizzie asked surprised.

"No, I'm American," Darcie confirmed, catching her breath.

"Well, yes. I meant that. I mean, you actually speak English? I thought you were Spanish?" It was all she could muster, despite her head spinning with a million questions. *Like, firstly, what the hell was she doing here? Why had she followed her?* "You followed me?" she asked, this time more sinister.

"Of course, I did. What're you trying to pull? You realize you're in the middle of a freaking third world country with a trunk that probably cost more than a damn house in these parts?" she cried exasperated.

"*Excuse me!*" she scorned. "Last time I looked, I didn't need rescuing from *anybody*. You have no idea who I am. And for clarity, just because you fell for my straight sister's bullshit doesn't mean to say we're all the same. You *don't* know what you're doing," Lizzie said, clearly not taking her on.

"I think you'll find you're the one who doesn't. You are going to get yourself murdered." She immediately cringed at the way she spoke about the people who paid her wages. "Seriously, you don't know what you're doing, this isn't—" Darcie heard a loud bang and screams. She grabbed Libby's hand before the confusion in the sounds hit home. There were shrills of laughter and... *Wait, what?* Darcie turned around, still holding Libby's wrist, and watched a herd plummet towards her, shouting screams of, "Miss Lizzie!"

"Like I said, I'm a big girl, and *not* my sister," she said, pulling her arm free. "Maybe it's best you leave now." The excitable children ran into her. "Wowzers... Guys, you are going to break a bone, or five." She laughed, ruffling some hair, and regaining her posture.

"Bonjour." A larger mixed-race lady stood and kissed Lizzie three times on each cheek. Darcie heard Lizzie say something in French, or maybe it was Creole. She knew Haitians spoke French, but believed it was a different form of French. It was her understanding they called it French Creole, if she was right in her thinking.

"Do you speak French?" Lizzie asked.

"No," Darcie said, suddenly aware of the situation.

Libby said something to the other woman in French. "S'okay, lady," the larger woman said, smiling kindly to Darcie before telling the children to now speak English.

"Come, come," she said, as the children all tugged Lizzie and her suitcase into the building.

Darcie was still super confused by the situation as everyone chatted animatedly around her. The prissy, stuck up "princesses" of the families they normally crewed for were most definitely *nothing* like this girl. She was so completely different to anyone she'd ever met before. Darcie watched with interest, analyzing how each of the children interacted with the beautiful woman, how the adults addressed her. Like she was one of their own. Her head spun a little, and all she could do was watch.

*

Bloody hell, if she really felt the need to be here, she wished she wouldn't continue looking so gormless, Lizzie thought. Before Lizzie had a chance to address the situation, one of the children bounced into her. "Hi James, you got big this year. How you doing? You still studying hard?"

"Yes, Miss Lizzie. I read that the doctors, they all write with the fountain pen. It's a pen with separate ink. I sent you a letter about it," the boy said widely." I'm gonna get one when I get big." He smiled widely, telling her his story.

"You did, indeed. And I may or may not have a little surprise for you." She raised an eyebrow, watching the little boy's entire face light up. Lizzie watched him, feeling her heart swell. She looked over to Miss Lovelie and Miss Roseline before addressing the children.

"Come on then, move back?" Miss Roseline insisted.

She rolled her eyes, laughing fondly. Lizzie unlocked the case, and watched with delight as the children began jumping, clapping, and laughing delightfully. It was a sound she never became bored of.

"Okay, okay, sit down a moment, and let me get this into some semblance of order," she instructed, watching the children do exactly that. Other than her patients, Elizabeth had very little dealings with children back home, but when she walked through London on her way to work, the children she saw were so unlike the children before her. *They didn't know what it was like to feel like all your Christmases had come at once by receiving only a pen,* she thought sadly.

Lizzie looked over at Darcie, who now sat next to Miss Lovelie, still looking wide eyed. She threw a ripple chocolate bar to Darcie, who didn't see it coming. It hit her on the head. They all giggled, and a surprised Darcie feigned injury, getting more laughs from all of them.

"You looked like you wanted some chocolate," Lizzie mused, raising an eyebrow.

"Please, please, Miss Lizzie, me too, me too!" She could hear the cries as the children raised their arms as high as possible in a bid to get some chocolate from her.

"Sorry." Lizzie pulled an apologetic grin to Miss Lovelie and Miss Roseline.

"It's okay, this ain't no different to any other year." Miss Lovelie rolled her eyes, giggling. Lizzie began distributing the fun size chocolates and threw them across the floor. The kids all dived in and swapped their favorite varieties.

Confident all the children had some chocolate, she went and sat on the floor alongside Darcie, Miss Lovelie, and Miss Roseline. Pulling her knees up to her chest, and getting comfortable, she tuned out the mmm's and ahhh's behind her and addressed the women. "So, how've things been?" she asked seriously.

"We still here," Miss Lovelie said with the same level of seriousness.

"Dieu Merci," Lizzie said, nodding.

"Yes ma'am."

"I wish you'd let me help you, Miss Lovelie."

"Quiet, child," she insisted, holding up her hand to prevent any further discussion.

Darcie watched thoughtfully, considering their dynamics. This upper-class, aristocratic, important surgeon, being told to... pretty much shut up, by a woman who probably spent her entire life earning the equivalent of a day's pay for Lizzie.

"You know how this works. I'll stay quiet for now, but at some point, we will discuss it," she said seriously, before a dimple formed, and her smile grew. "For now, it's present time!" She clapped excitably, pulling the case closer to her with all her might, and leaned on her knees. She picked up the smaller bag inside it and put it to one side. She held up two giant multi packs of crisps and threw them closer to Miss Lovelie. "In my country, we have a million varieties of crisps... I mean, chips," she corrected herself, informing Darcie, who looked over at her suspiciously.

"*Beef and onion*? Who even eats beef with onions?" she said flummoxed.

"We do, regularly." She rolled her eyes to Darcie. "One large, *British,* Cadburys whole nut bar. The biggest I could find for the lovely Miss Lovelie." She winked. "And the biggest bar of Toblerone for Miss Roseline." She handed over their gifts as two young girls came over to Miss Lovelie and whispered into her ear. Miss Lovelie smiled kindly, and spoke to them in Haitian. They rushed off with a soft smile to Darcie, who looked confused.

Lizzie continued to rummage through her case, retrieving a handful of books and handing them to the women. "The newest bestsellers back home," she said, watching as they excitably cast their eyes over the book descriptions. She switched the case around to the unopened partition, revealing half a case of clothing, footwear, pens, pencils, coloring books, and pads, and watched Miss Lovelie raise her eyes and shake her head.

"Miss Lizzie, you *can't* keep doing this. We only *need* you here."

"No, you don't, Miss Lovelie. You like me here because you're kind and loving and like to see me, but whether you accept it or not, you also *need* this. The kids do," Lizzie said shyly as the older woman softly stroked her face.

"Thank you. You are, and always will be, the most beautiful soul." She nodded her head to further confirm her words.

"Hey James, come here a moment, please," Lizzie said. James put his writing book and pen down, and shyly walked towards her.

"Yes, Miss Lizzie?" he said quietly, watching her hands twist the wrapped package in her hands.

"This is for you," she said, handing over the box.

He looked at the brightly wrapped box, stupefied as he carefully tore the paper little by little. The children, with inquiring eyes, gathered around them. Darcie watched silently. Bar the slight noise of the painfully slow paper ripping, the whole room was silent. This kid looked like he'd never received a personal gift before, something just for him. Something papered that *he* could open. It was reflective of the Willy Wonka movie when the child opens the candy bar, almost as if in slow motion. Her heart broke at the scene before her and a lone tear fell from her eye. She felt a squeeze to her leg from a dark hand belonging to Miss Lovelie.

"Parker?" The little boy said, bringing Darcie back to the moment. "What's Parker, Miss Lizzie?" He read the name of the navy box inscribed with the brand name.

"Well open it and have a look." She smiled.

He checked all sides before realizing how to open it, spied the bright, silver fountain pen, and suddenly gasped aloud. The boy ran back to the far end of the room and rummaged in a backpack, before rushing back and skidding on the floor next to Lizzie. He carefully opened the paper, looking between his picture of a fountain pen, and the real thing. "It's real? And it's *mine*?" he said uncertainly.

"It's real, *and* it's all yours," she said, putting her arm around his slight waist. "But... you have to continue studying hard, and one day, you will be a doctor too."

The boy smiled broadly as he desperately held onto his new present, and rushed into her arms. "Mesi, mesi, mesi!" He kissed her rapidly, repeatedly thanking her.

"I mean it. You need to focus on school now. You want to be a doctor, it's very important now."

He sat up proud and tall. "I promise. And then someday, I'm gonna be an even better doctor than you are," he said, causing them all to finally laugh at the emotional situation.

Miss Lovelie said something to her class that Darcie didn't understand and they all ran off with James to look at his new pride and joy.

"This one was about to flood us all with them tears. I thought we must stop for a moment," Miss Lovelie pointed to Darcie, who was discreetly rubbing her eyes and trying to hide the blush.

"It's just hot in here," Darcie said shyly.

"Well, it'll be even hotter when you get some good ole Haitian food inside you." She winked, touching her shoulder gently before turning to Lizzie. "That was too much, Elizabeth."

"I know. You're addressing me in full to make it known that I'm in trouble?" she questioned Miss Lovelie. "It really wasn't too much. It could have been a Montblanc instead of a Parker. Far more expensive." She smirked. "Come on, let's start on lunch." She held out her hand to help up the elderly woman.

"You're never too old to learn some manners, and to respect your elders. No speaking back," Miss Lovelie reprimanded her, trying to hide the slight smile.

"They like this all the time." Miss Roseline came and sat next to Darcie, giggling.

"They are?"

"Mhmm," she drew out. "So… You are Miss Lizzie's girlfriend?"

"Oh, no. I only just met her," she said, noticing the curiosity on the other woman's face. "Sorry, I'm one of the workers on the yacht. She pretended to be sick last night... clearly to do this. And then I saw her running through town with a Louis Vuitton case. No disrespect, but I thought she was going to get herself in trouble."

Miss Roseline nodded seriously. "I understand," she considered lightly. "She does it each year."

"She does?" Darcie spun her head round.

"For the last seven or eight, maybe. She brought her lover the first year, but it is my belief that her family drove her away."

"I can well believe it," Darcie said as they sat in silence for a few moments. "She isn't like them." Darcie broke the silence as she watched Elizabeth assist the elderly woman to the kitchen area. "She's unlike any of the people we have. They are just... just... so *horrible*," she said sadly.

"That beautiful lady does not belong there, and our fear is at the age she is, she will never escape. She cannot stand up to them."

Darcie allowed the words to settle, feeling a pang of emotion as the memories of the last few days with the Barrington family filled her.

Chapter Eleven

The morning went by with games outside, and more gifts for the children. Cars and action figures for the boys, journals for the girls, and some cheap underwater cameras for when they went to the beach. They all helped in plating the food to each of the children before the four adults sat down at their own table. Darcie felt Lizzie's hand slip into her own. Her breath quickened before realizing it wasn't being taken to hold; she was taking it to say grace. Darcie hadn't said grace a day in her life, but out of respect for the women and the situation, she lowered her head silently, quietly saying Amen when Miss Lovelie had finished.

*

Lizzie tucked into the Creole cuisine, murmuring sounds of delight. "Gosh, I've missed your cooking."

"Well, maybe you should come work in Haiti's hospital. Then you can come eat with us more than once per year." She lifted an eyebrow.

"I'd come work here with you before I worked at the hospital."

"It's not right to give up your life."

"With my money we could do so much good for you and the kids."

"And they still won't have parents. They have as much love as they are going to need. Money does not buy you happiness."

"Nor does a family," she said flatly, allowing silence to hit the table.

Darcie watched the sadness in her eyes. She'd seen it from day one, but this time it was different. It was the absence of love from a real family. Darcie swallowed the lump in her throat and thought about her own family. *Her mom would smother Lizzie if she were here listening to this, and her pops would probably go straight to his office and source information on emancipation. They would love her, but then who couldn't? She was perfect.* Darcie dropped her fork loudly on the table. "Oops, sorry," she said embarrassed, inquisitive eyes watching her.

"We lost you there hmm, Miss Darcie?" Miss Lovelie asked softly.

"Yes, I'm sorry. I was just..." She paused, unable to verbalize her words.

"Thankful for everything you have?" Lizzie muttered, as she met her questioning eyes. She hadn't said it with malice. It was simply understanding.

"Yes, I never knew about places like this. Well, obviously I knew they existed, but you presume that they're just like in movies and TV shows. You don't expect that they're real, that there are amazing people that should have the world and don't," she said sadly. "I'm sorry, I don't mean to sound disrespectful."

"You don't. The children have food, water, education, a bed to sleep in, and all the love they each deserve. They are each lucky in their own way," Miss Lovelie confirmed

*

The day had gone too fast. *As it always did,* Lizzie thought. The children teased her about having a girlfriend, which interestingly felt quite nice. A couple of the girls made Darcie friendship bracelets out of brightly colored threads, so they each had gifts to take when they left.

"It's time, eh?" Miss Lovelie said with a matching sadness to her eyes.

"It is," Lizzie said solemnly. "Miss Lovelie, thank you for your kindness and love once more. Please let me—"

"Child, do not dare," she warned.

"Miss Lovelie?" she pleaded. "It's unsafe. The window?"

Is getting fixed Tuesday," she said.

"She's not lying," Miss Roseline added.

"Please? I want to help. My parents just paid as much money on a two-week holiday as for each of you to have a five-bedroom house built. I have enough money to do good, and for once, I want it to serve a purpose."

"Child, must we do this every year?"

"I like the normality," she said defeatedly and opened her purse. "How much are the stamps?"

Miss Lovelie slowly maneuvered to a bag on the table, removed a slip of paper, and handed it to Lizzie. She checked it out, removed some notes from her purse, and handed a check to Miss Lovelie.

"There's 15,000 Gourde here. The slip shows a little over 9,000," Miss Lovelie said, handing the money back.

"I know, but you may want to write more this year." She smiled widely.

"Not a chance, lady," she said, giving it back.

"Well, you can take the 10 and be done with it. There's no discussion to be had," she said. For the first time there

S.L. Gape

was some strength to it. "There are a couple more things. I brought you an extra bag of medical supplies this time. I know you'll be able to use them. And I believe you had a big birthday which you failed to mention?"

Miss Lovelie shot a darting glare to Miss Roseline before looking back to the younger woman. "When you reach a certain age, they all become a number," she said.

"Well, not in my eyes. Being as you never let me help, I have a gift that I hope you'll like."

"You're very naughty; you don't listen to me."

"I think you'll find I do, Miss Lovelie. If I didn't, you'd all be living in a palace. As I said, it's a birthday gift for you, for your 70th," she said, handing the wrapped present over to her.

Miss Lovelie carefully opened the gift and pulled back the paper, revealing the picture of a camera on the box. "No, this is too much," she said, already handing it back to Lizzie. Truth be known, the cost of the camera could've been enough to keep them all fed for a year, but she wasn't about to tell her that.

"Don't be silly. I know you don't like expense. It's a good brand, but still relatively cheap."

"From the girl who earns more an hour than we get a year?" she said pointedly.

"Let's not do this. I must leave. I won't be back for another year, and you had an important birthday. I want you to be able to capture these moments. Yes, you have memories, but now you can keep them and treasure them," she said, hugging Miss Lovelie tightly before she could refuse any further.

"See you next year, my beautiful girl," Miss Lovelie said with tears creeping through her eyes. Darcie stood awkwardly, feeling like she interrupted a personal moment.

She focused her eyes on her deck shoes. "And you... my other beautiful girl. It was wonderful to meet you." She smiled, pulling Darcie in for a big bear hug. "You do me a very big favor," she said as a direction instead of a question.

Darcie nodded.

"You look after Lizzie while you're with her. Make sure she's safe, and try to make her smile on the vacation," she said seriously. "And you ever wanna come back to visit when you're in Port Au Prince, then please do." Darcie couldn't help the swell in her heart, and knew there would be plenty more visits here for her.

*

"Well, I guess as you've been with me all day after following me here, we may as well share a cab back," Lizzie said, walking to one of the men who was already approaching her, shouting, "*Taxi, taxi!*"

"Yeah, makes sense," Darcie said quietly.

The journey back was quiet. Solemn. Very fitting of the day, and the feeling in the air. The taxi ride was short, and they made their way back onto the yacht. It wouldn't be long before her parents returned, and she couldn't face an evening with them pretending everything was great. Nothing was great. *Her life was rubbish,* she thought sadly.

"What time will your folks be home?" Darcie asked, breaking the silence.

"Not too long now, I imagine," she said quietly. "At least I get to say I'm still sick tonight. Another one down."

"You're not coming to dinner?" Darcie asked disappointed.

"No, I don't feel like it," Lizzie said.

S.L. Gape

"Oh. What do you mean another one down?"

"Another day down. One less to contend with," she said seriously. "Goodnight, Darcie." And just like that, she disappeared out of sight.

Darcie felt broken and empty. It was the most gut wrenchingly painful experience of her life, and in that one short day, she realized how unbelievably lucky she was. She had the world, and she was utterly thankful for it at this moment in time. She wiped the tears from her face and pressed call on her cell.

*

"Hey sweetie, we were just talking about you."

"Hey, Mom. How's it going?"

"Better than you it seems. What's up, baby?"

Darcie spent the next 40 minutes divulging the day's events to her parents. Her parents were saddened to hear about Lizzie. *Or* Libby. She wondered why her family called her Libby, and the women and children referred to her as Lizzie today. She decided to go with Lizzie. *It was softer,* she thought. Her parents, like Miss Lovelie, said that she needed to ensure she looked after her as best she could throughout the vacation and be there as a friend, because she clearly needed one. She tried not to go into too much detail about Lizzie, and what she looked like. She already knew her mom would know she was smitten with her. Darcie ended the call, finally feeling a little less sad. She grabbed a bottle and decided to act on instinct, breaking the golden rule for the second time in so many days—going to guest quarters.

Chapter Twelve

Lizzie heard a knock at the door. She knew her parents hadn't returned yet, but the knock was firmer and harder than her mystery "gift giver." She opened the door, and saw Darcie standing in front of her.

"Hi. Umm, well I'm kinda not supposed to do this... come to your room, but—"

"But what... you're trying to get through us all?" Lizzie uttered, immediately noticing pain flash through the beautiful, turquoise eyes.

Darcie felt a pang of guilt and *hurt* rush over her. "I..." She stopped, admitting defeat and turning away.

"Wait!" Lizzie shouted, grabbing Darcie's arm and watching as the blonde woman turned slowly to her, eyeing the hand on her skin, and immediately feeling loss when she moved it away. "I'm sorry, that was uncalled for. I'm deeply embarrassed by my words. As you saw, today was hard for me. It was unacceptable for me to behave that way," she said somberly. "What can I do for you, Darcie?"

"It's okay," she said quietly. "I feel pretty shitty, so I can't begin to imagine how you must be feeling. Hence my visit," she said, holding up the Appleton Rum and two crystal tumblers.

"One condition."

"I'm not going to hit on you," she said seriously.

Lizzie felt a jolt through her body following the tartness of Darcie's words. Who could blame her after she'd just spoken to her that way. "Good, you're not my type." She smiled a little. "But I wasn't going to say that. I was going to ask if we could substitute the glasses for teacups?" She smiled.

Darcie laughed a little at the confusing words. "Sure thing." She handed her the rum before jogging off with two glasses in hand.

*

Darcie returned to find the door slightly ajar. She knocked gently before entering the room, noticing a faint smell of the expensive perfume Lizzie wore, and took in the surroundings. It was her favorite room of the boat, offering the best views on the private balcony, which is exactly where Lizzie was now.

"Teacups as requested," she said, stepping out onto the balcony, and holding them up for the woman to see.

"Thanks. Who knew it could be so refreshing in a teacup." She giggled.

"Yup, who knew?" Darcie watched as Lizzie poured them both a cup full. "Role reversal here; I should be doing that."

"I'm not like them, you know," Lizzie said, soft and sad.

"I know, Lizzie. Do you mind if I call you that?"

"No. And thank you. It's important that people recognize I'm not like them."

"I recognize it. I recognize it a whole heap. Can I ask you something?"

"If you wish."

"Why do you go by so many names?" She chuckled, trying to make the somewhat personal question, a little less personal.

Lizzie smiled a little. "My name's Elizabeth, but my family have always called me Libby. I realized from an early age that I was different. Was it not for the fact I look so much like my family, I would've been convinced I was switched at birth. I wanted to do something for me, so I decided I was going to change my name. I guess I wanted to have some control of my life, just for once," she said consciously.

Darcie waited through the silence before stepping in. "And so, they refuse to call you that?"

Lizzie looked at her carefully, realizing she'd already said too much, and was conscious that it was becoming too serious. "No, I just never had the courage to tell them." She giggled.

Darcie noticed the falseness of the laugh, but decided to go with it, and not push her. "Right. Well, I think it's kinda cool. It's like your own little secret. Like, this is who you really are. You're Lizzie, and then with your family, you're Libby. A bit like superman." She laughed. "Lizzie saves the world and Libby travels the world."

"I don't save the world," she said seriously.

"You saved their world today," Darcie said simply. "And you would if you could, I can tell," she stated. They both heard the voices of her family's return, choosing not to comment as Lizzie's body shivered. Darcie broke the silence before Lizzie's mood had further opportunity to deflate. "So, can I ask you something?"

"Again? You're full of questions, aren't you?" She lifted her glasses and smiled to Darcie.

"Funny girl! What was the money about today? With Miss Lovelie?"

"Ahh." She laughed. "She simply refuses to accept money I offer each year. I try to, because like I said today, I know I could make a positive impact with money that means nothing to me. Each year I pay for her stamps, so she can write to me. She's very old school, and I must say, I much prefer writing a letter; it's far more personal than texts and emails that we've all gotten so obsessed with. I know she wouldn't waste a single penny on anything, unless it was for those children. If it's something for her personal contentment, it's not deemed as priority. So, the stamps are mutually beneficial." She smiled. "I love it. She sends me a couple of extra letters from the kids too and now, hopefully, I can get her to send some prints from the camera."

"Yes, the camera. Which cost more than an annual salary as a deputy crew manager on a luxury yacht." She laughed.

Lizzie looked over to her and saw her wink, choosing not to acknowledge the value of the gift. "She'll never know, and everyone needs a little extravagance once in their life. Especially on their 70th."

"Can I ask just one more?"

"Blimey, what is this, 20 questions?" she teased. "Go on, last one."

"It's an orphanage, right?"

"Correct."

"Well..."

"Wait, I said just one more." She grinned.

"Cut it out, smart ass, that wasn't my question."

"Wow, do you speak to all of your luxury guests like that?" she mused.

"Only the normal ones." Darcie smiled.

"Good comeback. I like being normal. Proceed then, question master," she flirted.

"If it's an orphanage, then they must have ways in which you could anonymously donate money for them," she said, wondering if this was too personal. "You know, if it means so much to you."

"Also correct, but she would know it was me. And I wouldn't do that to her, out of respect. I desperately wish I could do more to help, but she is so defiant, and I feel I'd be defrauding her. She's so adamant that it's my company that they want and nothing else. It means more than anything in the world to me that I could be so important to someone that an annual visit impacts their life."

"I think you impact many more people's lives," she said quietly, letting the words hang.

"I told you no hitting on me," Lizzie said, trying to further lighten the mood.

Darcie looked at the woman interestedly and rolled her eyes. "You're a giant douche. And on that note, you think it's safe for me to leave your room? I need to get some work done, or my boss will kick my ass."

"I think you'll be safe to exit, yes," she said, already feeling a loneliness from Darcie's impending departure. Lizzie watched as Darcie left the rum, and made her way towards the door.

"Darcie?" Lizzie called to her.

Darcie felt her body shiver, hearing her name in the beautiful, English voice. She turned around to see Lizzie leaning against the doorframe of the balcony door. Her beautiful honey blonde waves, like tendrils, gently danced against the sea breeze. "Um, yeah?" she said, her mouth dry.

"Thank you," she said softly. "For today, for looking out for me. Albeit, unrequired, but all the same. And thank you for staying with me. Miss Lovelie will be very happy."

Darcie cringed at her shoulder shrug to Lizzie, feeling as though she'd gone back 20 years. "How so?"

"Because you're keeping her promise to keep me safe and happy on my holiday," she said softly, looking up through her eyelashes. Darcie felt her breath disappear from her lungs, as she watched the vision before her. She wanted to scream and shout, *I'll always keep you safe and happy*, but shook the confusing thoughts from her head.

"Well, I can very honestly say, Dr. Lizzie Barrington, that the pleasure was most *definitely* all mine. Don't drink too much." She winked and left her room.

Lizzie listened to the resounding "Dr. Lizzie Barrington" in that soft, American voice. She looked down at her fingers, unable to resist the slight smile forming on her lips.

*

Darcie needed to take a quick shower, and grab a fresh set of uniforms before checking the internet and getting to work. Part of her felt guilty for what she was about to do. By her own admission, she would've loved to help, but didn't want to disrespect Miss Lovelie.

She sat on her single cabin bed, and searched through Google, getting the details she required. Looking at the beautiful smiling faces of Miss Lovelie and some of the children, she immediately felt her heart swell. Darcie grabbed her wallet, and pulled her card out before typing in the digits. She checked the details once over as she hovered her finger over the submit button. "Well, regardless of Lizzie, this is the right thing to do for *me*," she said aloud and pressed submit. Hurriedly, she closed the lid of her laptop and left her room.

Chapter Thirteen

"Oh, dear God," Lizzie said to the room, feeling the effects of the rum. "Jesus, you're a surgeon, what were you thinking?" She eyed the half empty bottle of rum at her bedside table.

It was a little after six and she desperately wanted to do some snorkeling before she had to spend a day with her family again. Plus, the fresh sea water might help her hangover. *Or drown her,* she thought simply. *Hmmm either would be a win.* She put on her suit and left the room. She was getting more confident. Her tan was deeper, so she went only in her bikini instead of a cover up this morning. Since she was only jumping straight into the water, why wouldn't she? *And hopefully Darcie would see her.* She liked the way the woman looked at her with those startling, beautiful, turquoise eyes.

"Hey, beautiful. You feeling better today? We were worried about you yesterday," Deek said.

Lizzie looked at Darcie, confused.

"Yes, how're you feeling? Your parents said you had heatstroke and we didn't see you all day." Darcie stepped in, hoping that Deacon and Jose Luis would buy her lie. She hated lying to them, but this was a secret she felt was important for Lizzie to keep.

"I'm fine," she said quietly, liberated by Darcie's actions. "On a plus, if I go back out and it happens again today, I get another day of freedom tomorrow." She winked, taking the

71

coffee and snorkel equipment from Deek and Jose Luis. "Maybe next time I can fake it and spend a day with you three." She looked back over her shoulder, noticing the watchful eye of Darcie. She slowed her pace, allowing her sufficient time to get a good look. *She would make Darcie see the error of her ways from sleeping with her sister.*

*

Lizzie was as far out as she could safely be. It'd been a perfect morning, and she was disappointed to see the back of Haiti. She suddenly felt like the current and the temperature had changed around her body. She sensed a presence near her, lifted her head up, and turned around, pleasantly surprised and equally happy to see a beautiful, tanned body swimming towards her. Her darkened blonde hair, with strips of white, floated all around her. God, she couldn't be more beautiful if she tried. Lizzie noticed her near nakedness from her bikini and scorned herself at her desire to see more.

Darcie smiled as much as she could with a mouthpiece in and tapped her watch twice with her fingers, watching as Lizzie looked down and gave her two thumbs up.

Lizzie watched as she held five fingers up, and made a beckoning motion with her fingers. Lizzie looked down at her own watch, checking the time concernedly before feeling a thumb gently stroke her forearm. She looked up to a smiling Darcie, who gave a quick wink, and swam off smiling.

Did she have time? She didn't know. But she could lie for England, to people who didn't care enough to ascertain if it was the truth or not. *So why the hell not?* Lizzie quickly followed Darcie, her feet pedaling as she was directed by the beautiful woman to a snug spot she'd missed throughout the morning. Lizzie swam in rapid circles as she took in the incredible marine life around her, stopping as she watched a rigid Darcie. She looked up and waited for her "okay", wanting desperately to swim up to her and repeat the position from a few days earlier. Lizzie sighed. There wasn't a bloody chance in hell she was going to go there with a woman who slept with her straight, bratty sister only mere days ago. But she could at least be friends with her. She gave her a thumbs up and dived down, exploring the new marine life at her fingertips.

Chapter Fourteen

"How are you feeling today?" Vivvi asked her sister as they sat down for breakfast. "Better, thank you. Still not 100%, but I have some work to do, so I'll just keep out of it today given we're spending the day sailing. Far too risky with the breeze. How was the tour yesterday?" she asked without giving anybody the opportunity to comment. It felt quite exhilarating, taking control of her life for once.

"It was interesting. We saw a few places from last year, and father visited the hospital," she said uninterestedly. "We visited the Caribbean Jewel store, and pretty much kept them in business for another year."

Lizzie nodded her head, feigning interest in a response, and noticed Darcie walking towards them with a slight smile. "Doctor and Lady Barrington, would you care for some coffee?" she asked, smiling politely.

"Yes," they both said in unison. Lizzie cringed at the lack of manners from her family. Darcie did the rounds to the entire family in receipt of the same response before reaching Lizzie.

"Doctor, would you care for some?" she inquired, placing her hand on the back of the chair and brushing her back.

"Please," she said, unable to control her breathing as she moved her body further back into Darcie's hand. *What was she doing? This was not good. There was absolutely no way she was going there when Bella had been there! Jesus,*

Bella would love that—the prospect of Lizzie having her sloppy seconds. She felt a further brush, before Darcie's hands finally slipped away.

Lizzie spent the remainder of the evening barely speaking, which was not particularly difficult with her family, thankfully. There was the occasional knowing smile between her and Darcie, causing her to frequently jump. *At least she's making it bearable,* she thought. She couldn't help but like Darcie. She had fun with her. They spoke candidly, with nominal reserve and she seemed relatively normal. Lizzie rarely met people who were like that. The people she met were usually like her family, those of whom, she was expected to befriend. Of course, these were the ones she had no interest in, or they just didn't approach her because in their opinion, she was not comparable to them. Either way, Darcie was nice to her, offering her a friend for the duration, and in this situation, she preferred that more than she preferred the copious amounts of alcohol the deck provided her to get through it. Granted, it wasn't ideal, but things could be far worse.

*

Lizzie looked down at her phone vibrating and was thankful that dinner was over. She discreetly removed herself from the table and rushed off, answering the call with a sense of urgency.

"Miss Lovelie, *Miss Lovelie!* What's happened? You never call me unless it's an emergency!" she cried.

"We good," she said flatly. "Was it you?"

"Excuse me?" Lizzie said confused.

"Please tell me no, Lizzie."

"Miss Lovelie, you aren't making any sense. Start from the beginning. Tell me what's happened. Please, Miss Lovelie, I'm with my family. I don't have much time," she pleaded.

"Today, I have been informed that an anonymous donation of $30,000 went into the orphanage. I want to know if it's from you."

Lizzie couldn't help but gasp. "*Really*? This... *wait*. You thought it was me?"

"Miss Lizzie, you always ask to give money, and this time no different. How could I not think it was you?" she said sadly.

"Miss Lovelie, I'm not going to lie, I'm very happy. But I'm incredibly disappointed you'd even ask me. I could give you that twice a year, and if you'd allowed me to, I would've done it for the past seven. I could do it without my bank fund being compromised and equally without my family even realizing. How long have you known me? When have I ever disrespected you? Or, outside of the minimal money you allow for the stamps, given you money when you've told me not to?"

"It wasn't you?" She sounded sad, yet startled, and something else Lizzie couldn't put her finger on.

"Miss Lovelie, this is incredible. I need to come back."

"You can't, Miss Lizzie. You can't risk it. You go, your family will cause issues. I will speak soon," she said. "Goodbye, Miss Lizzie, god bless your soul."

Lizzie walked back a little dumbfounded, trying to take in the words. She couldn't be bothered with the mass pretence as per usual. "Right, I'm going to bed," she said to her family.

"Now? It's not even 9:30?" her mother questioned.

"Yes, well, I was unfortunate to have lost an entire day of sun, so I'm hoping that an early night will get me ready for The Virgin Islands tomorrow. You know it's one of my top spots." She smiled knowingly and left her family to continue with their evening.

Lizzie made her way to her room, and got out of the dress she was wearing. She put a pair of jean shorts on and a Skinny polo shirt before discreetly leaving again. She had an idea of where to go, knowing that her destination was never near where her family would be. She snuck past the area that she was certain were private quarters—the ones she could see from her room—thankful that they were all still working upstairs at the disposal of her exploitative family.

She reached the end of the mid-level deck, noticing the steps down to the overhang that housed the water sports equipment. She considered making her way down there, noticing its sheer darkness, but thought better of it. Lizzie continued walking around the area before spotting the ladder that lead to the very top of the yacht. She climbed up, taking in the vast area, maneuvering her way through the functional aspects of the yacht. "Bingo," she said lightly, noticing a large flat area, with a bit of an overhang facing the opposite end of the boat, and more importantly, away from her family. She sat down, allowing her legs to dangle from the overhang. She sighed happily to herself as she took in the beautiful sound of the waves quietly breaking, and the luminosity of the moon lighting the large expanse of water.

Lizzie became lost in her thoughts, revisiting her time with Miss Lovelie and the kids. She was a complete mixture of emotions from the discussion they'd had. *A $30,000 donation?* It was hard. She knew she could give that and provide so much for the people who meant everything to her. On the other hand, they finally had an incredible amount of money that meant so much, and she couldn't do anything about it. She couldn't even be there to assist. More importantly, she couldn't take any praise for it. She'd always considered Miss Lovelie's feelings, and had never experienced such a sense of respect for your elders where... where it was worthy. She sighed heavily as she lay flat on her back.

Chapter Fifteen

Lizzie heard faint footsteps coming towards her, barely noticing her surroundings until she felt vibration underneath her back. She spun up and around, blinking fiercely, trying to ascertain who was before her. Jesus, if it was any of her family, she was totally screwed. In the complete literal sense.

"Lizzie?" said a recognizable American accent.

"Darcie?" She looked back and blinked. "Sorry, my eyes are still adjusting. What are you doing here?"

"I could ask you the same. Were you sleeping?"

"No, I've just been staring at the stars."

"Right. Want me to leave you?"

"What are you doing here?"

"I come here most nights when the..." She stopped, realizing who she was talking to. "Erm, when the family is able to take care of themselves," she said. "What about you? I thought you went to bed?"

"Nope, just needed some *me* time. So, tell me, which is it?"

"Huh?" Darcie sat next to her.

"What do you call us?"

"I'm lost," Darcie said reluctantly, watching the blonde woman turn and raise an eyebrow to her.

"Of course you are. You stopped talking when you were going to say who you wait on, so I'm intrigued. Let me guess. Hmmm, the pains... no, far too polite. The... no, still too soft..."

"Lizzie, I wasn't going to call you and your family anything," she said, barely convincing herself.

"Oh, I've got it!" She jumped excitably. "The bolloxy, bastard-headed Barrington's! I love it," she said, clapping animatedly.

"Dreads... but I may prefer yours." She laughed, taking a swig of her beer and looking out at sea.

"Dreads?"

"Yes. It's not specifically your family. We call good families the 'supes' and bad ones the 'dreads.'"

"Well, that's a bit rubbish. Mine was far superior."

"This is kind of a weird conversation to be having with you."

"Well, maybe for you," she said distantly.

Darcie sat in silence for a moment. "Yours may be better, but if my back's turned, and I say 'the bolloxy, bastardhead Barrington's asked me to do this,' and one of them walks in, there's no way out of denying I'm talking about the people responsible for my pay check," she said. "If I say 'the dreads said this,' I could just be talking about Deek."

"Good plan, I like it," she said, looking back out at the water again, and sighing softly. "It's really beautiful, isn't it?"

Darcie lifted one knee to her chest and paid attention to the beauty around her. "Yup, sure is. Sure beats looking out a window from your office."

"Or a dead body," she said bluntly.

Darcie sat there in silence, unsure what to say.

"I'm sorry, I didn't mean to spoil the mood. I can leave," Lizzie said, attempting to get up.

"Why are you here?" Darcie grabbed her arm.

"I told you, I wanted some me time."

"I mean here specifically."

"Virtually, every yacht I've been on since the age of fifteen, I've found a hiding spot. I guess you can say I'm good with nooks and crannies," she said.

Darcie spat her drink out, and wiped her mouth, feeling a flush of embarrassment on her face.

"Well, aren't you the rude minded one? I meant on the yacht! And in hotels, homes, basically anywhere I'm forced to be with them," she said sadly.

"I don't have a rude mind. Actually... okay, maybe a little." She laughed in hopes of lightening the mood.

"I told you, no hitting on me. You missed your chance when you went after my sister," she said flatly, folding her hands in her lap.

"I never chased after her for the record."

"Can I ask you something, Darcie?"

Darcie felt her stomach drop, knowing what was coming. How did she explain it without making it worse? "Sure, I believe I owe you three." She smiled, watching Lizzie's eyebrow raise. "Now who's got her mind in the gutter? Go on. If I can't hit on you, then we should probably get our heads out of the gutter."

Lizzie looked at her seriously. "Speak for yourself, lady."

Darcie ignored the comment. "So, what's the question?"

"Before, when you were talking about my family, why did you talk as though I wasn't one of them?"

"Because..." she said, considering her response. "I guess because you aren't like them. I talk to you like you're the same as me, I guess." She looked over at Lizzie and noticed the slight smile on her face. "You want some?"

Lizzie looked down at the bottle, ignoring the excitement in her tummy at the thought of Darcie's lips being around it. "Tut tut, offering a 'dread' a mouthful of your beer." She laughed, grabbing the bottle from her hands, taking a large gulp, and relishing in the ice-cold liquid. She wondered if it'd be the closest her lips would ever get to Darcie's.

"You're very cheeky," Darcie said, taking the beer back, desperate to put her lips where, seconds ago, Lizzie's had been. She watched Lizzie watch her as she slowly took a long gulp of the drink they shared. Part of her wanted to get more to drink so she could spend more time with her, but that would mean they wouldn't be able to share a bottle. *Unless she got the hard liquor. Then of course they could still drink more.*

"What are you thinking?" Lizzie asked, bringing Darcie back with a blush that she figured was construed as some form of S.O.S.

"Um nothing," she said shyly.

"Your head was in the gutter again; I can tell by the fierce blush." Lizzie snatched the bottle back from her, drinking more, and laughing as she noticed a deeper shade of red cross over Darcie's golden face.

"You know for someone who's trying to stop me from hitting on you, you sure do flirt a lot," Darcie said, turning her body around to face Lizzie's.

"I know, but I'm allowed. I never went elsewhere after I saw you," she said, lying back down and staring up at the stars, leaving Darcie open mouthed.

"Well, I never expected you to look at me!" she yelled, jumping up with her bottle and rushing off.

Lizzie sat there quietly, lost in her thoughts and the gentle waves of the ocean. She thought back to only moments ago, where she'd felt the wetness of Darcie's lips around the bottle neck. *She'd never know. She was never going to go there after Bella.* She laughed as she considered asking her sister about the ins and outs of their sordid night of passion together. Lizzie sat up quickly, feeling as though she would be sick at the prospect. Why did she have to think those things? It happened, and she couldn't change that. Lizzie heard footsteps rushing up the steps, and turned around to see Darcie walking towards her. "You've come back?"

"I never left. I don't quit that easily, chica. Just because a beautiful woman thinks I went elsewhere, I deserve the opportunity to at least provide my side of the story, and to right my wrongdoings." She winked light-heartedly. "I just figured we needed harder liquor." She held up a bottle of tequila.

"Good lord, woman, are you purposely trying to get me drunk?"

"*Me*? What would make you think that?" She winked again. "You think I'm trying to have my wicked way with you? As if," she said, handing the bottle over.

"You couldn't locate any glasses?" She smirked, noticing the flush again.

"Um, I was concerned of getting caught. I figured I'd just go to my room where nobody would see me."

"Or maybe you just wanted to share a bottle with me." Lizzie laughed and playfully hit her shoulder, noticing the embarrassment on Darcie's face.

"Cut it out already! You want some or not?"

"You're so easy." Lizzie laughed, taking the bottle and opening it. "No pun intended."

"Right, so at what point did you convey you were into me?"

"*Excuse me?*"

"When. Did. You. Let. Me. Know. You. Were. *Into.* Me."

"No need to be sarcastic! I didn't, why? What makes you think I'm into you?"

"Gimme a break. And quit giving me shit because I fucked up and fooled around with a woman that *did* hit on me."

Lizzie watched the woman's demeanor. She couldn't establish if she was annoyed by Darcie chastising her or if Darcie was simply messing with her, if she should let it go. "I'm sorry, I didn't mean to offend you."

"You didn't, Lizzie. But you don't think I'm kicking myself that a beautiful, amazing, gay woman may have been into me? That before I had a chance to discover or explore that, I accepted a proposition elsewhere? This doesn't happen," she said. "I get it, and if it's any consolation I regret it, but I can't change it. I think you're darn awesome, and I made a promise to your friend, which I will stand by if you allow me to."

Lizzie went to speak before closing her mouth again. "She'd love to know that. Despite her falling out with me," she mumbled, deciding to change the subject. As much as she couldn't deny that Darcie was beautiful, and she was hugely attracted to her, she knew in her heart she couldn't go there. While the whole Bella thing was bad enough, she simply couldn't bring herself to face the psychological trauma of Darcie targeting her sister first.

"Why? What's going on? Why is she pissed with you? You want some?" she asked, pointing to the bottle.

"Oh, nothing. Yes, please."

"Look, maybe it's best I leave," she said more as a statement. "I don't want to upset you. You get enough crap up here. I'll leav—"

"Please don't. I can't... I'm sorry," she said sadly.

"I can't change it, Lizzie. I wish I could. I'd change it a million times over, but I can't. Also, I can't be punished for—"

"I know, I know. I'm sorry. I'll never mention it again."

"I'm not saying that, Lizzie. If you wanna ask me anything, I swear I'd answer you truthfully, but..."

"I know." She sighed, feeling disgust as she recognized some of her own family's traits in her behavior. "Look, if you wanna leave, that's fine. I know you guys have a long day."

Darcie looked at Lizzie. How could she even begin to comprehend someone having to deal with a life like this? *Was this becoming more than she could handle?* For some reason, she was so desperate to protect her. "Only a long day if I can come snorkeling with you," Darcie said, lifting her leg under her, taking a long swig from the bottle, and leaving it between them.

Lizzie was thankful that even after being so dreadful, Darcie gave her yet another olive branch. The woman was beautiful, and Lizzie was going to lose her if she continued this petulant behavior.

"I like this," she said, pointing her finger to the tattoo on her leg.

Darcie gave a sarcastic laugh. "Yeah, sure you do."

"Why would you question me?"

"It's not really that I'm questioning you. I just saw your face when you spotted it is all."

"Oh," she said confused. "Ohhh, I didn't realize you'd seen that. Look, that wasn't what it looked like. I personally love it. I could just imagine what my mother would say." She sighed.

Darcie chuckled a little. "Yeah, I could imagine too. Not really the environment for visible ink."

"Well, like I said, I like it. I've always wanted one." She playfully snatched the bottle out of her hand.

"*Really*?".

"Yes, I did tell you that."

Darcie lay on her side, facing Lizzie, and put her head in her hand. "So, hit me. What would you get? Or did you not quite get that far yet?"

"Yup, I have," she said, following her actions.

"So, what then?"

"I want 'live the life you love' on my side."

"So, let's go get it tomorrow."

Lizzie looked at her sadly. "Thanks, I'd love that—"

"But?"

"How could I? My parents would see it."

"Well, next vacation, get yourself one-piece suits and then we don't need to worry."

"What makes you think there will be a next one?"

"Because you told me they have one every year."

"What makes you think *you'll* be on my next one?" Lizzie smiled.

"I'll make sure I am. And I won't make the same mistake twice."

Lizzie looked at her seriously, noting the sincerity in her eyes. "Cool," she whispered.

Darcie knew it would've been a big step for her, so she decided not to dwell, and just merely float over it. "So, next year I'm taking you for your first tat?"

"Apparently so. I'm sorry about before," Lizzie muttered.

"Forget it. Tonight's been awesome. Thank you," she said, offering the drink.

"You're thanking me?" She laughed.

"Sure am. I've never experienced this before. I kinda like it."

"I've always experienced this, but—"

"Say what? You mean you're giving me shit for having some fun, yet you do this on every vacation?" She raised an eyebrow in jest.

"Be quiet! I meant I've never had a friend on vacation, idiot," she reprimanded.

"Idiot? You really are the charmer, huh?"

"Only to people I like." She smiled shyly.

"So, you like me, huh?" Darcie smirked at her.

"Don't start. I like your company when I'm trapped on a boat feeling like Nick Nolte."

"Nick Nolte?"

"Yes, as in Cape Fear." She rolled her eyes.

"Right," she said amusedly. "Well, while your family can be a little self-obsessed and snooty, I'm sure they ain't trying to kill you."

"Hmmm," she said thoughtfully, looking at her watch.

"You need to go? What time is it?"

"It's just after 11, and no I don't, but feel free to leave if you have somewhere to be."

"Nope. Nowhere to be but here," she said simply, turning on her back and looking up at the stars.

"You guys work a lot. It must be tiring," Lizzie said, following suit, and assessing the formations above.

"Yeah, but it's great fun when you have a good team. Jose Luis, Deek, and I are really tight, and he takes us with him each season as his management team."

"So, how exactly does it work? My father said there's a crew of 26, but we don't really see that many. It just seems to be you three I can't get away from," she said amusedly.

"You're too funny! We're kind of a bit more prestigious than most other companies. Our values are that you get the utmost service from the highest level. So ultimately, the crew take care of making sure the boat is up to the standards that our customers expect and pay for. Ultimately, it's pristine, refined, and, well, perfect. You get taken care of by the management, which is why we tend to advise on fewer guests."

"Oh really? I've never heard of that. It's unusual to how we normally do it."

"Yeah, everyone says that. On the plus side, pretty much all of our guests leave and say they'll only travel with us again because of the added attention they get. It's unusual, but it's a service that we thought could make us stand out from the rest. And it totally does."

"That's really interesting."

"Sorry, I'm boring you," Darcie said, realizing she was talking to one of the guests about their service.

"No, you aren't. I was being serious," she said, turning towards her. "It's not boring. I find it surreal, listening to it all. So, serious question, are we allowed to be up here? I was on another yacht before and there was this major issue being up top because of a frequency or something?"

"Yes, with the radars. They spin off a lot. We're okay here, it's more over there." She pointed behind them.

"Oh right, good stuff. If I'm not going to get you killed, that's okay."

"Me? Not both of us?"

"Uh, oh yes, correct," she said, turning on her back again.

"You looking forward to snorkeling in the morning?" Darcie asked, not wanting to push Lizzie given how she seemed a little more relaxed than her normal reserved self.

"Yes." She smiled widely. "It's the only thing I enjoy about being here. Well, that and Haiti."

"Charming," Darcie said.

"Sorry, I didn't mean…"

"Chill, Lizzie, I'm kidding."

Lizzie took more to drink before holding it out to Darcie. "You want some more of this?"

"No, I don't think so. I should probably sleep. I have to be up earlier tomorrow, I believe?"

"Yup, if you wanna snorkel you do."

"I can live with that. Deek has asked me to swap days off, so hopefully I'll be there. It shouldn't be a problem."

"How do you get days off? I've never known that with the 'superyacht' crew."

Darcie laughed. "Yeah, well as I said, it's an entirely different concept with us. We operate differently, and since we've become so established, and been put on the map, we get to pretty much do what the hell we like. The guests get what they pay for, what they ask or *demand* they get, and equally, we get to run the show. So, we don't fuck about changing 15 times a day when we get like 10 minutes to ourselves all day, ya know? You see us wear the whites on departure, and then the rest of the time, it's casuals. It's easier for the guys to work, and easier for us to manage when we have to pamper and entertain guests solidly for like 18 hour days. It's tough going, so the fact that we offer a slightly more senior level service is definitely the way the yachting world seems to lean towards now. We're also fairly authoritative with ourselves, and that's highlighted before you pay a dime."

"Wow. I'm surprised my parents went for it."

"Your parents are old money. They're ostentatious. They don't care what clothes we wear or whether we take a day off. They care about this and this only," she said, grabbing the logo on her polo. "All they care about is getting back home to the golf club and bragging about spending 750 grand for a two-week vacation with the most prestigious and most expensive company out there." Lizzie watched her intently. "Umm, I'm sorry, Lizzie. That's completely out of line. I shouldn't have said that to you."

"I have no issue with what you said. Every part of it is correct. I just can't believe my parents paid $750,000 for this. I knew it was an obscene amount—it always is—but that really saddens me," she said. "More so when I consider the situation with Miss Lovelie and the kids."

Darcie noticed the change in Lizzie. She couldn't imagine what it must feel like for someone to feel so completely detached from their family, so *unlike* the rest of them. She always had this sadness in her eyes, aside from their day in Haiti. *What must that feel like to this young woman?* "Hey, how about we call it a day? It's late, and you've had a long one. Plus, you've got another tomorrow."

"Even longer if you're not about," she said nonchalantly.

"Well, it's no big deal. I can skip a day off this week. Haiti was kinda like my day off anyhow."

"That's very kind, but you don't have to do that for me."

"I didn't say I did. Come on, doc, let's get you to bed," she said, jumping up and immediately turning to face Lizzie, embarrassed. "Uh…"

Lizzie smiled sadly at her. "It's okay, Darcie, you don't need to say anything. Thanks for this evening," she said, kissing her cheek lightly. "Good night, Darcie."

Darcie felt a tingle on her cheek from where Lizzie's lips had been. "Goddamit! Sheesh! You idiot, Darce. You stupid, dumbass!" she said loudly. *Why the hell did she go near Annabella? What the hell was she thinking?*

*

Lizzie returned to her room and allowed tears to fall as she dropped to the floor. She pulled her knees into her chest, and let words spin through her mind. She felt like she was going to physically be sick. *How had her life turned out like this?* she thought, curling into the fetal position on the floor.

Chapter Sixteen

Lizzie woke with the sun shining brightly in her eye. She could feel it burning into her skin. *Where was she?* Her body ached, and she could barely open her eyes. She did as best as she could to move. Hitting her back against a wall, she turned around and saw the door. Suddenly, everything came flooding back to her. She'd returned to her room, and lay on the floor upset, not quite making the bed, nor closing the curtains. She remembered crying herself to sleep. It must be why she struggled to open her eyes. She checked her watch and sighed; she'd overslept. There was no time for snorkeling this morning. They'd be leaving any minute now.

Lizzie pulled herself up and made a service call, asking that some cucumber and two tea bags be brought to her room. She opened her balcony door and looked out to find the crew rushing around the deck, pulling and throwing ropes, and shouting orders at each other. She needed a shower desperately, and a massage. There's no way she could get one today while they were cruising. She wondered if anyone on board was trained when there was a knock at the door.

She opened it and saw Darcie standing there with a silver tray. "Lizzie, what's wrong?" she asked, concern in her eyes.

"Nothing, I'm fine," she said sadly.

"You're not. You've been crying, what's happened?" She pushed past her into her room, and ignored the rule about avoiding client's quarters—let alone *pushing* into their rooms—unless for work.

"I'm fine, honestly. I just had a bit of a bad night."

"How come? Did something happen when you came back? Was it me? Did your folks say something? You weren't snorkeling. I was worried," she said seriously. "When one of the stews said you'd requested this, I said I'd bring it instead. I'm glad I did."

"You're sweet. I'm fine, though. I guess the magnitude of your words concerning the cost of this vacation impacted me greater than I would've anticipated. I returned and just, well, pretty much collapsed there." She pointed to the floor by Darcie's foot where she'd slept last night. "Interestingly, I slept longer on the floor than I do in the comfy bed." She laughed cautiously. She could see the sadness and concern in Darcie's eyes and needed to stop her from worrying.

"I'm sorry," Darcie whispered.

"For what? You did nothing."

"I assumed you knew. I shouldn't have said how much they paid."

"Darce," she insisted, walking over to her side table and picking up her electronic devices. "I have a MacBook, a kindle fire, an iPad, and an iPhone. We have WiFi everywhere on board. I could've Googled it in seconds if I wanted to find out. There is nothing for you to feel guilty about." She squeezed her forearm kindly.

"*Maybe*. I hate seeing you like this, Lizzie. I hate seeing you so sad."

"Why do you care so much?"

"Because I really like you. I've never met anybody like you, and I enjoy just chatting and getting to know you. Plus, I've never met anybody that always looks so sad."

"You make me sound like I'm suicidal or something."

"Are you?" Darcie asked seriously. *How do you live a life when you're doing everything for everybody else? When you're a puppet in someone else's show?*

"I'm good, Darce. This trip is fucking hard," she said, watching Darcie's eyes widen at the swear word. "But it's two weeks, and I have a new bestie. Believe it or not, when I'm not trapped and at home in my own life, it's far easier. Please, don't worry. I had a dreadful day. If it's any consolation, this tends to happen every year after I've been to Haiti. This year Miss Lovelie looks older and frailer. I guess it frightens me that something may happen and she might not be here next year."

"Would you ever consider working over there? Helping the kids? Or like she said, go work at the hospital and spend more time with them?"

"I couldn't. My family would never allow it," she muttered.

"So? You're a grown ass woman. What do they do for you? You already said you don't care about the money, so *fuck* them!" she spat.

Lizzie noticed a darkness glaze over the woman's eyes. The soft turquoise that she loved to look at was replaced with something entirely different. "Please don't do this, Darcie. Don't make it harder for me."

They stood there in silence for a few seconds before the crackly Spanish sounded around them. Darcie pulled her talkie from the back of her shorts and spoke into it in Spanish. "I have to go, I'm sorry. I didn't mean to make you feel bad, but I made a promise to Miss Lovelie, and I stand by my word. Try and get some time today, or this evening." She went to the pad and pen on the side table, and scribbled something down. "Here's my number. If you can manage it, text me. I wanna see you," she said, kissing her on the cheek and leaving.

Lizzie pecked her the evening before, but put it down to alcohol consumption, and wanting Darcie to know she hadn't offended her. And maybe a little because she was gorgeous, and Lizzie would've gone all out to have a two-week fairy-tale romance on board had Darcie not pursued her sister. But she liked the fact that Darcie said she wanted to see her. Truth be known, she wanted to see her too, but she wasn't about to tell her that. Darcie had pretty much demanded to see her. Interestingly, her entire life had been filled with people demanding and dictating her, and it was infuriating. *So why did it feel different with Darcie? Why did it feel warm and exhilarating?*

Lizzie thought about Alex Carter, her only experience with an American woman when she lived in the states for her placement year at Uni. It seemed to be the American way. Brits were far more reserved, or maybe uptight was a better term. Her experience was that Americans were direct and to the point. She liked that. She was completely smitten by Alex instantly. There was something about her that infatuated Lizzie. They went off into a whirlwind romance where, just like Darcie's ability, it took her away from the real world. Or *her* real world. She was confused and scared, enjoying the friendship growing between them.

*

Lizzie pressed call and hit the speaker button on her phone, placing wet bags over her eyes.

"Hello? What's wrong, Miss Lizzie?"

"Hi, Miss Lovelie." She giggled. "How are you?"

"I'm fine, child. Are you okay?"

"I'm fine, don't panic. I just wanted to check in."

"You never check in. What's going on?"

"Nothing," she said quietly.

"You lie," she accused

"I just wanted a friendly voice to talk to."

"About Miss Darcie?"

"Excuse me? Why would you ask that?"

"I saw the way you looked at each other."

Lizzie didn't know what to say. "I just want a friend to talk to, I suppose."

"You love her?"

"What?!" she shouted. "Of course not, Miss Lovelie. I don't love her, but I guess I like her. I can't go there for one reason or another, but I like spending time with her. And Miss Lovelie, she's keeping her promise to you. I don't think I've ever experienced someone so thoughtful, and kindhearted."

"So, what's the problem?"

"I don't know what to do."

"About what?"

"Her."

"What do you want to do, sweet child? If you're asking me, you like her. If you don't want to risk things, or if the past is causing you to doubt it, then take a friendship. It's more than you have, and better than nothing."

"Valid point."

"Have I upset you?"

"Gosh, no. I'm serious. Thanks, it's a valid point."

"Good. I should go. Come see me soon?"

"I promise, Miss Lovelie. I won't leave for so long this time."

"Take care, we all love you."

"I love and miss you all too, Miss Lovelie."

*

Lizzie got ready for a day by the pool. She was happy after her discussion with Miss Lovelie. She needed to sort herself out. She couldn't change the situation, but what she could do is enjoy the next eight days. And that she would. Equally, she'd enjoy the friendship that Darcie offered. Like Miss Lovelie said, she can have an ally *and* someone to get her through the vacation.

"Hey, gorgeous girl," the Caribbean whispered.

"Hi, are you okay?" she asked, kissing Deek on his cheek quickly. Jose Luis walked up behind him and she reiterated the action.

"We're good, girl, how you doing?" Deek asked.

"I'm good. I'm hoping to sneak off and spend some time with you guys." She winked, walking over to her family, who were already comfortably seated at the pool. Once again, she wished that life was as different as she pictured in her daydreams.

"Good morning, Elizabeth, how did you sleep?" her mother inquired.

"Fine, thank you, Mother." She removed a towel and unrolled it, placing it on her lounger. "Did you all have a good evening?"

"Yes, it was lovely. Shame you missed it." The comment had her mother's typical edge to it.

"Indeed," she said, pulling her phone from her Prada beach bag. Lizzie opened the phone, and checked her emails, noticing Darcie's tattooed leg walking towards them. She put her sunglasses on, and continued checking her emails with the odd, sneaky glance at Darcie working around her family, making them cocktails, and offering champagne.

Darcie was stoked that she'd put her glasses back on before coming out here, as she tried desperately to avert her gaze from Lizzie's toned, tanned body, those beautiful, long, wavy, blonde curls falling over her shoulder. When she'd first seen the sisters, she couldn't believe how beautiful they were. But the more she'd gotten to know Annabella and Lizzie, the more she realized they were nothing alike. Bella had become uglier, and Lizzie was even more stunning than she'd first thought. "Champagne or cocktail?" Darcie asked, leaning over Lizzie, smirking a little as her back turned away from the family.

"Could I possibly just get a sparkling water, please?"

"My gosh, you really have no idea how to vacation sister," Vivvi shouted. "Have some Dom or a mojito or something."

"I think I had a bit too much last night," she said without thinking.

"Last night, Elizabeth? You were in bed before 10." Her mother eyed her questioningly.

"Oh, yes. Maybe the sun then. I'm still not feeling great after the other day." She stood up and dove into the pool.

Darcie smirked as she walked off, hearing Lizzie's lie. She liked having this little secret. She usually confided everything in Jose Luis and Deek, but it just didn't feel right. She wanted to keep Lizzie's secret. *Her secret. Their secret.*

*

Deek relieved her to go change, and prep for the evening ahead. She quickly showered and grabbed a freshly ironed shirt. She sat on her bed, crossed her legs, and opened her phone. She'd left her number with Lizzie, and was disappointed that there was still no message.

Darcie lay back on her bed, pushing her hands behind her head as she had a thought. She sat quickly, smirking to herself as she recalled Miss Roseline's words. She pulled at the cupboard and rummaged through everything before finding what she was looking for. Bingo.

Darcie lay upside down on her front with the pen in her hand, thinking considerably as she tapped the biro pen across her temple, trying to think what to put in a letter. Miss Roseline had said Lizzie was a bit old fashioned like that. She liked letters—writing and receiving.

Darcie picked up her phone and Googled what to write in a letter and scanned over the results. "Seriously, dude, what are you doing?" she scorned herself. It didn't need to be war and peace at this stage, just a small note. That was fine. *Was this a love note?* Oh, screw it. She already knew Lizzie would like it. She grabbed the pen again, pulling the paper closer to her, and began writing.

Missed you today. Get your folks to the sky lounge and meet me at the toys overhang at 10.30pm -Dxx.

Was it enough? she thought. Yeah, sure it was. Lizzie would like it. She totally knew she would. Darcie left the room and discreetly slid the note under Lizzie's door, before rushing back up to her team.

*

Darcie's absence hadn't gone unnoticed by Lizzie, more so because she was left with her family. Every time anyone said anything about her, she jumped into the pool and chose to ignore them, which she was certain would cause a great deal of telling off later. She was becoming far less patient with her family. She just needed to get through the family time and enjoy herself with her own little vacation wherever she could.

Lizzie had spent hours with her family, and now felt suitably intoxicated. It was the only means of getting through the pain with them all, but she did it. Now she only had a short 30 minute turnaround before the evening meal. She'd gone for a new theory this evening. Drink lots, which would mean less tension with the family. The more intoxicated she was, meant the less time she had to spend with them that evening. Being she was the only worker left in the family—a chief surgeon—it would be a suitable excuse for not being a heavy drinker, just like Daddy hadn't been when he was still practicing. She just needed to *pretend* to drink. She wanted to stay relatively sober, so she could bump into Darcie again. Unfortunately, the alcohol was already taking an uncontrollable effect on her mind, and if she was honest, her libido.

*

Lizzie entered her room, noticing the slip of paper on the floor. She threw her towel onto the bed, opened the paper, and read the message.

Looking forward to seeing you at the toys overhang tonight -Dxx

Lizzie smiled at the note. She was speaking the truth when she'd said she wanted to see her. She needed to sober herself up, and quick. She only had 10 minutes to finish her hair and find something to wear, something that would knock Darcie out. She'd have to get upstairs to the exterior deck without her parents causing a scene for her tardiness. Why did she wear the sequin dress the other night? She rushed through her wardrobe trying to find an outfit. *"Perfect!"* she squealed, pulling out a dress.

Lizzie dried and curled her hair, allowing her large, soft waves to fall over her shoulder. She pulled the cappuccino t-shirt dress over her head, placing the long silver dress necklace around her neck, and sprayed some perfume. "Bugger, where're my shoes?" she said aloud, rushing around the room, desperately searching for her suede ankle boots. She felt a pain in her arm. "Bollox!" She rubbed her right arm that had taken a hit from the wardrobe door. *God, she needed to refrain from drinking this evening, or she just may fall overboard.*

Lizzie made her way up to the outer deck after carefully putting her shoes on. She could see her family talking at the table, the gentle glow from the moonlight and candles illuminating the stunning scene. Following her lateness, a few more insults were sure to come. She quickly hid behind the wall so her parents couldn't see, and whistled lowly to the deck crew talking in the kitchen. She noticed the tattooed leg. God, she wanted to feel that again. *Stop it, Lizzie*. She whistled again, this time caught their attention.

Darcie walked towards Lizzie's peeking head. As she reached her, Lizzie pulled her out of sight, only for the two to fall backwards through the swinging door into the main saloon, and onto the couch. "Double bugger," Lizzie said, hurting her lower back this time. She was barely able to acknowledge it, as all she could think about was Darcie between her legs and so close to her face.

"Erm, you coulda just said you wanted me on top of you," Darcie said smirking.

"Bugger off," she replied.

Darcie stood up, unable to ignore the way Lizzie's short dress had lifted, revealing her tanned thigh and slight glimpse of black lace underwear. She immediately felt a flush in her face. Her eyes traveled up the disheveled woman. She reached her eyes, and noticed Lizzie raise an eyebrow to her. *Crap*, she thought, instantly moving and holding her hand out to help her up.

"Pervert!" Lizzie squealed, frowning as they were face to face. The heeled boots gave her a slight edge to Darcie's height this evening. "I was just going to ask if you could provide me with ice water, whenever I ask for gin this evening?"

"Well, after that scene, I would have done so anyhow." She arched her brow and pushed the door open for Lizzie. "After you, doctor." Darcie smirked, paying close attention to the departing view.

*

Lizzie hid the smile from her face as she walked down to the outer deck dining area to meet her family. She slid in beside one of the stewards who poured them all some water.

"You're late," her mother said sharply.

"By three minutes. Some of us have to work," she said, instantly regretting the response. This was why she didn't drink with her family; she couldn't control the truth from coming out. However, seeing Deek and Darcie opposite of her, both open mouthed, was a sight in itself.

"I don't like your tone, dear," her mother seethed.

"Well, Father, what do you think? I've been reconsidering my decision of going into medicine in recent months. When I'm held up with work while on vacation, it becomes tiresome. The intention was to follow in your footsteps, but—"

"Enough of this!" he shouted. "You're here now and had little time to get ready. Marjorie, leave Elizabeth alone. She can't help being delayed when she's working. You need to refrain from this anarchy you have over Elizabeth's work. She's bound for incredible things, and will drive this family name in continuance within the medical profession. Excuse me, captain, when will dinner be served?" he asked pointedly, ruling out any further discussion on the matter.

Lizzie knew that wasn't a win, particularly. Her mother would no longer be able to admonish her, but equally, the atmosphere was ruined for the evening, which meant it would only be longer and harder. She was fairly amused by the reaction of the staff though.

*

The staff served their dinner as the menial chit chat continued amongst them. Lizzie was broken out of her wandering mind as she heard the sweet, American voice. She looked around the table, reconfirming the narcissistic behavior of her family before looking up and smiling widely at Darcie.

"Would you like a drink, Doctor Barrington?"

"Yes, a gin and tonic would be lovely." She smiled sheepishly.

"Cucumber in it also?"

"Perfect."

"Sure thing."

"Oh, Darcie, is it?" Bella said, interrupting her sister. "Could you possibly make me another champagne cocktail?" She smiled angelically. "Here, the same glass will be quite sufficient."

"Darling, there's no requirement to use the same glass. They should have plenty, the money we've spent," their mother said.

"Quite alright, Mother." She turned her back to her and confronted Darcie face to face. Lizzie couldn't help but watch the interaction between them, feeling a wave of sickness come over her.

She couldn't be sure, but she was slightly confident that Darcie wasn't engaging in whatever her sister was playing at. She noticed the frequent glances Darcie issued her, ensuring she captured her gaze each time with the faintest of smiles. Lizzie watched as her sister discreetly handed Darcie the glass, making sure to touch her hand.

Darcie eyed Lizzie cautiously as she felt Bella stroke her hand with the exchange of the champagne flute. She immediately stepped back, confirming Bella's request, and walked away, making a conscious effort to assure Lizzie once more that she wasn't going to make the same mistake twice.

*

Bella's actions heightened throughout the course of the evening, and it was evident that the cause for that was due to some irritation between her and Oliver. It was typical of her sister. Have an argument, then feel it's appropriate to turn your attention elsewhere. Darcie kept refilling Lizzie's pretend gin and tonic through the duration of the meal and maintained a very dignified distance from her sister. Lizzie didn't have a hold on Darcie, and if she wanted to go there again with Bella, she was in no position to say or do a single thing.

"Can I please have some champagne?" Bella asked one of the younger stews, who rushed off in obedience.

Lizzie looked up, as the young boy poured champagne into her glass, and saw Darcie eyeing her intently. She had sadness in her eyes and Lizzie didn't exactly know what for. Darcie spun around, and the following moments seemed to unravel in slow motion. Darcie's rapid spin caused her to bump into a stew carrying a tray of flutes. She lost her footing while attempting to rescue the tray, and several glasses smashed into her hand.

Lizzie looked aghast as her family merely turned their heads, displeased at the disturbance of their after-dinner coffee and cigar fest. She noticed the staff rush around her and saw the white towel quickly turning a deep shade of red. "Father, please, excuse me. There appears to have been an accident with one of the crew; I'm going to offer my assistance."

"Okay, Libby. Call me if you need some senior assistance," her father said, barely looking up. Lizzie rushed off, rolling her eyes at her father's egotistical response.

"Hi, I just saw what happened. Let me see," she said, moving to the stool where Darcie was.

"I'm fine, just a small cut. We have medics onboard," she said, nodding her head to Deek, who ran up the stairs two at a time with a first aid box in tow.

"Please, it clearly isn't fine. Look at the blood you're losing."

"Got the suture kit, boss," Deek said.

"The suture kit? Bloody hell, show me now, Darcie!" Lizzie demanded, feeling numerous eyes on her.

Darcie couldn't bring herself to argue back. She felt tired and the blood-stained towel didn't go unnoticed. She pulled the almost red towel away and heard gasps as the "z" shaped cut showed two flaps of skin lifted open.

"Holy fuck!" she yelled, stunned. "Darcie, you need to go to the hospital."

"Look, we've had worse things happen here." She covered it a little. "I think I need to lie down."

"Woah, easy, girl," Deek said, grabbing her and carrying her to the couch.

"Libby, can you manage?" her father shouted in.

"Yes, fine! Give me the equipment. I'll see to it."

"Lizzie, it's fine. It's no big deal," she said, hearing her parents' requests from outside. They merely looked disgusted and continued like nothing had happened, like they should still be waited upon.

Jose Luis knelt beside Darcie and said something in Spanish, to which she nodded. He looked at Deek who responded with the only two words Lizzie understood: "Si, capitan."

"Libby, are you sure?" Her father walked in.

"Yes, of course. It's my job."

"Darling, this is not your job. Do hurry, and make sure you put some gloves on," her mother said, a look of disgust on her face.

Darcie began to speak before noticing the look on Lizzie's face, and immediately stopped. She couldn't blame the woman. They were friends, and she wanted to help. Her mother openly insinuated that she was some disease-ridden junkie.

"I need to get downstairs, Deek. This isn't the right environment."

"Okay, mon. Come," he said, getting one of the young deck hands to help get her downstairs.

Lizzie grabbed an ice bucket, some towels, a bottle of water, and a bottle of tequila, hoping that's all she needed. She followed them all the way down to the deck below. "You sure you got this?" Deek questioned Lizzie carefully.

"I promise, I'll take great care of her," she said, looking around at the tiny space. "Maybe we should've taken you to my room. There's very little space here."

"We manage okay," she said warily.

"Okay. Darcie, I need you to sit up for me a little." She poured some water onto one of the towels and put it in place of the blood ridden one.

Handing a glass of water to Darcie and instructing her to drink, Lizzie opened the medical bag and box, pulling out the instruments and equipment she needed. "I think you'll need to go see a doctor tomorrow," she said seriously.

"Cool, is that my date I finally get?" She laughed, sipping the water.

"I don't know if I'll be able to get off here to go with you," she said seriously.

"I wasn't talking about getting off. I was talking about seeing you, being as you're a doctor and all that."

"No, a real doctor."

"You're not a real doctor?"

"Oh, bloody hell, be quiet and let me sort this first."

"Woah, you're trying to fuck about with me when you aren't a doctor?"

"Be quiet. I know exactly what I'm doing," she said, dismissing Darcie, and feeling a flush color her face at the resounding words in her head. "I am a real doctor, but I meant, a doctor with a practice and real equipment and treatments."

"I trust you," Darcie said, holding her gaze.

Lizzie lifted the towel and noticed the uncomfortable reaction from Darcie. "I'm sorry." She gently pushed the folded flap back into the correct position. "On the plus side, you have a Harry Potter scar. People would pay thousands for that." She smiled softly and focused her attention on the utensils beside her.

"Awesome," she said quietly.

"Are you okay? Do you want anything before I begin?"

The young deckhand reappeared at the door. "Cap said to come and assist if you need it," he said, wide eyed at the sight before him.

"You wanna come over to this end bud and keep me company?" Darcie asked, mindful of his pale demeanor.

He rushed past Lizzie, kneeling on the floor at the bedside and focused on Darcie. "You alright, boss?"

"Yeah, I'm a tough cookie."

Lizzie was concerned with how drowsy she appeared to be getting. "Could you please make sure she's getting plenty of fluids?" she asked the boy. "Darcie, first I'm going to anesthetize it, then I'll clean it up—which may sting a little—and stitch it back up for you. Darce, you aren't going to be able to use it, or get it wet for a few weeks because of the stitches. I don't know if you'll be able to continue on here."

"I get it. I'll speak to Jose Luis in the morning."

*

"Thanks for this."

"It's fine. How you holding up?"

"I feel pretty crap if I'm honest," Darcie said sleepily.

"Yes, I bet," Lizzie said, taking the gloves off. "She's good now. Maybe you could tell the captain she needs rest this evening?"

"Yes, doc," the deckhand said.

"I can't quite work out if he's crushing on you or terrified of you." Darcie smiled.

Lizzie walked over to the door and locked it, making her way back over to Darcie.

"You scared me tonight," Lizzie said sadly, kneeling up to face her.

"It's nothing. It happens all the time."

"I'm pretty sure it doesn't. Look, I should let you sleep. If you need anything—"

"Please don't. Just stay here for a while?" Darcie pleaded.

Lizzie knew she was not herself, and wondered how she'd feel knowing that? *She had such a strong character and was asking for her to stay. Would she recall it in the morning?*

"Of course," Lizzie said. "Do you want anything?"

"Just what I can't have," she whispered.

Lizzie looked at the woman, whose face was pale. She poured some water on a hand towel and dabbed it to her perspiring forehead. "And what's that?" she asked, equally as quiet.

Darcie turned to face Lizzie, looking at her intently and wondering how to respond. Her hand throbbed, but before she had an opportunity to further consider a response, she heard a ringing in her ears, and squinted a little.

Lizzie looked at her apologetically as she checked her phone.

"It's okay, I know you gotta go. Thanks for looking after me," Darcie said.

"I don't want to leave you," she whispered.

"Me neither, but your folks will be on your back, and it's not worth it. I'm sorry we couldn't meet tonight."

"We did, silly."

"Not like how I wanted."

"How did you want it?" Lizzie stood looking at her, her phone ringing again.

"Go."

"I'm so sorry," Lizzie said, giving her all into an apologetic look.

"Don't worry. Thanks for tonight."

"Anytime. I'll text you so that you have my number. Contact me if you need me. Take care, Darcie," she said, kissing her forehead and stroking her thumb over the wound.

"I have the full use of two legs, no way I'll text you. I know you love letters, so I'll drop a letter off."

"Don't you dare. Text me you have a letter, and I'll come."

"Loaded statement, lady. Go before your mom brings in someone to quarantine me for all my diseases."

"I don't care. Rest well, Darce."

"Thanks, Lizzie. Take care."

Chapter Seventeen

"I've decided Libby has a new lady friend," Vivvi announced as Lizzie returned, steadily checking her phone.

"*Excuse me?*"

"Well, you're spending less time than usual with us. You're late. You're on your phone and laptop constantly. You definitely have a girlfriend back home," Vivvi said.

"Darling? Is this true? Oh, how wonderful! When can we meet her? Let's take her to the golf club. Oh, I hope she isn't like the last one," her mother said in one breath.

"I don't know what you mean," Lizzie replied.

"Oh my gosh, she so does. You've never been able to lie." Bella smirked.

Lizzie could feel the tension running through her system. The only override was the fact that her family looked happy. They thought she had a girlfriend, and that it had nothing to do with a certain beautiful, American, which meant that she could enjoy a friendship with Darcie without worrying. Equally, they were being unusually easy-going about her not spending as much time with them. *This could work in her favor.*

Lizzie missed the barrage of questions being thrown at her. She wasn't in the mood to deal with her family right now. She couldn't stop thinking about Darcie, and her hand. And while they were happy to jovially interrogate her all night, she realized she may be able to grab another evening without them.

"I'm not having this conversation right now." Lizzie stood up.

"She has got a girlfriend!" Vivvi clapped her hands together.

"You are excused for this evening. Tomorrow, I want to know everything, including what family she is from," her mother said.

Wonderful, a night filled with story making. Albeit, a night away, as it was still relatively early, she thought as she left the table.

*

"Good evening."

"Hi, have you seen or heard from Darcie?" she asked the young deck hand who'd assisted her earlier.

"No, doc, I think she's sleeping. You want me to go check on her?"

"No, it's fine. Thank you."

Lizzie returned to her room, wondering whether she should go and check on Darcie. She'd texted her earlier but received no response. She was concerned about her welfare, so as a doctor, surely she was only doing her job. Clearly, it had nothing to do with the fact that she wanted to be near her again, looking after her, and... feeling her skin. *Jesus, this was not good.* She had a week left and she literally didn't know if she had the will power to remain only as friends. She was completely enamoured by Darcie, and that was never going to end well. She could risk developing feelings, and never seeing her again, but she wasn't sure she could move past the whole sister thing. On the flip side, she could refrain but then always wonder what it'd be like to kiss her anywhere other than her cheek or forehead. How it would feel entwining their fingers, feeling her soft skin against her own. Or Darcie's lips on her own. She imagined her lips were soft and tasted of citrus from her infatuation with lime water. She wondered how Darcie would kiss. *Was she the type of woman to take the lead? Would she start slow, before increasing the pace or was she more of a tease? Start and end slow, leaving her desperate for more.* Simply put, Lizzie was screwed. Somehow this woman had completely captivated her. She opened the door to her room and sadly closed her eyes. *Seriously, what was she going to do?*

She needed to stay away. It's the only way she would be able to control herself. Opening her eyes again, she breathed in deeply. "I can do this, I can do this, I can do this," she said aloud, feeling determined with her mission. Stepping forward, Lizzie heard a slight crunch under her foot. She could already feel a smile disobeying her and forming on her lips.

A little note for my lovely doctor to say thank you for looking after me. Feeling a little sorry for myself. The thought of you receiving a letter, making you smile, made me feel a little better. -Dxx

"Oh bugger," she said aloud as she slammed her head against the bed. Lizzie removed her shoes, grabbed her key and travel pack, and left her room.

*

Darcie could feel the medication wearing off. *Sheesh, she was in some kinda pain.* She lay staring at the ceiling, which was oddly not mere centimeters from her head, like

113

the usual bunks the cabins consisted of. She wondered if Lizzie had managed to escape her family and seen the note yet. *And if so, did she sit there thinking she was a dork? God this woman was chewing her up inside. Why the fuck had she hooked up with Bella? Yeah, she was hot, but nowhere near as much as Lizzie. Lizzie had hidden depths.* The disgusted look at her tat on day one wasn't, in fact, a disgusted look. She read her all wrong. And despite all else, Darcie was 99% certain that something would've happened between them. But did she really want to get involved with someone that she could see something more with? *Jesus, what was she thinking?* She needed to stop. Lizzie made it perfectly clear that she wouldn't go near her because of Bella. The English doctor was well on her way to capturing her heart, and she couldn't let that happen. No, she'd be good, the friend Lizzie needed. Well, that's if Jose Luis let her stay. *He may not wanna pay for her if she couldn't do her job,* she thought sadly. *Stop it, be strong.* "She's just a pretty face, she's just a pretty face, she's just a pretty face..." she said aloud, trying to convince herself this was true, upon hearing a light tap on the door. Darcie froze. *Who could it be?* "Oh fuck, please be that pretty face," she whispered, making her way to the door and opening it.

"Hi," Lizzie said.

"Doctor Barrington, after hours extra care?" Darcie smirked.

"Behave, I'm here on a purely professional level."

"Sure, you are," she said.

"So, how's things? How're you feeling? Have you kept hydrated? You shouldn't have gotten up to drop the letter off," she insisted.

"Wow, authoritative *and* a million questions. Did you smile?"

"Excuse me?"

"When you saw my note, did you smile?"

"I did, but—"

"No buts. I asked a question, you answered. And in response to your initial one, yeah, I'm okay. I'm in a little pain, but as I mentioned before, I have two legs, both of which work perfectly fine. It was no issue with the letter."

"You're so cheeky."

"You love how cheeky I am, and you can't deny it." Darcie pointed her finger at her.

"You think you know me. You think I like unruly ladies, but I can assure you, you're quite displeasing."

"Your eyes tell a different story, lady. Tequila?"

"You *cannot* drink. You went through surgery a mere few hours ago," Lizzie scolded. "And what exactly are you referring to with my eyes?"

"I know, but as they say, worse things happen at sea. It's fine, I'm good." Darcie smiled kindly.

"Eyes," Lizzie reiterated.

"God, you're very demanding, I just meant... it doesn't matter."

"It matters to me."

Darcie looked at her seriously. "I'll tell you when I'm not so drugged up. I feel unsafe saying certain things, but I promise I'll tell you."

"I'll accept that. And my point entirely about the medication and alcohol," she said seriously.

"I like you being all authoritative."

"Stop flirting. There's no veto just because you're unwell."

"Well, that's no fun. And here I thought my favorite doctor would give me some extra TLC."

"Your favorite doctor would've had you not—"

"I get it, I get it, I get it. We don't need to go over it again," she sighed.

"I'm sorry, that was unfair of me. Do you need some more medication? I brought my medical bag. I have some that are stronger than over-the-counter meds."

"Ahh the pluses of befriending a *super doctor.*" She winked, laying down on her bed. "Do you mind?" She pointed to the bed.

"Hardly a super doctor, lady. Of course not. Apologies, I shouldn't have come. I'll let you—"

"I wanted you to come. I was waiting for you to come," Darcie said simply. "And you're *my* super doctor."

Lizzie stayed quiet for a moment, revisiting her chat with herself a short while ago.

"What are you thinking?" Darcie questioned.

"Erm, nothing."

"Why can't you just tell me?" Lizzie looked at her contemplatively. It's about your twin again, isn't it?"

"My what?"

"Twin?" Darcie asked confused. "Your sister? Bella?"

"She told you we were twins?"

"No, I did... I just thought... what, aren't you?"

"No! But you've just made my day." She giggled light-heartedly, glad that the mood had lifted.

"Why? I can't believe you aren't twins! You look virtually identical."

"Clearly, I'm the better looking one though." She winked.

"Without a shadow of a doubt," Darcie said.

"Well, given my sister tried her utmost to get your attention all evening, making it blatantly obvious that she would like a repeat of her first day, please feel free to tell

her you thought her older sister of six years was her twin."
She laughed.

"Six years? Jesus, no way! You look awesome for 34, and I'm not just saying that. Also, I have no interest in Bella. I learned from my mistake. It'll be one I never make again, I can assure you. I'm aware how I fucked up," she said sincerely.

"I wish I could get over the fact you slept with her." Lizzie fidgeted with her fingers in her lap.

"You do?"

"I do, but I... just don't know how to. She's always been the typical younger sibling, making a conscious effort to try and belittle me, get me into trouble. She's vile, and nasty. I couldn't bare her finding out. She'd make my life misery."

"Why do you put up with it all, Lizzie?"

"What choice do I have? They're my family."

"They aren't a family. That isn't how family treats each other."

"It's only Bella. We have the eldest, youngest sibling rivalry going on."

"I disagree. Ryan and I don't treat each other like that," Darcie said simply.

"Is that your brother?"

"No, my sister. I'm American; we call dudes, Kelly, and chicks, Ryan." She laughed.

"Do you have a brother named Kelly?" she asked, entertained.

"No, it's just Ry and me."

"What's she like?" Lizzie pulled her legs to the side, getting comfortable.

"She's cool. She's super hot..."

"Oh yeah, as opposed to you?" she said immediately, embarrassed at the slip of her tongue.

S.L. Gape

Darcie smiled shyly. "You think I'm hot then, huh?"

"Be quiet. Continue…"

"Yes, ma'am. She was always totally popular, and every guy loved her and the girls wanted to hate her, but she's super smart, and super adorable. She's the nicest person you'll ever meet. She wasn't your typical bitchy prom queen. She was cool."

"Wow, don't suppose she's gay and single?" Lizzie winked.

"Straight and married, with kids. But she has a nearly as awesome, gay, single sister." Darcie winked back.

"So, do you have nieces or nephews?"

"One of each. Typical Ry. She always wanted one girl and one boy. Most people never get that, but Ryan did."

"Does that bother you?"

"Hell no, she's my best friend. We did sex baby dances throughout each pregnancy."

"*Sex baby dances*? Do I *want* to know?" she asked, laughing.

"It's not as bad as it sounds. A bit like a rain dance, but she wanted a boy first, to look after the girl, so we did 'boy' dances, and then 'girl' dances with the second pregnancy." She smiled.

"And it worked?" Lizzie asked surprised.

"Nuh uh. Addison came first; she's ten now. Then Nate; he's seven."

"Do you speak to them much?"

"Every other day. And I have a Skype date on Saturday nights for family night."

"What's family night?" Lizzie smiled, leaning in closer.

God this girl was killing her. She'd never taken her family for granted, ever. She'd never been in a situation before that made her feel like she took for granted how

118

lucky she was to have the family she had. Everyone she knew, everyone she'd ever met, had a family that they loved and cherished, but here was this amazing and incredible woman, whose family treated her like she was less than worthy of being one of them. "Pretty much everything it sounds like. Family night is a night with the family." She smirked. "We always chose Saturday for family night growing up—"

"How old is she?" Lizzie asked interestedly. "Sorry, I didn't mean to interrupt."

Darcie forgot about her pain and tiredness from talking to Lizzie like this, until she attempted to move towards her and leaned on her hand. "Fuck!" she squealed.

"Jesus! Darcie?" Lizzie jumped over the small distance between them on the tiny cabin bed.

"I'm fine, don't worry," Darcie said, smiling to her, using her uninjured hand to squeeze hers a little. "Listen, you don't ever have to apologize to me for interrupting. I love that you're interested." She took a leap and touched Lizzie's face with a gentle stroke before moving back. "Ryan's 37, and I'm 35. In case you wondered," she said sheepishly.

"I did. And what does she do?"

"She's a pilot."

"Oh, really?"

"Yup, sure is. She's awesome at it too. She's done it for so long that she's got an awesome little gig now where she pretty much does a bit like a nine to five doing internal. And she's just been approached to become a personal pilot."

"My gosh. Wow, so both of you will be committed to a life of pain and torture with the horrifically wealthy?"

"It's not so bad. But yeah, hopefully she'll get it. They're offering a pretty decent package."

"Big traveling family, then?"

"A little, I guess. Mom and Dad vacation a lot and come visit me, but they didn't work in travel like we do."

"Do they still work now?"

"Nah. Mom was a high school teacher, and pops, well, bit of a long story."

"Why?"

"Don't you have something better you could be doing? Rather than listen to me talk about my family?"

"No," she said simply. "Unless you need to sleep?"

Darcie smiled, wishing she could just grab her and hold her all night long. "My pops wanted more than anything to be an attorney. He spent his entire life dreaming big, but part way through school, my grandpa died, and he had to step up and take over the ranch. He had to quit school, and help my grandma. He did good though. When Ry and I started kindergarten, he worked on the ranch during the day and took part time night classes. He had to pretty much start afresh because so many years had passed..."

"And did he? Do it?" Lizzie asked keenly.

"Sure did. After a couple years, my grandma decided the ranch was too much for her at her age and wanted my pops to follow his dream. She sold up and paid his tuition fees and made him go full time. It was on the basis that she moved in with us for the duration, so she could help my mom out with everything, and so that her career didn't suffer. It was awesome. We've always been a real tight family, and I have some awesome memories with my grandma."

"Is she still alive now?"

"Unfortunately, no. She passed away about 10 years ago."

"I'm sorry," she said sadly. "But what fantastic role models. Do they mind that you do this?"

Darcie watched Lizzie, completely engulfed in the conversation. "No, they're happy. I was a partner at the biggest law firm back home. I left home to progress my career, and before I knew it, I was obsessed. 18 hour days, and in my folk's words, 'driving myself into an early grave.' During one of our family nights, and after way too much liquor, my mom and Ry got upset that I was going the same route as pops. He worked so hard to make it that he was completely obsessed by it. They worried so much about him. Well, we all did. And then I did the same. It made me put things into perspective, you know? I didn't even enjoy my job, I just wanted to follow my dad because I knew he'd be proud of me. He worked so hard to follow his dream. The problem was, he would've been proud of me no matter what. We were in his office one day, and he asked me, seriously, what my dream was and why I wasn't following it," she said. "I completely had to rethink my life."

"That's..." Lizzie stopped.

"Normal?" Darcie continued.

"Actually, I was going to say nice."

"Yeah it is, but Lizzie, it's also normal. I wish you could meet my family. I'm sure you'd love them. They'd love you for sure."

"That sounds nice. Why do you think they'd like me?"

"My mom would literally fall in love with you, and mother you to hell." She laughed. "There's nothing not to love," she said quietly. "Have you ever been to the states? Sorry, ridiculous question. Of *course* you have."

"Yes, but not in so many holidays. I lived in the states for a while," she said shyly, concerned about the conversation.

"You *did*? No way! Where?"

"Massachusetts."

Darcie eyed her cautiously. "Cambridge?"

"Yes," she said pointedly. "Anyway, don't try to ignore the 'partner' at the biggest law firm comment."

"You were cherry picked for Harvard?" she asked, amazed.

"You were a super-duper lawyer for the biggest law firm on the planet," she stated matter-of-factly.

"Not quite."

"Yes quite!" she added. "So, tell me the story of law to stew."

"On one condition."

Lizzie eyed her cautiously. "Go on."

"I need to lay down. Come here?" Darcie asked kindly, and pointed to the small space between herself and the wall.

"That's very little room."

"Good thing you're skinny," she said. "I promise I won't hit on you."

"Not that skinny. That's obscene; I'll virtually be on top of you."

"That's my deal. And then I'll tell all." She smiled.

Lizzie wanted to argue back, but the alcohol and adrenaline infused day made her veer more to do it than not do it. She lay down beside Darcie in the slim bed. "I do believe I have obliged," she said nervously, feeling the closeness between them. "So, there's a story to tell?"

Darcie wanted to say so many things, but knew she was unable to. "I like this," she said quickly, ensuring Lizzie didn't have a chance to respond. "I was kind of a big deal back home. That sounds arrogant, I'm aware, but lots of firms came after me. As I said, I was doing 18 hour days, even weekends. It was silly. After my pops asked me about my dream, I knew I needed to consider it. My pops was so sad. He didn't want me to follow him, he wanted me to follow my heart like he did. After a long discussion, I realized I loved to travel. I was passionate and curious about it. I'd always wanted to travel and explore, and I'm not afraid to admit, I do kinda like my luxuries, so this seemed like the sensible option. My boss had a charter, so he put me in touch with the company on the basis that, when my 'temporary insanity' was over, I'd go back. My pops was disheartened that I felt I had to do the job just because he did. He was super stoked I quit to do this. He and Mom both were so worried I'd lose out on the whole love and marriage stuff though. More so because being a lawyer didn't really allow for that. When I said I was doing this, they were kinda stoked. They felt that this would capture my heart and someday I'd meet a girl who would too."

"And do you think that?" Lizzie asked seriously.

"I didn't, no."

"Didn't? Past tense? So, what's changed?"

Darcie was desperate to say so much, but she couldn't. "Who knows," she said simply. "Tell me something that nobody knows."

"Like what?"

"Anything you can trust me with."

"Ummm, I'm not sure."

"There must be something. Do you trust me?" she asked, watching her seriously.

"I'm a strong believer of innocent until proven guilty, and not vice versa, and you've done nothing to make me think I can't trust you. I would even go as far to say that

I've likely never trusted anyone as much as I have you," she said softly. "That sounds stupid, I suppose."

"I disagree. It's the nicest thing anyone's ever said to me. Thank you. Tell me something then," she repeated, noticing the discomfort in Lizzie's expression. She didn't want to retract what she'd said, but she wanted this amazing woman to know that she didn't only have Miss Lovelie and Miss Roseline in her life to trust and talk to. Darcie took her hand in her own and stroked her thumb across her fingers, encouraging her to talk.

"I used to wish and daydream that I'd been switched at birth. You know, with another family, and that one day they would come and rescue me, and I'd have a nice, normal family. A family a bit like yours. People that didn't demoralize me and make me feel so worthless," she said simply.

Darcie was speechless. She'd never heard anything so sad come from someone so incredible. She needed to speak. She *really* needed to speak, but couldn't think of a single thing to say that would make this better.

"Anyway, it's stupid. I was a kid. I only have to put up with this once a year and a few dinners here and there. Luckily, they think I'm dating someone back home, so they're giving me some leeway on my early nights." She smiled, but Darcie could see the pretence behind it. Lizzie mastered that art after 34 years of feeling as though she didn't belong. It afforded her the ability to easily hide behind a smile.

"So, if you could do anything, what would it be?" Darcie asked quietly, still stroking her fingers.

"What do you mean?"

"Like, any job in the world."

"I don't know. I've never thought about it."

"Well, do. I'm intrigued to know." Darcie smiled.

"Okay, bossy pants." She smiled, ignoring how nice the feeling of Darcie holding her hand was. "Do you trust me?"

"Well that depends," Darcie responded.

"On?"

"On whether you're asking in general, or if your head's in the gutter." She smirked.

"My head's never in the gutter for your info. And stop flirting, I keep telling you."

"Flirting? You think I'm flirting with you?" she said, laughing. "Come on girl, you would know if I was flirting with your ass."

"Oh really?"

"Yeah, really," Darcie said confidently.

Lizzie wanted so bad to be strong, but she felt completely exposed having just told Darcie everything she did. Now all she wanted was someone to make her feel good, and worth something. "Enlighten me, oh experienced one," Lizzie said, arching a brow to her, unable to contain the smirk at Darcie's shocked and concerned glare.

"You think you're so clever." *Get a grip, Darce*, she thought to herself.

"*I'm waiting*. Allegedly, you were *not* flirting, but I'm intrigued as to how you would..." She pulled her hand from Darcie's and raised her finger to her mouth in contemplation. "...what was it you said? Ah... 'flirt with my arse?'"

Darcie lifted her hand and brushed the backs of her fingers over Lizzie's cheek. She used the very tip of her finger to gently run up towards her hairline, as she slowly pushed her fingers through Lizzie's long waves. She pulled back a little and looked at her with intensity. Darcie didn't question for a moment that Lizzie would be able to see the heat in her eyes. Darcie knew that Lizzie liked her eyes; she could tell from that first time in the water and each time they were together. She smirked a little as Lizzie's eyes searched her own in desperation. The closeness between them allowed Darcie to easily spot Lizzie's increasing chest movement.

Darcie moved her hand down to the base of Lizzie's dress, upping her game a little. She looked down to where her hand was hovering, seeing Lizzie's eyes widen as she followed Darcie's look. She didn't know what Darcie was going to do, and it was written all over her face, her eyes darting between Darcie and her hand.

Darcie licked her bottom lip, pulling it in and biting a little. Lizzie was fixated on her, causing her to forget about Darcie's hand until her fingers grazed her thigh. Lizzie gasped loudly. Darcie smirked a little more, watching Lizzie's lips. She leaned forward, and as she reached Lizzie's face, she diverted, placing her lips against her ear. "I love this dress," she whispered, stroking the material again, ensuring that once more her fingers grazed her thigh. Darcie could feel her own heart racing, hoping and praying that Lizzie wouldn't be able to resist her. At this moment in time, she'd give just about anything to kiss her. Darcie moved back into her initial position, looking at Lizzie and wondering what she was thinking.

Lizzie could barely catch her breath. She wanted so badly to take a leap. Before she could ponder any further, they both jumped at the knock on the door. "Sweet Jesus!" Darcie hurtled, panic stricken. She turned back to look at Lizzie who was oddly bemused with the situation. "I am not happy about this," she said, watching Lizzie move to the opposite bed and put her medi bag on her lap.

"Hey, dude." Darcie smiled sincerely to Deek as he walked in.

"Yo, girl, how's it going?" he asked. He looked at Lizzie. "Hey, doc. I believe you saved this gorgeous girl," he said sincerely, patting Lizzie's shoulder.

"Not quite. I just did my job," Lizzie said shyly.

"Modest girl, yeh, mon?" he questioned Darcie.

"Totally," she responded, watching an embarrassed Lizzie.

"Look, I should go and leave you to catch up," Lizzie said.

"No, I'm busy working. Cap just told me to come down and check you were feeling okay. I'm glad the doc here checked on ya. Thanks for looking out for her. She's a good chica, and we need her," he said sincerely.

"Not quite sure that will happen though, buddy. Don't be surprised if I get shipped off tomorrow," she said seriously.

"It's that bad, doc?" Deek asked Lizzie, concerned.

"It's pretty bad. She won't be able to get it wet or use it for a couple of weeks. Minimum."

Deek looked concerned, hearing the radio sound in his back pocket. "I gotta run baby girl, I'll speak to cap. Doc, please do anything you can to keep her here," he said, kissing both girls on the cheek and rushed off, slamming the door behind him.

"Are you okay?" Darcie asked.

"Will you really have to go?"

"It's highly likely. I'm deputy, and if I can't do my job, he isn't going to want to pay me as well as another employee to come down and do it."

"Oh," she said quietly. "Do you need more painkillers before I leave?"

"You're leaving?" she asked sadly.

"Erm, probably for the best. You need your rest."

"Or you could stay?" she blurted out, wide eyed. "Sorry, of course you don't want to. Why would you stay in here when you have the room you have? I'm sorry, I just didn't want what could potentially be my last night to end like that. Umm... sorry, I sound like a sexual predator. Let me start again." She sat on the bed opposite Lizzie and looked directly at her, taking a deep breath. "It got a little awkward from Deek coming in and interrupting... *whatever*. I'm being a goofball. We were having fun. I don't want you to go feeling like I'm a jerk, or that I was gonna jump your bones, is all. I just meant we could have my last night talking and goofing around like before. Erm, not goofing around like fooling around..." Embarrassed, she shook her head.

"I'll stay," she said quietly.

"You will?" Darcie asked surprised.

"Do you need to go to sleep now?"

"Nope, I'm good. You?"

"No. You owe me a secret," she said simply, and returned to her previous position.

Darcie smiled a little. "How so?"

"You asked me to trust you, and I told you something. Now it's your turn."

"Okay. Let me think," she said, laying down opposite Lizzie and feeling nervous suddenly. Darcie was conscious not to get into Lizzie's personal space, which was particularly hard in staff quarters. "I know," she said bemused. "I'm an awesome flirt, you can't deny that. That was some awesome skill before Deek interrupted us." She laughed, raising her eyebrows.

"Okay, so you're a devilish flirt, and a colossal tease," she said. "That is *not* a secret."

"Ah but the question is, am I a colossal tease that you can resist?" She winked.

"Tell me the secret and I'll tell you my answer."

"On one condition."

"Excuse me? You don't get to make conditions. You owe me one," she said, looking at her turquoise eyes dancing. "Get your head back out of the gutter."

"It's out," she said sadly. "What if I ask nicely?"

"What, for me to give you one?"

Darcie coughed in surprise. "Now whose head is in the gutter? I meant, if I ask nicely, would you let me have a condition?"

"Ask nicely, and I *may* allow it."

"You like being in control, don't you?" Darcie smirked.

"Hardly. Outside of work, where I'm paid to make important decisions, I've never been in control of anything."

"Authoritative was probably a better word choice. I didn't mean to offend."

"You didn't. So, come on. Secret!" she demanded.

"If I tell you, will you go on a date with me? No funny business. I'm a good girl, ya know." She smiled.

"Why would I go on a date with you? You slept with my sister. That doesn't constitute '*good*' in my opinion," she said light-heartedly. "No less, you thought she was my twin. You can see how this looks, yes?"

"Yeah, I guess," she said defeatedly. "For the record, that's my secret. I wish I'd never slept with her. I wish I'd never saw her advances. I wish I'd never gone near her."

"You realize the entirety of that statement completely contradicts itself, don't you? Your one wish would be that you hadn't slept with my sister, but in turn, for giving me said piece of information, you want to take me out on a date, where 'allegedly,' you won't try and have your wicked way with me... because you aren't that type of woman." She laughed.

"Sheesh, you sure *you* didn't study law? Okay, okay. I give in. You have my secret, and I have no date."

"If you stay on board, I'll give you a date," she said simply.

"What's happened to you? Are you teasing like I was before?" Darcie laughed.

"Nope. I'm equally as good at teasing, should I wish to be. And that shall be identified when you take me out on my dream date. I have grand expectations; you flirt plenty, then tease plenty. I'll also flirt tremendously, and when you're disheveled and horrendously desperate to take it to the next level, I'll merely walk away, leaving you with absolutely nothing," she said, raising an eyebrow.

"Well that's plain evil. How're you gonna tease me?" She winked.

"You'll find out." She smirked.

"You're *super* evil, I can just tell." Darcie smiled at her.

Lizzie decided she'd act on instinct and play Darcie at her own game. She leaned forward, moving slightly past Darcie's face and towards her ear. She smelled her hair, hearing Darcie take a deep breath. "You. Have. No. Idea," she whispered. "*No* idea." Lizzie moved back into position, simply smirking as she lay flat on her back, happy with her actions, and the intended outcome. "Gosh, I'm tired," she said, lifting her arms up to yawn, an action she knew full well would cause her t-shirt dress to raise just enough, teasing Darcie a little more.

Darcie was just about to respond to Lizzie, when she noticed her yawn and stretch. She looked down the length of her body as she stretched out, and noticed the base of where her dress rose. Darcie's breath quickened, spotting her black lace shorts.

"Darce?" Lizzie called amusedly. "The question is, after catching you check out my lace, French knickers, can you be trusted in the same bed as me?" She smirked.

"I hate you," Darcie said to her, rolling over, and sighing.

"You would *love* to hate me, but you can't quite do it because you secretly want me. *Bad.*" She laughed. "*Real* bad."

"You need to go to sleep. Or drink. You're far less naughty when you're drunk."

"I know. So, what's the sleep situation?"

"None." Darcie smirked.

"Here or there?" Lizzie pointed to the two beds.

"Well, this is my bed. But I've always been taught to share, so I'm happy for you to stay here with me. Maybe it's a good idea; you can protect me from hurting my severely damaged hand. Equally, if I leave tomorrow, I'll have a good last memory to take home," she said seriously.

"Are you really going to keep using 'going home tomorrow' like that?"

"What, as guilt? Sure am." She winked.

"You really think you might go?"

"Maybe," she said, looking away from Lizzie. The chances of her leaving were incredibly high, but she didn't want to tell her that. It would seem like Darcie was trying to get laid on her last night. She'd get Lizzie's details for sure, but no way would she try and trap her.

"Let's hope not," Lizzie said sadly.

"Yeah. You okay sharing with me? Or do you wanna go over there?" she asked seriously.

"As long as you keep your hands... *hand,* to yourself."

"No promises. I'm taking no responsibility given you showed me your lace panties."

"Good night, Darcie."

"Good night, sexy girl." She giggled, turning off the light.

Chapter Eighteen

Lizzie woke around five. She had no clue what time they went to sleep, but she was surprised at how well she'd slept given her concern over Darcie leaving. Her eyes seemed to give something away, but she couldn't quite work out what.

"Sleep okay? In your short dress and sexy panties."

Lizzie couldn't help but smile. "Good morning. So, I figure you're a morning person," she stated. "Do you have a problem with my short dress and sexy panties?"

"It's not good for a lesbian, least not in this tiny bed."

Lizzie laughed. "I'll wear pajamas next time. How's your hand?"

"Well, I'm pretty darn sure it wouldn't hurt this much had it been amputated."

"Bloody hell, really? Let's get you more pain killers."

"No," Darcie said, stopping Lizzie. "I didn't want to say anything last night, Lizzie, but if I were Jose Luis, there's no way I'd keep me here. Let's just have this. Weirdly, you take away the pain. God, I sound so dorky."

"A little. But a cute dork," Lizzie said, turning to face her.

"So, it may be a little inappropriate, but can I get your address?"

"Why, are you planning on showing up on my doorstep?"

"Not unless you ask me to. Miss Lovelie told me you love letters, so I figured I could write you. I figured you'd prefer it to text, emails, or phone calls."

"You're so trying to win my heart." Lizzie laughed.

"I was hoping I already had." She winked.

Lizzie laughed, hearing her phone vibrate. She opened the message and sighed a little.

"You gotta go, huh?"

"Unfortunately, I do. The car's here. Would you like me to say I'm ill again?"

"No, it's fine. I'll get ready and go speak to Jose Luis."

"Do you really think you'll go?" Lizzie asked, unable to hide her sadness.

"Honestly, I don't know. But if I was captain, I'd send me packing for sure."

"Even at your level?"

"More so at my level. Unless you have some miracle way of making it better, I'm out of action," she said sadly.

"If I did, I would've done it already." Lizzie took a pen and pad on the opposite bed and began writing on it. "As requested," she said, handing the slip of paper to Darcie.

"Willow Place. That's cute. Very British." She laughed. "Thank you."

Lizzie got up and took Darcie's hand, squeezing it a little. "I genuinely hope you're still here when I return. Goodbye, Darcie."

"Goodbye, Lizzie. Thanks for everything. I'll miss you. A lot."

"Me too. You've been the best distraction, and in the short while I've known you, an incredible friend," she said, pushing the lump from her throat.

*

Lizzie walked back to her room feeling empty. It was the closest she'd ever gotten to semi enjoying these holidays, and now Darcie potentially had to leave. She pondered whether she should've just bit the bullet and swallowed her pride last night. The closeness between them seemed imprinted on her brain, and she found it difficult to stop the "what ifs" about the entire scenario.

Lizzie entered the room, and fell onto her bed. Her parents had arranged for a car to pick them up in 40 minutes, and she was supposed to meet them for breakfast beforehand. She so desperately wanted to pretend to be sick, but knew that she'd probably need to do it again before the week was out. On the plus side, she really did adore the Turks and Caicos Islands, and at least she had a couple of days there before the confinement on board with her family, and their journey back home, commenced. Sighing defeatedly, Lizzie forced a smile on her face and motivated herself to get ready for the day ahead.

*

"Where were you?" her mother asked upon meeting them.

"What do you mean?"

"Breakfast. We aren't stopping for lunch until two pm. Your father has already arranged a late dinner for this evening."

"Oh, yes of course. I didn't really feel very hungry, so I thought I'd sleep a little longer."

"Maybe my dear sister has been up late FaceTiming her lover," Bella said sardonically, leaving her with their mother's eager questioning.

*

Lizzie rushed towards the transport in a bid to get to the back and avoid her family. She wasn't particularly interested in speaking with anybody, and tried to wash over the sadness embroiling her at the prospect of never seeing Darcie again. *Seriously, what the bloody hell was wrong with her?* She sounded like a love-sick teenager, and she wasn't in love with her, so what was the issue? *That Bella had gotten there first,* she thought. She should've just ignored that and had some fun with her. *It'd been a bloody long time, so who could blame her?* She leaned back against the headrest and allowed the cold air conditioning to relax away the questions.

"Libby? Libby? *Elizabeth*?!" her mother shouted, pulling her out of the nice dream. "We're here. Everybody's waiting for you!" she scolded and stepped off the bus.

She wondered at what point her family would ever stop treating her like a four-year-old. She grabbed her handbag and rushed off the bus, following her family and the guide that would escort them around for the day.

"Are you okay, Libby?" Ollie asked.

"Erm, yes, thanks."

Ollie looked at her seriously. "Right then, very well," he said, walking off speedily towards her sister and their father. She sighed heavily, already feeling the wrath of her family.

*

"Isn't it beautiful? Can you imagine this being where you wake up every morning?" Bella spoke frantically.

136

"Well, maybe one day we can look at buying a place. There are some incredible properties. We could do a family place. Libby can bring her new love interest," her mother said. "Elizabeth, what is wrong with you? You normally love it here, and you've been... well, quite frankly, miserable and intolerable all day."

"I..." Lizzie didn't know how to respond. They were correct; she hadn't been happy all day. Her mind was elsewhere, and she didn't know how to contend with that.

"Elizabeth has been unwell. I saw her last night and this morning. I told her she shouldn't have come today, but she insisted on the basis that it's one her favorite destinations. It's apparent she still isn't better, hence the somber mood," Oliver said simply.

"Well, why didn't you say anything?" her mother asked. She wondered what it must feel like to have a mother question with concern and trepidation when her child felt unwell?

"I told her to. I even said I'd advise you all. I don't mean to be rude, Libby, but I know Bella and I are enormously delighted of this afternoon's agenda. I rather think you'd be best off returning to the Iconica. Maybe sleep it off," he said simply.

Lizzie wanted to argue with him. How *dare* he? However, she may have gotten the "get out clause" she'd been desperately searching for. She loved this place, but she'd just rather explore it with someone else. *Was that someone else Darcie? Or was it just someone who she could enjoy those things with?* She'd probably just as easily enjoy it alone.

"Maybe that's for the best. We don't want you holding us back, and you clearly aren't enjoying it. Plus, I don't want to run the risk of you making us all ill. You've been frequently ill throughout this holiday, so maybe you need to go and visit one of your doctor friends when you return. Your father could get you in."

"Yes, I guess so," she said sadly.

Lizzie's father called their guide over, whispering something to him. Within minutes the man rushed off, phone in hand, and ushered out to a waiting car.

She stayed quiet on the return to the boat, annoyed at how they'd dismissed her. Ollie saying she would *ruin* their day. *Who the hell did he think he was?* After everything else, the prospect of returning to the boat made her feel worse than anything. It killed her not knowing if Darcie would be there. She gave the driver $20, thanked him, and returned to the yacht, feeling more jittery with each step she took.

*

"Hola. You okay, Miss Libby?" Jose Luis looked up from the paperwork he was completing as she boarded Iconica.

"Yes, I wasn't feeling too good..."

He held up his hand to stop her momentarily as crackling sounds went off. She heard Spanish come through his radio. "Sorry, sorry..."

"It's okay. Is um... is Darcie around?"

"Si, si," he said manically into the radio. "No, she gone," he said, squeezing her shoulder as he moved past her quickly. Just like that, it felt like her world came crashing down.

*

Lizzie snuck into the galley, took a bottle of tequila, and made her way back to her room to change. After opening the door, she immediately looked to the floor, a sadness creeping in at the lack of note. She changed into denim shorts and a plain vest and brought a bottle of tequila up to the top deck, her new hiding place. The place she'd shared with Darcie only nights before.

Lizzie loved the sea. The sound of the waves, the beautiful variances of blues caused by the depth of the ocean, and the formation of the coral reefs. They were moored now, so the lack of wind was enormously distinctive. To the extent that she almost considered taking the risk of going down to the pool, or snorkeling. It was a difficult decision as she really didn't want to see anybody.

Opening her phone to her messages, she looked at the lone text from herself to Darcie last night, following the accident. She considered texting her, wishing her well, asking if she was okay. But she didn't text back last night. Maybe Darcie didn't really like her that way. *Why was she so insecure?* Darcie had mentioned on numerous occasions she'd regretted the situation with Bella. Additionally, Darcie referred to her personal love of letter writing, and while she hadn't texted her back, she had, in fact, sent her a note.

"Why, oh why, oh why?" Lizzie said out loud, frustrated her thoughts were preoccupied by the beautiful blonde. She opened the tequila, and took a large gulp before undressing down to her bikini, and lying out flat.

She'd never really had anyone. Well, *friend* wise. Her cousin Kate was okay, but she was in Berkshire, so they rarely saw each other. She'd lived in such a shell all her life that her friends were chosen for her. She limited them to social functions only. She'd also considered them more like acquaintances than friends. She'd had a couple of long term relationships—in which they had nothing in common—around a year or two each, but again, they were either chosen for her, or she'd chosen them herself, and the reality of her family would soon send them running. Darcie seemed different though. She wanted to be her friend, despite her family. She *was* her friend. She'd had a real, genuine friend for the first time in 34 years, who'd met her family, and stayed her friend despite all of that. And now she was gone. Worse still, if her sister didn't act like a tramp, maybe it could've been something more. Lizzie thought back to last night, to sharing the bed. Jesus, had they not both been so trim there's no way they would've been able to share it. Although, she was pretty sure that deep down, she would've somehow managed it one way or another. All of it was amazing. The closeness to another woman, the smell of coconut shampoo on her hair as the soft locks settled next to her face, and the smell of suntan lotion on her skin. She'd missed that. And *kissing*. God, did she miss kissing. She could've just kissed her when Darcie was showing of her flirting skills, but they were interrupted. *Darcie had been... bloody amazing.* Lizzie confirmed several times that because of Bella, there was no way she'd go near Darcie. She was pretty sure she could see the want and heat in her eyes, yet she never once pushed Lizzie. If she'd had, Lizzie was unsure as to whether she would've had the will power to refrain. *Those eyes would get her anything. And those lips. Those amazing, soft lips.*

She hit her head on the floor harder than anticipated, inwardly shouting at herself for the constant thoughts of Darcie. *She would not do this. She could not do this.* What she could do is thank Darcie for opening up so much to her.

Lizzie awoke to the sounds of her family's laughter returning from their day out. She'd often questioned why her family could all be happy as one, but *she* never had. They weren't particularly *nasty* to her. Well, maybe a little off, but harsh was too harsh. Maybe a little unkind, a little *too* vocal with projecting that she was clearly nothing like any of them aside from her looks. She was around 13 when she finally acknowledged that it didn't bother her; she wasn't like all the other children she knew. They fit in, she didn't. But she'd never been like the rebellious ones at boarding school who acted up when their parents showed them little to no attention. Her father was proud of her, she was aware, but she simply had to do as he said. Like it, or lump it. She couldn't connect with her mother and sisters. They were nothing alike, mostly because, unlike her and the career in medicine that'd been carved out for her, they'd never worked a day in their lives for anything. Of course they couldn't connect. They were all readily available to highlight her refusal to be a part of their interests, escapades, *and* the family.

She'd had too much sun. Sleeping and drinking in it never ended well. And now she had to try and get through the evening. She could potentially continue the illness, but it would only mean further disparage tomorrow. No, she needed to go to dinner this evening, get it out of the way, and start anew tomorrow.

Clothes in one hand and tequila in the other, Lizzie could only imagine what her mother would say. Bloody hell, she was the epitome of what her mother would deem as "cattle class." *Her favorite saying.* Everyone was cattle class to her mother, unless of course, they were of some noble stature.

She couldn't think about that now. She needed to focus on something positive, or at least ordinary. *What to wear?* she thought. *What would she wear this evening?* The darker the clothes, the more significant the tan. Which meant if she wore it well enough, she may be able to feign "sunstroke" and lose a few more days to break it down a little.

She rushed back to her room, so her parents wouldn't check up on her. She immediately stopped, noticing the not so empty floor this time. She froze as her heart beat faster. *It couldn't be.* Jose Luis had already confirmed she'd left. She ignored her dry mouth, and opened it, smiling widely as she recognized the writing immediately.

You owe me a date. I'm staying... -Dxx

Lizzie read it, re-read it, then re-read it again. Even after six or seven times, it still gave her the greatest smile. Eventually, she threw her belongings on her bed, and rushed out, uncertain if she'd even closed her door.

She arrived at Darcie's door, feeling somewhat dizzy, and slightly nauseous. She was unsure if it was the drink, the sun, or the situation. Either way, her body defied her as she realized she was knocking on the door. Lizzie heard the door unlock, and everything played out in slow motion in her mind. The door opened, and those turquoise eyes lit up at the sight of her. "Hey…"

Without giving Darcie an opportunity to continue with pleasantries, Lizzie dived at the woman, pushing her against the slimline wardrobe at the end of the beds, putting both hands at either side of her face, and pushing her lips hard against Darcie's.

*

Darcie opened the door to find Lizzie standing in front of her, her eyes widening at the stunning woman. Before she could understand what was happening, Lizzie's lips were on hers within seconds. Milliseconds. It took Darcie a moment to adjust to the situation. She'd waited so long for it, but the action completely took her by surprise. Stunned beyond belief. She refused to waste time thinking and enjoyed the moment. She put her hands around Lizzie's waist and pulled her in closer. Feeling, and living in the moment of Lizzie's soft, bare, skin against her hands drove her insane. She'd finally gotten what she wanted. *What she'd been craving.*

Lizzie's lips started to hurt. She *had* to stop. Slowing down the pace, she paused before pulling away from Darcie, leaving her hands in place. "This. Changes. Nothing. I'm still not sleeping with you, for the record," she confirmed, watching Darcie's eyes.

"If you make out like that, I don't care. You look super hot by the way."

Lizzie blushed, remembering she ran out with only her bikini on.

"You also look super cute when you blush."

"Please stop."

"Why? You should know you're beautiful."

Lizzie looked down to her feet. "I'm sorry," she said, moving her hands away from Darcie's face.

Darcie pulled her closer into her, watching her eyes widen. She kicked the door shut with her foot. "Well, I'm not," she said simply, and kissed her again, enjoying the fact that Lizzie didn't pull away, but engaged in the kiss. Darcie turned Lizzie around, pushing her against the cupboard, intensifying the kiss further. She was desperate to run her hands over her barely clothed body, but didn't want to push it. She knew she wouldn't be able to stop if she started. Darcie felt Lizzie's hand move back up to her cheek, and the most tender of strokes graze her face. The contact changed the dynamics and the direction it'd been going. Darcie slowed down the kiss, and moved her hands to Lizzie's waist. Her skin was so soft to touch. She grazed her thumbs over her tummy, and pulled back from Lizzie, looking at her intently. "Hi," she whispered.

"Hi, yourself."

"You okay?"

"I am." She smiled a little. "And you?"

"Pretty damn fine." She winked and brushed her fingers through her hair. "So, that was a pretty awesome hello."

"Yes, clearly the prospect of never seeing you again impacted me more than I'd have imagined," Lizzie said openly.

Darcie smiled softly, looking at the blonde waves she ran around her fingers. "I didn't think my day could get any better after the doctor gave me the paperwork to stay on board, but I can categorically state, you just improved it."

"I'm glad. Maybe I need to go find the doctor to thank him?"

"You have any of that left, you keep it for me, and nobody else," she said seriously.

"There's plenty left."

"Good." Darcie blushed. "I wouldn't have left without saying goodbye you know. You've made too much of an impact on my life. I've never met anyone like you before."

Lizzie stared at the woman. Part of her wanted to say she probably said that to all the women, but the way that Darcie looked at her didn't tell her that.

"You think I say that to everyone?" Darcie asked seriously.

Lizzie smiled a little.

"Yes, then?"

"How do you read me so well?"

"Maybe we were destined to be together. Maybe I'm your destiny, your fate. Maybe I was the one sent to save you." She smiled, grazing her bare shoulder with the back of her fingers.

"Really?" She smirked.

"Stranger things have happened. Do me a favor?"

"Of course," she said seriously, moving her arms from around Darcie's neck and taking her hand in her own.

"Don't come to my room and kiss me like that in a bikini again. Especially if I'm not allowed to make the most of this body."

"I don't know if I want to comply with that." She smirked. "For the record, it wasn't intentional. I was on the top deck, and when I returned and saw your letter, I knew you were here. I spoke to Jose Luis earlier when I returned. He said you'd gone, so I couldn't believe it. I literally ran down here to see for myself, clearly missing a thing or two," she uttered shyly.

"On the contrary, you couldn't have shown up in a better way, or with a better welcome. With a delivery like that, I'm not complaining. And no, I'm not being a pervert," she responded seriously.

"So..."

"So..." Lizzie smirked.

"So, do I get to make out with you at the end of our date now?"

"Who says you get a date?"

"I do. You got a problem with that?"

"Bossy, aren't you? I have no problem with that. What are we doing?"

"Not sure yet. Can we reschedule last night's meet? I had a plan. I'll make up my mind, and make some arrangements."

"Of course. 10:30 still?"

"Perfect."

"Wonderful. Right, well, I suppose I must let you get on with work. I'll get ready and get the evening meal with my family out of the way."

"Well, I'll make it as pain free for you as I can." She winked.

Lizzie watched the sincerity in Darcie's eyes. "How very gallant. I thank you for the benevolent attitude. I imagine that such kind gestures are therefore warranted of some specific gratitude this evening?" She raised a brow.

"I have no idea what you mean. I have a duty, *and* a promise to uphold," she saluted.

"Well, if that's the case…"

"Cut it out," Darcie quipped, pulling her in and pressing her lips against Lizzie's. She kept it slow, without hidden meaning. It was sincere, and what Darcie had dreamed about for days. She pushed Lizzie away, her lips moving with hers before looking back. "Now go. Get that cute butt out of here." She screwed up her nose and waved her hand at Lizzie.

Chapter Nineteen

Lizzie found it difficult to not pay any attention to Darcie. She avoided her glances in a bid to not make her family suspect anything. Mainly because she wanted the privacy to fully enjoy it, but also because she didn't want to be in a position where her family might involve themselves. They'd have a million and one remarks to make about Darcie, despite knowing nothing about her. Irrespective of anything, even if she was the richest woman on earth, in their eyes she wasn't of noble birth or belonging, and they'd have no issue making that vividly clear in front of Darcie.

She sat there quietly as her family filled each other with the tales of their day and all the beautiful places they'd visited. Property hunting formed part of the day, after Lizzie had left them. She played around with her food, moving it from side to side on her plate, and not eating very much. She carefully eyed her family one by one as they huffed at the stews who tried to do their jobs around them. Nobody had spoken to her all evening. Granted it'd only been approximately one hour, but given the fact she was sent home poorly earlier, you'd deem it would impart perfunctory interest. *Clearly not.*

Lizzie looked up, and noticed Darcie watching her intently from the door. She smiled softly at Lizzie, and felt bad for the sadness in her eyes. She sat up straight and pulled herself together. She needed to focus on the end of the evening, and whatever Darcie had planned for her. Catching her eye again, she lifted the empty flute. Darcie came over with the bottle of champagne, and filled her glass promptly, purposely closing the gap between them so she could brush her foot against Lizzie's bare calf. Lizzie's back straightened at her touch. Darcie moved around the table, filling up the remaining glasses.

"So, you are feeling better now, Elizabeth?" her mother questioned.

"Excuse me?" she stammered.

"*Better*? You're no longer unwell?"

"Oh right. Yes, a little better. I think the sun has caused me some difficulty this year, which is quite unusual. I don't feel right in myself."

"Well, what's wrong? I can diagnose and treat," her father said stiffly.

"Father, you are a surgeon. I'll have it looked into when I return."

"I'm the greatest surgeon of our time!" he spat indignantly.

Lizzie noticed his stiffness, followed by a knowing glance between Darcie and Jose Luis. There was nothing about her family that surprised her any longer, nor people's views and perceptions of them. She suddenly felt deflated, and embarrassed that Darcie had witnessed that.

"I'm not feeling so great after all. I will return to my room, I think," Lizzie stood, and watched her parents faces turn steely.

"Elizabeth, you have been drinking, and you just said you were feeling better. This is family dinner, and I will not have you ruin it!" her father yelled.

She watched her mother's glare. *How could any parent dislike their own flesh and blood so easily?* "Sit down now,

Elizabeth!" her mother spat, and just like that, the pair of them returned to the laughter at the other end of the table, delighting in the enjoyment of the day like they hadn't just belittled her in the most treacherous manner.

She drained the last of her champagne, feeling embarrassed at the castigation. Sitting quietly, she took herself back to about 20 years ago, around the time she realized she was gay, and starting to develop a crush on one of her polo team mates. Something had happened. She couldn't recall what now, but her family had somehow devastated her, belittling her in front of Freya. It was the worst. It was at that point, she made a promise that she wouldn't allow them to hurt her any longer. She'd realized she was different. Maybe it was her sexuality, maybe it was the fact that she was different in more ways than one. But whenever they treated her this way, she closed herself off, refusing to allow them to upset her.

*

Darcie made her way to the back of the boat, appreciating the beautifully lit underlighting. The variations of color from the underwater lighting, and the brightness of the moon were the only two things illuminating the area. She couldn't help but think it was perfect. A perfect spot since Lizzie had given her the perfect kiss this afternoon. She carefully stepped down the ladder, jumping onto the overhang, and scattered a few random candles about. She was grateful of the grandiose vessel, and the space it offered. The overhang housed lots of toys, including five jet skis, which meant it was plenty big enough for them to hide.

Darcie sat there a while, enjoying the stillness of the night. The soothing sounds of faint waves broke around her. She pulled her phone out, noticing it was 20 minutes to 11. Lizzie had returned to her room a while back, and unfortunately, yet again for her, it hadn't been a great night. Maybe that's why she'd bailed, leaving Darcie feeling deflated and sad. She couldn't do anything for Lizzie, and now she wouldn't even get the chance to at least try and cheer her up. She opened the phone to her messages, opting not to go for a handwritten note this time around.

I guess you've decided not to come down. I can't say I blame you. I wish I could see you, and hold you tight, like you did for me last night. Sleep well, Lizzie. Xxx

She grabbed the tequila and took a deep gulp, lying down and enjoying the gentle rocking of the boat.

*

"Hi." Darcie heard, opening her eyes, and noticing an angelic Lizzie illuminated by the moon and candlelight around them.

"*You came?*" She sat up surprised.

"Yes, I wasn't going to. Which I guess you established, given your message," she said somberly.

"Yeah, I kinda figured," she muttered. "What changed your mind?"

"Honestly?" Lizzie sat down next to her.

"Always."

"I didn't want to lose out on the only enjoyment I get, which is when I'm with you. I'm sorry, that sounds ridiculous, but it's the truth. Why should I miss out because of the embarrassment and shame they continue to enforce upon me?"

"It doesn't sound ridiculous at all, it sounds as though we're on the same page. I don't think you should feel any embarrassment and shame though," Darcie responded.

"You saw the way they spoke to me. The way they treated me, chastised me. All in front of you and the team," she said, taking the tequila, and downing a large amount.

"You wouldn't ever do anything, would you?"

"What do you mean?"

"Um, nothing," she whispered.

"Harm myself?" she asked quickly.

Darcie's head spun around. Her eyes desperately searched Lizzie's, praying that she wasn't about to say what she thought she was.

"No. Don't get me wrong, I've often wondered if... I don't know how to verbalize this. Please don't think I've ever considered committing suicide because I haven't. I guess I've always wished I could be out of this situation, and that regularly leads to... probably inappropriate thoughts," she said.

"Like what?"

"Darcie, would you mind if we didn't discuss this? I'm fairly over today, and I don't feel in the right frame of mind to start discussing my home life."

"Sure," she mumbled, feeling bad. "I'm sorry."

Lizzie ignored the apology. She just couldn't do this right now. "This is beautiful," she said, looking around her.

"Yeah, it's kinda why I said we should come here. It's one of my favorite places." She sloped down again.

"Yeah?"

"Yeah, it's awesome."

"It is. I love the variances of color with each underwater light. These people must be incredibly rich, designing these super-yachts. The finish is incredible," she said, looking at the symmetrical underwater spotlights. The two closest to her were bright pink, the two in the middle, bright blue, and the two farthest away, an effulgent lime.

"Yeah, it's kinda why it's my favorite spot. All those lights." Darcie smiled softly. "Maybe we should give it a go. Or just buy our own and rent it out," she said nonchalantly.

Lizzie looked at her carefully. "I'm not so sure my eye for design would get me very far, but I'm game for getting one. I'm more inclined to refuse the rental option and just escape and sail around the Caribbean."

"Sounds awesome."

"Yeah," she said quietly, as she lowered her body to match Darcie's.

"Would you like to do that?" Darcie asked seriously.

"Probably not. Yes, to the escape—that would be phenomenal—but I think I'd get cabin fever doing it permanently. I love it like this, but I think maybe a month or two would be enough for me."

"Yeah, I get that," she said. "So, what would you do?"

"In terms of what?"

"Well, you have the money. You have the degree, *and* the experience to pretty much ditch that poor excuse of a family, and set up anywhere. So, what would you do and where would you go?"

"I don't know. I used to daydream about teaching back in the states."

"*Really?*" she said, turning to face her.

"Yes, but I don't want to do that. I've never *really* wanted to do that. I've just spent my entire life hopping from one daydream to another to get away from the life I'm in."

"You don't know what you wanna do?"

"It's difficult, really. I've never allowed myself to think seriously about that. Why would I? I can't do anything about it. I'll never be able to change my life. Thinking about it is just a form of torture."

Darcie nodded her head contemplatively, without giving a response.

"You disagree?" Lizzie asked quietly, looking over at her.

"Well, that's not my place."

"Okay, so tell me what you'd do if you were me?"

"But I'm not Lizzie, so that would be unfair for either of us. It's easy for me because I haven't spent 34 years through these atrocities. My family is…" *How could she sit there and tell someone who had experienced such a life, that hers was awesome?*

"Amazing?" Lizzie finished. "You can say it."

"No, I can't because I'm not so sure I can deal with the emotional consequences of going down that route. Not from you. You seem hardened to it, which kills me even more."

"I love the way Americans say route," she said.

"You do? I kinda like how you say it, especially the enunciation of your 'T's.'" She smiled.

"Do you think you'll do this forever?"

"Yachting?"

"Mhmm."

"No, definitely not. I've done it a while already. I love it, but I need to put down some roots. I want what my folks and Ry have."

"You mean children?" Lizzie looked at her squarely.

"Not necessarily."

"What do you mean, then?"

"A girlfriend. A partner. A wife. Someone I can share my life with, some day."

"But you don't want children?" she asked again.

"Why, do you?"

"What relevance is that?"

"None, I guess," she said quietly.

"No, I don't think so."

"I'm unsure too. I *love* kids, but I just don't know if they fit into my life. I love the spontaneity of life. I want to be able to come home after work and sail away just me and her, whoever I end up with. Or call Ry, and get a ride someplace cool. You're restricted with spontaneity when you have kids, you know?"

"Yes."

"But in the same respect, when I think of growing old, I don't know how I feel about it just being my wife and me on holidays. Like, no excited children on Christmas morning, or just the two of us eating at Thanksgiving."

"Hmmm. Yes, I guess."

They sat there in silence for a long time, listening to the waves, and dissecting each other's comments. Lizzie had never thought about it like that. As much as she always wished she could get out of Christmas with her family, it was a large, celebratory event in their household. Their gifts were typically of more value than a family home in some countries. But money wasn't everything; she'd give it all up tomorrow.

"I think I'd adopt," Lizzie said after a while.

Darcie felt a lump in her throat. She didn't want to respond. She already knew Lizzie well enough to know that would be her way of saving someone, and she couldn't help but wonder if it was because she felt *she* should've been saved. "Anyway, holidays aren't so important. I'd much prefer to be in a Hooters with a large beer and big ole bucket of wings," she said light-heartedly.

"*Hooters*? Oh my word, please tell me you're kidding."

"Hell no," she said incredulously.

"Bloody hell, maybe I should cancel this date."

"Nuh uh. You already committed," she said confidently. "Did you never go to Hooters in Boston?"

"No, why would I have?"

"Well, for starters, you're a lesbian." She laughed.

"You're so tacky."

"Hardly. The food is awesome. The beer is awesome. You'll have to come visit me back home, and I'll take you."

"I'm quite sure I can manage without."

"Now you're just being pretentious. It's not tacky. Sure, the staff wear skimpy uniforms, but it's awesome and fun. The atmosphere from the sports, the staff, and the food— it's super fun," she said seriously.

Lizzie wondered if she offended Darcie. "Well, next time I'm in the states, I'll check to see if you're in, and you can take me to a Hooters," she said quietly.

"I wouldn't force anyone to do anything they didn't want to. I'm not like that, but I also think that trying everything once, within reason, is a necessity. It's probably one of my favorite restaurants, especially for downtime."

"Wow, you sound like a Hooters marketer." She laughed. "And likewise, if you come to the UK, be sure to advise me so that I can take you to my favorite restaurant."

"Well I best get saving."

"Don't start with that. You already told me that you're *also* rich and enjoy your luxuries."

"Not quite rich, but correct in that I do like the occasional extravagance. Especially a fine dining restaurant. So, where are you taking me, then?" she asked amusedly, crossing her feet at her ankles.

"Well, *there's* a load of confidence."

"You offered to take me on a date. I'm never gonna pass that opportunity up. The first break I get, I'll be over to London." She smirked. "So... *where* are you taking me?"

"I knew it was a bad idea giving you my address." She smiled softly, turning on her side to face Darcie. "It depends how we feel when you arrive. As much as I like the occasional fine dining experience, I tend to opt out. I love South American food. I love flavorful foods—meats, spices, vegetables. I love Argentinian, Brazilian, Mexican, Portuguese, Pakistani, Singaporean, Malaysian. My favorite thing is going to the London markets on a Friday night, and wandering through. Stopping at the food stalls, trying lots of different things, getting involved in their way of life. It's incredible to lose yourself at the Caribbean festivals while Brazilian carnivals are happening around you. It's an opportune time to get lost in the laughter, fun, and happiness of some of the most basic things. Drinking with complete strangers, and dancing in the street is one of my all-time favorite things to do."

"Sounds awesome, I can't wait."

"How's the hand?"

"Still sore, but okay for the minute." She smiled. "Hey, thanks for coming down tonight."

"I'm glad I did."

"You are?"

"Yes."

"Me too," she whispered.

"So, you decide what happens on our date?" Lizzie asked.

"I have."

"You have? How exciting. Tell me more. I haven't been on a date outside the UK before," she said excitably.

"Well, hopefully I can do good."

"Let me know what we're doing and I'll tell you."

"Good try, but no," Darcie said smiling.

"*Really*? Nothing?"

"Don't try that rubbish with me."

"I don't know what you mean."

"Sure, you don't. I can't tell you anyway, as I kinda need to get other people involved. I'm not so sure whether I'll get the buy in," she said secretly.

"Well that sounds ominous. It won't get you in trouble, will it?"

"Nah, worst case they'll just refuse. I'll come up with another plan, just on borrowed time now, you know? But I'm confident it'll work out. You gonna be okay to pretend to be sick again? Your family seemed a little harsh tonight."

"It's fine," she said. "Thank you for this; it's very kind of you."

"What? Asking a hot girl to come on a date with me, and her agreeing? Hmmm, yeah, I'm mother fricking Teresa."

"Americans are so sarcastic." She rolled her eyes.

"Well, that's a fairly sweeping statement. I'd have to disagree; that's our humor. Brits are totally sarcastic."

"Rubbish."

"We'll argue about it on our date." She laughed.

"I should probably get going though. I need to spend some serious time trying to work out how to be sick again," she said.

"Look, I don't want you to get in trouble," she said, feeling the oddness of her words. *She'd not said stuff like that since being a kid,* she thought.

"It's fine, it's not a case of getting in trouble. It's ensuring my story's believable, and equally, so that I don't get the third degree. Maybe I'll say my girlfriend dumped me." She smiled.

"They won't let up on this chick back home, huh?"

"You do realize there *isn't* anybody back home, right? Bella told them that, and given I've never spent as little time with them as I have lately, they believed it. I'm sleeping late, skulking off early, and getting 'sick.' Ordinarily, I'm sick for one day—in Haiti, and that's it. I just put up with them for the rest of the time. This time obviously has them questioning everything since I'm not around far more frequently," she said. "All because a certain someone is a little more interesting." She smiled.

"*Really?* Awesome. I was a bit concerned."

"About what?"

"That you may have someone back home," she said quietly.

"And if you had someone back home wouldn't you wish to speak to them regularly? Given my time is spent with you or my family, that would've been fairly difficult to maintain, no?"

"Fair comment. I apologize; I have no right to question you."

"It's fine. So, what's the plan for the date? I'm relatively excited for the surprise. What I need to know is, am I throwing a sickie tomorrow, or the next day, or when?"

"I'll tell you tomorrow."

Lizzie eyed her suspiciously.

"As I said, I'm kind of relying on others. I'll discuss it with them this evening and let ya know tomorrow, if that's okay?"

"Of course. Well, I best get my brain to use. Maybe I'll use baby oil tomorrow and get sunburnt. That's always an easy excuse." She laughed.

"Yeah, great idea, and then we can share a date in the hospital," she said, rolling her eyes.

"I'm kidding. Good night, Darcie, and thanks for making me feel better." She smiled sincerely.

"Wait, no kiss?" She jumped up.

"Sorry, of course," she said, kissing her cheek.

"You're kidding me, right?"

"Not at all. You'll get one at the end of the date as promised."

"But that could be two days away yet."

"Well, you'll enjoy it even more then." She giggled and climbed the ladder to leave.

Darcie slid back down onto the floor, shaking her head. *This god damn woman,* she thought, unable to stop the smile forming across her face.

Chapter Twenty

Lizzie hadn't seen Darcie since the evening before. It was a beautiful morning for snorkeling, despite not seeing a great deal. But she hadn't seen Darcie, which was unusual. She told her she'd have to discuss details about the date, and wondered if it'd taken her off the boat. Either way, she was now at breakfast with her family, unsure whether or not she needed to feign illness. Oddly, Jose Luis kept looking at her strangely, which further disturbed her. *What did he know? And what exactly was happening?*

"Lord Barrington, when you finish breakfast, please come to the bridge. I need to speak with you," Jose Luis said seriously as he eyed Lizzie. Her heart raced. *Had Darcie told him? What if he was annoyed, which had resulted in her being sent home? Was he going to tell her father? Her life wouldn't be worth living if this was happening,* she thought worriedly.

Lizzie pulled her phone out, wondering if she should text Darcie. *What did Jose Luis want to speak to her father about? What would her parents do if they found out about this?* She needed to look at flights home. She could say that there was an issue at work that required her to leave. Her father wouldn't check while here, and then hopefully he'd forget about going for someone's blood for ruining his family holiday.

"Water?" Lizzie heard over her shoulder. She looked up to sparkling, blue eyes.

"Please." She smiled. Reaching out her fingers, she discreetly grazed Darcie's leg. Lizzie sat back and relaxed. *She was still here.*

"Are you actually coming out with us today? Or are you still feeling too poorly, Elizabeth?" Vivvi asked her. Lizzie looked up at her sister. She glanced at Darcie, who made a very discreet nod, and looked back to her family, confirming she'd be there. She had no idea what Darcie was planning, but either way she had to face today with her family.

"Where are you going, darling? You haven't even finished breakfast," Lizzie's mother questioned her father.

"No time for eating, the captain needs to see me. It's time for us men to sort what needs to be sorted," he said, arrogantly walking off.

Chapter Twenty-One

"All, there has been a development with the weather, thus, eliciting a change to the schedule. We have to cut the Turks short, and make our way back. I won't bore you with the specifics; you won't understand," her father said conceitedly. "The direction it's headed has allowed us to have one final day back in the Bahamas, and the captain has arranged for us to be taken to an exclusive island—one of the most beautiful out there it seems—and to stop off at Pink Sand Beach on our return. We'll spend the morning here, and the remainder of the day will be on the move. If you wish to see anything specific here in the Turks, then I trust that you'll all concur it is better to go separately. Elizabeth, you will come with Mother and I," Lord Barrington ordered.

"Well, actually, if we have limited time here, I'd rather stay and do some snorkeling; it's one of my favorite destinations—bar the Bahamas—to snorkel," she said.

"Well, I don't think you should be snorkeling alone…"

"Actually, Lord Barrington…" Jose Luis stood tall next to him. "I told Elizabeth that she can snorkel with me," he said seriously, softening his glare and smiling the most brilliant smile to the charter. He held out his hand. He was completely charming, and somehow managed to get her father to back down.

Unfortunately, the look her father gave her said that this wouldn't be the last she'd heard of it. "Fine," he said stiffly.

"Great, how long do we have here? I'll go and get changed now." She looked between the captain and her father.

"Senor?" her father said to him.

Darcie stood forward in front of Jose Luis. "It's Captain," she corrected. "Lord Barrington, the captain will be leaving at a quarter after 12. If you and your family would like to visit the island pre-departure, then you have approximately four and a half hours to do so." She nodded curtly and left, making a conscious effort to stand up against the arrogant A-hole, who not only belittled his own flesh and blood, but also disregarded her own boss's rank and status.

Dear god, if they found out about Darcie, Lizzie's life really wouldn't be worth living after that little execution. "Great, I'll go and get ready. I wouldn't mind going a little further out than the port," she said hurriedly, leaving her family.

Lizzie sat on her balcony with her coffee as she waited for her family to leave the boat. A sense of relief fulfilled her. Finishing her coffee, she went inside to continue getting ready, fully confident they'd gone. She changed into her bikini, grabbed her underwater camera, and made her way to the top of the deck.

*

"Hi," Lizzie said quietly.

Jose Luis nodded at her and said something in Spanish to Deek, who nodded courteously and left the three of them alone. Lizzie could feel her breathing increase, and nerves overtake her entire body.

"Doctor Elizabeth, calm down," he said, placing his hand on her shoulder. He said something to Darcie, who rushed off and returned with a bottle of water, stroking her hand concernedly.

Lizzie watched him intently, wondering what he was going to say. She sat down and took some water. "What is it that you want to say?" she asked stiffly, probably the only manner likened to her family.

"Elizabeth, please calm down," he said sincerely. It's not my place to reprimand you. It's nobody's place; you are adult too. I'm not happy about this, lying to charter guests. But circumstances happen beyond our control sometimes. And this time, I will do. You need to be careful because if this is found out by your family, we have big problemo. *You* have big problema," he said carefully.

"No, Captain. You don't have a problem because the worst that would happen is that you wouldn't get a tip from my parents, and if need be, I can double what they'd have given you anyway. After 34 years of this, it's not like it's new to me. I know how to contend with it," she said sadly. "Am I able to go out alone, or do I have to stay on board?"

"Why would you have to stay on board?" Darcie asked, confused.

"Because I didn't know if the captain stepped in with my father because of our situation."

Darcie spoke to the captain, who looked at her, confused. "You no need to stay on board, doctor. But I no come with you. Darcie and you have time together," he said seriously, and walked off with a gentle nod.

"Gracias!" Darcie shouted after him.

"For what? What is it?" Lizzie asked.

"He's told the drivers to notify him when your family is en route. He'll call us when we need to return," she said sheepishly.

Lizzie stood still, unsure of what to say or do. The morning so far had been spent worrying about her family finding out, being told off by the captain, and Darcie only just now showing up. She was a quivering wreck. She had a little time with Darcie and the ocean, and she'd make the most of it as best she could.

"Shall we go, then?" Lizzie eyed Darcie seriously.

"Sure. Let me just get my liner," she said.

"You're what?"

Darcie smiled. "My waterproof liner. I can't get it wet, remember?" She held up her hand.

"Bugger, of course you can't. Oh, I'm sorry, I—"

"Don't sweat it," Darcie said, grabbing her arm and stroking it slightly. "I have one. Give me five minutes." She smiled.

Darcie was back moments later, still attempting to put on the liner alone. "Can I help?" Lizzie asked.

"Sure," she said happily.

"Are you sure this is wise, Darce? I can go alone."

"No way. You wanna take the jet ski? You'll have to drive. Or we can take the small boat? I can drive that."

"The boat, I think."

"Cool," Darcie said.

"Is that okay?"

"Sure thing. You ready?"

"Yes, thanks for this. I'm glad you're coming with me," she said sincerely.

"Me too. Come on, let's get outta here." She kissed her quickly on the cheek.

Lizzie moved quickly in the water, but Darcie was unable to keep up with her given her arm. The last time she looked up, Darcie was on a board, paddling around. She looked bored, and for that, Lizzie felt guilty. She had to babysit the woman, unable to enjoy any part of it.

Lizzie swam up behind Darcie as discreetly as possible. She listened to the woman as she sang lightly, nodding her head. She couldn't help but smile at her relaxed mood. "Having fun?" Lizzie barely finished the sentence before startling Darcie, who hurtled towards her.

Darcie fell entirely on Lizzie, tugging them both underwater. Lizzie pulled them up, grabbing a coughing Darcie. "You okay?" she asked concerned.

"You trying to kill me?" Darcie said flustered.

"Sorry, and no," she said sheepishly. "It was way more impressive in my head."

"Yeah, I bet. Well, I think I at least deserve a kiss now, given you nearly drowned my ass."

"Oh, you do? You are an incredible exaggerator, aren't you?" She laughed.

"Quit talking and start kissing, lady." Darcie eyed her carefully. Lizzie was just about to move in when the phone began to ring from the waterproof case around her neck.

"Guess Lady Luck isn't on your side. You'll just have to wait a little longer." She laughed.

"You're killing me."

"Yes, Darce." She rolled her eyes. "You tell me frequently."

They made their way back to the boat absentmindedly. "You okay?" Darcie asked concerned.

"Yeah, fine. It was a fun morning. Thanks again."

"No worries. Shame I couldn't enjoy it some more, but I'm glad you had fun. You wanna go have a secret drink when we get back?"

"Actually, I'm going to respectfully decline. I want to sort a few bits."

"Oh right. Yeah, sure," Darcie said disappointed, switching the engine on.

"Relax, sweetie. It's nothing to do with you. I've had a little idea that I'd like to see if I can put into practice to make my final days here somewhat bearable." She smiled.

"Bailing on your family, and leaving here with me?" Darcie said expectantly.

Lizzie looked at her carefully before smiling and squeezing her knee. The dynamics were changing between them, which concerned her, but she didn't want to think about that now. She enjoyed their time together, and their secrecy allowed them to enjoy it fully, without the obsessive intrusion of her family.

*

Lizzie lay on her bed, considering her options. If she did this, and it fell through, she was... quite frankly, screwed. But, she may, just may, pull it off.

Lizzie pondered the situation. As it were, she'd never been at this stage before. A stage where she was confident in taking on her family. Taking a deep breath and sitting up in her bed, she made a call, awaiting the international dial tone.

"Hi boss, you okay?"

Lizzie smiled, listening to the concern in her voice. "Yes and no," she murmured.

"Liz? What's going on?"

"I'm okay."

"You're not."

"I *am*, calm down. You still got that friendship with Doctor Mac?"

"A little, why?"

Lizzie breathed in heavily, relaxing into her pillows as she explained everything to her assistant.

Chapter Twenty-Two

"You're late!" Her mother spat as Lizzie walked up to the dining table, feeling Darcie's eyes on her.

"Yes, work stuff," she said easily. Lizzie noticed Darcie's staring eyes, and ignored her mother. It was the way Darcie was looking at her; she couldn't help but smirk. *Clearly, her choice of city shorts and chiffon top with chained straps was the right one,* she thought. Seemingly, they were making a bit of an impact on each other.

"What's the issue now?" her father quizzed. "Is everything okay?"

"Yes, it's fine. A few issues at the hospital. Nothing they can't handle, though. I don't need to return." She smiled and thanked the stew for the water put down in front of her. "So, what is the situation for tomorrow?" she asked her father.

"We'll meet around seven for breakfast. The bus will pick us up at 7:45 sharp, and we'll return at approximately five pm. I've also arranged for a beach barbeque..." He stopped, feeling a vibration on the table. Lizzie looked away from her father, ensuring that she play the best role of her life. She looked at the phone with concern, declined the call, and looked back up at her family. "Is everything okay?" her father asked.

"Yes, I'm sure," she said. "Will we still return to Miami on Tuesday, or will we return home earlier?"

"Tuesday still, yes," he said as the phone vibrated again.

Lizzie repeated her earlier actions. Looking at the phone with a little more concern this time, she declined it once more, and ignored her mother's deep sighs. She stimulated concern and confusion as she moved her food around the plate, and slowly began to eat.

*

Darcie was certain she was sponging the granite clean as she tried to discreetly establish what Lizzie was doing right now. *God she looked hot tonight.* She had four days left with Lizzie, and that was all. She was spellbound by her, and she didn't know what the hell she was going to do about that. The thought of Lizzie leaving bummed her out. Massively. Darcie was brought out of her thoughts as she heard the mouth clicking sound behind her that Deek always made. She looked over her shoulder slightly, feeling his breath at her ear. "Ya know, ya keep watching the doc like that, ya gonna give away whatever ya got going on with the cap, and our diversion," he said.

"What are you on about?" she said, turning fully to him.

Tutting and rolling his eyes, he stopped, and shook his head. "You got it bad, girl."

"You're tripping," she said.

"*Whatever.* Just stop watching her, or her family will click, and you in trouble," he said softly, stroking his friend's shoulder.

"Dammit," she muttered to herself. Grabbing the jug of water, she made her way back out on deck, and replenished the Barrington's drinks. She could feel the intensity at the table as they discussed the next day's events. Lizzie was completely engaged in the conversation, which scared

Darcie. *A lot*. Her phone constantly rang, and Darcie didn't know if it was rehearsed or the real deal.

*

Lizzie noticed the uneasy look on Darcie's face as her phone began to ring again. It was time though. She couldn't do anything about Darcie right now. It was the third phone call from back home, the final call. She looked up at her father, stealing his attention, and ignored her mother's scowl. Her father nodded curtly, and Lizzie got up and left the table, answering the phone as she walked off. "Doctor Barrington," she answered, praying this worked. She needed tomorrow to be perfect, for her *and* for Darcie.

She engaged in the conversation on the phone, away from her family. She needed to make it believable to them, because if it didn't work, she was… well, she couldn't think about what the next four days would be like for her.

She checked the table as she walked back towards them, passing Darcie as she did so. Her family was completely preoccupied, so she grabbed her wrist, and gave it a gentle squeeze. She couldn't wait to spend time with her tomorrow, albeit, it was what she'd originally been trying to avoid. But it was done. She couldn't keep thinking about that. No matter what the conflict was between her head and her heart, there was a pull she just couldn't fight. Or maybe she didn't want to fight. She watched the smile form, and those blue eyes grow. Her demeanor changed from the concern it'd been before. It was softer, calmer. She ignored the increase in her heartrate, and the tingles in her tummy. So help her god, she was going to get out of tomorrow if it killed her.

"What's happened?" her father asked.

"I've been working on a project. Specialist research on intracerebral hemorrhages. It's what I was doing when we first arrived. They want me back home. Someone's come in—"

"I can assure you right now, you will *not* be returning without the family. This is a family holiday, and you have already ruined it by your lack of commitment, and preoccupation while here. If it isn't sickness, it's work. I will not have people hearing that you left the family holiday early—"

"Enough!" her father demanded, scowling at Lady Barrington. "You do not make these decisions. I don't care what anybody thinks about her leaving early. I will make a call, and find out the absolute necessity for her to leave. Elizabeth is a prodigy in the medical world. She needs to continue the legacy of the Barrington name. I will be retiring soon, and she needs to continue to make sure she can be as good as me! Who called you?" he asked Lizzie. "Who requires you? I will contact Dr..."

Jesus, the last thing she needed was her father calling the CEO and demanding that someone's head be readily available to hang on their wall. "It's fine. I've managed to get around it. I'm not going home. I'll be in work first thing on Wednesday morning on the basis that I'm teaching and researching only."

"Ah, good. Glad to hear it. So, we are all happy." He raised his hands around the table, informing his family the discussion was over.

"Erm..." She coughed, watching her mother's deathly stare increase. "It's alright if I stay, on the basis that I interconnect with them for the research convention tomorrow," she said, noticing Jose Luis, Deek, and Darcie astounded by the situation. Lizzie had experienced this before. They were frozen, uncertain what would happen next. If her father would become a crazed figure, or her mother, demented.

"Well, none of us will go then, and you and I will interconnect," her father said.

Lizzie heard the grumblings of her mother and sisters, and knew she had to cut in before her father literally became enraged by it all. "Well, the weather has already ruined part of the trip. The Bahamas is fantastic. You can go to an exclusive island, and Pink Sand Island. It's meant to be far more superior than Horseshoe Bay that we went to in Bermuda." This was untrue; she actually had no idea if it was far more superior, but again, the lies just kept coming. "It seems illogical for all of you to waste the final day at a destination that the crew have purposely redirected us to in order to avoid ghastly weather, and prevent us from enjoying the final part of the break. We have the entire following day here on the boat. I won't be able to rely on the WiFi here, so I'm going to rent a conference room somewhere, and expense it. Plus, if I get done early, and since I was sick the day you all bought jewelry, I can go diamond shopping," she said, praying that she'd grabbed the attention of the women to get involved in her perjury.

"There you are then," her mother said, accepting the plan. "Rupert, Libby hasn't got any jewelry to take home, and will be sat in a room working all day. Surely, if you haven't been part of the research program there isn't much requirement for you being there?" she asked simply.

Her father stood grandly. Lizzie couldn't help but look at Darcie as the boat waited for his response. "Gentlemen, let's go to the sky lounge," he said flatly. "It's time to open the Cubans and pappy." He left them all wondering what the answer would be.

Lizzie had been thrown to the wolves. Her mother's look of disdain was anything but well-hidden, and she was glad of the distraction when the vibrations on the table commenced once more. Lizzie took great satisfaction in her mother's newfound actions that resembled the devil. "Take that and go!" she spat. "You have already ruined too much of this holiday. Just leave."

"Happy to," Lizzie said without thinking, immediately regretting it and awaiting the impending wrath of her mother.

Lady Barrington stood so fast, the chair slammed to the floor, the sound resounding throughout the open area. She stormed up to her daughter, the intensity of her heels slamming on the wooden deck. "Who do you think you're talking to? I am your mother, and I command you to speak to me with the dignity and respect with which you were raised. Now, go to your room. I don't want to look at you for the rest of the evening!" she slammed.

Lizzie left, noticing Jose Luis grab Darcie's arm, her face turning various shades of angry. She smiled to her, raising her eyes in accomplishment. She opened her phone up and redialed her assistant, Abby, after missing her call.

"Hi."

"Did it work?" Abby said.

"Yes, I'll call you later, if that's okay?" She made her way back to her room, pushed her head against the door, and allowed her nerves to finally release. She needed to sort the Darcie situation first. She grabbed the pad and pen, laid on her bed, and wrote a note.

Operation date day is complete... Super excited for tomorrow, hope you have got something great planned. I have high expectations. Xxx

Folding the letter, she walked to Darcie's room and slid it underneath the door. She really hoped Darcie wasn't unhappy or concerned. This was her life. It had been her life for 34 years; this wasn't an unusual occurrence.

Chapter Twenty-Three

Darcie was fuming; *nobody* should be spoken to in that way, least of whom by your own family. Sheesh, your own Mother. She was literally on the way to getting her ass fired at this rate. She was second in command, unable to do her job because of her injured hand, and about to go crazy with the charters. *What the fuck was she thinking? Clearly, she wasn't. That was the problem.* She'd never witnessed anything like that before. They mentally abused their own child. *Who the hell even does that?*

Jose Luis sent her back, and told her to finish for the night. It was the worst thing that could've happened; she had to sit alone in the tiny cabin and dwell. Arriving at the cabin, she slammed the door and focused on her breathing, desperately trying to control her anger. She moved towards her bed, feeling the paper below her bare foot. Kneeling to the floor, she opened the paper, and read Lizzie's note.

She sat down on the floor, leaning her head against the door, and reread it. The girl was a hopeless romantic with the love letter thing, but she kind of liked it. She wasn't going to let the situation drain her mood. She had tomorrow to look forward to, and she'd do anything and everything to make sure Lizzie had a wonderful day. She was confident that what she planned was perfect for her. *Oh, dear god, this girl had her. She was in some kinda trouble.* Darcie grabbed a pen and paper and wrote a return note.

Hey doc, thanks for my note. I'm totally aware of your expectations, but surely just a day with these 'pretty blues' is enough for ya haha. I'm super stoked, and I really hope you'll like it. P.S. thanks for the letter. I needed it! -Dxx

Darcie put the letter under her pillow, grabbed her keycard, and made her way to Lizzie's room. She pushed the note under the door, smiling at the prospect of Lizzie's reaction when she got it. She ignored the fact that she was practically skipping back to her room. She prayed that Lizzie was still up; she could really do with some mutual letter writing. Even if the last time she wrote a letter was when she was eight, it still made her giddy. *Who knew?*

*

Lizzie got out of the shower, deciding she was going to plan what she'd wear for her date tomorrow. She wasn't sure what to wear, or take, even. She'd have no choice, but to text Darcie and ask her. As she walked back into her room, she noticed the paper on the floor, immediately smiling as she read it. She was so screwed. She'd tried so hard to keep away, or stay in control with Darcie, but the fact remained that she was hugely attracted to her, and bloody excited for tomorrow. She couldn't keep overthinking it all. It was done. Darcie had gotten her date, as promised, and tomorrow she'd forget about everything and just go with it. After all, she only had four days left. She grabbed her pen and pad and wrote back to Darcie.

I'm surprised you didn't say "what's up doc" in your letter, with that daft American humor, "pretty blue." My expectations are fairly low; we'll be in one of the most

S.L. Gape

beautiful destinations in the world. Surely you can't do that bad, can you? Why did you need the letter? Are you ok? Was it what happened with my family? If so, please don't let that concern or affect you. It's no issue. Also, what do I need to wear and take tomorrow? I hope you're ok, pretty blue. I sent your letter with a gift. Smell the paper. It's my perfume... I know, you're missing me haha.

She smiled at the words, hoping that Darcie didn't think she was completely lame. She changed into her bed shorts and vest, sprayed the paper with her favorite perfume, and rushed down to Darcie's room. She was so desperate to see her, but knew the build-up, and the anticipation of their old-fashioned communication methods would make tomorrow even more perfect. She smiled giddily as she pushed the note under her door.

*

Darcie fidgeted on her cell, trying to stop the abundance of thoughts rushing through her mind about the following day when she heard a paper slip under the door. She looked down, unable to control her smile, and trudged across the small vicinity to unfold the paper. Darcie could already smell Lizzie's expensive perfume on it. She lifted it to her nose and closed her eyes, allowing the fresh scent to fill her senses. Darcie read the words, laughing at her goofiness. She liked their nicknames for each other, the fact that she called her "pretty blue." It made her think that maybe Lizzie was succumbing to her charms. Maybe they would be able to… get to know each other. She sniffed the paper again, and leaned back against her bed. God, she wanted to see her, and smell her, and kiss her and… "Dammit!" she said aloud. *She was completely done for*. Darcie grabbed her pen and paper off the side table, and started writing again.

Pretty blue, huh? Sounds like you're kinda crushing on me there, doc. I was feeling crappy, but it's done now. A certain cute doc got me over it, so thank you! I'm now suitably happy. Tomorrow, wear swimwear and whatever you feel comfortable in. I don't mind; you look beautiful in whatever you wear. I'm looking forward to it. I just hope I can give you a good day. P.S. thanks for the perfume, best gift ever. Good night, Lizzie. Dream wonderful things.
-Darce xxx
P.P.S. Turnover; it's sealed with a kiss. Sorry, you turned me into a dork. x

She was *such* a dork, but she grabbed her lipstick anyhow. Putting the nude pink onto her lips, she pressed them against the paper before dashing back off to Lizzie's room.

*

Lizzie lay on her bed, trying to watch TV, and ignore what her heart seemed to crave and pray for, which of course, was Darcie. Her feelings rushed through her veins. She didn't want to be in this position—eagerly anticipating a letter… flirtation, lust, whatever it was. But it seemed she had no control. The heart wanted what the heart wanted. She smiled as another note came through. *I'm so not crushing on you*, she thought, reading the first words. *I so am crushing on you,* she corrected herself. She read it numerous times, debating whether or not to respond. She decided she couldn't not, grabbed her pen and paper, and began writing back.

Yes, pretty blue, I love it. I will now officially abstain from using Darcie ever again. And "crushing" on you? Really? As if. You should be so lucky!! Thanks for the update on attire. That sounds easy enough, and thank you for the kind words. Albeit, I've never attended a date without making an effort, but I'll try. I'm glad you're feeling better, and I hope I contributed to that. No worries re the cologne/perfume. I'm glad you liked it. Thank you in return for sealing it with a kiss. For the record, I like dorks.
-Lxxx

She couldn't stop looking at the lipstick print on the back of the letter. Darcie's lips had been there only moments before. There's no way she was going to be able to resist kissing those lips tomorrow on their date. But more importantly, she'd be spending a day with Darcie in a bikini. Kissing was the last thing she needed to worry about.

The night was spent with exchanging letters into the early hours, each one definitively longer, containing their newfound, obligatory perfume and kisses. Each woman felt a longing inside them as happiness and excitement spread throughout their veins. Sleep was, of course, inconsequential. Neither wanted to stop their activities, yet both wanted the day to be upon them.

*

Lizzie woke a little after seven am. She wasn't going to breakfast, and she hoped and prayed that when she went down later, her family had decided to go without her. She hadn't gotten around to choosing an outfit last night, so she switched the shower on, and went through the wardrobe to decide what would suit the day ahead. Having made her choice, she pushed aside the fear of her parents and the nerves of the day, and got into the shower.

*

Lizzie's phone lit up with an incoming message from Darcie. She slumped on the bed, and began reading the message, sighing heavily with relief. Her family had just left. *God, she needed to take her assistant Abby to the Ivy when they returned.* That was it. Nothing could stop them from enjoying the day to its entirety now.

She had 10 minutes before she had to meet Darcie at the port, a bid so as not to get the crew involved. Buckling the metal clasp of her gladiator sandals, Lizzie checked herself one last time, choosing to ignore her sudden wave of nerves. She assessed the outfit, happy that the lemon Ralph Lauren chino shorts complimented her tanned legs. The navy and lemon striped chiffon vest finished the outfit off perfectly, adding a touch of elegance to her daywear. It was rare she felt worthy and attractive, but of the rare occasions she did, today was one of them. She sprayed some serum into her hands and ran them through the messy blonde waves she'd created earlier. She plumped it further, adding a little extra volume before grabbing her beach bag and leaving the room.

*

Lizzie rushed off the boat, grateful she hadn't seen any of the staff. She was a few minutes early, and not 100% sure where she needed to meet Darcie, but hoped it'd be easy enough to navigate. As she walked along the dock, she immediately noticed Darcie standing with her back to her. Taking a deep breath, she privately assessed the beautiful woman. *Those legs. Bugger, bugger, bugger. Just... those legs.*

Darcie appeared to look... nervous, which surprised Lizzie. She fidgeted on her feet, switching her weight from one to the other. Her hands did the same, from being wrapped around her wrist, to messing with her hair. Lizzie couldn't help but smile. She was glad it wasn't just her dominated by nerves. Darcie was wearing simple flip flops with a cute brightly colored ankle bracelet. She wore short faded denim shorts, and a white vest with a large number "1" on the back, the name "Booker" printed above it. Her arms looked incredibly tan against the gleaming white, as she stood in front of the Atlantis resort. Lizzie took the final steps to join Darcie, coughing slightly, and reached for her arm. She noticed her back jolt slightly, and her shoulders rise. Darcie took a deep intake of breath before slowly turning to face her.

*

Darcie tried to concentrate on the Atlantis resort; it was easily large enough. It was still one of her favorite hotels, and she frequently spent time wandering through, or going to Aura with Deek and some of the crew. Despite watching the world go by in one of her favorite places, she still couldn't stop fidgeting from her nerves. *What the hell was up with her? It was a date, one date. She'd had plenty over the years, so what was the big deal?* She heard a gentle cough from behind her. Darcie knew it was now or never as she inhaled deeply and turned to face the beautiful Lizzie.

Darcie could feel her heart rate increase to what she felt was dangerously fast. Lizzie looked stunning, and *she* looked completely underdressed in faded denim shorts and a basketball jersey. She could feel a flush come over her, and now felt more uncomfortable than ever.

"You look gorgeous," Lizzie said to her, smiling slightly.

"Yeah, um sorry about that," she said awkwardly, avoiding eye contact.

"*For what?*" Lizzie asked confused, gently raising her chin to force Darcie to meet her eyes. She looked sad, those eyes looked sad. "What's the matter, 'pretty blue?'" A glimmer of a smile appeared.

Darcie considered her eyes, sighing lightly. "Well, I planned an informal day, and I just feel a little underdressed now, I guess. And you look...*wow*. You look incredible."

"*As do you.*" She grabbed her shirt at Darcie's midsection, and pulled her in. "As. Do. You," she whispered, and kissed her cheek slightly. "So, what's 'Suns?'" She pointed to the word on the front of her chest.

Darcie relaxed immediately after Lizzie's words and actions. "Come on, doc." She pulled Lizzie, laughing. "And this," she said, grabbing her jersey, is my basketball team."

"*Your* team?" Lizzie asked impressed.

"Easy, doc. Not my *actual* team. Remember how I told you I was from Phoenix? Well, Booker..." she said, pointing her thumb over her shoulder, "... is my favorite player for the Phoenix Suns basketball team."

"*Really*? Well, that's exciting," she said happily. "I'll have to have a bit of Google fun when I get back home. So, what's the plan for today? Can you tell me yet?"

"Sure thing. There's *so* much to see and do here, like super awesome stuff, but I figured you've done most of, if not all of it. I've kinda gone for a real simplistic day. I hope that's okay? I mean, your folks have pretty much gotten the best day ever here, but I figured you wouldn't have heaps of fun on a date with me *and* your family." She smiled widely, a glint in her eye. "It'll be kinda relaxed, but hopefully, fun for you."

"Sounds perfect." She smiled. "Where to first?"

"Here." She pointed at the bridge of the Royal Towers of the Atlantis Hotel.

"A hotel room?" she questioned sarcastically.

"Shut up..." Darcie rolled her eyes. "Come on, goofball," she said, grabbing her hand, and weaving her in and out of the crowd.

*

A short walk later, they arrived at the entrance of the waterpark. Darcie dropped Lizzie's hand and pointed behind her. "*The waterpark*, not a room. I'm not that much of a douche." She laughed.

"Well, I don't know. Nothing surprises me with you." She jokingly bumped into her.

"You are quite safe, doc. I have no interest in sleeping with you," she said casually.

"Of course not." She smirked. "On the contrary, your body language told me otherwise in bed the other night." She giggled.

"Nope, I'm serious." She held her hands up in defence towards Lizzie. "You don't need to worry. There is no part of me that is going to try and hook up with you in the next four days..." she said seriously. "Oh, for clarity... by 'hook up,' I mean have sex with. I'm gonna go all out with the kisses, though." She leaned in to Lizzie, who turned her head quickly, causing Darcie's lips to land on her cheek. Darcie looked up confused, and noticed an odd look on Lizzie's face, who urgently watched the people around them. She was embarrassed. *Was it the fear of running into her family, or just the crowds of people?* Darcie didn't want to push her about it. She was a lady for Christ's sakes, and the definition of reserved. Of course she wouldn't want to make out at the entrance of an aquapark in front of crowds of people. "Come on, doc. Let's go have some fun."

Lizzie sighed with relief as she watched hurt flash across Darcie's eyes before dissolving into understanding and comfort. Lizzie had never really fit in with anyone or anything, so trying to ascertain who she was in this environment was already out of her comfort zone. She smiled, allowing Darcie's hand to push her lower back softly, and guide her through.

"You wanna go change in the bathroom, or are you happy to do it here and lock it up?" Darcie asked, nodding to the locker she opened for them.

Lizzie shook her head and started unbuckling her sandals. "I'm fine here," she said, getting ready. She got out two $20 bills and debated where to put them when she looked up and noticed Darcie's smirk.

"You sure you don't wanna go change inside?" Darcie asked.

"No, why?"

"You just look like you're stalling."

"Oh no, not at all. Just wondering where to store cash at a waterpark."

"You don't need to worry; it's cashless. We aren't here all day. We'll stay a few hours, and then get outta here to go grab lunch and drinks somewhere else. If you need anything before then, it's cool. We'll come back and get a card." She smiled softly.

"Oh, um, right. Okay, thank you," she said shyly.

"You okay?" she whispered.

"Yes, just new to this."

"No worries. Come on, let's get into our suits and go have some fun."

Lizzie smiled slightly, and put her sandals in the locker. She didn't necessarily feel uncomfortable getting changed. Darcie had seen her numerous times in a bikini, but there were also children everywhere. It felt completely out of her comfort zone. They were two 30-something's *without* children, and it felt a little odd.

"Are you sure you're okay?" Darcie asked concerned. "We can leave; I just thought it'd be fun."

"No, seriously, it's absolutely fine. It's just full of... children," she whispered.

"You don't like kids?" Darcie asked puzzled.

"No, it isn't that. It's just... will we not look odd being the only adults without children here?"

"Ahhhh, got it. Don't sweat it, doc. You ever been to Disney World? Scrap that. As if you would," she said, rolling her eyes. "Look, when we get out there, I can assure you there will be heaps of adults without kids. Just like at Disney, if you ever go." She smiled. "Come on, get undressed, and we'll go take a look. You don't like it, we'll move on."

"For someone who doesn't want to sleep with me, you seem incredibly keen on getting me naked." She laughed, unbuttoning her shorts.

"You're so bad." She rolled her eyes, trying to avert her gaze from Lizzie getting undressed.

Lizzie smirked and took her top off, folding it neatly, and placing it in the locker. She stopped lowering her shorts any further upon catching Darcie's eyes.

Darcie watched Lizzie unbutton her shorts, revealing the low cut, hot pink trim against her tanned tummy. Her shirt came off next to reveal the matching hot pink bandeau top. She hadn't seen this bikini before, and she looked super-hot. Darcie, unfortunately, was a hot mess. She looked up at a smirking Lizzie, who'd caught the way she was looking at her. *Shoot,* she thought, turning her back to Lizzie and continuing to undress herself. *Had she messed up by going casual?* She was way underdressed compared to her, but it was too late to worry now. She'd just go with it. Darcie placed her clothes and flip flops in the locker and searched her bag for the camera and selfie stick while waiting for Lizzie to finish.

Lizzie pushed her bag into the locker and turned back to Darcie, her eyes wide. "I…" She stopped, looking Darcie up and down. "*Really?*" she said incredulous. "You chose to wear that?"

If Darcie hadn't noticed the heat behind Lizzie's stare as her eyes roamed her body, she would've felt even more self-conscious about her outfit than she'd been before. But now, after seeing the way she looked at Darcie, she felt a little better and more than happy to have some fun with it. "You okay?" she said smirking.

"Yes, of course," she said, ignoring her body. They were at a waterpark, and while Lizzie had never been to one before, she was pretty sure from what she'd seen on TV and in movies that when Darcie went down the slides, she might lose that bikini. But maybe that wasn't such a terrible thing. Darcie turned back to the locker and attached the key wristband to her ankle. Lizzie felt like she was being tortured. Not only was she on a date with, quite possibly, the most beautiful woman she'd ever seen, but she was also wearing the sexiest, white, Ralph Lauren bikini with tiny, multi-colored ponies on it. The white against her body, a body that's in the sun year-round... well, she was suitably screwed. To add insult to injury, when Darcie lifted her tattooed leg up to tie the key around her ankle, she was completely blown away by her body.

"You ready?" Darcie smirked at her.

"Be quiet. Yes, are you taking the camera? Oh my god, and a *selfie stick*? God, you're such a tourist." Lizzie laughed.

"Not so much, I just thought it'd be nice to have some fun with it, ya know? Shut up, anyway. Come on," Darcie said, grabbing Lizzie's hand and pulling her excitably.

"Where are we going?" Lizzie squealed as she was dragged through the crowds.

"To the fastest and biggest slide first, of course." She looked at her questioningly. "Is that okay?"

"Erm, I guess. I've never been on one before, though."

"Okay, follow me. I have a much better idea." Darcie grabbed her hand and squeezed it gently before diverting them in a different direction.

*

"How about this for your first go?" Darcie pointed to a ride with a double doughnut.

"Perfect," Lizzie said excitably. "Thanks, you really are too much."

"In an enjoyable way, I hope?"

"Of course." She winked, and pulled her to the queues. "You wanna ride up top or bottom for your first time?" Darcie asked as they waited in line.

Lizzie looked at her confidently, leaning into her ear. "Ordinarily, for my first 'ride,' I'm *always* on top."

"You're such a tease, you know that?"

"I don't know what you mean." She smirked. "Ohhh, come on, it's us," Lizzie said excitably, rushing to get the double doughnut. Darcie watched the woman; she was captivated by her, allured. She rushed after Lizzie and held the inflatable in place, so she could get on first. Once Lizzie was in, Darcie jumped on behind her and wrapped her legs tightly around her waist. She clicked her camera on and pushed them off down the shoot, awaiting their imminent screams and shrills.

Darcie held the selfie stick up as best she could as they rose high up on each side from the twists and turns of the corners. She was desperate to capture the moments of intense laughter and squeals from Lizzie, who, she was highly confident, was having a great time.

They reached the bottom in no time. The doughnut toppled over and the two women went flying underwater. They resurfaced and laughed uncontrollably, trying to maneuver the hair stuck to their faces, and the water that managed to go down every orifice the wrong way.

Lizzie giggled heartily. "That was probably the coolest thing I've ever done."

"Come on, we need to get out of here before we get squashed by the next two coming down." Darcie laughed, pointing back to the water swishing swiftly out of the chute.

"What do you mea—" The next doughnut flew out over their heads, drowning Lizzie by the heavy splash of water that followed. She turned to look at Darcie, somewhat resembling Cousin Itt, and heard loud giggles. Darcie's soft hands moved the hair from her face.

"You'll be glad to know, I got all of that too." She laughed, waving the camera in front of Lizzie.

"Evil." She winked. "Come on, where to next?"

Darcie tried to ignore the feel of Lizzie's hair between her fingers. When it was dry, the long, messy waves were beautifully soft. Honey blonde locks with lighter streaks from the sun. But now it was wet, and still just as soft, the color more ash-like. Light streaks gently clinging to her tanned, bare shoulders.

"Are you going to stop staring?" She smirked and shook her head.

"Uh, um…" Darcie stuttered, embarrassed.

"Come on, gorgeous, let's go have some fun," she said, pulling Darcie out of the water. "So, where to now?"

Darcie smiled. "Well, we can do that again, except this time I ride up front? Or we can go do some single chutes? There's also another slide that goes through a shark tank," she said.

"A shark tank? You can bloody well bugger right off," she said seriously.

"It's okay, I'll protect you. Come on."

"Well, there's more fat on me than you, so I can't imagine you'll do such a good job. They'll totally come after me first."

"First off, there is no fat on you. You have an incredible body. Second, we're in one of the biggest hotels in the world. They wouldn't make a ride that has, maybe 3,000 rides per day, unsafe." She rolled her eyes. "Lastly, I told you I'll protect you, so I'll *protect* you," she said, dragging her off to the next ride.

*

"My tummy hurts so bad because of all the giggling," she said, pushing her hair behind her ears.

"Good, I'm stoked you enjoyed it. I thought you would, but I was still a little unsure," she said shyly.

"Well, you can be rest assured, it's truly been the most fun I've *ever* had. And the best date I've ever had," she said shyly, linking her arm through Darcie's. "So, it appears I've built up quite an appetite. Would you like to go get some food?"

"Well the day isn't over yet, so how hungry are you? If you can hold out, we can go dry off on the beach for a half hour, and then leave. But if you can't, we'll go get cash and—"

"*No way*. If you have an itinerary, I can wait. Let's hit the beach." She smiled.

They returned to the lockers to collect their belongings before making their way to the beach, and Lizzie ran ahead. Darcie grabbed the towels, and walked hurriedly in the direction Lizzie ran in, noticing the proud smile on her face for grabbing the double sun lounger.

"Good going," Darcie confirmed. "Lift up." She opened the towels, and placed them carefully on the bed to lay on. "You need sunscreen?"

"If you wouldn't mind?" Lizzie stood up, turning her back to Darcie. Lizzie tried to relax, but after the morning that she'd had she was, simply put, smitten. *How could this gorgeous, sexy, kind, amazing woman, be interested in her? Want to do all of this for her?*

Darcie rubbed her sweaty palms down her bare thighs, trying to control her breathing before applying the sunscreen on Lizzie's body. She couldn't remember another time she was this nervous, and felt completely paralyzed. She squirted some lotion into her hands, and applied it gently onto her shoulders and back. Applying a little more this time, she rubbed it into her lower back and sides, unable to ignore the slightness of the hot pink bottoms. Darcie ignored everything running through her body, and rubbed her hands over Lizzie's lower back, once again trying desperately to control her impatiently wandering hands.

"You quite alright there?" Lizzie asked, looking over her shoulder and down at a wide-eyed Darcie.

Darcie looked embarrassed. "Uh, um, sorry," she said, quickly kneeling and wiping her hands against her thighs. "Whatever. Do me, please?" She immediately looked at Lizzie, and felt a redness cover her face. *Shit.* "Would you mind putting some on my shoulders, please? I'll be fine everywhere else." Lizzie lifted the bottle to squeeze, hearing Darcie's shock. "That's *too* high…" Darcie started, noticing the look on Lizzie's serious face as she folded her arms across her chest. "Hey, do me a favor, don't cross your arms like that in a bikini." She unfolded them. "And alright, fine, doctor. I'll put the spf 30 lotion on. Come on, do me."

Lizzie chuckled at the terminology.

"I meant lotion… *lotion.*"

"Sure, you did." Lizzie giggled a little, turning Darcie around, and taking in the view from behind. The Ralph Lauren bikini she wore was incredibly complimentary to her body, and now here she was, *exactly* like Darcie, unable to take her eyes off her. More specifically, her lower region.

Lizzie's eyes scanned her lean, tanned, and partially tattooed legs, moving all the way to the dark creases defining her pert buttocks.

Lizzie tried to shake off the situation, and began rubbing the lotion into her body. Her skin was soft, and Lizzie felt as though her fingers burned as she explored her body. The problem wasn't the exploration of the lotion rubbing; it was the unequivocal desire to explore it in an entirely different fashion. "Okay, I need to stop this, or I'm going to end up with all kinds of problems. Which isn't good, given you don't want to sleep with me any longer." She laughed.

"In my defense..." Darcie said, copying Lizzie by getting onto the double sun lounger, and lying on her stomach. "...I never said I didn't want to sleep with you. I said I wasn't going to try and sleep with you in the next four days."

"Ahh, so you do want to sleep with me?" She arched a brow to Darcie. "Let me get this straight. You tell me you don't want to sleep with me, on the basis that I might come running after you for sex? Is that what this is? Some reverse psychology?" she said, smirking.

"Listen to me. I... will... not... sleep... with... you... before... you... leave."

Lizzie looked at her, confused by the comments, and purposely refused to engage in the conversation. If Darcie was being serious, the last thing she wanted was to seem desperate, or worse still, be the instigator when she'd been adamant that she wouldn't go there. "Thanks for today," Lizzie said seriously, laying her head on her arms and facing Darcie.

"No worries, I've actually had an amazing time myself. Better than expected."

"You didn't anticipate having an enjoyable time?"

"Hell no, of course I did," she said, shaking her head before replicating Lizzie's position.

"Okay," she whispered.

"I've had an amazing day with an amazing woman," she said shyly. "And FYI, you are killing me... being half naked this close to me." Darcie moved her hand forward slightly, gently stroking the tip of Lizzie's forefinger.

Lizzie glanced up at the gesture before looking around them, and noticed a sigh from Darcie. She looked at her, her eyes wandering aimlessly. "I'm sorry," Lizzie whispered.

"Why?" she asked, turning back up to face her.

"Because you're clearly miles ahead of me when it comes to tactility, and I can see the frustration in your eyes over that."

"It's not about that. It has nothing to do with that. I've been with women who like to be discreet; I have no issue with that. I guess, it's just... I don't feel that you're doing what you..." She stopped. "Hey, look, it doesn't matter."

"No, tell me."

"Lizzie, I don't want to jeopardize today, and the day we've had."

"So, it's something unpleasant?"

"Nooo... hell no," Darcie said, reaching for Lizzie's hand, and waiting for her to move it again. She saw a sadness in her eyes, and felt crappy that she'd made her feel this way. "Look, I didn't mean to be harsh. All I meant before was sometimes I feel like you do certain things because it's all you've known. For example, feeling awkward when I touch you because it's not appropriate in your life as you know it, as opposed to *you*, yourself, who wants to be tactile. Anyway, let's leave it. It's irrelevant. You do what you feel conformable with and I'll follow your lead, okay?"

"Okay," she said. They sat there in silence for a while, looking at each other. "I'm sorry if I hurt you."

"You didn't, you never could. *Ever,*" Darcie said seriously.

Lizzie digested what Darcie said. She wondered if there was any truth to it. She didn't know, but she wished she could let go a little. "Are your eyes real?" Lizzie asked, breaking the silence.

"*Excuse me*?" Darcie laughed.

"I meant is that your real color, or are they contacts?" She rolled her eyes at her initial question   .

"Ahh, right. Yeah, they're my real color. No contacts, colored or otherwise. My mom's got the exact same. I got them from her."

"*Wow, really*? Interesting," Lizzie cringed, wondering what exactly was interesting about a mother and daughter having the same eyes.

"Is it?" she said, reaching into her bag. Darcie pulled out her phone and began swiping through it. She leaned in closer to Lizzie and showed her a picture. "See?" She pointed to an older version of herself.

"Wow, your mother is very beautiful. She looks lovely," she said, searching the picture. "Is this Ryan? She's cute."

"Ahh, payback, right?" She winked. "And yeah, Mom is awesome. She's always been the best. I'd love for you to meet her. I think you'd like her a lot."

"No payback, thank you very much. And yes, I'm sure I'd like her very much." She laughed.

"What are you laughing at?"

"Well, I just can't imagine this super hot shot lawyer in court, throwing in an 'awesome' midway through her close." She laughed again.

S.L. Gape

"For real, you can't? Well, when I move to London and become a hot shot lawyer, I'll invite you to see and hear it for real." She raised an eyebrow sarcastically.

"London? *Really*? Interesting. And yes, I can't wait. Be sure to also throw in a 'cowabunga.' It would make for some incredible viewing."

Darcie laughed loudly, amused at Lizzie's words. "Cowabunga? You know people don't say that, right? Well, not since *Saved by the Bell* and, maybe *The Ninja Turtles* in the 90's. I know you love your TV, but really?" She laughed.

"Hush your mouth."

For the record, I was very eloquent when I was in the courtroom, but when you go from Wall Street to a yacht, then things kind of change. It's all about being adaptable. It's part of yachting."

"Really? I can just imagine 'awesome' coming up in many a conversation with the rich and famous," she said, rolling her eyes. "Anyway, tell me more about London."

"Sarcasm will get you nowhere." She pointed seriously to Lizzie. "Hmm London, I don't know. I'm considering maybe running away and being a hot shot lawyer in the London offices. At least that'll give me a chance of sweeping a certain beautiful woman off her feet, and running off into the sunset with her."

"Ohh, interesting. Well let me know when you're intending on visiting, and I'll ensure Bella is alone." She winked.

"You're an idiot!"

"But a cute one." She raised her eyebrows animatedly. "I can see it in your eyes."

"What... *these* sexy eyes?"

"Bugger off," she said, picking up Darcie's phone and swiping to the camera. Lizzie leaned in, laying her head on her shoulder, and directed the lens on them. "Smile," Lizzie said. Darcie looked at the screen, admiring the simple, yet perfect photo. Both women looked completely happy and comfortable. "Today's been perfect, everything about it. I thank you from the bottom of my heart," Lizzie handed her the camera, stroking her thumb over Darcie's hand.

"Well, thank you too. I've also had an *'awesome'* day." She rolled her eyes playfully. And I know that it's gonna be crappy when you leave, but I'm glad I had this. I genuinely mean that," she said, mimicking Lizzie's actions, and noticing for the first time all day, the woman relaxed. "Tell me about your work."

"What about it?"

"How did you get into it? Tell me what you do, what you like about it, anything. Everything."

"It's fairly boring."

"Nothing's boring about you, Lizzie."

Lizzie felt a blush creep, and a flip in her tummy. "That's very kind," she said, leaning down to her hand and kissing it softly.

"Well, I'm a nice girl. So, tell me."

"There really isn't too much to tell. I didn't really have any choice but to go into medicine. My parents already had my future and life planned before I could walk. My place in medical school, my place on the board. Everything, really..."

"So, what if you were dumb?" she asked.

"Excuse me?"

"Well, what if you weren't intelligent enough to do it? What would've happened then?"

Lizzie pondered the question momentarily. She'd never thought about that before. "I don't know. Maybe they would've thrown me to the wolves." She smiled.

"That isn't funny," Darcie said seriously.

"I'm sorry. I don't know is the honest answer. Maybe sent me to a better school with extra tuition, who knows. Luckily, we didn't have that problem. I must say, I do believe there's a large element within intelligence that depends on the teaching, if that makes sense? I mean obviously you have to have a brain." She smiled softly. "But I went to boarding school. I had some of the best professors, teachers, and lecturers of anywhere in the world. Throw 10 to 15 hour days of studying, seven days a week into the mix, it was unlikely that I wouldn't have been intelligent enough, I suppose."

"Do you like it?"

"I like helping people."

"But do you like your job? Would you have personally chosen it?"

"I save people's lives for a living. I'm one of the top neurosurgeons in the country, and if I didn't like it, I wouldn't be able to do it. It's incredibly pressurized."

"I don't buy it."

"Excuse me?"

"I don't buy it. You can work a job you don't enjoy, irrespective of whether you're saving lives. I spent over five years keeping major criminals out of jail because I thought my dad wanted that for me. It was everything I was against both ethically and morally, and I got up every day and did it. I didn't particularly enjoy it, but I did it. I did it damn good. So your excuse of 'doing' it as justification for 'liking' it... nah, I don't buy it," she said simply.

Lizzie looked at her carefully. "I don't want to argue," she said quietly.

"I don't want to argue either, and I'm sorry you feel that way. I wasn't trying to argue, I was making a point. I'm sorry, I didn't mean to seem confrontational," she said sadly, noticing the concern in Lizzie's eyes.

"No, I'm sorry," she said, feeling the inexperience of situations such as these.

"I just hate how you've lived a life for others for 34 years, and you still won't admit it. It infuriates me. I'm sorry, let's stop. I've ruined your day now," she said, moving her hands and putting her phone back in her bag.

"You haven't," she said, grabbing Darcie's hand again. "I love that you care enough to be... vocal about it. Honestly, I don't know if I like my job. I do it because it was contrived for me. I've never allowed myself to consider what else was out there because why would I? To further damage me? Every time I thought of something, I stopped. I mean, don't get me wrong. As you know, I love my TV and movies, and I went through stages of wanting to be a policewoman, a firefighter, a pilot, a deep-sea diver, a pathologist—gosh, all sorts." She giggled. "But I never actually stopped and seriously allowed myself to go into any level of detail of the thought. I couldn't have daydreamed of being something else because it would've just tortured me. And now... well, I'm 34. Medicine is all I know. What else do I do?"

"Run off to the Caribbean, and be a stew. Or a lifeguard in an aquapark. Or a doctor in Haiti. Or a teacher in Haiti. There's all manner of options."

"I can't even get a day off without lying or feigning illness, so how exactly do you propose I do that?"

"Stand up to them. Emancipation..." Darcie watched the flicker of hurt in her eyes. "I'm sorry," she said again. It'd been a fantastic morning filled with laughter and happiness, and now all she was doing was hurting and upsetting Lizzie.

"It's okay. I don't expect you to understand. You've been lucky enough to... look, I don't want to discuss this. I apologize, Darcie. Maybe we should just go back?"

Darcie felt pain shoot through her heart, and a pang of guilt cross her body. She looked down to her hands, wondering how she'd messed it up so badly. "You don't need to apologize, I'm the one who was out of line. I don't have the right to say any of that stuff. I don't know what's come over me. I apologize. I was rude, and I've just wrecked the best day of my life. Come on, I'll take you back," she said.

"Why are you so concerned?" Lizzie asked seriously.

"Concerned about what? I don't understand."

"Why do you keep pressing me about my life... or lack thereof?" she asked cordially. "Why? Tell me. I need to hear it."

Darcie felt pain at the question. She looked down at her fidgeting fingers over the edge of the sun lounger. "I don't know," she said softly. "I'm not doing it to be nasty, and I certainly don't mean to come across as shitty. I guess I've just never met anybody like you. You're different from the rest. You're amazing, kind, honest. I guess I just don't like that you don't get to live your own life. But when I say it out loud, it sounds like I'm doing the exact same thing. Like I'm trying to control you, and your life. I guess I just wish I could make you see that you can break away and live the life you want. I hate to see sadness in your eyes, or the way they speak to you. The way you say you don't allow yourself to daydream about different jobs. The lack of emotion when you tell me that you spent your childhood wishing that someday someone would knock on your door and tell you that you were switched at birth. I hate it all. I hate that you're the most amazing person I've ever met, and I can't give you everything. God, I'm sorry. I don't know what I'm saying. Just ignore me. Come on, we're dry now. Get ready, I'll take you back."

"No."

"Huh?" Darcie said confused.

"No, I don't want to go. Granted, it's gone slightly skewwhiff, but you either continue with the day as planned or I'll go out myself."

Darcie looked at her confused. She was standing up to someone or something, for what Darcie imagined, was maybe the first time in her life. "Erm, well, would you like me to come, or should I leave you?"

"I want you to come," she said seriously.

"Do you like nachos?"

"As long as they're chicken." She smiled.

"Come on, let's get outta here," Darcie said, thankful that Lizzie was not the type to hold a grudge. *Even after she royally messed up.*

"So, where are we going?"

"We're going for a walk to another island." Darcie smiled.

"We're walking to *another* island? I'm desperately hungry."

"Come on," she said, laughing and grabbing her hand. She quickly realized what she was doing, and let go. "It's only like 15 minutes."

"Thank the lord. I'm very close to wasting away. We're just going for lunch?"

"Nope. It's the next part, but also simple, as the day was intended. Come on, you'll see soon enough."

"You're very mysterious," Lizzie said, grabbing Darcie's hand and holding it tightly. She watched Darcie look down between them, and up again with a shy smile. It'd been an odd day, and she didn't want it ruined for whatever reason. She could tell by Darcie's line of questioning that she wasn't intentionally setting out to hurt her, or trying to be antagonistic. For now, it was about having fun, enjoying whatever was in store for her.

Chapter Twenty-Four

A giant grin formed on Lizzie's lips. "There's a seven foot statue of a giant frog sitting on a lifeguard seat in front of us."

"Yup, with people queuing to have their photo taken on it. You want one?"

"Erm, I'm okay for now," she said confused. "Is this where we're going?" She looked at the brightly colored bar faced toward sea, with music screaming out of it.

"Sure is. Come on, have some faith in me," she said, looking into her eyes and squeezing her hand a little. Darcie ignored the flip in her tummy.

As they walked towards the loud music through the bar, Lizzie noticed the people around them noisily drinking, laughing, and enjoying themselves. There was a variety of ages. Plates of food filled the tables. Groups and couples wore beads with shot glasses around their necks, balloons made into different things on their heads, and drank from giant, plastic glasses filled with different colored drinks. The inside area was dark, housing a stage with several people racing to finish their drinks the fastest. An excited host egged them on loudly into the microphone, and the crowd of people at the foot of the stage all shouted and cheered. Lizzie was mesmerized; she'd never seen anything like it. Not in real life, anyhow. It wasn't even two in the afternoon, and everyone appeared to be severely inebriated.

"Here," Darcie said, breaking Lizzie out of her trance.

"Sorry."

"For what?" Darcie asked amused.

"Leaving you, walking off. What is this?" Lizzie asked reluctantly, taking the bright blue, tall cup filled with a bright red slushy drink inside it. She read the words "Senor Frogs" on it. *What was a Senor Frog?* she wondered.

"Who knows? I asked for a yard of anything strawberry." She laughed and took a sip out of the oversized straw. "Mmmm, definitely tequila. I'm guessing a strawberry margarita."

"You got me a *yard* of tequila before two in the afternoon?" she asked appalled.

"Looks like it." She smirked. "Welcome to Senor Frogs, Lizzie. Cheers, here's to a fun afternoon."

Lizzie looked at Darcie, and sipped through her straw. She held the cup out for Darcie to tap with her own. Cheers erupted across from her and she looked around to see what was going on. "What's happening?" she asked as Darcie stepped onto the seat at the bar and out of the way. Several people wearing variations of Senor Frogs t-shirts and lanyards with staff cards attached, grabbed a chair to stand on, holding bottles of multi-colored mixtures. The conga song began, and the host from moments earlier now led a conga line, blowing his whistle loudly as he weaved in and out of his colleagues who poured drinks into the customers' mouths. The guy tried to grab Lizzie, who shyly moved back, sloping further into the bar. She heard Darcie's comforting laugh and noticed the man on the bar pouring a drink into her mouth. She swallowed the drink, giving Lizzie a smile and a nod. He moved toward Lizzie without giving her a chance to refuse, and leaned the bottle over her head. She didn't have a clue what she was supposed to do, but heard cheers around her. She closed her eyes, and hoped for the best.

Her taste buds felt electrocuted by whatever culmination of alcohol had gone down. She lifted her head, hearing more cheers and claps as she wiped her mouth and looked at Darcie shyly, who gave her a simple wink. "Come on beautiful, let's get you some food before you pass out on my sorry ass," Darcie said, leading her toward the tables overlooking the water and the port.

"Have you ever worked on a cruise ship?" Lizzie asked Darcie, settling into her seat.

"No," Darcie said, admiring the mega Disney cruise liner. "Have you been on one?" Darcie asked distantly.

"A Disney cruise? Yeah, watching Dumbo under the stars was the best night of my life." She smirked

"You goofball," Darcie said, throwing the napkin at her. "Chicken nachos good for you then?"

"Absolutely perfect." She smiled.

"So, what did you think of the waterpark? Was it okay?"

"Honestly?" Lizzie said sincerely, noticing the nervous nod of Darcie's head. "It's the best date I've ever been on. I've never been to a waterpark before. I was really concerned at first because of the number of children, and thought it may be odd, but it was incredibly fun," she said with a large grin. "And the company was also okay, I suppose." She winked.

"You're on fire today, huh?"

"Always." She smiled. "So, tell me about this place," Lizzie said, interested.

"What do you mean?"

"Well, you've brought me here for a reason. Why Senor Frogs?" she inquired. "Please don't think I don't like it. It's just that it's so different from anything I've ever experienced. I mean, a conga shot line at two in the afternoon is not really something my parents would approve of."

"Honestly, that's why I did it. I don't care if your family would approve. You aren't your parents; you're nothing like them. You're beautiful, and funny, smart, sweet..." She stopped, noticing Lizzie's embarrassment. "I'm sorry, I didn't mean to weird you out. My point is, you aren't like them, and I think I know you well by now, and I thought you'd love the simplicity of all of this. I wanted to give you just one day in your life, for you. Something that I felt would make you feel down to earth and normal. Something *you* could enjoy for yourself. After seeing you in Haiti, it was clear to me you don't need all that glamour and aristocracy, so I wanted something kinda basic, but equally fun. And Senor Frogs is so easy going. They mostly have cruise ship passengers in here, which makes it lots more fun. You know, all these loud yanks partying hard in the afternoon." She laughed as she made fun of herself.

"It's somewhat insane, I must admit, but it's very fun. I already can't believe all the alcohol I've consumed in the last 10 days, but then you take me out and feed me a yard of tequila?" She laughed. "I wonder if this is your theory... Spend all day telling me you don't want to sleep with me, and then get me so inebriated that I end up throwing myself at you."

"Ohhh yes, of course. My plan has been blown." She rolled her eyes, sipping on her cocktail. "Oh, and hey, please don't throw yourself at me. I don't know that I have that much will power to resist." She laughed.

Lizzie poked her tongue out at Darcie's sarcasm. "It's horrifically busy, isn't it?" Lizzie said, looking at her surroundings.

"Yeah, is that okay? We can find someplace quieter, if you'd prefer?"

"No, I'm enjoying it. Plus, the nachos..." she said, pointing to the table next to her, "...look bloody amazing. Plus, I've learned to *love* people watching." She smiled widely. "You can learn an awful lot about someone just by watching them." She raised her eyebrows in a way that Darcie found seductive.

"Oh really? There seems to be a hidden meaning to that statement. Pray tell." Darcie leaned back in her chair.

"*Hidden meaning*? I have no idea what you mean." She smirked, enjoying the easy flirting. Just as Darcie was about to respond, their food arrived. "Bloody hell, is that a normal portion?" she whispered to her.

"Yup. Dig in," she said, handing Lizzie a plate. "So, come on, enlighten me. What were you going to say as our food arrived? What have you learned from *me*? From watching me?"

"That's an awfully confident assumption," she questioned, arching a brow, and taking a bite. "Ohhh wow, these are yummy. What makes you think I've been watching *you* specifically?"

"Because if you enjoy 'people watching' as a *norm*, then there's no way you wouldn't check out the person you're into," she said, making inverted commas with her fingers.

"*Wow*, you really are full of yourself, 'pretty blue.'" She laughed.

"Not really," Darcie said seriously. "You're on a date with me. You keep going on about me not wanting to sleep with you, you have a pet name for me, and *you* came to my room and kissed me first when you thought I'd left. I think those could easily be construed as *you* being into *me*." She smirked.

S.L. Gape

"Gosh, you really can tell you're a lawyer." Lizzie laughed. "Seriously, as much as your chef is incredible, I'm so done with the fancy stuff. This..." She pointed to the nachos, "...is my guilty pleasure. I'll be in the gym for a month, though. I'm literally in love," she said happily.

"Awh shucks, you are? Thanks," Darcie mused, pretending to blush.

"You're such an idiot," Lizzie rolled her eyes, stifling the laugh.

Darcie grabbed the waiter as he walked past, ordered another two drinks for them, and raised her eyebrows at Lizzie. "A yard of rum now, doc."

"You did not!" she said wide eyed. "I still have this!"

"Well, drink quicker. I've seen how much you can knock back," she muttered sarcastically. "So, you go to the gym a lot?"

"Very bossy, aren't you?" Lizzie rolled her eyes. "Not as much as I should, but I don't drink all that often at home. I'm not able to with the shifts and hours I work, and I don't smoke or take drugs, so I'm not all bad. I try to eat as healthy as I can to ensure I'm in good condition both mentally and physically. I maybe go twice a week. I can't bare it, if I'm perfectly honest. I'd rather have a pool and swim in the water frequently."

"You don't have a pool?" Darcie asked surprised.

"It's a bit difficult to in London." She giggled.

"Of course, yeah. Stupid thing to say. Sorry," she said shyly.

"Don't be silly. You have nothing to apologize for." She placed her hand on Darcie's and stroked her thumb softly. Darcie tried to ignore the flip in her tummy at the out of character contact. "So, did *you* have a pool?" Lizzie asked, removing her hand and taking more nachos.

"My folks don't, but my apartment block did. It was one of the main reasons for buying that one. I've always loved the water."

"Obviously." She smiled. "What's happened to your apartment now, then? Did you sell it?"

"No, it's a rental now."

The next drink came over in a different colored plastic cup this time, and Lizzie dove in to taste it. "Mmm, excellent choice. It's very nice."

"Thank you. Today's been perfect; we're in the Caribbean, the sun's shining, and we've got good music, tasty food, and a beautiful view," Darcie eyed Lizzie intently, watching a blush fill her face. "Your choice next time."

What, date or drink?"

"Drink, obviously. The date is definitely yours, as it'll be in London, and I've not seen any part other than the offices when I've visited." She raised her eyebrows.

"Long way for a date, isn't it?"

"Matter of opinion. You told me you'd take me on a date, so I guess I've got to come over."

"And tell me..." Lizzie asked seductively, leaning closer into Darcie. "Will you sleep with me there? Or is this an indefinite thing?" She smirked.

"Well, I guess that depends on how good the date is." She leaned back, slowly and seductively taking a sip of her drink.

"I best get my thinking cap on then, huh?" She'd love Darcie to come visit her, albeit it was obviously, incredibly unlikely.

"Yes, you best. And I think it's best we change the subject. Being intoxicated brings back recollections of you half naked in a hot pink bikini all day, and that smile really makes not sleeping with you difficult."

"You're quite safe. As I said, irrespective of what you're now 'alleging,' I'm equally not prepared to sleep with you. Though I on the other hand, have a valid reason for that."

"*Whatever.*" Darcie rolled her eyes. "On a serious note, are you going to be okay with your parents? Ya know, lying to them? Will it be okay?" she asked concerned.

"It'll be fine, Darce. Please don't worry. My mother won't get involved as she'd have no idea how to anyway. My father is genuinely interested in the project because that's all he really cares about. I studied neurobiochemistry, so I do a lot of research programs on it. I'm sure he won't question my detailing because he'd have to admit that I know more about neurology than him. I'm officially stuffed. I literally couldn't eat another thing," she said, changing the subject.

"Sheesh, you really are super intelligent. And yeah, you did good. I'm glad you liked them. I was going out on a whim with the basic thing."

"I love it. I've had the best day ever. The yards of spirits clearly help. I may need to intercept the continuation of yards though, or I won't make it home." She smiled.

"We can get some beers," Darcie said carefully. "We need to keep some liquor room for the next place, anyhow." She smirked.

"We're going somewhere else?"

"Yup, just one more place, and it's close to Iconica, so we can just rush back when your family is on their way."

"Oh, delightful! How exciting. In that case, I most certainly need some beer. Do you want one?"

"Yes, are you done? I'll get them to clear this away, and ask for some Dos Equis."

"Some what?"

"Dos Equis. It's a Mexican beer. Great with Mexican food."

"Oh, lovely. I'm just going to have a quick look in that shop if we're going elsewhere shortly, if that's okay?"

"Sure thing."

*

Lizzie could feel the effects of the alcohol. She wandered around the store, picking up numerous souvenirs. She wanted everything. All of it did, and would forever, remind her of the perfect date. A day they'd had together. Lizzie noticed a top like the basketball one Darcie wore. Smiling widely, she decided to get it as a gift for her. Next, Lizzie found some bright, casual shorts with a picture on one of the legs of a drunk frog on a beach holding an empty bottle of tequila. She couldn't help but chuckle and picked that up too. As she made her way to pay at the cash register, she noticed the lanyards the employees wore around their necks, giggling at the prospect of exchanging her NHS work one to a brightly colored lanyard with the words, "one tequila, two tequila, three tequila, floor." *Gosh, her father would literally disown her. It was worth a go,* she thought. Lizzie saw a plain, white polo with a small Senor Frog's, Bahamas logo on the left chest. It was like Darcie's work tops. She checked through the sizes, realizing how long she'd left Darcie before picking up two and paying.

"Sheesh, you can give a woman a complex leaving for that long," Darcie stated, eyeing the two bags full of mementos. "Anything you *didn't* buy?" She laughed.

"Yes, I may have gotten somewhat carried away. Note to self, don't go shopping while intoxicated. Have you seen the shop? It's fabulous. I am suitably happy with my purchases, which will now always remind me of you and our perfect day." She smiled shyly. "Oh, bloody hell, you didn't think two yards of different spirits was sufficient?" Lizzie held up the shot glass full of what she assumed was tequila, given the salt and lime accompanying it.

"Actually, it wasn't me. Apparently when you ask for a check in this place, they feel the need to provide a shot of tequila." She grinned.

"Are we doing it?"

"Damn right we are. Salut," she said, holding up the tequila.

"Dear lord," Lizzie held up the glass. "Do you not do it correctly?" She picked up the salt, looking at Darcie intently as she slowly licked her hand and poured some salt on it. The deep gulp Darcie took while watching Lizzie hadn't gone unnoticed. "Salut," Lizzie said, smirking as she downed the tequila and sucked on the lime slice.

This woman, Darcie thought. She leaned in closer to Lizzie. "I think maybe we need to cut you off," she shook her head, downing her own shot.

"Where's the fun in that? Shall we go after this?"

"Yeah, sure," Darcie smiled, enjoying the simplicity and comfortability of the day.

They drank the remainder of their drinks—Darcie insisting on paying as it was her date—and left the lively bar in pursuit of their next adventure.

Chapter Twenty-Five

"So, I'm walking to another island again, yes?" Lizzie asked amused.

"Sure are. It may help sober you up." She winked at Lizzie.

"Hey, cheeky." Lizzie bumped her shoulder as they walked down the main street, passing shops with vendors who called them in to buy gifts.

"There's one of the diamond jewelers. You wanna go in? You mentioned to your family you might visit."

"Hmm, so I did. I'm not particularly fussed, not unless you want something. I can treat you for today," she said kindly. "I'm sorry, I didn't mean that to sound like I was trying to buy you. I know you can afford it. I didn't mean to be rude."

"Stop overthinking," she said seriously. "You don't need to do that, and I knew what you meant. I'm not really a diamond kinda gal anyway. Wouldn't really fit with my Suns jersey." She giggled. "But come with me, I have an idea," she grabbed Lizzie's arm and ushering her inside a local store. Darcie directed her towards the back, where they had several stands of casual bracelets, necklaces, and anklets. "I don't *need* anything from you. You being here has been perfect enough, but if you're adamant, you can get me one of these."

"Thank you, me too. I've had the best time. And yes, I'd love to." She smiled widely. "Pick one."

Darcie looked at the different varieties for a while before choosing a coral shell necklace. "I like this one. Will you choose one too?"

"I don't need one. I wanted to get you one to thank you for today."

"I know you don't need one, but you'll be leaving soon, and I wanna know you have something from me that I can think about you wearing. Something that makes you think of me," she said sadly. "Not just the memories of today."

"We've really made this difficult for ourselves, haven't we?" Lizzie responded.

"What do you mean?"

"Well, we've continued to get closer, knowing as you say, that in a few days it'll be over?"

"Do you think it'll be over?" Darcie asked seriously.

"How can it not be? You live on a yacht and travel the Caribbean. I live in London."

"I don't know. I know we can't have a relationship, but I'd love to stay friends and talk to you regularly. And as I said, as soon as I get some time off, I'm coming straight to London."

"Maybe you need to go back to law and transfer to the London office," she questioned, handing Darcie the turquoise and neon yellow material ankle bracelet. "This one, please."

"What, so we can live in marital bliss?" She left the statement hanging. "Thank you," she said, taking it from her hand and walking off.

"I'm not even going to respond to that sarcasm, lady." She rolled her eyes.

"What makes you think I'm being sarcastic? Come on, let's get a move on. Your family will be returning shortly, and I want us to have some more fun," Darcie confirmed, choosing to change the subject.

"I can't imagine how much more fun I can possibly have. Have I thanked you for today?"

"Yes, plenty."

*

They walked back over to Paradise Island, and Darcie led the way into the next bar.

"We're going to Margaritaville? We need *more* margarita's?" she laughed, walking into the bar.

"Sure, we do. You can never have enough margaritas." She winked. "You wanna sit over there by the pool?"

"Yes, definitely. Shall we get in?"

"You wanna?"

"Me, tequila, and you half naked again? Of course I do." She winked.

"You are very naughty, Doctor Barrington."

"As I've already said, you have *no* idea. Shall we?"

Darcie rolled her eyes, removed her clothes, and headed straight for the pool's swim up bar.

Lizzie watched Darcie saunter off in that bikini again. It was hard enough this morning, but now having been drinking, it was an entirely different situation. She got undressed, and followed Darcie into the water, swimming up behind her, and splashing her playfully.

"Hey!" Darcie squealed, turning around in her chair and passing a drink to Lizzie.

"Yay, more alcohol." She winked, sipping a little, and nodding in appreciation. She stood up, standing between Darcie's legs as she leaned over her to put her drink down, making a conscious effort to graze her breast against Darcie's shoulder.

"Are you *purposely* trying to destroy me?" Darcie asked seriously.

"*Destroy you?*" she quizzed.

"Half naked, wet, *and* rubbing your chest against me?" Lizzie smirked at Darcie.

"Lizzie don't you dare do, say, or think whatever it is that's giving you that glint in your eye," she said seriously.

"I honestly don't know what you mean." She lowered herself into the water again, and moved closer to Darcie, taking a hold of each of her ankles underwater.

Darcie looked down into the water at Lizzie's hands around her legs. "Getting brave, I see, doc." She arched a brow.

"Seemingly, I can't help myself."

"Lady! Lady!" shouted a staff photographer, aiming a camera at them.

"Oh, no thank you," Lizzie responded shyly.

"Erm… yes, please." Darcie dragged Lizzie up and put her arm around her shoulder. The photographer took several pictures, telling them he'd be back in a while. "Thank you," Darcie smiled kindly.

Lizzie looked at her puzzled, slowly acknowledging the playful transformation cross her face. The next thing she knew, she was underwater. Lizzie felt water rush up her nose, and pain shoot up her head. Their bodies brushed against each other as she came back above water, coughing, and spluttering a little. "You are in so much trouble for that," she said, pushing her hair back and eyeing Darcie evenly.

Darcie smiled at Lizzie as she'd come up from being dunked, noticing the light-hearted nature and playful side to her. "I can't wait," Darcie smirked, unable to take her eyes off her body. The drinks were completely overtaking her, and while she'd been desperate to not go near Lizzie, she no longer knew if she'd be able to keep her hands off her.

Lizzie couldn't help but smirk at the confidence growing within her, particularly as she watched the glazed look cross Darcie's face. Those incredible, blue eyes roamed her body. She approached Darcie confidently, deciding to have more fun with her. "You won't be saying that later. You thought my teasing was treacherous before? Well, I'm going to come to your room this evening, after we've spent all day, semi naked and intoxicated together, and then I'll show you what teasing really is. I'm going to tease you to hell and back, just so you're aware," Lizzie purred.

"I can't wait." Darcie raised her eyebrow with a sly grin. "Come on, let's get a seat. The bar's getting busy," Darcie responded, grabbing their drinks and walking to a table in the water.

*

They sat contentedly at the table, sipping their drinks, and watching the boats in the distance. The pool wasn't overly crowded outside of the bar area, but there were pockets of people. She noticed two women at the table next to them. They were likely a couple of years older than Darcie and herself and were clearly a couple. Equally, neither had any qualms about making that glaringly obvious. Lizzie hadn't ever been tactile, and because she rarely went out, or associated with other gay people, she'd not had any exposure to the openness that was on show right now. They weren't being improper or tasteless. No part of them flaunted their sexuality in front of others. They

S.L. Gape

were just being... well, normal. They were laughing, and drinking with the occasional, discreet touch, or knowing glare. *They were in love, and nobody else around them mattered.*

Lizzie had gone out with a girl back in her 20's who she went to Brighton with for the weekend. It was the only time she'd been, and they'd gone to a gay club where there was a great deal of tactility. In fact, it was probably a bit too much for her at the time, but here, it was different. *Or was it? Maybe it was just her age having mellowed her.*

"Does that bother you?" Darcie interrupted her thoughts.

"Sorry?" Lizzie questioned as she turned to face her.

"That couple... does it bother you? You know, because they're a couple?"

"*What?* Of course not. Why would a gay couple bother a gay woman?" she asked confused.

"I don't know, just saw something in your eyes. That, and you were staring."

"Interestingly, it's still relatively new to me, I suppose. People being open, yet not open, if that makes sense?"

"Sure."

"It's nice. It's normal. Like, they aren't any different to that couple over there." She pointed to a straight couple laughing with the occasional kiss. "I don't think I've ever been in an environment where it's not like feeding time at the zoo. Where it *is* just normal. The 'I love you, you love me, and this is life' normal."

"So, you're saying you *love* me?" She laughed.

"You really cannot have an adult conversation, can you?" Lizzie rolled her eyes.

"I can, actually, but not when I see sadness in your eyes, a sadness brought by something I have no way of fixing. I try and make you laugh to ease the moment," she said seriously.

"Thank you," Lizzie smiled shyly. The music increased, and the staff danced with shots around the pool area. She watched them, and moved her head back, this time deciding to engage in the drunken fun.

The employee shifted the drink to Darcie, and Lizzie waited until she was swallowing it to tickle her. Darcie began to cough and cover her mouth, spluttering the neon liquid. She sat wide eyed, watching a giggling Lizzie dive off in between the tables and swim away from her. Darcie followed Lizzie and swam fiercely after her, hearing a squeal as she grabbed hold of her leg. She pulled Lizzie's leg up and threw her over and back underwater, watching her reappear with her hair in disarray, still giggling uncontrollably. Lizzie tried to push Darcie under, but was unable to. Darcie grabbed her and dunked her again.

"Oh my gosh, how *strong* are you?" She smiled, dipping her head back underwater to regain control of herself.

"Living in New York, ya gotta be tough," Darcie confirmed, swimming closer to Lizzie and grabbing her hands underwater.

"Does that mean you'll protect me if we go?"

"Of course, I'll kick some serious ass for you." She laughed. "You'll have to clean me up after, though. Bloodied knuckles and all." She screwed up her nose.

"Ohhh, lovely. I'll come to your rescue," she said, playing with Darcie's hands. "I'll come in my scrubs."

"Oh, you will? I can't wait to see you in your scrubs," she flirted.

"Oh, you can't?" She stood up in the water so that Darcie was eye level to her chest. "Well, I'm sure I can arrange that. I'll need to think about what I want you to show up in, but this wet in a skimpy bikini is definitely top of the list." She smiled, swimming back to the table, and retrieving their melting drinks.

Darcie joined her and sat again, enjoying the sun beating down on her face.

"Excuse me, would you mind taking our photo?" a woman next to Lizzie asked.

"Yes, of course." She turned the camera to the two women she'd paid attention to earlier. They were huddled closely, smiling at the camera. Lizzie took a couple of pictures and handed the camera back.

"Thanks, those are awesome," the woman said, showing her partner.

"No problem, I hope they're okay." Lizzie smiled politely.

"They are."

Lizzie sat next to Darcie again, and felt their fingers brush against each other. She looked up at her and smiled.

"So, where are y'all from?" one of the women asked, pulling them out of their moment.

Lizzie looked over at the woman. "London."

"You are? Awesome. You're a cute couple."

They both blushed as Darcie leaned forward. "Actually, we *aren't*," she confirmed. "And I'm not from London. Just her. It's just a date." She smiled softly towards Lizzie.

"Oh wow. You guys look super cute together, like you've been dating forever. Where are you from?" one of the women asked Darcie.

"Phoenix, Arizona." She sipped her drink. "And y'all?"

"Chicago," they said in unison. "So, how did y'all meet?" They moved to Lizzie and Darcie's table. "Ya mind?

"No, please sit," Darcie offered. "You wanna tell?" She pointed at Lizzie.

"Cat got your tongue?" Lizzie winked playfully, enjoying how even sexier Darcie's voice was when she gained a stronger, American accent. "On a boat. I'm currently on vacation here. Well, here being a slight piece of misinformation. I've been traveling through the Caribbean, and I do believe this one diverted the trip for our date," she said, raising a brow.

"You did? Ohhh, how sweet."

"Oh, that's gotta be love," the other woman confirmed

"Woah easy, I've known her for 10 days. Chill with the U-Haul jokes." Darcie laughed.

"It's okay, she already told me she loves me." Lizzie nodded at them, laughing.

"Say what?" Darcie spat her drink. "I did not," she responded playfully outraged, unable to stop herself from smiling as she watched Lizzie finally show a flash of who she really was. *Who she should really be.*

"You did, too. Earlier you said, 'I love you, you love me, and we'll live in marital bliss,' or something like that." She smiled widely. "I'm sorry, she's also taken me out all day to get drunk."

"It wasn't really how the conversation was going for one, and if you remember correctly, I did say 'marital bliss,' but *you* said, 'I love you, you love me,' goofball."

"I still think she did, but it may be the drink," Lizzie whispered to the two women who looked amused. "Oh, I'm sorry, how rude of us. I'm Lizzie. This is Darcie. What are your names?"

Darcie couldn't help but allow butterflies to unravel. *This woman,* she thought for the millionth time today, and throughout the charter.

"I'm Kelly," the taller, more athletic woman said, holding out her tattooed arm to shake Lizzie and Darcie's hands.

"And I'm Jamie," the shorter, curvier woman said. Her hair was cut short, and unlike Kelly, she appeared to have no tattoos. "You two are the cutest," Jamie stated, clearly a bit more of a romantic than her more masculine partner.

"So, how long have you guys been together?" Lizzie asked interested.

"17 years." Kelly looked on lovingly.

"*Wow*. That's... wow... how beautiful."

"Sure is."

"So, you're a Suns gal?" Kelly directed the question to Darcie. "I noticed your top when you arrived. You know what us lesbians are like, always drawn to other gay folk." She laughed.

Darcie laughed, nodding in agreement. "Yup, it's true. And yeah, Suns through and through. Bulls?"

"Yes ma'am."

Lizzie looked confused before Jamie stepped in, and confirmed they were talking about basketball. "Oh, I see," she said, feeling Darcie's hand slip behind her, and gently stroke her back.

"Kelly is a physical ed teacher," Jamie confirmed, affirming her reason for the sports interest.

"Really? That's awesome," Darcie responded keenly. "And you, Jamie?"

"I'm a stay at home mom."

"Oh wow, you have children?" Lizzie asked excitably.

"Yes, they're the best," they both said in unison, laughing shyly together.

"Are they here with you? Well, not Margaritaville, but in the Bahamas?"

"No, they're home with Kelly's folks. It's just a short break for our anniversary."

"Hey, congrats, you guys," Darcie held up her drink to them.

"So, is it your 17th anniversary, then?" Lizzie asked, touching her glass to both of theirs.

"No, our 17th year together was last year. It's our 10th *wedding* anniversary... today," Kelly muttered shyly.

"You're married? And it's your 10 year wedding anniversary *today*? Oh my gosh, how wonderful. We need to do something!" Lizzie turned to Darcie excitably. "Oh, two kisses..." She clapped her hands, downing the last part of her drink.

"Two kisses?" Darcie asked confused. "Is that some kind of British thing?"

"I'm not so sure my 10 year wedding anniversary would go so well if I'm kissing other chicks," Kelly said, equally as confused.

"Nooooo, you're confused. I don't want to give you 'two kisses.' Well, I do want to give you two, but not of what you're thinking. Look, there." She pointed. "They have a bucket of the 'two kisses,'" she pointed to the metal ice bucket with a beer logo on the side and several bottles of beer hanging out.

"Dos Equis?" Darcie laughed. "You're so cute. You mean, let's get a bucket of Dos Equis, which looks like 'two kisses,' as opposed to kissing up on these lovely ladies?"

"Yes, of course. I have no interest in 'kissing up' on them." Lizzie squirmed at her poor attempt of an American accent. "While you're both incredibly beautiful women, there's no need to worry that I'm going to start suggesting any kind of 'keys in bowls' scenario," she responded,

S.L. Gape

embarrassed. "I just don't speak Spanish, and only heard of these beers today. Oh, and then forgot the name."

"Well, I for one, am happy you don't wanna go elsewhere, but *I'd* kinda prefer two kisses." Darcie winked.

"Oh, you guys... you're super cute together," Jamie said.

"Thanks. So, you fancy some new friends to celebrate with? I'll go get the beer," Darcie offered.

"Yeah, if you're sure you guys don't mind the intrusion of your first date?"

"It won't be the last," Darcie responded coyly.

"I'll go help her, baby," Kelly said, kissing her wife quickly on the lips, and swam after Darcie.

"You guys make an incredible couple," Lizzie stated as she and Jamie sat down.

"Thanks, she's awesome. I'm so lucky. She makes me feel like I'm the most beautiful woman in the world, which kinda helps." She laughed. "Even when I was fat and gross when I was pregnant she did," Jamie said bashfully.

"I'm convinced you were not fat and gross. It's beautiful to watch. So how many kids do you have?"

"Three boys." She rolled her eyes. "My world is owned by sports," she laughed. "They're awesome though, and I wouldn't change it for the world."

"How did you meet? I'm sorry, we only just met; I hope you don't think I'm prying."

"Hell no. To new friends," Jamie held up her bottle of beer to Lizzie.

She looked at her empty glass, stole Darcie's, and tapped it against Jamie's. She put her finger to her mouth, and whispered 'shhh' to her new friend.

"I was a sports therapist before we had kids and she came to my clinic for help with a sports injury," Jamie smiled lovingly. "We were a bit like you guys, and well…

224

just had something special really quick. Like this instant connection."

"That's beautiful," Lizzie responded.

"Thanks. So, when do you leave?"

"Three days," she added despondently, realizing that today would soon end.

"*And...* then what?"

"I don't know. I really don't, I have... nothing back home."

"So, why go back?"

"Well, it doesn't really work like that, does it?"

"Sure, it does. *Love's love.* It's 2018. The states legalized same sex marriage. You can move there if you have nothing back home. You could go work with her. Hell, you could go work in the Caribbean if that's what she does for a living. There's plenty of options," she said, like it was the easiest thing in the world.

"Not quite practical, though. I don't know. She talks like there's no way it'll end here. I like that, but it scares me a little."

"The only thing I'll say before they return is don't take it for granted. Don't risk losing it, and don't overthink it." She smiled as Darcie and Kelly walked back over with numerous drinks in their hands. Lizzie looked at her seriously, unable to say anything further as the others returned.

"I had nothing to do with this," Darcie handed Lizzie a shot.

"You're kidding."

"Nope."

"What's up with you Americans?" Lizzie said, shaking her head.

"Well there's a prejudiced attitude." Kelly laughed.

S.L. Gape

"Hardly. It was the same way when I lived there; you drink shots without mixers, and like they're going out of fashion."

"You lived in the states? Where? I told you it was easy," Jamie said simply, ignoring the confusion in Kelly and Darcie's eyes.

"Near Boston. Anyway, here's to a wonderful couple on their beautiful 10 year anniversary. May there be many more to come." Lizzie held up the shot.

"Here's to new friends. And *soul mates*." Jamie raised her glass, smirking at Lizzie who shook her head.

"Baby, behave." Kelly said. Lizzie watched the eye contact between Kelly and Darcie, wondering what they'd discussed at the bar.

"You okay?" Darcie whispered to Lizzie.

"Yes, fine. You?"

Darcie noticed the sudden change in her demeanor and wondered if Jamie had said something to upset her, or if something else had happened. She turned her water pack over, and checked her phone to make sure Deek or Jose-Luis hadn't messaged her. "Yes, just feeling rubbish about it all coming to an end I suppose," she responded honestly.

"You are?"

Darcie looked at her seriously before leaning in and stroking her face. "I won't apologize for how I feel about you, Lizzie." She kissed her lips softly.

And in those few words uttered, Lizzie knew her life had changed forever. *What the hell was she going to do?* She pulled away from the tender kiss and looked at Darcie, who desperately searched for something. *Maybe an answer,* she thought.

"Sorry about that," Darcie answered shyly to Jamie and Kelly.

"Don't be. It's super cute. You guys should stop by Chicago when you're there next?" Kelly offered

"Well, I'm not so sure we'll be in town, but we can certainly arrange a visit," Darcie said, lacing Lizzie's fingers in her own.

"Yes, awesome. I'd love for you to meet the boys."

"Me too," Lizzie muttered, noticing the phone vibrate on the table. Darcie checked it, and sighed sadly.

"You okay?" Kelly asked.

"Yeah, we just need to leave," Darcie groaned.

"Can't you guys stay?" Jamie asked.

"No, the boat needs to get moving."

"You guys are gonna come visit Chicago, yeah?"

"Yes, if you promise to come to London," Lizzie responded sincerely.

"We'd love to."

"With the boys," Lizzie added, downing her beer. As they got out of the water, the worker who'd photographed them earlier reappeared, apologizing for the length of time it'd taken. He showed them the key ring with their happy faces filling it. She handed the man some money, and gave Lizzie a photo. "For you," she said simply.

Lizzie looked at the picture, noticing how Darcie's eyes stood out far more than her near naked body. She hung onto Lizzie's body, a pose that expressed so much meaning. "Thank you," Lizzie said sincerely.

Darcie looked at her, wanting to say so much. They held up their bottles to Jamie and Kelly, wished them a happy anniversary, and made their way back over to Iconica.

*

"I hope you've enjoyed the day," Darcie questioned, leading her to the boat.

"More than you'll ever know," she added despondently.

"Is everything okay?"

"Yes, fine. Just... yes, it's fine."

"No, it isn't." Darcie stopped and grabbed Lizzie's hand. "Honestly..."

"Don't do that. Please don't do that to me. Just be open with me. Tell me."

"It's just... reality setting in once again."

"Right... Yeah, I guess it is," Darcie replied with equal sadness.

"Seriously though, thank you. Thank you for the best day ever." Lizzie smiled softly.

"No, thank you, Lizzie. It's been... life changing."

"Are you working this evening?"

"Yes."

"Will you come get me when you're done? I don't care what time it is."

"You're not coming down?" Darcie asked sadly.

"I'm a mess, and I can't deal with my family telling me so. Initially, I was going to say I finished early and enjoyed beer and sun in their absence, hence my drunkenness, but..." She stopped. Lizzie grabbed Darcie's hands, entwining their fingers and resting them on her waist. "How can I possibly be near them, and allow them to ruin this day that you've created for me? This perfect day, Darce," she said, smiling softly. "No, I'd rather deal with the wrath tomorrow." Lizzie put her finger to Darcie's lips to stop her from speaking. "Shhh, 'pretty blue.' Don't say a thing. You've created perfection, and I need to *end* on perfection. Thank you again." She kissed her softly. "Come get me when you're done. I don't care what time it is or if you must break my door down. Promise me?"

"Well, I can't promise I'll break your door down, but I can promise I'll come get you. I'll always come get you, Lizzie."

"Wonderful. Thank you," she said, kissing Darcie, and pulling tightly on her hands which still wrapped behind her back.

Chapter Twenty-Six

Lizzie obliviously looked out to the blackened sea, the tiny ripples illuminated by the moonlight. In the distance, the hotels ashore were lively. Flicking her biro against her forehead, she distantly pondered what else to put in the letter to Miss Lovelie, hearing a faint knock at the door. She put her pen down and cracked open the door.

"Hey," Darcie said seeing her.

"Hi." She smiled softly. "Are you okay?"

"I guess. Are you?"

"Yes, you want to come in? I have wine, if you'd like some?"

"Um, no thanks to the wine. Of course, to the coming in." Darcie smiled widely.

"You okay?"

"Yeah. Tough night. I've had a chance to sober up, so I don't really want to have a double hangover at five am tomorrow." She looked at the balcony. "You busy?"

"Not too busy for you," she said shyly. "I was just writing to Miss Lovelie," she answered. "So, why a tough night?"

"No reason. You want me to leave you to your letter?"

"No," she answered quickly. "Did my family say something?"

"Why do you ask that?"

"I feel like you're being slightly standoffish with me, and I can only presume it has something to do with them."

"No, I can't blame them for this."

"So, what happened? Did I do something?"

"No, god no," Darcie rushed into Lizzie's arms. "You didn't, I promise."

"Well...it doesn't matter." She sighed, wondering what had changed.

"Your family was talking so naturally about leaving. I guess after that, and today, it just hit home."

"Yes, it's suddenly becoming a reality." She looked down to her partially packed suitcase in the corner, noticing the sadness in Darcie's eyes when she saw it. "Do you regret it?"

"What? There's so much I regret, Lizzie."

"Such as?"

"Let's not do this. Not now. Not after such an incredible day."

"Was it really?"

Darcie looked into her eyes seriously, trying to read their blankness. "It *was* for me," she answered sadly.

"Me too. That's why I wanted it to end just as well."

"Oh god, you're not going to try and sleep with me, are you? I don't think I can abstain."

"I'm not." She laughed. "All bets are off. I won't torment you, or try to sleep with you. But I do want to in one sense of the word," she said seriously.

"What do you mean?"

"Please, will you stay with me this evening? One last time? I don't think I'll get the opportunity of escaping again."

"So, we may not see each other again before you go?"

"Potentially, yes. I'll probably have to be there all day and night. I've been given enough crap. But it'll be back to secrecy, hidden glances and touches, and maybe...

hopefully, an hour in the water, or in our spot on the top deck at the end of the day. Beyond that, I've made a promise to take you on a date if you come to London." She smiled.

"*When* I come to London," Darcie confirmed.

"So, will you stay with me tonight, then?" she asked softly.

"No," Darcie advised, quickly noticing the hurt in Lizzie's eyes. She grabbed her hands and smiled softly. "I have to be up at 5:30 because of today, so can you come stay with me? Plus, if today's the last... time, I'd much prefer you stay at mine. I know I don't have all of this..." She pointed to the room, "but it's less space. We can be—"

"Let's go to yours, it's..." Lizzie shyly wrapped her hair around her finger, looking sheepish. "Cozier," she added.

"My thoughts exactly." Darcie kissed her forehead.

"You go ahead. I'm guessing you'll wanna get ready, or shower, having been at work. Plus, I just need to clear up, and shower quickly myself. I smell horrendously of citronella from being outside."

"Oh, at least somebody got a bite of you." Darcie smiled, looking slightly awkward.

"I'm assuming that was meant slightly more coquettish than cannibalistic?" Lizzie raised a brow.

Darcie rolled her eyes. "Hurry, Lizzie. I'll see you soon."

Lizzie couldn't help but laugh at her. "I'll be a few moments, and then I'll be with you."

"Okay then. I shall see you ma lady, in just a few moments." Darcie laughed at her attempt of a posh British accent.

"Leave now, or you'll regret it. Are you forgetting the minuscule area we'll be sharing this evening?"

"Okay, okay. I give in," Darcie kissed her lips quickly. "Hurry up, it's late, and I need cuddles." Lizzie couldn't help but grin at the comment she knew Darcie would've normally found difficult to say.

*

Lizzie had been out of the shower for a few minutes. She sat cross legged facing her case in a vest and her new Senor Frogs shorts. She'd run a million times through her head if there was anything they could do. *Was it wise to spend the night with her? Would something happen? And why did Darcie keep talking about going to London? She didn't like her law career, so she wouldn't come for that, and she couldn't come without anything. They were just delaying the inevitable.* She was shaken from her thoughts upon hearing the message on her phone. Finally getting up, Lizzie moved and checked the message from Darcie, simply asking if she'd forgotten about her. She grabbed her key card and left her phone as she made her way down to Darcie's room.

*

"Hey, you." Darcie opened the door.

Lizzie eyed Darcie, wondering if there was anything she wouldn't find her attractive in. "Cute PJ's."

"I'm wearing an undershirt and briefs," Darcie responded confused.

"Well, you're a delight."

Darcie laughed at her. "Yeah, that was pretty short. I'm sorry." Darcie pulled her in. "You smell nice."

"Thank you. Did you go to Stanford?"

"I did." She smiled. "Given I have to get up in a couple hours, are we gonna go to bed or stand here talking all night?"

"Oh, you really are full of joy this evening."

"I know. Rubbish night, as I said. I'll be fine when I get to sleep in your arms." She turned towards the bed. "Look at that, you've turned me into a dork."

"Maybe I like dorks," she responded confidently, removing the silk robe and squeezing into the cabin bed.

"I know, you told me. That's why I'm happy to go with it." She considered Lizzie's clothes. "Some of your new purchases, I see?"

"Yes, reminds me of good times."

"Me too," Darcie said, instantly putting her arms around Lizzie as she slipped into the bed next to her. "You really do smell awesome."

"Behave."

"What do you mean? I'm not misbehaving. Just telling ya," she answered. "I'm gonna miss this."

"Me too. You don't seem yourself. You seem all out of sorts."

"I don't know what's happened to me. I'm going home next month."

"*What*? For good?"

"No, I spoke to my mom and cap earlier and... I'm gonna go visit is all. He asked if I wanted to go after you left, but the next..." She stopped, pushing the lump back in her throat. "The next charter is a large group. I don't want to leave the crew, especially as I've been so crappy on this one."

"I'm sorry, that's my fault," Lizzie said sadly.

"It's not your fault I broke a cup and trashed my hand, and now I can't work fully."

"Maybe."

"I don't think you know what you've done to me," Darcie whispered.

"Oh you mean making you fall for my incredible charm?" Lizzie tried to lighten the situation. She didn't want her perfect day to end in a sea of sadness. She put her hand under Darcie's vest, and felt the softness of her skin. Lizzie watched Darcie's breathing come to a halt as she closed her eyes, embracing the touch. It was hard to miss the sadness fill her face. Lizzie closed the very small gap between them and kissed Darcie, slipping her hand around her neck, her leg between her thighs, and pulled her closer. She sustained the kiss as their bodies conjoined.

They stayed that way for a while, deep rooted in each other's bodies and embroiled in the kiss. Darcie didn't want the day, the kiss, the night, or the charter to end. No matter how hard she tried, she couldn't stop the complexity of emotions at Lizzie's impending departure.

Chapter Twenty-Seven

Lizzie woke to the pull of her body brought closer to Darcie's warmth. "Don't leave me," Darcie whispered into Lizzie's ear. She didn't want to make her feel uncomfortable, or embarrassed, so she stayed still for a moment longer. Darcie's body tightly spooned her own and her hands were high up her stomach. She wriggled backwards, closer into Darcie's body. "Good morning, beautiful."

"That's an incredible way to wake up. Good morning yourself, beautiful girl. Did you sleep okay?" Lizzie asked, still wrapped in Darcie's arms with her back against her.

"How could I not?" She wrapped her outer leg around Lizzie's. "I've decided if I stay like this, and keep my eyes closed, then it doesn't need to end."

"Good theory. I'm stealing it." Lizzie giggled.

"Do you think we could be like this forever?" Darcie asked seriously.

"Do you think we have enough money to run away and stay like this forever? You'd have to give up all of those luxuries." Lizzie laughed.

"My luxuries? Says the woman with a house on her wrist. We may need to live in a shack."

"It's doable, if I can stay like this." Lizzie cuddled further into her body. "You realize if you pull me any closer, I'm going to be on top of you?" She giggled.

"You say that like it's a bad thing," Darcie giggled, tickling her stomach and hearing her squeal. Lizzie desperately squirmed as Darcie continued teasing her, tightly holding onto her body. She was barely able to move. Darcie could happily listen to Lizzie's cries of laughter forever. Her squirms became more erratic as she tried hysterically to move from the persistent tickles. As the women's twists and turns increased, Darcie changed her angle, and both women froze, silenced by Darcie's hand fully cupping Lizzie's breast. Darcie heard her gasp, and felt Lizzie's body react to the unintended touch, her nipple rising beneath her hand. She tried desperately to ignore the stir inside her. She couldn't sleep with her. She was desperate to, but she'd made a promise not to. She didn't want to make things worse. Lizzie seemed to purposely push her breast further into Darcie's hand. She increased the pressure with her touch, feeling Lizzie accept the attention. Before anything else could happen, they were stilled by the loud rings of an alarm sounding.

"You *cannot* be doing this to me," Lizzie groaned.

"I'm afraid so," Darcie whispered. "I'm sorry. My god, I'm sorry. I don't even have any extra time."

"Do not do that. Do *not!*" Lizzie ordered. "I simply cannot... my word, I'm so incredibly turned on. I can't just stop and forget it." She turned in Darcie's arms, noticing the removal of her hand from her breast. "We simply cannot just leave it there. I don't care what you promised yourself."

Darcie couldn't help but slightly smile. "Stop trying to make me misbehave. I have to go to work."

"But do you? Like, really, *really,* do you?" Lizzie moved forward a little, taking Darcie's hand, and placing it on her bottom. She watched Darcie's eyes close and her breathing quicken. She wanted it as much as Lizzie. She could tell by her eyes.

"We can't. I need to…" Darcie felt Lizzie's lips press firmly against her own, and her hand slip underneath Darcie's vest. She couldn't help but groan as she embraced the kiss, and revelled in the feel of Lizzie's rear.

"Not again!" Lizzie cried as the alarm sounded once more.

"Babe, you have no idea how much I want to do this, even though I really did want to try and refrain, but cap will seriously kick my butt if I'm late for work. I'm quickly on my way to getting my ass fired," she pleaded.

"Charming, so you get to second base and then ditch me?" she asked, raising her brow.

"Don't be like that."

"I'm kidding. I know you have to go, and I certainly don't want you getting into trouble."

"Shit, this is literally the dumbest thing I've ever done," she said, untangling her body from Lizzie's and lifting the cover. Darcie pulled her shorts back down where they'd risen in all the tomfoolery, noticing Lizzie watch her intently. "Good view…" Darcie responded.

"Well, it *was*."

"Actually, I meant for me," Darcie said, nodding toward Lizzie's raised top, revealing part of her breast."

"Oh," Lizzie shyly pulled her vest down.

"Spoil sport," Darcie said, leaning down and kissing her. "Fancy coming and washing my back?" Darcie laughed.

"You are very mischievous. And no, you had your chance, I'm afraid. You've lost the opportunity to get beyond second base now," Lizzie answered, getting out of the bed.

"Well that's not fair game. I guess it just means I'll have to get to London quicker." Darcie put her hand to Lizzie's cheek and pulled her in for a tender kiss.

"Can't wait," Lizzie embraced her affections.

Chapter Twenty-Eight

Lizzie lay on the bed taking in her surroundings. She could hear the bustle of Miami outside of her window, and distantly reflected on the past two weeks. Nearly three decades of these holidays, or any holiday with her family in fact, and the events of this one were incomparable to any she'd ever experienced. Unfortunately, the affairs of the heart had come to an unwelcome end. She went to her balcony one last time, leaning over and catching sight of Darcie and Deek cleaning up. She felt a sadness overcome her once more.

Lizzie felt a vibration in her back pocket, pulled her phone out, and read the message from Vivian telling her to hurry up. Her family was keen to leave. She pushed back the sickness and sadness currently flooding through her body, and zipped up her cases. She grabbed the bottle of perfume from the clear plastic bag required for airport security and lay it next to the envelope. Lizzie grabbed a pen and wrote on the envelope 'Iconica Team.' She grabbed the Senor Frogs carrier bag, and carefully laid out the white polo shirt she'd bought days earlier. She sprayed her perfume all over the top before folding it up and placing it back into the bag. Lizzie moved her luggage outside the door and rushed down to Darcie's room one last time, placing the bag on her door knob. She touched the door, thinking back to the memories of them in Darcie's room.

She made her way back up to her family, trying with all her might to build the strength to get through the next 15 hours.

"Where have you been? I told you all to be here at 0900," her father stammered. Lizzie ignored the snide remarks, and pulled her gladiator sandals onto her feet. She looked up and saw Deek and Darcie watching her intently. Lizzie hated seeing Darcie sad. She wanted to do something, but was completely unable to for obvious reasons. They hadn't seen each other since the morning after they spent the night together a few days ago. They'd managed to sneak glances across the room, minimal discreet embraces, but unfortunately, hadn't had any alone time. Lizzie smiled at the beautiful woman in her formals for one last time, remembering the impact she'd had on Lizzie, just two weeks earlier.

"You okay, girl?" Deek whispered to Darcie, who'd turned away from Lizzie to prevent her from seeing how sad she was.

"Yeah," she whispered back. She'd not seen Lizzie look unattractive since day one, but today her short, dark, denim shorts, gladiator sandals, and white, silk symmetrical top made her look like a goddess. Her golden tan and matching golden angel waves left Darcie feeling like she should chase after her, and insist they run away together.

The captain requested them for departure, and they acknowledged their instruction, making their way to where the Barrington family was getting ready to depart.

*

Jose Luis led his team to the bow of the superyacht, immediately standing tall as he confidently and firmly shook Lord Barrington's hand. He discreetly placed an envelope in his pocket and stepped forward, curtly kissing Lady Barrington on both cheeks.

Lizzie felt bile rise in her throat as they said their goodbyes to the staff, and watched Annabella embrace Darcie. The rigidness on Darcie's frame was obvious to Lizzie, and she ensured that her eyes were permanently fixed on her. Lizzie couldn't help but feel touched that Darcie made such a gesture.

She got to Deek who held onto her tightly. Her family and the deck hands departed the boat with their luggage as Lizzie moved from Deek to Darcie. Deek and Jose Luis maneuvered their positioning so that none of Lizzie's family could see them.

"Thank you for an incredible holiday," Lizzie muttered, squeezing her hand tenderly.

"Thank you for an incredible charter," Darcie replied. "Call me when you get home?"

"Of course. I'll miss you."

"For real?"

"Yes, of course. Gosh, more than I can even begin to converse."

"Me too," she said sadly. "*Me too.*"

"I should go." Lizzie pulled her in for a tight hug, feeling the strength in Darcie's grasp. She felt a soft kiss on her temple, refusing to allow Darcie to see her sadness.

Lizzie turned to Jose Luis and embraced his big arms around her. He said something in Spanish, which she didn't understand, but nodded knowingly when she pulled away. "Be happy, doctor," he offered kindly.

"Thank you, all of you. You've…" She tried to hold in her emotion. "You've changed my world," she whispered sadly, and just like that, she was gone. Iconica, and the team, were officially out of her life.

*

Lizzie was thankful for the night flight, certain her family would soon be eye-masked up, and lying down, ready for their journey home. She took the seat furthest away, and cozied into it, watching the men busy themselves around the runway in the intense heat.

She reminisced every moment that she and Darcie had shared. Gone was the initial concern of the situation with Bella. Something had happened—clicked—between them. She and Darcie connected on a different level, in a way that was new to Lizzie, a way that she'd never known before. Which was why, of course, it made it even more heart-breaking. The sounds of the engines roared, and the aircraft slowly started reversing.

*

Darcie stood at the bow of the boat watching the bus to the airport drive off. She held on tightly to the bar, feeling a pressure in her hands. She felt a hand at the small of her back and turned to face Jose Luis. He nodded warmly to her, putting his arm around her shoulder. They stayed there silently for a brief time as they watched the bus disappear.

She realized that in the real world, people don't come running back to declare their undying love and run off into the sunset together. No, in the real world, a wonderful time is had. A fantastic time. And then it ends, just like that. *Like it was all a dream.*

Pushing the sadness aside, she pulled herself together, and made her way back to her room to change out of her formals. She could see a plastic bag hanging from her door, and noticed the large, green frog on it. Quickening her pace, she couldn't stop smiling. She reached her room, grabbed the bag, shut her door, and moved onto the bed. Closing her eyes, Darcie could already smell Lizzie in the air. She felt a lone tear fall from her face as she opened the bag, revealing a rush of perfume. Darcie pulled out the polo shirt with the small Senor Frog detail on the chest and held it up to her nose, taking in Lizzie's scent. She lay down, resting her face on the shirt, and lost herself in all their wonderful memories. She pulled out two envelopes, one with her name on it, and the thicker one for the captain and the team. She was annoyed that Lizzie had done that. She could already tell it was cash. She opened the envelope and took out the small note.

I wasn't sure if or how much my father would leave, but given that this charter and this team were absolute perfection, I couldn't leave without showing some gratitude. -Elizabeth. xx

It was formal and clearly not what Darcie was expecting. She'd done it for the staff. It had nothing to do with her; that was clear. She opened the other envelope and pulled out the lone sheet of paper, smiling as more of Lizzie's perfume filled the room. *She must have used a whole bottle,* she thought.

I didn't want to write you war and peace, but equally, you're now aware of my love for writing and therefore, it felt incumbent of me to proffer a final note. Darcie, Darcie, Darcie, where to start? You are without a shadow of a doubt, the most incredibly, beautiful woman I've ever met. Truly, if I was asked to name the world's most beautiful woman, you would forever be at the top of my list. The most wondrous part of that, though, is beyond your visible beauty. You are the most incredible woman I've ever met. Your courage, humor, wit (sarcasm), and strength is enriching. I only hope I can one day have some of those awe-inspiring qualities. You've made the greatest impression on my life, and you've given me a holiday of a lifetime. I forever hope you'll stay in touch, and will await the day you come to London and allow me to take you on my very own date. Stay happy, beautiful Darcie, and refrain from hiding those beautiful eyes. Actually, scratch that. If there are any females on your charter, firmly hide those 'pretty blues.'

Fond affections and growing emotions will allow me to forever delight in all you gave me. Warm wishes, -Lizzie xxx

Darcie turned her face into the soft material of the shirt she bought for her and closed her eyes. She relived only a few days earlier when Lizzie was in her bed and the perfume filled the small space. She wished she'd said so much to Lizzie before she left. She wished she could've made her see that she was so incredibly strong, that she could fight her parents and not allow them to try and control her the way they did. She reread the final line of the letter and felt an emptiness inside her. "*Fond affections and growing emotions.*" She couldn't dwell on it now. She'd been rubbish on this charter, which she'd never done before, but she needed to get back up to the team. They only had a day and a half before the next guests arrived. Darcie gave the envelope to the captain, apologizing for the delay, and walked off to start her cleaning duties.

Chapter Twenty-Nine

Lizzie didn't sleep at all on the flight; she hadn't even laid her seat down. It seemed the entire 10 hours were spent mesmerized by the light on the wing. It was the only thing that allowed her to daydream about Darcie and what they'd had. Unfortunately, she was going to pay for it later that night when she had to go back to work.

*

Lizzie retrieved her luggage, and left her family as she made her way out through departures. It'd been raining as she landed. A*n accurate representation of her feelings right now,* she thought.

"Lady Barrington," the driver called pleasantly. "How was your break?"

"Amazing. Thank you."

"Home?"

"Please," she stated quietly and stepped into the car, allowing him to close the door behind her. She switched her phone back from airplane mode and waited for the reception to appear.

Hi, as requested, I've landed. I hope you are well, and aren't working too hard :) x

Lizzie sent the message hoping that it sounded relatively light-hearted. *A complete disparity to her actual feelings.*

Hey... I've been thinking about you. How was your flight? Can you speak? If not, don't worry. Xxx

Lizzie smiled at the immediate response.

Yes. The flight was... bearable. I can, however, could you possibly wait 25 minutes? I'll be home then. I don't want to speak in front of the driver. If not, I'll call you now? x

Yes, that's fine, the charters don't arrive for a couple of hours so I have some time to spare. I'll continue writing a letter for you. xxx

You're writing to me? That's lovely. When will you send it? As soon as I get home, I'll call you. I'm very much looking forward to hearing your voice. xxx

Me too. OK, I'm gonna leave you while I just sort a few things and I'll be back in 10. Ya fancy FaceTiming? Or not really?

I'd love too. Speak to you shortly. Xxx

*

Lizzie got into her apartment a short while later and dumped her bag in her room. She unbuckled her sandals and lay on her bed, dialing Darcie's number immediately. "Hey."

"Hi, are you okay to talk now?"

"Yup, I've been waiting on you. You didn't wanna FaceTime, huh?"

"Oh bugger, I forgot," she confirmed. "Shall we switch now?"

"You're too cute. Yeah sure, let's do it... I miss your face already."

Lizzie hit the button, and they switched over to FaceTime.

"Hey, that's better. You look cute. Are you in bed?"

"Partially, yes. I'm lying on it. I need a shower first, and then I'll sleep until work this evening."

"You're gonna shower, huh? You wanna take me with you?" Darcie raised her eyebrows.

"I'm pretty sure that iPhones aren't waterproof."

"Hmmm, note to self... buy you a waterproof one."

"Be quiet. So, how's it been?"

"Quiet, rubbish, sad... Oh, thanks for my top by the way. I love it."

"You do?"

"Yes, I really do. I wore it in bed. I love being able to smell you so close to me. Shame it's not for real, but there were a couple times I woke up and thought you were here with me."

"You did?" Lizzie whispered, turning onto her side, and resting the phone against a pillow.

"Uh huh. You look like you're lying right next to me."

"I so wish I was, Darce," Lizzie said sadly. "I'd give anything to have you here next to me."

"I know, me too. I've been feeling a massive emptiness ever since you left. I just want you back here."

"Wish I could be."

"So, do it then."

"If only I could."

"You can. You can do anything you want. I gave up everything when I wanted to change things. You can do anything if you really want to."

"Okay, so then what?"

"What do you mean?"

"Well… so, I tell my family; they disown me. *Whatever*. Then what? What are you asking of me?"

Darcie watched her closely. "Forget it, I'm just being dumb. I don't know what I thought. I guess I just never met anyone that's treated the way you are with your family. It's fine. Anyhow, what time you working tonight?"

Lizzie noticed the change in her voice, and desperately wanted her to explain what would happen after that. *She just wanted to know how Darcie felt, if it was the same as her*. If Darcie was missing her because there were no guests on Iconica, or if there was more to it. If she wanted to take *whatever* this was out of the holiday romance/fling situation. "Around seven pm. I'll get some sleep and then go in."

"You need to go?"

"No, definitely not. Unless you do?" Lizzie questioned. "I'm very tired, but would prefer to stay up and talk to you. As long as you're free."

Darcie hated that she was being like this. *Especially to Lizzie*. "I'll be free until the minute I have to leave." She smiled. "I just may need to get changed while we're talking."

"Really? Is this because you want to pay me back?"

"For what exactly?" Darcie smiled knowingly.

"The teasing."

"I have no idea what you mean," she said with a sly, lopsided grin that made Lizzie want to screenshot her phone and keep the picture forever.

"Tell me about this letter."

"No, you have to be patient. My mom always said that patience is a virtue."

"Do you know what that means?" Lizzie shook her head dramatically into her phone.

"Are you actually asking me that? You know I'm not some dumb 'yachtie' right?"

"Ouch, that's a bit of a sweeping statement. Yes, I know you're intelligent. I just wondered if you knew?"

"Sure, I do. I'm telling you that being patient makes things more incredible."

"Like what exactly? Your letter, or something else?"

"Are you always this inquisitive?"

"Yes, it makes for more fun." Lizzie giggled.

"*Really*? Is that so?"

"No, I'm joking. I'm normally incredibly serious. In fact, I think the only time I've ever been less than serious was during the date you took me on."

"Maybe it's a sign you should let go more often."

"Maybe it is. I'll have to have a little look at that swipe right thing."

"*Tinder*? You've just crushed my heart. Less than 24 hours of leaving me, and you're ditching me for some skank hoe on Tinder?"

"Wow, 'skank hoe?' And ditching you? I didn't realize you were mine to ditch."

"You didn't ask if I wanted to be yours to ditch."

"Okay, so hypothetically speaking… if I'd asked you to be 'mine to ditch,' would you have accepted said request?"

"No," she answered simply, noticing a flicker of hurt cross Lizzie's face. "Not if you'd put it like that. Why would I want someone to have me, just to ditch me? However, if you'd requested in such a manner that *wasn't* like you were gonna ditch my ass as soon as I said yes..." She laughed.

"Okay, *Little Miss Sarcasm*. Take two. Hypothetically speaking, if I said, 'would you be mine' when I left, what would your answer have been?"

"Yes, of course," she responded simply. "Um, hypothetically speaking."

"Well, hypothetically speaking, I really wish I'd known that. I'm just saying."

"Well, that's a very American statement."

"Really? I wasn't aware of that."

"Well, probably not. I just didn't expect to hear it from you. I like it, it's cute."

"You think I'm cute?"

"You know I think you're cute," Darcie muttered. "Super cute. And sexy as hell. I'm bummed you left without letting me show you just how sexy I find you."

"Are you being rude there 'pretty blue?'"

"I don't know what you mean. I'm just saying that if you let me show you, then maybe we wouldn't be having a hypothetical conversation is all."

"Are you saying that if I'd had sex with you, then I wouldn't have wanted to leave without making you my girlfriend?"

"Erm, no. You make me sound super arrogant. And I—"

"Relax. I don't think you're arrogant. In fact, I think it's actually very sweet. I just wish you would stop with the comments about sex. Do you know how hard it is..." Lizzie stopped.

"Yes?" Darcie smirked.

"Be quiet."

"I can't. Do I wanna know how hard *what* is? That you didn't sleep with me? Tell me."

"Come on, behave," she said as they both heard the crackle of Darcie's walkie talkie. "You need to go, huh?"

"I do. And you need to sleep. Wish I could be snoozing with you."

"Are you sleepy?"

"No, goofball." Darcie rolled her eyes. "You wanna catch up again tomorrow, or are you busy?"

"Nope. What time works for you?" Lizzie smiled sincerely.

"I don't know, what time do you get off?"

"You really need to stop with the euphemisms and sexual talk."

"What do you mean?" Darcie asked sheepishly.

"*Really*? Stop forgetting I lived in the states too. Anyway, you go babe. I need to sleep. I'll be home around nine or ten in the morning. What time will your break be?"

"I don't know, it depends on what demands they have. And the weather could be a problem, so text me when you return and I'll be able to tell you when I can talk. Is that okay?"

"Of course it is. As long as I can speak with you."

"You can speak to me anytime, cutie."

"Thanks, I miss you."

"You too, gorgeous. Dream sweet, sexy girl."

"Have fun, Darce."

Darcie lifted her fingers to the screen and stroked it gently. She blew Lizzie a kiss, and just like that, the first day without Darcie beside her was on its way.

Chapter Thirty

Lizzie woke up at five pm, her head throbbing. She was far more tired than before she went to bed. She adjusted her eyes, and the realization set in that it was all over; Darcie was a mere memory. Not allowing herself to get upset, she got up to shower, and turned on her work phone, awaiting the notifications to come flooding in. Her tummy told her she needed to eat, but the prospect of food made her feel sick. She'd make coffee and eat at work.

Lizzie put her scrubs on and put her coffee machine to work. She picked up her bag and quickly checked her phone, tapping her fingertips on the side impatiently. She opened the message sent by Darcie while she was sleeping, ignoring the dancing in her tummy. Lizzie laughed loudly, opening the message to see a selfie of Darcie in her obligatory smart shorts and polo shirt with the words, *"In case you're missing me. xxx,"* written underneath it.

"You're insane, pretty blue," Lizzie said to the emptiness of the room. She opened the phone's camera and angled it so the selfie incorporated a full-length picture of her in her scrubs. She sent the picture to Darcie and attached a text.

In case you were wondering what I look like in my scrubs ;) xxx

She grabbed her coffee and left the apartment, allowing her smile to linger.

Chapter Thirty-One

Lizzie walked in from a 15 hour shift and wondered at what point everything would go back to normal. The vacation and memories were nothing but ad hoc thoughts to cross her mind. Her feet burned, her arms ached, and her head pounded. She checked her phone again, a sadness overflowing from the lack of contact from Darcie. The contact had become less and less over the past couple of weeks, and she still couldn't help but regularly check for their intermittent messages. She pressed the crushed ice button on her fridge, and topped it with water, picking up the post and checking through it. Lizzie felt her heart leap as she recognized the personalized handwriting and Bahamas post mark.

She sat cross legged on her bed, stroking her thumb over the envelope, thinking of how her thumb pressed where Darcie's would've been. She slowly tore the paper away, already smelling the very distant scent of Darcie. Lizzie allowed tears to drop as the pain of Darcie's absence overcame her. She pulled out several pieces of paper, noticing the pink writing. She couldn't help but chuckle at the abnormality of the pen color. Lizzie lay down, and opened the sheets of paper, feeling irrevocably touched at the beautiful gesture. She switched on her playlist, sliding down the bed, and began reading the letter.

Pre-Date…

My Darling Elizabeth,
(Oooh I love that! how very British!); sorry, I'm being a dork, I'll behave.
So, I've written this in two parts. Part one is now. (Not that you know what 'now' is), but part one is tonight. The night before our first (but hopefully not last) date. I hate to ruin this moment of 'romance,' but by god, I'm nervous as hell. The only thing that's kept me going is that I've just spent time with you and god, you amaze me. And turn me on. Sorry, that's not very romantic. So, I just wanted to tell you... you truly are the most incredible woman I've ever met, and I am literally dying inside at what you are going to think about tomorrow and my choice, but as you read this, who knows where we'll be or what will have happened. What I do know is that it was my sole intention to give you a little bit of fun and what I wish to be the best day of your life. I just hope you see it for what it is. As I lay here now, writing part A of my letter, I can't help but sit here breezily, allowing my thoughts to wander at the prospect of a second, third, fourth, and fifth date. I hope as you read this, you're wishing we'd had that. But anyway, let's move on... So, tonight, you looked freaking awesome and I really enjoyed us being all secretive. I can't wait until tomorrow. And on that note, I'm gonna hit the hay, as I want a fresh face for tomorrow.

Lizzie smiled at "Part 1" of Darcie's letter, and turned it over to read the next sequence of words.

So... that worked... not!! It's nearly two am, and I've been through my entire closet trying to find the right thing to wear for tomorrow. And I know whatever you show up in you'll look amazing, and everything I try on, I'll look lame. I've decided on my outfit. I've gone for it. Because otherwise, not only am I gonna look lame, but I'm gonna look crappy from a lack of sleep.

3.17am.

Ok, so now I can't sleep because not only am I panicking about what to wear, now I'm freaking about if you'll like it. I know you like simple, so why am I worrying? I wonder if you'll ever tell me it's shit? Hmmm, so this has become less 'love letter' and more 'journal'... Erm, not that I am writing a love letter, more of a note. Holy shit, I need to stop thinking and writing. The thoughts are coming thick and fast, and I don't wanna miss them, but now I'm speaking rubbish. And I can't rewrite it because then I'll have to redo all the nice stuff from earlier. Holy shit, girl, you need to get with the times. I know it's romantic and stuff, writing a letter, but if this were a text or email, I'd be able to delete all this now. Jesus I've just written you half a page of a love letter (yes, I'm going with it!) to say that I spoke shit. I bet you're reading it now and thinking that's a whole heap of my life I'll never get back!! Unless you're not reading it. You could have given me a phoney address. Oh yes, it was far too perfect to be real. Hmmm, I wonder where it'll go? Is anyone reading this? God, if you are reading it, you must think, PSYCHO ALERT! PSYCHO ALERT!

Ok, note to self, writing love letters makes me a little crazy. Well, now that I have so much more to freak out about, I'm gonna try and get back to sleep. This is obviously never gonna happen, because now I'm worrying that you won't like my outfit choice, or my date choice, or if you'll get this, if you live where you said, and everything I already wrote. On that note, at 3.31am, somewhere outside of the Bahamas, Darcie is signing off.

6.54am Yayyyyy, I managed to sleep. For like an hour. By the time you read this, we will have had our date, so I'll apologize now for thinking it was wise to take you out drinking! I may well have just lost any potential of providing you with the date of your life. So, I'm back to writing to tell you I'm as giddy as a giddy kiddy can be. Yeah yeah, I'm not a kid. But I'm super excited, and I can't wait. I just hope you like it. Right, I have to get up and do some work for LORD AND LADY BARRINGTON. If I could eyeroll now, you know I would!! But I don't care today, because I know what's to come. I'll write you more later, xxx

Lizzie re-read the note, giggling once again at the nonsensical and warped mind of Darcie in the middle of the night. Taking the next sheet, she breathed in deeply and began to read.

Post-date....
I genuinely do not know where to begin. You're amazing, my god, you're amazing. You have literally given me the best day ever, and I can't help but feel disappointed and upset as I consider the implications of you not being with me every day from here on out, after the day you gave me today. The normality of meeting gay friends, partying, and daytime drinking together. The laughter and shrills from you going down the water rides. The delight on your face as you slid through the shark filled tanks, your legs wrapped around my waist. Gooooodddd, your legs wrapped around my waist. How perfect that felt. Everything was perfect. Everything was just as I'd imagined it would be. I just hope you felt the same way. You've somehow changed

everything, Elizabeth Barrington. And I don't quite know how to feel about that.

Lizzie allowed tears to drop as she held the letter close to her heart. It was the best day of her life too. *Every part of it.* It was the perfect date, with the perfect girl. Darcie was everything to her. *She was…* Lizzie shook the thoughts aside. *She couldn't do that, how could she?* Lizzie sat up, reading the letter again and again, each time noticing a little extra detail to it. She finally managed to get to a place where the letter brought more happiness than tears. She closed her eyes, and smiled at the recollections of the perfect day that Darcie created for her, how she could relive it all by her description. Lizzie picked up her phone and opened her messages.

Hi, sorry for the late contact, I hope you're well. I've missed not speaking with you. I wanted to say I've just returned home to a beautiful letter after an incredibly long shift. You've made my day. Thank you again, Darcie. Xxx

Lizzie hated the way it'd become so formal between them. She didn't know how and when that had happened, but she still missed her so much. All she wanted to do was be with her like they'd been a couple of weeks prior at the waterpark. She wanted the normality of everything, exactly like she'd described. Lizzie was pulled from her thoughts as the notification of an incoming message came through.

Hey you, I've been waiting for you to get it. I was debating flying over to hand deliver a new one :) I hope work is okay. Sorry it's been long and crappy. If I was there, I would give you a big, long massage, and you could tell me all about your day. I'd stroke your hair and snuggle up until you fell asleep in my arms. Xxx

Lizzie read the message and smiled. It was beautiful. Despite them having not spoken properly, a single message picked her up entirely. She wanted to have exactly what Darcie described, but she wasn't sure how that'd ever be possible.

How do you always make it ok? That sounds so nice, I wish I could have that right now. xxx

Lizzie heard the phone ring immediately and saw Darcie's name appear. "Hi," she answered awkwardly.
"Hey, what's going on? You okay?"
"Yes, why?"
"Because you don't seem it. What's happened? Has something happened with your family?"
"No, seriously, I'm absolutely fine. Well, apart from being tired from a few too many long days. But tomorrow is my last shift for a while, so that'll sort that. How are you, Darcie?"
"Ya know," she responded quietly.
"No, I don't. Tell me."
"Umm, just... well... ya know."
"No, I just told you, I don't. Tell me. Talk to me."
"You didn't seem to want to."
"It wasn't that I didn't want to. I just... I don't know. I didn't want to keep hurting you. We seem to be getting closer, as opposed to..."
"And you don't think there's a reason for that? Like maybe it's fate or something? We met for a reason, Lizzie. Everything happens for a reason."

S.L. Gape

"I'm sorry. I don't know what to say. I don't dispute that it happened for a reason. You've opened so much up to me, my life, my family…"

"So, why is it not enough?" she asked sadly.

"For what, Darce? For what?"

"For me. For us. Why isn't that enough?"

"It's not as easy as that. I'm sorry, I am. It just…"

"It's fine, Lizzie. I shouldn't have raised it. I don't want to fall out with you. I missed not talking to you. So, what's been going on at work, then?"

"Oh, nothing. It's just been busy and I've worked a lot. As I said, I finish after tomorrow and have some time off. How's work on your end?" Lizzie asked, choosing not to enter the difficulty of the conversation.

"Fine."

"Any hot girls for you to pass the time with?" Lizzie immediately regretted her words. She said it comically, but it wasn't funny, and she knew there was an edge to her question. She awkwardly awaited the silence to fill, listening to Darcie's soft breaths.

Darcie sighed heavily. "Um, I should probably go. I have to be up soon, I just wanted to check that you were okay. Good night, Lizzie." She hung up.

Lizzie immediately felt sick to her stomach. *Why had she said that, and why had Darcie reacted like that? Was there someone else? This would be her second or third charter since her family left; it was entirely possible. But if she didn't want anybody else, everything she'd just said, all those heartfelt words, were like a stab to the chest. Why had she said that?* Lizzie couldn't handle feeling this way. She'd never known a time where she was constantly this sad. Darcie was the closest friend she'd ever had, the nicest person she'd ever met, and she knew Darcie would do anything for her. More importantly, she made her think that the two of them could take on the world. *Just the two of them. Together.* Still in her scrubs, Lizzie turned over and closed her eyes, ignoring the tears slipping through, and the loud grumbles of her tummy.

Chapter Thirty-Two

Lizzie woke to the sound of her alarm, still feeling physically sick. Checking the time—3:45am—she realized the reason for feeling ill might be that she'd not eaten in about 18 hours. She checked her phone, disappointed there was no message from Darcie. *She couldn't blame her.* She'd made less and less contact with her since she'd returned home, and every time they spoke, Darcie always tried to engage in a "them" conversation about their feelings. But of course, Lizzie ignored it, not even entertaining the thought, though she would've loved to think it was at all possible. Truth be known, Lizzie was the one that had pushed Darcie away after probably being the one to pull her in, in the first place.

"You can't think about this now," she said aloud, getting up, and getting ready for work. She was on a seven, seven shift, but opted to go in early, acutely aware that she needed to eat something before she started.

Chapter Thirty-Three

Lizzie's head spun, the pain agonizing as she felt Jack's strength gripping her. "Elizabeth, Elizabeth. Calm down. Stop! STOP!" he yelled, firmly holding her, and eventually calming her down. She looked down at the cut on her white top under her scrubs, the red liquid growing rapidly. "Jesus, what's going on?" He looked around the room at the contents she'd just thrown. She pulled away and picked up the medical trolley. "*Lizzie, stop!*" Jack pulled his colleague and friend up off the floor. "I'll sort it. Let's get this first." He assessed her cut. "I think you'll need a stitch or two. Come on, let's get you cleaned up. Do you want to go grab a quick drink and talk?"

"No, thank you," she whispered, wiping tears from her eyes, and refusing to look at the wound.

"What's going on? You don't ever react like this, Liz. You're probably the only one of us that can hold it together in times like these. Jesus, it's why you're the best in the country. What happened in there? We all did everything we could. We can't win them all; you know that," he said seriously.

Lizzie simply shrugged her shoulders. She didn't know what to say, but he was right. She was the strongest. She oozed professionalism. Well, at least around her team. When she went home, she'd deal with the consequence of keeping it in, the emotional hardships that came from the job. This time was different though. This time she'd walked

out, savaged a cart—medical equipment and medication—
and in the process, wounded herself.

"I'm worried about you. I haven't ever seen you like this
before. You're working too much and you're not the same.
You need to see someone. Go visit a doctor."

"I'm with them all the time," she snapped, inhaling
harshly from the anaesthetic jabbing into her skin.

"You know what I mean. *Your GP*. What's happening?
You know, your father has put us all on watch, following
your holiday. He said you were ill a lot, that we needed to
monitor things and let him know immediately. I'm starting
to think he has a point."

Lizzie watched Jack's eyes carefully, seeing his concern.
He was probably the closest person she had to a friend.
She'd only ever had one drink with him before, but they
tended to hideout together on the rare occasion things didn't
work out right during a shift. The truth was, he was far from
a friend. She didn't have any. She never had, not since she
was a kid when they were forced upon her. She'd never
once had a single real friend, someone she felt comfortable
enough to talk to things about. She pondered if she could
have a little more with Jack. *Would he give more than she
ever gave him*? He did always try. "Please, don't tell my
father about this," she asked sadly. "I'm fine, I guess I… I
don't know, maybe the job's just taking its toll."

"I won't say anything." He squeezed her thigh. "Please
promise me you'll talk to me or someone if something's
going on, though," he asked as he began to suture the
wound on her forearm.

"I will. I have a few days off now. I need them."

"Yes, I agree. Why don't you take off now? You're
working too hard. You're a consultant. You should be

delegating, especially with all the research you've been doing. You want me to give you a lift?"

"What, around the corner?" She smiled sadly.

"It's raining," he said, concerned.

"Jack, don't worry please. It's the first procedure that hasn't worked in a while. Plus, it's the first after my holiday, and I've worked six days solid doing a minimum of 15-hours. I need a break."

"You sure that's all?"

"Yes."

"Okay, I'll take your word for it, for now. But if things don't improve, I mean it," he stated seriously.

"Okay, okay. I get it."

"So, what are you doing with your days off?"

"Oh, you know… sleeping, eating." She rolled her eyes. "Oh, and something very much out of the ordinary tomorrow." She smiled softly.

"Yeah?" he asked interested. "What are you up to?"

"I can't tell you, I'm afraid. Are you still coming on Saturday?"

"Yes, unless anything untoward happens."

"I'll reveal all then. Thanks, Jack. I'm sorry about earlier. Please don't tell my father," she insisted.

He looked at her seriously. "I won't, but I won't commit to that being a permanent promise. You're concerning me," he said seriously. "Get shopping tomorrow. You're going to need something to cover that bandage."

"I know, I will. And thanks again."

"Lizzie?" He grabbed her undamaged arm. "I know we don't really communicate out of work, but please call me if you need anything, even if it's just to thrash out the 'if's, but's, and why's' of tonight."

"Thanks, you're a good guy. Goodnight, Jack."

*

Lizzie left the hospital, allowing the rain to fall on her skin. She strolled the 15 minute journey, desperately hoping the rain would clear her head. She loved the smell of summer rain. *That damp, summer smell.* A hint of grass, and of course, in London, fumes; she found it comforting.

She reached her apartment and eagerly checked the post-box, disappointed at the lack of further communication. Sighing heavily, she defeatedly made her way inside, wondering why she thought there would've been more post. It was only yesterday that the letter had arrived from Darcie, and it was an extensive one at that. Biting the inside of her cheek to prevent the tears from coming, she patiently waited for the lift to reach her floor, so she could get inside her apartment. It'd been the worst week, and as time went on, her heart broke a little more each day. *How could so little time spent with someone make you feel this way? So impacted?*

She opened a large bag of crisps, put them into a bowl, and poured herself a large glass of wine. She needed to get over Darcie in a bid to improve her lifestyle. She was drinking more and eating far less, and when she did eat, it was pure rubbish. Tonight would be no different. It was the least healthy of dinners, but it was already after eight pm, and she refused to start cooking now. She grabbed a handful of crisps, and took a large gulp of wine, allowing it to infuse her body as she made her way to the shower.

*

Nautical Delights

Lizzie moisturized her legs aimlessly after the lengthy shower. She sat with her hair wet in a pair of men's oversized tracksuit bottoms, and another one of her oversized Senor Frogs t-shirts. She took the wine and crisps to bed, switching on the TV, and tried desperately to forget everything clouding her mind. *Clouding her judgement.* She couldn't stop thinking about last night's phone call. She opened her phone to photos, and scrolled to the picture of Iconica and the crew. She'd only gotten one photo of them at Margaritaville, but not a single photo on her phone of the two of them together. Darcie had taken all the photos on their date. *She wondered if she should text her and ask her to email them.* She may tell her to bugger off, given how last night had ended. She was upset with herself for not calling Darcie back or even texting to apologize for her behavior last night. She deserved more than that, and it was unfair of Lizzie to mistreat her so greatly. She picked up her phone before allowing the alcohol to influence her decisions, and opened her messages. The least Darcie deserved was an apology.

Hi, I'm very sorry for the way I behaved yesterday evening. I was tired and had a bad day, not that it was any excuse. I was trying to be humorous, and I apologize for that. I guess it was my way of dealing with things. I'm also sorry I've left it until now to contact you. That was incredibly stubborn and petulant of me, and has played mentally with me all day. I'd like to thank you once again for your letter; it's under my pillow and I'm going to re-read it after I send this. Good night, Darcie, sleep well. xx

She pressed send, hoping that when she woke the following morning, it would maybe brighten Darcie's day the way Darcie's letter brightened hers. Lizzie poured more wine, hearing the text alert. Trying desperately to ignore the thump in her chest, she awkwardly opened her phone, fearing the response.

Hi, I should apologize, too. I've been worried ever since that you'd think my words meant that there was someone else, and my god there isn't!! It's hard with the time difference, our jobs, and the distance. More importantly, it's hard because of the uncertainty between us. I just wish things were different. I wish there wasn't a nothingness, I wish there was a somethingness. I'm glad you liked my letter, I've kinda gotten used to writing them now. I like it. I hope work was okay today. Take care, Lizzie. Xxx

A somethingness? she wondered.

Well I don't think you have anything to apologize for, but why don't we just both accept the other's apologies and go from there? I'm unsure what a 'somethingness' is, though. Is this an American term or just a Darcie term? I think I get you. And yes, I really liked it, a lot. It's helped after a day like today, so I thank you from the bottom of my heart. Why aren't you sleeping? Xxx

Lizzie saw the grey dots appear before Darcie could've even fully read the message, but she was glad. She could use some downtime with her right now.

Cause I'd rather speak to you. So, tell me what happened today. Xxx

Oh, nothing more than the norm. Lost a patient, smashed up a room, which resulted in a wound to my arm. But I'm home safe and sound in bed with wine, crisps (chips), and Senor Frog's clothing. You know there's nothing that makes me happier. :) xxx

Lizzie was reluctant to press send, wondering if it was appropriate. She stopped overthinking and sent the message, waiting to see if she'd respond. The word "delivered" changed to "read," and as she attempted to turn the phone over, it rang throughout the room.

"Hello?" Lizzie asked confused.

"What's happened?"

"Excuse me?"

"You said you hurt yourself. What happened?"

"Oh, right. I'm fine, Darce. How are you? You sound tired."

"Don't do that."

"What?"

"Sweep stuff under the carpet. I wanna know. I'm worried, and I wanna know you're okay."

"I'm fine, sweetie. I had a difficult procedure, which is why I was given it, but it was pretty low risk. It was a certainty, or so I thought, but complications arose. We lost the patient, so I took it out on the medical cart and equipment, and a few of the tools didn't take to it kindly. I only had four stitches—"

"You had *stitches*?!" she blurted.

"I'm okay, Darce. Please, don't worry about me. It's the norm for my job."

"Maybe losing a patient, but I'm pretty sure that having stitches on duty isn't." She sighed.

"Okay, okay, you win. Please don't fall out with me. I don't think I can stand anymore."

"I'm sorry," Darcie whispered.

"It's fine." She sipped her wine. "So, how come you aren't asleep? It's late there."

"I couldn't really sleep. I have the morning off, so it's okay."

"Really? How's that?"

"Umm," Darcie answered awkwardly. "I need to go revisit the doctor."

"What? Why?"

"It's okay…"

"Do not dare do that when you've just forced it out of me. What's going on?"

"I just have an infection in my hand."

"What do you mean? Send me a picture now. Or put me on FaceTime!" she demanded.

"Calm down, Lizzie. It's wrapped up. It was bad, but I'm going back tomorrow. It's fine. So, tell me more about work. I've never heard you sound so sad."

"Please don't try and change the subject. Don't insult my intelligence by doing that. You were just calling me out for doing exactly this, for playing it down," she advised sadly.

"Okay, I'm sorry. Look, how about we promise to be open with each other?"

"I can do that."

"Last week, I was helping get one of the jet skis that was stuck, and my hand got caught on it. A small amount of the stitches reopened, just a little. A couple of days later it was painful and swollen. Cap told me to go check it out, and I didn't. The next day, it was seeping, so I'm gonna go back to the doctor just to be safe. I'm okay. I think I'll just get a shot and some antibiotics. Can you talk now?"

"I am talking. That doesn't sound good. You need to call me when you go in, and I'll tell you if they're giving you the correct advice. Where are you? Will it be a legitimate practitioner?"

"Baby, calm down..." Darcie stopped, realizing what she'd said. "Sorry."

"Don't be, I liked it. I missed it... I miss you, Darce."

"Me too," she said sadly.

They sat there in silence for a while. Lizzie sipped her wine and ate a crisp, waiting for Darcie to say something.

"Oh my god, what the hell is that noise?" she asked.

Lizzie laughed. "Sorry, I forgot."

"You forgot? What is it? Are you eating something?"

"Sorry, I *did* tell you about my five-star cuisine. I'm having crisps and wine for dinner.

"That doesn't sound too healthy."

"Well, I don't have a top chef cooking for me anymore, do I?"

"I'd cook for you if I could," she added sadly. "So, what are you eating?"

"Mature cheddar and red onion crisps. What would you cook for me?"

Darcie gave a little laugh. "One of my first memories of you is eating chips."

"Really?" Lizzie laughed, sliding further down her bed to get comfortable. "When?"

"Your first night, when your mom balled you out in front of everyone. I was cleaning up, and saw you on your deck. You were eating chips and a candy bar."

"Oh gosh. Well, yeah, I have a thing for junk food. It's my dinner this evening. And no doubt I'll eat some rubbish tomorrow, too. Although, there is a beautiful sandwich shop not far from me that does the most amazing wraps, with some crisps of course. I can eat and go." She laughed.

"Wow, you like those chips, huh? So, you don't have to work tomorrow?"

"No, I'm off for a few days, and then in for one. Then I'm off Saturday for a party," she groaned.

"You're not happy about a party? There may be some hot girls," Darcie said quietly.

"Would you want me to do that?"

"I can't stop you from doing what you wanna do."

"And you think I want to do that?"

"I don't know. I hope not," she murmured.

"I don't want to. I want to…" Lizzie stopped.

"You want to what?" Darcie pushed.

"It doesn't matter."

"Why do you always do that? I hate it. It's been hard enough with you just walking… look, it doesn't matter. I should probably let you go. You need to sleep. It's late, and you worked a lot," Darcie stated.

"I'm fine, I won't sleep even if I wanted to. I need to relax. This is my evening. If you need to go, that's fine. You should sleep."

"I don't want to sleep. I don't want to go, but equally, I don't want you to undervalue my feelings. And if you're gonna do that, then I *should* go."

"And what exactly are your feelings, Darce?"

Darcie silently contemplated how to answer that. "That I want what I can't have." She sighed. "Lizzie?"

"Yes?"

"Please tell me about your day. I haven't known you to be like this. You're scaring me. You sounded fine last night. I know we only texted each other, but other than our… parting words, you were fine. After losing your patient, what happened today that was so bad you smashed everything up and cut yourself?"

Lizzie sighed, desperately wanting to push Darcie further on what it was she wanted. She really didn't want to relive what happened at work, but something convinced her to open up. "As I said, it was a difficult procedure. My colleague Jack—he's one of the senior neurosurgeons—and I were on it, and there was a complication. I don't want to go into too much detail…"

"Well, I wouldn't understand anyhow." She giggled.

Lizzie let out a small laugh, and moved the crisp bowl, laying further into her bed. "I could teach you. You're incredibly intelligent. Basically, it was a craniotomy. Do you know what that is?"

"Is that when you treat a brain tumor?"

"Well, one of them. There are different variations. It's a lengthy procedure, and similarly, it's the one used with high profile cases. It's basically where you remove part of the skull to either further establish details of the tumor, or remove the tumor in part or full. There was a leakage of the cerebrospinal fluid, which is the fluid that cushions our brains. It's rare, but unfortunately, dangerous. To cut a long story short…" She stopped, breathing in deeply and swallowing the lump in her throat.

"Baby, you okay?" Darcie felt like she should use the term again. Lizzie had been struggling enough already, but when she heard Darcie's sexy American accent and soothing voice call her baby, it was simply too much for her to bare. She tried desperately to conceal her low sob, but Darcie cried out in despair. "Lizzie? Baby please, are you okay? Talk to me, please! You're scaring me."

"I'm fine," she said amidst sobs. She relived the day's events, filling Darcie in on the procedure failing, the leak that lead to the brain swelling, and consequently, the patient dying. They failed their duties as doctors. She failed her duty as one of the top neurosurgeons in the country, and that resulted in her smashing up the room and wounding herself.

Darcie wiped a tear from her cheek as she lay in bed, holding the top Lizzie bought her to her nose, desperately craving the smell of her. If she could, she'd jump on a plane right now just to get to her and hold her tight. "I'm so sorry. I wish so bad I could hold you, and make it better—stroke your head, tickle your back, and kiss you slowly," she responded seriously.

"I'd love that, Darce. Especially right now. I so wish I could have that now."

It broke Darcie's heart, and she didn't know how to deal with it. "You want me to come visit?"

"Don't be silly, you can't."

"I can. If you want me to, I'll be there as soon as I can."

"It's fine, I'm just being silly. That just all sounded so nice."

"Alright, then. I'll see if I can make you feel better from here. Are you sleepy?"

"I'm drained."

"Okay, good. Get yourself comfortable and in bed."

"Erm, okay."

"You done?"

"Yes."

"Good. Grab a spare pillow and turn on your side. I like to do this and imagine it's you I'm snuggling into," she said shyly. "Put me on speaker and lay me behind you, so that my voice is in the distance. Have you done all that?"

"Yes. Do you really imagine the pillow is me?"

"Yes, every night," she stated simply. "Now close your eyes." She waited for Lizzie to hum her confirmation. She could hear her movement in bed as Lizzie got herself comfortable. Darcie lowered her voice this time to a simple whisper. "So, think back to Atlantis. We're not at the park, just close by. We're looking at the boats as we walk, hearing the shrill of laughter, and happiness fill the air. We can smell the scent of vacation, the mixture of coconut sunscreen, beach, and chlorine. It's busy. Real busy. I'm holding your hand, guiding you in and out of the crowds, but not back to the boat. Not this time. This time we're not there for a secret, 'one day' date. We're vacationing together, just like normal couples. We go get a Jamba Juice, swapping flavors every few minutes, and giggling. I get my favorite banana berry juice. It's a hot day, and we're already in tune with the Caribbean way. We're laughing, strolling along, hand in hand. This time though, you don't mind holding hands. We're caught up in the moment. We don't care about anyone around us. Instead of making our way back on the boat, this time, we don't. We aren't there to return to Iconica, or any other vessel. We are there for us. We're enjoying a beautiful vacation alone in the Caribbean. We spend days exploring, chilling on the beach, rubbing sunscreen onto each other. Mmmm, I love massaging that into your upper thighs, discreetly grazing your cheeks. We sneak up to the room to make love in the afternoon. We make out when nobody is around. In the evenings, we drink beer on the balcony and watch the sunset as we talk to each other, learn more about each other. We get ready in our room, listening to music and laughing together, applying our makeup and sharing curling irons. In the evening, we enjoy everything the Bahamian nights bring. We do evening sunset cruises, and enjoy the perfection of the picturesque, romantic setting. We visit the straw markets, and barter for gifts for our home together. We take a bus down to fish fry and enjoy the party atmosphere with the locals. We enjoy fine dining in beautiful settings some nights, and Dominos pizzas with pjs, movies, and early nights for others. It's the perfect vacation, with the perfect woman…" Darcie noticed the slight change in Lizzie's breathing. She waited a few moments and realized that Lizzie had relaxed into sleep. "Good night, baby girl, sleep well," Darcie whispered, ending the call.

Darcie switched off the light to her room, and pulled the pillow closer to her, fighting the tears edging out. How she wished all that could be true. She nuzzled her head deep into the pillow and allowed her mind to drift to the dream she'd just spoken of.

*

Lizzie pulled the pillow closer to her, feeling a beautiful sense of comfort and ease as her body and mind awoke. She stopped dead, remembering that it wasn't real. Darcie had talked her to sleep. Lizzie told her about her day, had gotten upset, and Darcie steered her to equilibrium. So much so, she'd fallen asleep during the call.

She adjusted her eyes, and opened her phone. It was still on the call list, Darcie's name sat boldly at the top. She wanted to speak to her desperately, but had no idea what time she was going to the doctor. She decided to text her instead.

Good morning (afternoon), how are you? How's the hand? So, shocker, that was the best night's sleep I've had since the last date I went on :) thank you for doing that.

Nobody has ever done anything like that for me before. The only downfall was when I woke up thinking I was on vacation with my hot girlfriend... and then you weren't there!! Hope your hand is ok. If you get a chance to talk today, I'd love to hear from you (if you want, obviously). I have an appointment at 12:15, but it should only be an hour or so. Take care, Darce, and thank you again. Xxxx

She ignored her doubt about the words she'd sent. She was elated. She felt so incredibly happy, and rather excited about the afternoon. She wondered if she would ever see Darcie again, but desperately hoped she would.

Refusing to waste anymore time lazing in bed, she got up, put on some music, and went into a full cleaning mode. She didn't want to stay and stare at her phone, or even dwell. She wanted to make the most of her days off, try and regain the happiness that'd been so short lived in her life. The happiness she felt on Iconica.

During her cleaning spree, Lizzie heard a notification come in and smiled, seeing Darcie's name. *She'd never been overly fussed on texting and emailing before, but given the fact that she was unable to write to her, she was enjoying it.* She opened the message with a smile on her face.

Oh my god, you remember that? Sheesh, how embarrassing. The hand's fine. The doctor gave me some antibiotics and some cream. It's pretty painful, but I'll live. :) what's your appointment for then? You getting some pampering? Yeah, I can talk. Lemme know when you're free? Xxx

Lizzie was excited about getting a chance to speak to her later and decided to refrain from telling her about the appointment. She could FaceTime her later and reveal all.

Unfortunately, no pampering. And yes, I remember that part. I can't quite recall what the last thing I remember was? I remember the making love ;) that led to a magnificent dream FYI. I like the idea of chilling on the balcony together with a beer, and you being naughty about rubbing lotion into my bottom. I loved it, I loved it all. You're the most amazing woman I've ever met. I wish you were here, so we could have all of that for real. xxx

Can you talk? Darcie replied, wanting to speak rather than text after reading Lizzie's words. Within a few seconds, her phone rang and Lizzie's smiling face on the waterslide filled her screen. "Hey, you," Darcie answered her cell.

"Hi, are you okay?" Lizzie asked.

"Yes. When I ask to speak to you, you don't have to always assume something's up. It may be that I just wanna hear your voice." She laughed. "So, what would you do if I were there?"

"I knew you were naughty."

"Actually, that's all you. I wasn't being naughty at all. I meant 'what would you do' in the literal sense. As in, where would you take me? What would we be doing today? Where would be our first vacation?"

"Hmm, likely story." She laughed. "Well, if you were here today, I'd sneak out and leave you sleeping, so I could make you breakfast in bed. Then we could stay in bed, and watch movies, and pig out. Around midday we'd get up and take a walk down South Bank along the Thames with coffee and pastries. Then we could go play rounders in the park for the afternoon, and enjoy some fresh watermelon with stolen kisses as we sit against a tree before returning home early evening. We'd open a bottle of wine, take a long, hot bubble bath together—"

"Okay, I'm moving to London," Darcie interrupted.

Lizzie laughed. "Sounds nice, I think."

"Yeah, it does. So, hypothetical question… if I'd asked you to date me before you left, would you have said yes?"

"Well, I don't know, because it didn't happen."

"I know that, but if you went back to our date, and I said, 'be my girlfriend,' what would you have said? Hypothetically, of course."

"Of course, hypothetically. I don't know. I guess, logically, I would've questioned the 'how and why,' but I probably wouldn't have been able to resist you, especially after the best day I'd ever had. Equally, I wonder if I would've had the strength to decline it, and not explore that option."

"The strength? So, you wouldn't have wanted it?"

"Sorry, that was the wrong choice of words. I think I would've said yes."

"Right…" Darcie answered distantly.

"Does that bother you? Did I say something wrong?"

"Not at all. Guess it's just a little disappointing."

"What is?"

"Me, not having asked you. I could be laying here on the phone, talking to my girlfriend
right now. Anyway… what appointment do you have later?"

"Well, hypothetically speaking, if we did that, then how would you be now?"

"What do you mean?"

279

S.L. Gape

"Well, how would things be different?"

"Lots of phone sex." She laughed.

"Oh my goodness, you're sex obsessed."

"I know, what's up with that?" She giggled. "On a serious note, I don't know, I guess it'd just maybe..." She stopped.

"Maybe what?"

"God, you have no idea what you do to me. I literally feel like a kid sitting here all nervous and tongue tied." She sighed. "I don't know, I just feel maybe it'd be easier, you know? If you were my girlfriend, I'd know that I'd see you again, I guess."

"You don't think you'll see me again?"

"I don't know. I don't know if you even want to see me."

"I do!" she blurted quickly. "Sorry, that was a bit—"

"Awesome," she interrupted before Lizzie had a chance to respond. "I'm glad you want to because I really do. I'd fly out tomorrow if I was able to."

"What, so you could have your wicked way with me?" She laughed.

"Hmmm, that's a pretty awesome thought, but I wasn't thinking that. It's you with your mind in the gutter now. As much as I hate hate hate to do this, I do have to leave. I have to get back to work."

"That's probably a good idea. You may start with the whole phone sex thing," Lizzie responded seductively.

"Yeah, I can just imagine you doing that." Darcie noticed a long silence. "Wait, you'd *do* that?" she asked astounded. "Maybe I should call in sick."

"Stop misbehaving, I said nothing of the sort. Get yourself to work, I have stuff to do."

"Please tell me it's real stuff, and that's *not* a euphemism."

"Darcie... hmmm, what's your surname?"

"That's random... It's Paxton. Why?"

Lizzie considered the name. "Well, Darcie Paxton, will you please get your mind out of the gutter? Go to work and I'll speak to you later, if you have time."

"For sure. Take care, gorgeous, I'll speak to you later. Miss you." She smiled into the phone, replaying their parting words in her mind.

*

Lizzie couldn't stop looking in the mirror. It was strange. She wondered what Darcie would think. More importantly, what her parents would say. *If her parents ever found out, they would kill her.*

She couldn't wait to speak to Darcie later. They'd sent a couple of texts to each other throughout the day and agreed to speak when Darcie got off her shift. It was frustrating the hell out of her, fidgeting and trying to keep herself busy. She utilized the opportunity to go shopping and find an outfit for Saturday's party that would keep with her family's high standards, and cover the wound from yesterday.

Chapter Thirty-Four

"Hey, you," Darcie said, hearing Lizzie's voice.

"Hi, how are you? How's your hand?"

"It's still fine, sweetie. Stop worrying. How are you? What have you been doing in my absence?"

"Not much. I cleaned my place and went shopping."

"You cleaned?" Darcie asked surprised.

"Yes, why?"

"I don't know, just assumed you had a maid, I guess."

"Charming," Lizzie answered playfully. "I don't like the idea of someone rummaging in my home. I'd rather do it myself. But if my parents ask, I do. How was work?"

"Yeah, I get that. Not bad, but busy. I'll be happy when I get some time off. I'm tired."

"You have some time off?" Lizzie asked inquisitively.

"Yeah, next month."

"Ah, right. Um, are you doing anything? Like maybe a trip to London?" She giggled nervously.

"I'd love to, Lizzie, but I've already booked flights to go back home…"

"Oh gosh, yes, silly me. I remember you telling me. It's okay, it was a silly idea…"

"No, it wasn't. The next break I get, I'm coming straight to you, okay?"

"Okay. Well, it'd be good to see you," Lizzie confirmed, quietly thinking about how good it actually would be to see her. "Do you need to go? You must be busy."

"Nah, they're out on the island. I'm here on cleaning duty. Well, I should be, but I'm not doing much except thinking about and missing you," she announced sadly. "I wish we were like what I described last night. I wish I was there with you, in your arms. Next to you for real, smelling your perfume, instead of the just faint smell of you on the shirt you got me."

"Are you okay? You sound sad."

"I am, but I'll deal."

"Maybe you should get back to work. Look, before I go, can you talk tomorrow?"

"Unlikely, I'm afraid. We have a full day—mini cruise party. It'll be a late one by the time we get back on board, probably after one am. But if that's not too late, I can call."

"Actually, I'll already be in bed. I start work at three am the next morning," she said sadly.

"Right. That night, then?"

Lizzie sighed, desperately hoping Darcie didn't feel like she was pushing her away. "I probably won't get finished until late, and I think you'll probably be in bed by the time I'm home,"

"Right. No problem…"

Lizzie stepped in before she had a chance to dampen their moods. "Friday?" she asked desperately. If nothing else, Darcie would know she was as keen to talk to her too.

"It's arrival day, so it'll be hard. How about Saturday?"

"I'm sorry, I have a family event all day." She sighed. "This is shitty."

"Well, if you want, I'll text as much as I can. I know it isn't the same, but…" She paused. "But I'll definitely try so that I get to speak with you."

"Yeah, me too. You know you don't have to talk to me if you don't want to," Darcie stated.

"What if I do want to? I want to get in my pajamas, go lay in bed, and talk to you like we're together, like you did for me last night. If that's okay with you?"

"Of course it is."

Chapter Thirty-Five

It'd been the worst few days for Lizzie. Not speaking to Darcie was way harder than she'd thought. Things changed that night. They'd been on the phone for nearly five hours, each sharing what they'd do if they were able to live like a normal couple. It made her want the one thing she so desperately wanted, and knew she'd never have.

She got out of the shower and flip flopped her way to the kitchen, taking the milk and crumpets out of the Tesco bag. She put them in the toaster and made herself a cup of tea. She felt sad. The prospect of spending a day feigning happiness and pretending to be somebody she wasn't, filled her with dread and nausea. She flicked through the post, her heart stopping once more at the sight of another personally written letter. The only letter that was postmarked from Miami. She pulled the stool out to sit at her breakfast bar as the loud pop of the toaster announced. "Bloody hell!" she screamed nervously. "Jesus." She sighed, holding her chest. She buttered the crumpets and sat down with the letter.

Hey,
It's me again. I wanted to write you. I know you like the letters, and I find them oddly therapeutic. I apologize that it's not a nice, uplifting one.

Lizzie stopped, unable to continue. She felt physically sick. *Why was it a bad letter?* What was she going to say to her? There's no way it would've reached her since their last conversation; it'd only been four days. Three really, given the time difference. She controlled her breathing and returned to the letter, waiting for the impending devastation to implode.

I wish it was. But the fact of the matter is, I can't find anything to be happy about. I've been reliving the last letters I wrote, desperately trying to regain those feelings of happiness and excitement. But instead, I've just watched you leave the boat. Watched you take your seat on the bus and drive out of the port. Gone… just like that. Out of my life forever. I don't know what to say, Lizzie, except you're truly amazing. You are my dream woman, and as I lay here and write you a letter, in the shirt you bought, tears uncontrollably deceive me as the heavy presence of your scent fills my room. It's breaking my heart that you're gone, that I don't know if I will see you again. I wish so much I'd asked you out. I wish so much I took you on a date sooner. I wish I'd asked you to stay, or told you that I'd go with you. I know this all sounds ridiculous. Jesus, we didn't even make love, but you have left me feeling like if this "us" goes away, it'll be the biggest mistake of my life. I want you, Lizzie. I don't know why you've made me like this, but if you said to come to you, I'd leave right now and come be with you. Whether it meant having to go back into law, or working behind a bar. As long as it meant that you were mine. And I was yours. The problem and most infuriating thing is that I never got to find out what page you were on. I don't know if you were really into me, or if I was just a holiday fling. I know this is wrong on so many levels, and completely confusing, but I don't know if we'll stay in contact, if we'll speak, or see each other, or what. On the basis that at this moment in time, I feel completely heartbroken and as though I'll never see you again, I can't possibly let you walk out of my life without telling you that you really are the most incredible woman I've ever met. You're my dream woman, and if I had my pick, you'd be the woman I got to go to bed with every night and wake up to every morning. You're my "one," Lizzie, and so as not to have any regrets in my life, I wanted you to know that. I also want you to know that, somehow, somewhere along the way, I have started to develop deeper feelings for you. I, um, don't really know how you will digest all this information, and I apologize for this bombshell. I just couldn't risk you not knowing how I felt. And god forbid, if I never speak to you again, I'll never forget you, and I don't believe I'll ever meet a woman who will measure up to you.

I'm sorry for the way I did this, just know you are everything and then some. And if I can't be the one to make you smile every day and tell you how beautiful you are and how loved you are from now to eternity, then I hope whoever the lucky woman is, fully deserves you.

Goodbye my perfection, I love you more than I ever thought possible. -Darcie xxxxx

Lizzie sat dumbfounded by the letter. The butter had unknowingly dripped onto her breakfast bar. She couldn't believe it. *She loved her. She wanted her.* She stood up and paced the room, completely obliterated by the letter. *What did this mean? What did any of it mean? What was she to do?* She went to open her phone messages, but decided against it. She couldn't get into this now, not before the day she was about to face. Darcie wouldn't know that she'd received the letter. She just needed to get through today, and spend some time working out what, if anything, she should do.

*

Lizzie arrived at the party a little late, but she was past worrying about her family's berating. She had no requirement to be here today. In fact, if she was entirely honest with herself, she wanted to stay in bed and talk to Darcie all night. But for now, she just needed to get through today without any further distress and then try and establish some next steps. *First, champagne,* she thought.

Lizzie downed a glass of champagne, put it down, and quickly retrieved another as she made her way outside, thankful it was at least a nice summer's day for the affair. "You're late," said a familiar voice. Lizzie plastered an obligatory, fake smile she'd have to hold for the next 10 hours, and turned to face her mother.

"Mother," she winced, air kissing her on both cheeks. "I'm not actually, I've been inside speaking to the Colby's. I'm actually on my third glass."

"Well, don't drink too much. I believe Victoria James has brought someone for you to meet. You need to find someone; you won't maintain those looks forever. Being too busy with work is unacceptable," she retorted.

"Libby, darling?" Lizzie turned around, immediately bumping into the air kiss coming her way.

"Victoria, how are you?"

"Amazing. I'm flying to Dubai on Monday to look at another horse. You'll have to come to Ascot next year. We missed you. My new pride and joy will be a good addition to my growing racing empire." She gave a fake smile.

"Great. Sounds fantastic. I will try my hardest." Lizzie looked up at the slight cough from the woman smiling politely next to her.

"Heaven's yes, I'm sorry. This is Suzanna. She's gay."

"Nice to meet you, 'Suzanna who's gay.'" She smiled oddly, noticing the snigger from the woman.

"Well, you two will definitely get on. You have a plenitude in common, so I'll leave you to get acquainted." She smiled, about to headbutt Lizzie again with another air kiss before Lizzie stepped back and looked at Victoria.

"Like what?" Lizzie asked.

"Excuse me?" she asked, clearly confused.

Lizzie could see, from the corner of her eye, the smirk on the other woman's face. "You said we have lots in common. Well, I'm intrigued to know what. Because as far as I recall, I haven't seen or spoken to you in around three years, which was the last time I believe I went to the golf club. So, what exactly is it that we have in common?"

Lizzie looked at the woman, who simply shrugged. "Well, the least you could do is be polite. I only did it to help your mother." Victoria stormed off. Lizzie sighed heavily, knowing there would be repercussions from her behavior.

"I'm sorry to be so rude." Lizzie turned to the woman.

"Please don't, I'm not party to any of this. Tori and I play tennis together. She invited me, but I wasn't aware of any of this. I have a girlfriend and was absolutely, under no circumstances, here today because I thought I was being set up."

"Really?"

"Yes."

"Jesus," she said, shaking her head.

"Look, don't worry, we'll catch up with her later. We'll say we've got lots in common and are running off into the sunset together. Maybe that way everyone will stop meddling."

"Good thinking. Sorry," she responded awkwardly.

"Absolutely no problem, not your fault. Have a wonderful day. P.S., your folk's estate is phenomenal."

*

Lizzie sat at a table talking to family friends for what felt like forever. In reality, it'd only been about an hour and a half. Thankfully, this was typical. They were so self-obsessed that they hadn't noticed the blankness on her face, the intermittent nods and smiles.

"Judith? Thomas? How are you both?" Lizzie recognized Ollie's voice. "Would you mind if I stole my sister-in-law from you?"

"See you soon," Lizzie kissed each of them. *This was all she needed now,* she thought as she followed Oliver away from the crowd, grabbing the champagne he'd just taken from a wandering server.

"Would you like to take a walk with me?" Oliver asked.

"Why?!" she blurted, immediately feeling regret when she saw the hurt in his eyes. She found this odd. "I'm sorry, that was rude of me."

"It's okay. I'd like to talk to you, and I feel it best to get away from here, I suppose."

"Of course," Lizzie responded apprehensively, as she followed at a slightly slower pace than her brother-in-law. He walked towards the lake and she had no idea what he was thinking. It even crossed her mind that he would try and murder her. She was clearly insane because there were about 1,000 people on her parent's premises, *and* it was her brother-in-law. She was shaken from her ridiculous thoughts.

"This was where I first kissed your sister. It was the most romantic place on the planet, in my opinion. I just fell in love with it. Apologies, that's somewhat of an overshare," he said awkwardly, leading them off again. "How are things, Elizabeth?"

"Busy at work, but okay, I suppose. And yourself?" she asked curtly.

"Yes, not bad. I miss the Caribbean, but of course that's the nature of returning home." He turned and smiled to her.

"This is true," she responded awkwardly, unsure what the hell was happening.

"So, you're probably wondering why, when we've never done this before, we are here walking around. I've been speaking to your father. He isn't best pleased with me." He turned and smiled oddly. "Have you ever been there?" He pointed his glass to the opposite side of the lake where a crowd of trees stood in close vicinity.

Lizzie wanted to demand what the hell he was playing at, but she saw the sadness in his eyes, the closed frown bringing his eyebrows together to become one. She stood beside him and faced the area. "Yes, when we were very young we'd play there. As I started getting a little older, I tended to spend a little more time there. *Alone,*" she confirmed.

"I remember an occasion." He chuckled to himself. "It was the day I decided I was going to ask your parents if I could have Bella's hand in marriage. 20,000 pounds I spent in total." He turned to find her nodding. "You know… on the ring. And then at least 1500 pounds on the best Cubans and bourbon I could find in Harrods," he said light-heartedly. "I love your family, and your sister. I fit. We all do. We all love being the best of the best. At the top of the ivory tower looking down on all those menials. But the day I chose to propose, I was hiding out in there. I sat there, thinking of the appurtenance that marrying into your family would afford me. I mean don't get me wrong, as you know, my family is equally as affluent and privileged, but bringing that together…" He shook his head proudly. "And do you know the best thing?" He looked at Lizzie, who, confused by the whole speech, simply shook her head. "When you get that with the most incredible woman you've ever met… well, that's what I would call game, set, match. But that day, I realized something. As I sat there with very little doubt in my mind, I watched you come over and spend a long time at your grandparent's bench," he stated, nodding towards the bench a few meters away. "It was at that point I noticed that you weren't like us. You don't revel in the prestige. You never did, Libby. I didn't understand that. At first, I thought it was because you were gay. We are in a very different age now. Nobody has an issue with your sexuality. But then I realized it was more than that. I…" He stopped and turned to look at her seriously. "Please don't freak out now. I've always classed you as a sister, despite you being incredibly distant and disparate from all of us." His eyes held a sincerity she'd never seen before.

Lizzie watched him carefully, and nodded lightly, intrigued by where this was going.

"I started paying more attention to you, almost studying you. Your reluctance to become involved, the sadness when you speak of your job—you don't have the same passion as your father—and the way you disassociate yourself from any part of the family. No part of you fits in," he confirmed, taking a long pause. "I found you a job." He quickly removed a slip of paper from the inner pocket of his jacket, handed it to her, and walked off.

Lizzie watched him walk away as she opened the paper and read the extensive content. *What the hell was Oliver playing at? What was he thinking? Was he going insane?*

*

"I don't get…" She rushed after him, unable to convey her words.

Oliver smiled confidently. "Guinea. Yes, beautiful part of the world. Desperately requiring doctors. Your father isn't best pleased that I found this job for you."

"Ollie, what exactly… why did you find this job for…" Lizzie quietened at his raised finger to hush her.

"He doesn't believe any of his children should live in such a place. Anyway, as I explained to him, you're currently chasing his tail on being the top neurosurgeon in the UK. I particularly liked my emphasis on the matter… with your 'recent' interview." He nodded to her. "Anyway, as you can expect, your father is thrilled at the prospect of his prodigious daughter potentially working towards being the principal neurosurgeon in the world to continue 'his' name."

"Oliver, what the hell are you talking about? How much have you had to drink?"

Oliver smiled slightly. "The difficulty with Guinea is, unlike Singapore and America. It's… I believe," he said distantly, holding his flute and index finger out to the openness. "…still a third world country. Thus, not such a place we'd all visit. Gosh, could you imagine if we told the golf club?" He smiled, realizing she was still completely oblivious. "It's unlikely the family would come visit there

S.L. Gape

on your two-year placement." He laughed obnoxiously, giving her a more serious look this time. "I mean, you could almost be anywhere in the world. London, Guinea, or even traveling around the Caribbean on a superyacht. A very fortuitous affair. Libby, you really are one of the most incredibly intelligent women I've ever met, but by gosh, you're slow at times."

Lizzie tried to piece together what he was saying, unsure if it was real or a set up.

"Elizabeth, please don't look at me like this is some sordid set up."

"I'm confused, Oliver."

"Go follow your heart, Elizabeth," he said simply, a kindness in his eyes she'd never seen before. "All this time I thought your heart lay with a beautiful woman in Haiti, but seemingly, if there was such a woman in Haiti then she must no longer be after turning your head at our very own deputy captain. For several years, you've feigned sickness in Haiti, hence the reason I provided you with some celebratory red the evening before—"

"*Wait*? You were the one that left the red?"

"Yes, I've known for at least three years it's a common trend of yours, so why shouldn't you enjoy an evening like we all did? Look, I don't know what else has happened, but I saw the way you two looked at each other. Go after her, fight for her!" he pleaded. "This isn't you." He nodded his chin to the party in the distance. "None of it."

Lizzie's head was swimming. She couldn't digest everything that was happening and being said. "So, you really left the wine?"

"Yes." He laughed softly, something that was entirely new to her.

"But why?"

"Because you are a fraction of who you are after you've spent time in Haiti. I don't know what or who is there, but clearly, something or someone important. It's the same as when you were with *her*, the deputy captain. Albeit, she's somewhat odd around my wife, but in most part, you two were completely enamored by one another."

"Why do you say around your wife?" She looked at him seriously.

"Come on, Elizabeth." He sounded insulted. She looked at him, uncertain as to what he wanted her to say or admit. "Don't look so concerned. I know my wife; she likes to get attention… elsewhere, on many different levels," he said nonchalantly. I saw the way the boat hand looked at you though, Elizabeth. Please don't ever doubt that look. She slept with Bella, but she fell in love with you."

"You knew?"

"Yes, Elizabeth. I schooled alongside three royals; I'm far from lacking intelligence."

"I'm sorry, I didn't mean that. I just don't understand why…"

"Why I'm still here?"

"Yes."

"Because as I said earlier, I am all of this." He aimed his arm at the area surrounding them. "*I am*. I fit here, Libby. I sit here comfortably. *I love it*, and more importantly, I love your sister. If she needs to have some fun elsewhere, occasionally, I'm fine with that. As long as she comes back to me."

"I can't believe I'm hearing this," she stated seriously.

Oliver turned to face her, smiling kindly as he placed his hands on her shoulders. "This isn't about us. Go get her, Lib, and if you're too proud to let it last forever, at least let it last for a couple of years, and come back to this nonexistence you currently choose to reside in." He kissed her cheek warmly.

"Why are you doing this?"

"Because irrespective of blood or not, I've always felt like you were my sister. I don't want you to feel alone, and I'll help any way I can. Just consider it, Elizabeth. Only you can take stead of your life. Consider your options, and if I need to be of assistance, I will do so. Just promise me one thing?"

She looked at him seriously. "Go on."

"I know we don't do this, but if you decide to take the job, then please take this and be sure to contact me if ever you need anything. Legal advice, money, flights—anything," he confirmed, handing her his business card.

"What are you two doing?" Bella appeared. Lizzie quickly pushed the business card inside her clutch.

"Hello, darling. I was just telling Libby here about a job I found for her that I spoke to your father about."

"Why?" she demanded.

"Just an idea. Come on my beautiful girl, let's go mingle," he said confidently, taking his wife's hand and leading them away. Ollie turned back to her and nodded his head curtly, leaving her completely confused by the situation.

Chapter Thirty-Six

Lizzie sighed heavily before leaving the hotel room and grabbing her holdall. She was afraid, but equally she'd always been relatively spontaneous. She wasn't afraid of doing things out of her comfort zone, but this was entirely different. She'd lied to her parents. Interestingly, with the facilitation of Oliver, which she never would've envisaged. But here she was, about to make the biggest transformation of her life, and take a risk she'd never taken before.

She pulled up to the marina and meandered to the location that she'd left a couple of months prior. Passing numerous yachts, Lizzie could finally see Iconica. Her heart suddenly beat out of her chest as the realization of the situation hit her. It was too late to go back now, and despite all the fears and insecurities running through her, she'd never felt so sure about anything in her entire life. A smile formed on her lips as she got closer and spotted the long, tan legs. Darcie had on the polo that she'd bought for her from the Senor Frogs restaurant. It rested perfectly at her hips, giving the slightest glimpse of her bikini bottoms as she cleaned the deck. She was stunning. Lizzie didn't doubt for a moment that she was doing the right thing, but she also needed to establish what it looked like beyond the next two weeks.

Lizzie reached Iconica and noticed Jose Luis walking over to Darcie, communicating as they always did in

Spanish. *She really did need to learn it.* She walked on board, coughing a little to get their attention.

They both looked up, and their faces dropped as Lizzie stood there with a bag in her hand. "Senorita Barr—" He started, as Darcie, stunned, dropped the jet brush washer, which proceeded to fly everywhere, ejecting water all over both Darcie and the captain. They rushed around, trying to get control of the wayward appliance.

Lizzie bit down on her lower lip as Darcie finally got control of it, noticing that both her and Jose Luis were visibly drowned.

"What are you doing here?" she asked, ignoring her sodden body, and looking at Lizzie surprised. Jose Luis walked over to her and kissed her on each cheek. He eyed Darcie squarely, and apologized for the uniform that wasn't as pristine as it'd been moments before.

"Hi, I was wondering if I could ask a favor?" she asked, looking at both of them, and ignoring Darcie's question.

"Si?"

"I don't suppose you would like an unpaid apprenticeship for two weeks?"

"*What?*" Darcie asked, looking at a confused Jose Luis.

"I'm not really very sure where I want to be in my career," she confirmed. "I was hoping I may be able to come with you on your next charter, visit some places, get some inspiration. I'll work the whole time, but I don't need the pay. I just want to ascertain what I want to do, and where I want to go." Darcie's face contorted with confusion, but Jose Luis began to question her. *Bloody hell, why couldn't she speak Spanish?* she thought, hearing the conversation between the two.

Jose Luis looked between the two women and said something else to Darcie. A smile crept up her lips. "No," she responded simply. Lizzie was unsure what "no" meant, but the smile on Darcie's lips made her heart beat clear out of her chest.

"Welcome to Iconica." Jose Luis smiled and pulled her in for a tight hug. In Lizzie's experience, charter captains were ordinarily quite uptight and reserved, but Darcie was right; this company was far more superior, and far less antiquated. Jose Luis, Deek, and Darcie were the three bosses, effectively, yet all of them were probably the most genuine and sincere staff she'd ever met. Lizzie watched Jose Luis walk away. She turned to Darcie, who stood silently staring at her.

"So, what's going on?" Darcie asked quietly.

"Exactly as I said. I'm unsure as to where I want to go. As much as I love Miss Lovelie and everyone there, I'm not entirely convinced Haiti is exactly where I want to live. However, wherever I end up, I'll need to be close enough that I can visit every couple of weeks."

"What about work?"

"I left," she said nonchalantly.

"And your family?"

"Long story."

"Did you disown them?" she asked wide eyed.

"Not quite." She smiled.

"Right. Um..." she muttered, digging her toe shyly into the wooden deck.

"Yes?" Lizzie raised a brow.

"So, what about me?"

"What about you?"

"Well, you're here."

"Incredibly observant, aren't you?" She smirked. "Yeah, Darce. I'm..." She paused, feeling for the first time ever that it filled her face, and reached her eyes. "Are you going to take me to my room, so I can change for work?"

Darcie grinned back widely, feeling like all her Christmases had come at once. "Erm, yes, sure," she confirmed, turning on her heel. "There's um, only space in..."

"Your room, yes. There's a reason I came to you," she said seriously.

"Oh." She'd not stopped thinking about Lizzie since she left. Now that she was here, she was a little embarrassed over the letter she'd sent her. They arrived at the room, and Darcie opened the door to let her in. "I'll let you get sorted and stuff. Sorry about the mess. I'll sort it out when I get back," she muttered seriously.

"Why are you nervous?"

"I'm not." She fidgeted.

"Well, your actions tell me different. Is it a problem I came to see you?"

"Hell no. I'm just..."

"You're just surprised I'm here, and you don't quite know how to deal with it? Equally, you don't know whether to continue where we left off, or whether I'm just here because I needed a starting point, and you're a good friend that's offered as such?"

Darcie looked at her, unsure of how to respond.

"Darce, for the record, you've been an incredible friend. But I haven't come here simply for a place to sleep or for just a friendship. *I want you.* I want an *us.* I can't remember a time I wanted anything else more. So, are you going to kiss me finally, or continue looking gormless?"

Darcie smiled. "You have quite the tongue, don't cha?"

"Sweetie, you have no idea." She smirked, pulling Darcie to her. Lizzie pressed her lips to hers, holding the position as they felt the comfortability of being as one again.

*

Darcie pulled away first and ran her fingers through Lizzie's blonde waves. "You surprise me daily," she whispered. "You first came here so... shy and stuff. And then you took complete control of yourself. You got confident."

"And you normally take the lead?" she questioned, rubbing her thumbs over the material of her shirt on her back.

"No, actually. Well, not in this environment. Mostly other people make the moves, but with you it was somewhat different. I felt comfortable with you."

"Felt?" Lizzie questioned.

"Feel." She smiled. "I love that you've become this person."

"I've always been this person, sweetie. I just tend to go into a bit of a shell around my family." She smiled somberly.

"Well, I'm charged I get to see this real side of you."

"Glad to hear it. Right, let me change and get some bits unpacked, and then I'll come upstairs for my duties," she confirmed smiling.

"It's fine, we're mostly done. You just get everything sorted."

"Don't give me special treatment, Darcie. I'm incredibly hardworking and if I'm not here to work, I'm certainly not staying. I'll go elsewhere..."

"Woah, easy," Darcie reacted, raising her hand. "I thought I was being sweet."

"I can do sweet. I love sweet, but being here with you and doing this is what I want. Let's just have some fun working and playing together."

Darcie looked at her seriously, debating which way to acknowledge the statement. Lizzie wanted to work. *And work she would*, Darcie thought. "You have 15 minutes. Then you can get that sexy ass to work."

"Yes, boss." She saluted. "Thanks. Oh, and Darce?"

"Yup?"

"How do I say that in Spanish?"

"What?"

"Yes, boss."

"Why?" She laughed.

"Because I can't speak Spanish, and you all speak Spanish to Jose Luis. I know I'll be with the normal deck staff as opposed to those in charge, but if I'm allowed to talk to him, I'd like to be able to say that."

"You will not be with the..." Darcie stopped, noticing Lizzie's frown. "Okay, already. Yes, you can speak to Jose Luis; he's very approachable. You can say it two ways. 'Si jefe,' which means 'yes boss,' or 'si capitan,' which means 'yes captain.' I can teach you some more over the course of your two weeks," she confirmed. "You're now down to 13 minutes." She slapped Lizzie's backside and rushed out.

Lizzie smiled, feeling slightly aroused by Darcie's authoritative attitude.

*

Lizzie changed into her running shorts and plain vest top. Leaving her sandals in the room, she made her way upstairs.

She found Darcie and Deek talking in the saloon area. "It's true, yeh, mon. How you doing, doc?" Deek asked, pulling her into a big hug.

"Hi, good to see you."

"So, you our personalized doctor?"

"Nope, I'm the unpaid apprentice." She smiled widely, watching his serious expression. He turned to Darcie who nodded in confirmation.

"I knew there was a reason I liked you. Well, I'll be looking forward to some celebratory drinks today when we finish. Unless, yo got plans already," he asked in his Jamaican twang.

"Not at all," she affirmed, smiling softly at Darcie. She didn't want to disassociate herself from the team if she was working with them. Equally, she'd never experienced anything like this before, and wanted the opportunity to enjoy it. "What would you like me to do?"

S.L. Gape

Chapter Thirty-Seven

Lizzie worked long, unsociable hours. Being a surgeon held a great deal of stress, given that people's lives were literally in her hands. *But bloody hell, this amount of manual labor was new to her. Clearly, this was how Darcie kept in such good shape.* She couldn't deny that she loved it. She enjoyed the camaraderie with her colleagues. She was strangely in love with walking around a boat without her shoes on, like the guests, barefoot with her peers. She loved the fact she was treated on an equal par as 20-year-olds who, a month ago, served her wine, and cleared away her silverware. And that it didn't bother them. They treated her like one of their own. They weren't rude, or derogatory. They included her. They squirted her with water, threw her in the pool, and poured vodka in her water when she was horrendously warm and in desperate need to hydrate herself. They treated her like they treated each other, and truth be known, she loved it. Never in her life had she felt so at peace with herself.

Jose Luis, or El Capitan as they all referred to him, had called them all in for a meeting. She was certain nothing could make her love the day more than she had already. That, paired with the closeness, the being a part of something was somewhat... overwhelming.

They sat in the dining area as he provided information on the guests arriving the following day. The team laughed and joked about which ones they were going to try and seduce as Jose Luis went through all the details of what was expected and required from them in their roles. He ended on an official introduction to Lizzie. They were thanked for their hard work, and advised they could have the night off, go into Miami for some drinks, and party.

The closest Lizzie had ever experienced to anything like this before was at university. Albeit, she probably could've counted the occasions on one hand, given that she was still closely linked to prestige and her family's allegiances. And of course, there was the lack of life from having to be the most studious at everything. This was entirely different, though. This was exciting. It was like what Darcie exposed her to on their date in The Bahamas.

They chose a sports bar in Downtown Miami to introduce Lizzie to real, American, "working-class" food and beer. She didn't want to say that living in Massachusetts for a year had already afforded her the opportunity to do this because it was a difficult conversation to have; if it hadn't been for Alex, she wouldn't have been given the opportunity. Alex made conscious efforts to take Lizzie further away where nobody could see them, to different districts. But tonight, she quietly enjoyed her new team taking such great satisfaction in the basic introductions.

Lizzie spent most of the evening getting to know Jose Luis and Deek better, while Darcie spent time with the rest of the team, enjoying sports on TV. She occasionally came over to make fun of the "three foreigners" who had no idea what was happening in the numerous sports games, and therefore, happily chatted instead.

*

"So, is everything okay?" Jose Luis asked Lizzie in his Spanish accent when Deek left the two of them alone.

"Yes, better than ever, actually. I must thank you. I know this was a big favor, and I really appreciate that you've done it for me. I promise I won't let you down. I will work my backside off, and I'll only be here for this charter. After that, I'll leave, and work it out on my own," she said sincerely.

"It's fine. Don't be worried, I'm happy you come back. We all worry about you," he responded with equal sincerity.

"I'm good, I love this." She smiled, pointing around to her team.

"You okay?" Darcie walked up behind her. "Capitan," she greeted politely.

He said something to her in Spanish and walked off, leaving Lizzie confused.

"He said he likes you... *a lot,*" Darcie whispered into her ear. "You okay?"

"I'm amazing. I love it. Today was quite frankly the greatest day of my life."

Darcie saw the sincerity in her eyes. It was hard to believe how something that meant *nothing* to some people meant *everything* to others.

"I'm glad," she answered nonchalantly. She didn't know what was appropriate to say or do, so she allowed Lizzie to focus on the excitement of it all.

"Are you okay?" Lizzie asked seriously.

"Yup, sure am."

"Did you mind I wanted to come out?"

"Nope, I wanted you to experience it."

Lizzie heard chants of shots come from her work colleagues. They headed towards her with what could only be described as a surfboard full of different colored shot glasses. "You may not say that when I'm up sick all night." She smiled to the young deck hand, wrapping her arm around her neck, and holding her glass to hers.

Lizzie looked beautiful in a denim shirt dress with a tie-up back. Darcie watched her, loving every minute of it.

*

The captain announced his departure to the team, warning each of them that they had an early start the following morning before the charters arrived.

Darcie nursed a lamb's navy rum with Deek, pondering what to do about Lizzie. She couldn't say it was time for them to go, but she was deputy; she needed to be semi responsible.

"We going?"

Darcie turned around to find Lizzie looking at her. "What... um..."

"You need to go; *you're a boss*. Leave the kids to have fun. Plus, I'm a little jet lagged, so let's go back," Lizzie announced.

Darcie smiled, pleased by the woman's thoughtfulness. Deek downed his drink and the three of them made their way back to the boat, enjoying the drunken, equivocal conversation en route. "One more for ta road ladies?" Deek asked when they reached the galley.

"It's up to you," Darcie questioned. "I could also do with a bite to eat to ensure tomorrow's successful."

"Oh god, you read my mind. I'm totally up for that. I'll really feel it tomorrow."

Deek laughed at the two women, and rummaged through the freezer. "Pizza okay?"

"Good with me." She looked at Lizzie.

"Bloody brilliant," Lizzie slurred, a little intoxicated.

Chapter Thirty-Eight

Lizzie woke up in the darkness of their room. The last thing she remembered was walking back to the boat, with a slight recollection of eating pizza. Her head banged, and she was sure she'd never consumed this much alcohol before. She pulled her phone up to her face. *3:49am*. Jesus, they needed to be up soon. Lizzie got up, and used the bathroom, trying to make as little noise as possible while she gargled some mouthwash in a bid to remove the horrific taste in her mouth. *Why did she feel the need to drink like others did?* Her job didn't really allow for it, so she never drank much outside of being with her family. She climbed back into bed, and turned on her side, pushing away the thoughts of sickness.

*

20 or 30 restless minutes went by, but she couldn't ignore the quiet snores coming from the other bed. Darcie had looked incredible this evening. The short, white denim shorts, and the bright blue halter complimented her turquoise eyes to no end. They'd somehow managed to end up drunk, and in separate beds. A far cry from the plans she'd envisaged for their evening on the 10 hour flight over. She desperately tried to ignore the noise, and the faint perfume smell coming from Darcie, but she couldn't. She couldn't spend any more time together only kissing.

Lizzie turned on her side and watched her body move as the tiniest amount of moonlight illuminated the small cabin. Lizzie pushed the fears out of her head, and made her way over to the other bed. She snuck in and spooned Darcie, taking in the coconut sun lotion, the fruit extracts of her hair, and the faint smell of her perfume. Lizzie was only in her knickers, and as she moved her body next to Darcie's in the tiny bed, she noticed Darcie had on slightly more clothing. A t-shirt covered her body. Lizzie moved her hand underneath the base of her top to her tummy, and gently stroked her fingers over Darcie's soft skin. *God, this woman was amazing. And sexy as hell.*

Lizzie heard a slight groan from Darcie. It wasn't an "awake" groan, but it gave her the courage to continue. She continued running her finger tips over Darcie's tummy, moving her way down to the top of her knickers, and feeling the elastic tight against her skin. She wondered if it was wrong to broach it this way for the first time, but equally she felt she'd let Darcie down on their moving forward. She was certain it would've happened had they not gone out, but it was her choice to meet the team properly. She pushed the doubts out of her mind, and continued roaming her midriff. She moved in closer to Darcie. *The woman literally made her feel alive.*

Lizzie's fingers roamed the soft, cotton material of her knickers, her nails gently running up and down, feeling what she'd been desperate to feel for such a long time. Pushing herself closer, she continued the up and down movement, running her nail between the slight split below the material. Lizzie noticed the change in Darcie's breathing, which had gone from barely visible snores, to deep inhales as the actions seemed to wake her. Lizzie continued her mission with slow, soft movements, fully confident that Darcie was awake now. After a few moments, Lizzie felt Darcie's top leg move back slightly, creating a more definitive division for her to run her nails over. Lizzie's breathing quickly coincided with Darcie's as she tried to control herself.

No one spoke a word, but Lizzie knew Darcie was awake as her breathing increased each time Lizzie's fingers reached lower. She could feel the dampness of her knickers and knew her movements had the desired effect. She felt Darcie move her leg again, letting out the tiniest of groans. She was confident she'd been given the seal of approval to advance. This time, she crept under the material, hearing a whimper. Her breathing heightened as she reacted to the brush over her smooth skin. She'd waited forever and a day for this moment, and suddenly struggled to pull herself together to continue.

She felt Darcie move again, this time upwards, which caused Lizzie's fingers to lay slightly at the entrance of her slit. Her breathing quickened as she lowered her fingers once again. Lizzie felt a warmth emanating as she gently eased her middle finger to the entrance. She didn't want to enter fully; she didn't feel the need to. She was confident that she could achieve all desired effects from minimal touch alone. She used her thumb to press down on her swollen area, and continued with careful precision. Lizzie loved the effect her movements appeared to have on Darcie. She could already feel her body starting to accept and react positively. She continued her actions at the same, leveled pace, noticing Darcie's body slowly and silently convulse.

Darcie finally took hold of Lizzie's hand to discontinue her actions, though she let it lay there. Her breathing was heavy, and jagged. She eventually removed Lizzie's hand and turned from her right side to her left to face her. "That

S.L. Gape

was a pretty awesome way to wake up. Clearly you don't suffer from hangovers," Darcie giggled.

"On the contrary, I completely do. But I couldn't stop thinking about making love to you, so I had to do something about it," she purred.

"I know that feeling." Darcie moved her hand towards Lizzie's mid-section, but Lizzie gently swatted it away. "What are you doing?" Darcie asked confused.

"Making you wait," Lizzie muttered simply.

"You can't do that, I'm turned on to hell."

"I think you'll find I can. You need to be patient."

"You can't. You're being a massive tease, plus, I'm sure you'll need relieving." Darcie's grin was barely visible from the faint moon.

"I can take care of myself... *if I need to.*"

"You would not?" Darcie questioned, shocked. Lizzie went quiet, allowing the words to settle, knowing Darcie's mind would be reeling right now. Darcie slowly moved her hand down Lizzie's body.

"I told you no," she stated firmly.

"You can't do this to me. You're being a huge tease. I need to. You need to. You can't do this."

"I think you'll find I can, and I will."

"*You wouldn't.* You so wouldn't take care of yourself instead of asking me to," she pleaded.

"Wanna bet?"

"Lizzie, you can't do this to me." She noticed Lizzie's hand move beneath the covers.

Lizzie ignored Darcie's pleas, desperately wanting to lure her in. She ran her hand over Darcie's bare leg before making her way between her own. She spread them and maneuvered her fingers comfortably, hearing Darcie's gasps.

Darcie moved in closer, allowing Lizzie to feel her erect nipples through her t-shirt. "I can't believe you're actually doing this to me. Why would you do this? You're such a tease," Darcie confirmed defiantly.

"No sweetie, this is not teasing. It's just foreplay."

Darcie gasped. *On a scale of 1 to 10, according to how turned on she was, she was currently*
at a 19.

Lizzie closed her eyes and relived moments before while satisfying herself, hearing, seeing, and feeling Darcie's desperate cries. Lizzie was fulfilled in no time at all, he heavy breathing filling the room.

"I can't believe you just did that to me," Darcie whimpered.

"You can't?" Lizzie turned on her side to face Darcie. She reached Darcie's knickers and lifted the material as she slowly pushed inside.

"Oh fuck," Darcie gasped, feeling Lizzie's wet finger slide inside her. She pulled her closer, allowing Lizzie's exploration to intensify. "My god, you're the most insanely sexy woman I've ever met." Darcie lifted her leg and wrapped it around her body, feeling her move faster and deeper. Lizzie's other hand shifted beneath her butt, and she pulled her in closer. Darcie rocked in tune with Lizzie's movements. She'd never known anybody to turn her on this much before. She tried desperately to hold out, but it was simply impossible. Lizzie utilizing and mixing her own arousal with Darcie's had pretty much sent her over the edge. She felt Lizzie's movements go deeper and faster, and pushed into the rhythms as she cried out into Lizzie's shoulder.

Lizzie wanted to stay like this forever, their bodies implausibly close and privately placed, Darcie's leg wrapped tightly around her. There was only one thing Lizzie could think would make this moment better, and that was Darcie convulsing around her tongue. Lizzie pulled away from Darcie easily. "I've thought about that since leaving the boat," she whispered, kissing her temple.

"I'm desperate to feel you, and taste you. You're driving me insane," Darcie pleaded.

"That's the point," she declared sardonically.

"My understanding of foreplay is clearly very different from yours."

"You're looking at it entirely wrong. I'm not talking about this not ending in intercourse. It's not about that. It's about creating the sexual arousal and desire as the lead up to sexual activity. Both emotionally and physically. You're saying you want to touch me. I think the direct quote was 'you're desperate to touch me.' Being unable to forms part of that sexual arousal. It increases the desire in you each time you're unable to touch me. Therefore, leading to that… hmm, how do I verbalize it…" She contemplated.

"You're mentally teasing me, and I'm going to mentally combust."

"Be quiet, silly. Besides, I was hoping you would physically combust." She laughed.

"You continue touching yourself in front of me, I may very well do just that."

"Take your clothes off," she whispered.

Darcie smiled, moving closer. "It's time for the main event, huh?"

"Be patient, darling girl. Not quite, I've just been dreaming of spending the night together, and snuggling with you naked."

"Oh, you're definitely a tease. You want me to be naked, squished up next to you in the world's smallest bed, our bodies entwined, and yet you still expect me to not touch you. Let me guess, it's all part of the foreplay?" She laughed.

"Are you always like this?"

"I'm sorry. I guess I've just never really been in this position before."

"What, lacking control?"

"No. Well, maybe a little, actually..." She stopped, deciding not to detail previous women she's been with. "But no, I meant more like people interested or invested in my turn, or sexual desires and stuff. I'm totally not communicating this right. I'm not making it out like I've never been loved or wanted, which is how it sounds. I guess, it's just been a while—"

"Since it's been more than a quick fuck with a straight, rich girl? Which is all you've had since yachting?" she simply asked.

Darcie went quiet, unsure of how to respond.

"I'm not stupid, Darce. I don't want to focus on the past, neither yours nor mine, but I'm aware that we both have them. Come on, let's just go to sleep. Thank you for tonight, today, the job. All of it," she whispered sincerely, kissing her lips.

"You're more than welcome. Thanks for coming back to see me. And tonight," she said. Darcie pulled her top and briefs off, and threw them to the other side of the bed.

"You don't need to..."

"I believe you have an item to remove."

Lizzie took off her knickers, copying Darcie's actions. She put her hand on her cheek and kissed her softly, yet passionately. "You sleep facing the wall, I believe?"

"Normally, uh huh."

Lizzie kissed her again, and then her forehead. "Turn over then."

Darcie turned over and lifted her head so that Lizzie could rest her hand under her neck. She moved closer to Darcie's body, and heard a gasp as her breasts pressed against her back. Lizzie cupped Darcie's breast and placed the other arm across her tummy, pulling her in close. Darcie sighed lightly, consumed by Lizzie and the moment she'd waited forever for.

*

Darcie woke as the sun slowly rose into existence. She'd slept well in Lizzie's arms, but she hadn't slept as much as she'd hoped. There were moments of desperation to stay like this forever, moments of fear as to what would happen after two weeks, and then moments of sexual frustration over her despair of wanting and craving Lizzie. She lay still, thinking about the night before. Lizzie, taking the lead, giving her the best sex she'd ever had. The teasing, the anticipation... Lizzie was totally right. She didn't know how she would be with her when they woke because she was desperately in need of her. She was absorbed by Lizzie, and the way she tried to explain it yesterday about the build-up, the "foreplay" as she called it, made sense. She had totally got her wired. Darcie turned into putty in her hands.

Darcie delicately removed Lizzie's arm from around her waist, instantly feeling the loss of the warm, naked body around her own. She turned over and kissed her neck softly, feeling a gentle toss beneath her. Darcie worked her way down a little farther, reaching the curve of her breasts and kissed her gently. She stopped at the edge of her nipple, making soft circles around the edge and feeling how they reacted under her tongue. Darcie bit down on the area and sucked softly, hearing whimpers emanating above. She noticed Lizzie's hand appear beside her as she clenched the sheets. She kissed a little further down her tummy, biting slightly as she did so. Darcie heard Lizzie's groans and pleas to hurry, which made her slow the process further, teasing her the way she had the evening before.

Darcie felt Lizzie's hips raise towards her mouth. She softly grabbed her hip bones, pushing her back down carefully. Continuing back up towards her breast, she stopped and gasped as the sun shone through to the slightest glimpse beneath the cover. Her eyes were torn, but she simply couldn't stop. *Not now*. She continued her journey, biting her nipple lightly. Lizzie's legs wrapped around her waist, pulling her down on top of her. Her hands scratched desperately at her back, and it took everything in Darcie to stop from racing through the motions. Between Lizzie's desire, and her own craving, she was hungry for her. Darcie removed the legs around her and grabbed Lizzie's arms, crawling back up to her face. She held her hands above Lizzie's head, her blonde hair falling lazily over her face. Kissing down her neck, Lizzie let out cries once more. "Elizabeth," she whispered, feeling a tremble beneath her. "You need to keep your hands to yourself and stop trying to rush me. This is *my* time now." She eyed her carefully, watching the glaze over her eyes. *She was desperate*. "If you don't stop, I'm not going to finish, and you know that no matter how desperately you think you can fulfil yourself, there's no way you'll be fully satisfied." She smirked.

"Oh, dear god," Lizzie whispered. It filled Darcie with even more confidence to continue the teasing Lizzie subjected her to. She kissed her way down her torso at the slowest pace. She was nowhere near where she needed to be, and there was no way she'd be able to hold out the way she wanted to; she was as much on the verge as Lizzie. Apparently, the woman was right; this version of foreplay certainly caused an increase in physical and emotional desire. Darcie made her way further down, kissing the silky-smooth skin at the top of her entrance. Lizzie seemed perfect for her in every way.

She pushed Lizzie's leg aside carefully. As she kissed down her inner thigh, she noticed the elevated level of sensitivity in the area and factored this into her movements. Lizzie literally squirmed under Darcie's sexual prowess. She lightly ran her fingertips down her inner thigh, feeling goosebumps raise. She replaced her fingertips with her tongue and ran it slowly upwards this time. Before she knew what was happening, Lizzie grabbed her head, pushing her in further. Darcie jerked back, and took Lizzie's hand in her own, moving up to face her. "It was your idea to enforce these teasing rules." She smirked. "Now behave, doctor, or I'll stop altogether."

"I don't think anyone's ever infuriated me more."

"Touché. But you gotta admit, nobody's ever turned you on more either." She raised her eyebrows.

Lizzie watched the glint in those beautiful, blue eyes. How was it possible that any person's eyes could be more captivating, more beautiful? She gulped loudly, and it surrounded the room.

"Behave baby, I waited a long time to make love to you," Darcie whispered alluringly, stroking her face. She returned to where she'd left off moments before, repeating the same action and tickling lightly down her inner thigh. This woman was so ticklish, and Darcie couldn't wait to save that for another time. She was beyond desperate now.

This woman drove her insane. She looked up to Lizzie, whose eyes cautiously watched her, hands still firmly tucked behind her. Darcie caught sight between her legs and lost the inability to breathe. Her body felt as though it was about to give way, but suddenly, she was brought to by a gentle touch to her cheek. Darcie looked away from the gleaming sex, and looked up at Lizzie, whose thumb stroked her cheek. Her smile was so pure. There were so many unspoken words in that moment, but never had Darcie felt so in tune with another. She turned her head into Lizzie's hand, blushing slightly. Taking her hand in her own, Darcie kept her eyes on Lizzie as she allowed her tongue to warmly direct her. Their eyes never deviated. Darcie pushed her legs a little farther apart, leaned down, and took one of Lizzie's lips between hers. She pulled and sucked the sensitive area, reveling the taste and feel of Lizzie on her. She occasionally stopped to run her tongue between the area before capturing her lip once more. Darcie would've loved to ignore the pleas and cries from Lizzie, but the recollection of making her wait last night, of making her watch her satisfy herself was mentally too much for her body to handle.

There was little room on the bed, and had she attempted to move her legs further apart, they'd both end up on the floor. Instead, she raised Lizzie's legs onto her shoulders, allowing herself to get the right angle to delight in every part of Lizzie. She felt her hips raise, allowing Darcie to fill her. Lizzie was beautiful. She was perfect. She was everything Darcie had ever wanted. She buried her head deeper and clenched herself in a bid to stop the waves coming over her. Lizzie was many things, but seemingly, knowledgeable in the bedroom department was top of the list. She was unable to take any more of the woman.

S.L. Gape

Lizzie's legs tightened around her neck, her body trembled, and Darcie lost control over her own libido as the pair simultaneously reached a euphoric state.

They caught their breathing, silently laying there satisfied. "That was…"

"Mmm hmmm," Darcie mumbled. "It sure was. Are you okay?"

"What, you mean aside from failing on my mission to make you suffer assiduously for my own personal gain, thus plummeting into a world of insubordination?" She smirked.

"Plummeting? That best be plummeting from a state of ecstasy." She giggled. "Anyway… you forgot to mention something."

"I did?" Lizzie asked, confused.

"Uh huh," she confirmed. "*This.*" Darcie pulled the bed sheets to the side. "Solo se vive una vez, huh?" Darcie spoke in her Spanish accent.

"Gosh, that accent turns me on immensely."

"I still can't believe you did it," Darcie questioned, running her finger down the side of Lizzie's body, just below her ribcage. "And I love that it's in Spanish."

"Well, I've always loved the language, and after seeing yours, and meeting you, and speaking with you that day, I just thought, 'you only live once,' seemed quite fitting. When I searched for it in different languages, Spanish was entirely the best," she stated.

"I love it, it's sexy as hell. Just like you," Darcie whispered, kissing the tattoo softly.

Chapter Thirty-Nine

Darcie woke startled, immediately smashing her head hard against the wall. "Shoot!" she squealed, holding her head in her hands, and looking up at a sheepish Lizzie.

"Sorry," she responded shyly. "I didn't realize you were still sleeping."

"It's fine. You just almost concussed me." She kissed her, still rubbing her head. "You okay?"

"Yes. Are you sure they'll like me? Like, are you really sure? I can't breathe."

"You knocked me unconscious because you're worried what my folks are gonna think?" she asked, stroking her face. "Baby, relax. They are literally going to love you. What is there not to love?" She smiled softly, moving away as she noticed another traveler watching them.

"I think I'm going to be sick. Maybe I won't go with you. Let's slow it down. We've only been dating two weeks. Maybe you go to your parents, and I'll just check into a hotel and we can meet when you have time. I can just go and explore Phoenix."

"Yeah, because I'm going to allow that," she giggled sarcastically.

"Mhmm." She looked away, distracted.

Darcie pulled her face up to look at her. "Lizzie," she said again, getting her attention.

"Sorry, yes?"

"Have you ever met a girlfriend's family before?" She already knew the answer as she
saw the change in her demeanor. Her back straightened into the airplane seat and her eyes grew sad.

"No, not entirely. I mean, I've dated friends of the family that I've been forced with, but I've never been introduced as a girlfriend per se. I've never physically done this."

"Okay, so let's hash this out. For starters, my folks are *awesome*. Granted, I'm biased, but they are. My mom is a typical mom; she'll shower you with love…" She stopped immediately, feeling guilty at the recollection that not all moms are *typical* because Lizzie's sure as hell isn't.

"It's okay. You can't watch what you say forever. Please, continue."

"I'm sorry. My family is great. There's nothing not to like about them. They're stoked about meeting you, Lizzie. Let's just go down, and have an awesome time with them. *Please?*"

Lizzie nodded her head slightly as the wheels hit the tarmac and the engine sounds increased. "Okay," she softly agreed, turning back to face the cockpit.

*

"You want me to get that for you?"

"No, I'm fine," Lizzie advised distantly, stepping in to grab her bag.

"My folks are going to think I lied to them if you turn up acting like this."

"I'm sorry. I just don't know how to act, how I need to be."

"How about you don't act? Just be yourself, and let everyone see exactly what I do."

Lizzie saw the seriousness in Darcie, swallowed her fear and concerns, and nodded simply. She'd adjusted to several tricky situations in her lifetime, so she'd embrace this. She had Darcie with her, and that's all that mattered.

They walked through the arrivals, Darcie eagerly scanning the hordes of people. She turned to face Lizzie with the largest of smiles forming on her face, and rushed towards a woman who looked like a slightly older version of her. *Jesus, she was her mother's double.* The tall woman wore relaxed clothes, giving off a soft and gentle look. A look her mother would have scrutinized up and down and refused to be in the same vicinity as. Her father was tall, slightly more rounded, and looked as though he'd been enjoying retirement. He was surprisingly dressed in khaki shorts, flip flops, and a brightly colored polo. She would have assumed he dressed more like her own father—suited, or in golf attire, given his reputable, longstanding career—but he looked normal, relaxed. He looked like he belonged on a superyacht with his daughter. Lizzie watched the smiles grow on Darcie's parents faces, feeling the warmth fill the airport.

Darcie rushed ahead to her parents, smiling back at Lizzie, and erratically gesturing her hand to hurry up. Lizzie felt a relaxation set in, her fears slowly subsiding as she followed Darcie. Before Darcie had an opportunity to make introductions, her mother wrapped her arms around Lizzie, squealing her name. As she moved out of the embrace, Darcie's father stepped in, kissing her on the cheek and removing the bags from her and his daughter's hands to take their cases.

"How are you both? You look great," her mother confirmed, looking to each of them as if she'd known Lizzie forever.

"Awesome. It's been a tough couple of months, especially with my hand."

"Yes, how is it Darce?" her father asked, putting their bags away.

"Great, thanks to this one," she replied, squeezing Lizzie's knee as they got comfortable in the back seats.

"*I know*. Thank god you were there, Lizzie. Is it okay to call you that, or would you prefer Elizabeth?"

Lizzie smiled at how much Darcie's mother knew about her. "No, Lizzie is fine. Thank you for extending the invitation to me. I've never been to Arizona before."

"That's a great accent you got there, Lizzie," her father confirmed, smiling into the rear-view mirror. "So, what you girls up to while visiting?"

"Seeing family," her mother offered, bemused.

"Calm down, mom, we've got plenty of time with everyone. We'll be spending a couple days out though."

"We will?" Lizzie asked surprised.

"Sure you will. Arizona is a great state. And if you haven't visited before, my daughter needs to take you to see some of the sights. There isn't enough time to do it all, but each time you're here, you can see a bit more. Where you going this time, Darce?"

"Um, I'll tell you later, pops." She winked at her father in the mirror.

"Oh, a surprise? Nice." He whistled.

"Ry will be over in an hour. They're staying for the night. She has a couple days off work. You guys okay to stay in the guest house?"

"For sure."

"Lizzie, I didn't get groceries yet. Tell me everything you like to eat and drink, and I'll make a grocery run after we get home," her mother confirmed.

"Oh no, please don't do that for my benefit. I'll just have whatever." She smiled sincerely.

"Don't be silly, it's fine. I'll get what you like. I know when we've been to the UK before, there are certain brands of tea, for example."

"Really, Mrs.—"

"Do not dare, lady." Her mother turned fully in her seat and pointed directly at her before slumping a little and winking. "It's Linda." She smiled.

"Okay, Linda." Lizzie laughed. "But seriously, I can drink anything. There really isn't anything specific I require."

"Lizzie eats plenty," Darcie chimed in.

"*Excuse me?* It's been three weeks, and you're already telling me I'm fat?"

"Uh, oh. Um… no, I didn't mean that," Darcie stuttered, seeing a smirk form on Lizzie's face. They all laughed at her. "Shut up." She rolled her eyes. "What I meant to say was, whatever we have for dinner tonight will be just fine. We can make a visit tomorrow to buy some stuff."

"Okay, sweetie."

Lizzie felt Darcie take her hand and grew uncomfortable as she noticed Darcie's mother watching their interaction. Darcie looked at her concerned, throwing a glance over to her mother. She leaned into Lizzie and whispered, "I've been gay a long time, Lizzie. My folks aren't bothered by it, but if it bothers you I'll back off."

Lizzie noticed her parents happily chatting away in the front, her father holding his wife's hand. Lizzie lifted her and Darcie's entwined hands to her lips, and gently kissed

Darcie's soft skin. She smiled and turned, quietly looking out the window for the duration of the journey.

*

"Hey, we're here," Darcie said to Lizzie as they pulled up the drive.

"I gathered." She smirked at her.

"You are so sarcastic." Darcie rolled her eyes.

"A bit like another young lady we know," her father stated, grabbing their bags.

"You have a beautiful home." Lizzie nodded to Darcie's parents, taking in the expanse.

"Thank you. You make yourself at home, okay?"

"Thank you," she responded shyly.

"Come on, we'll go and unpack before Ry gets here."

"Here you go, Darce," her father threw her two waters. She caught them confidently.

"Impressive." Lizzie laughed, smiling at her dad.

"We'll teach you all our tricks, Lizzie." He winked and followed his wife into the kitchen. "You girls can manage, right?"

"Sure pops, we got this. We'll be back soon.".

*

"Wow, is this where we're staying?" Lizzie giggled.

"Yeah, our own little hideaway. The kids love it, but Ry doesn't like them out here alone because of the desert, even with the locks on."

"What do you mean the desert? Well, I know what you mean in the literal sense, as I've just seen it. But I didn't realize you *lived* in the desert. What exactly does that mean?" she asked, concerned.

"Yes, my folks do live kind of close to it, but we're far more residential here. We do, however, sometimes have the occasional out of towner."

"Darcie, seriously, what the bloody hell are you talking about? Whom or what exactly might come and pay us a visit?" she asked, worried.

"Don't worry, babe, I'll protect you." She giggled. "Honestly, it's fine. Nothing will come in, okay?"

"But what could potentially come in?"

"Are you scared?"

"I live in bloody London where spiders are the size of a grain of salt, and the scariest things we have are…" She stopped, trying to think. "We don't have anything bloody scary—it's bloody London!"

Darcie couldn't help but laugh at her. "God, you're the cutest," she said, wrapping her hand around her waist. "Listen to me. We're on the outskirts of the desert. We get bark scorpions—although they're a rarity—tarantulas, and rattlesnakes. I've seen minimal in all my life. We'll put the air con on now, so we won't need the windows open, and I'll seal the doors with towels if it'll make you feel better. I can assure you, I'll protect you if anything comes in, but it won't." She smiled kindly, making a mental note that she'd grab some hiking boots for Lizzie for when they go out.

Lizzie walked like she was playing hopscotch, stepping in and around the tiled flooring, muttering "buggering scorpions" under her breath.

Darcie struggled to limit the sniggers as she listened to Lizzie's cussing. She hadn't thought for a second of the repercussions from telling Lizzie about those things; it was the norm for her. But Lizzie was right. She lived in London. She saw a bug maybe once a year. "Come on, you ready?"

"Yes," she said softly.

"Look, if it's that too big of a deal, we'll go inside and sleep on the couch, or my folks can stay here."

"*Oh, god no*, it's fine. You'll just have to hold me tight all night and protect me." She smiled.

"Always baby. *Always*," Darcie smiled, kissing her lips softly. "Come on, let's go have some fun."

Chapter Forty

"Hey, we're here!" said a voice from inside.

"We're out back, sweetie!" Darcie's mother called from the garden.

Lizzie sat up straight, feeling nervous all over again. "Stop panicking, sweetie. We already all love you." Linda squeezed her knee. "More raspberry lemonade?"

"Yes, please," Lizzie murmured, watching the family walk through the back doors. *Ryan was another stunning member of the family. Minus Darcie's incredible eyes,* she thought.

"Hey runt, about time you came back," Ryan said, dropping her bags and hugging her sister tightly.

"Well, you had plenty chances to come visit." Darcie slapped her sister playfully. "Matty boy! How you doing, buddy?" she asked, hugging and kissing her brother-in-law. She picked up a squealing Nate, and kissed him playfully.

"Hey, Darce, how goes it?" He kissed her on the cheek, and passed the iPad to his daughter, who comfortably sat on her grandma's lap.

"Awesome. So, Ry, Matt, Nate, this is Lizzie. Lizzie, this is dumb and dumber, and my fave boy on the planet." She tickled Nate.

"Erm hi, very nice to meet you all. You have a beautiful family," she confirmed.

"Ohhh, cool accent!" Matt chimed.

"That's what I said."

Lizzie was confused, looking between the family and the little girl, Addison. Darcie caught her eye and smiled slowly. She knelt in front of her niece, putting her hands to her face and scrunching up her nose to the giggling girl. Darcie kissed her lips softly before communicating to her with her hands. "This is my friend, Lizzie. Say hi," Darcie spoke aloud. Addison looked over at Lizzie and waved her hand shyly.

"Hi." Lizzie waved back.

"You want some raspberry lemonade?" Linda asked her family.

"Thanks, Mom. So… squirt, how much you gonna pay me *not* to let all your secrets out to your girlfriend here?"

"Ry, cut it out. Mom, tell her."

"*Mom tell her*? God, do you hear your girlfriend, Lizzie? *Dude*, you are so lame. So, what do you wanna know?" She turned to look at Lizzie.

"I don't think I need to hear anything after that little episode. You just snitched on your sister at 35. *Really*?" she responded playfully. They all laughed around the table. Immediately she was transported to a place of complete repose, finally allowing herself to settle in with all of them.

Lizzie felt something at her foot and immediately screamed, falling backward out of her chair. The moments passed rapidly. She saw Darcie rush beside her, helping her up as she felt a wetness brush her face. "*Jesus!*" she screamed, looking down, and seeing the big eyes of a small puppy licking her face, its head cocked to one side. It viewed her with the same oddity that the entire family appeared to view her with. Like she was crazy. "Erm, I'm really sorry," she stood quickly.

Nautical Delights

"I'm so sorry, I didn't think to tell you they have a dog," she said apologetically. "I forgot that they bring Lucky when they come stay."

"Lizzie we're sorry, we can put him inside," Ryan offered concerned.

"It's fine. I don't mind dogs. I mind my girlfriend telling me that there's the potential of killer spiders, snakes, and scorpions coming to get me in the middle of the night, and then something touching my leg not too long after." Ryan, Darcie, and their mother laughed at Lizzie, who eyed them in surprise. "*It isn't funny,*" she insisted, laughing along with them, unable to contain herself any longer.

Addison turned to Darcie and asked her a question. Darcie smiled at Lizzie before signing back to her niece, who laughed hysterically. Addison clicked her fingers under the table, and the dog rushed over, jumping up onto her lap, and causing her grandma's chair with all three of them on it to fall backwards this time. The two men quickly grabbed the chair and prevented them from falling. "All this before we even opened any beer." Matt laughed.

"Lizzie, if you're really afraid, we can stay in the guest house. You can take our room," Darcie's father suggested.

"No seriously, I'll be fine. As long as there are no more surprises." She rolled her eyes.

Darcie leaned in as they all talked amongst themselves. "So… I'm your *girlfriend,* huh?"

"Be quiet," Lizzie rolled her eyes.

"It's what you said… just saying."

"Yeah, because everybody has been saying it all day," She shook her head.

Darcie laughed, leaning in closer to kiss her. Lizzie didn't have a chance to worry about the "ifs and buts" before Darcie's lips were on hers.

"Dude, get a room!" Ryan shouted.

"Shut up," Darcie said, moving away, and mouthing "sorry" to an embarrassed Lizzie.

"Come on, who's up for family baseball?" Matt asked, turning to communicate with his little girl.

*

Lizzie came out of the bathroom, walking back through the kitchen, and heard the soft, American voice behind her. "Hey you," Lizzie whispered, turning into her arms and smiling.

"Hey, good looking. Are you okay?"

"I am. I *so am*, Darce. How are you?"

"All the better now." She leaned in and covered Lizzie's bottom lip with hers. She sucked it in a little, hearing Lizzie's soft groan as she pulled away.

"One good thing about being in the guest house is at least I get to have my wicked way with you later." She raised her eyebrows.

"Wicked way, huh?" She giggled. "I can't wait," Darcie winked, pulling away from the embrace, and quickly slapping Lizzie's backside. "Come on, I can't allow you to keep letting my team down."

They returned outside, Matt and Darcie's father, Robert, sitting on the step with their beers. "We thought you guys quit," Matt passed Darcie a bottle of beer.

"Nope, pep talk." Darcie laughed, playfully slapping Lizzie's shoulder.

"Oh, is that what it's called now?" Ry laughed, throwing the baseball to Nate. "Darce, for future reference, when you come back, maybe wipe off the lipstick after the make out session." She teased her sister.

Darcie wiped her lips furiously, turning to Lizzie and noticing her makeup free lips. "She wasn't even wearing any lipstick!" she whined, noticing Lizzie's embarrassment. Ryan laughed hysterically, high fiving her son. She walked over to Lizzie and put her arm around her. "I'm sorry, it's just what we do," she laughed, shrugging her shoulders. "She's super easy to poke fun of." She winked. "Okay, I'll give you guys a shot. Me and my girl are gonna have some girl time." She signed to Addison, who laughed, looking between Lizzie and her aunt.

Lizzie watched the little girl and her mum, who communicated and laughed on a blanket on the grass. "You okay?" Darcie whispered next to her.

"Hi," she responded, surprised. "Sorry, yes I am. Why didn't you tell me about Addison?"

"About her being deaf? I don't know, I guess it's just the norm to us now. Why, does it bother you or something?"

"Gosh, no. Don't be silly. It's just another thing I'll have to learn if I'm going to stay in your life," she said shyly.

"Well, I sure hope you are," Darcie answered embarrassed, aware that neither of them had discussed a future yet. "Maybe not so much Spanish, but signing for holidays and vacations."

"Oh really? Holidays and vacations, huh?"

"Yup, Thanksgiving will be here in no time."

"And how will we do Thanksgiving? Do we have barbecues? It's odd, I always think of Thanksgiving as similar to Christmas. You know, like silly jumpers, cold outside, et cetera."

"Do you do the Christmas jumpers thing?" Darcie asked intrigued.

Lizzie raised an eyebrow. "*Really*?"

"Well, I've never missed a Thanksgiving yet, but if you want that kind of experience for your first time, then I'll take you someplace else. We can get an Airbnb in New York, spend the morning in Central Park, and come home and cook Thanksgiving dinner together. Or go to Canada and do some skiing in the morning."

"No, I'd never ask you to not spend it with your family. Please don't ever think that."

"I don't. I know you'd never ask that. I'm just saying for our first one, if that's something we want to look at doing, then we can do that."

"Darce, is it weird that we keep doing this?"

"Doing what?"

"Making plans? Like we're together and... oh, I don't know."

"Well, I don't think it's weird. You've given up your life. You left your job, you lied to your family. You've been on the boat for two weeks, and cap said you can stay until the end of the summer if you want to. There's not loads more time left, and I wouldn't want to let him down, but if you don't wanna stay, that's fine too. I'm not losing you again, so we could leave before then."

"No, I don't want you to do that. If I decide to leave before then, I'll figure out where I'm going, and then you can come over if you want—"

"Woah, easy tiger... you read my letter, right? You know, the one I wrote you after you left? I'm never going through that again, Lizzie. Life is life. And when you meet someone you think you want to..." She stopped and sighed heavily. "Look, I'm not going to be without you until you tell me you don't want to be with me."

"That isn't going to happen."

"Hey, Darce, you gonna tear yourself apart at any point, and come spend time with your favorite niece?" Ryan interrupted.

"Sorry," Lizzie said awkwardly.

"Don't be silly. Come on, let's go see Addison." Darcie took her hand, leading her towards her sister and niece.

"I'm sorry, that was my fault," Lizzie responded, sitting down next to Ryan.

"Don't be silly, it's fine. I'm just having some fun with my sister. You want some?" Ryan pushed a big bowl of fruit salad towards them.

"Oh, yes please," she took a strawberry. "So, what are you doing?" Lizzie laid down next to Addison who was playing with her iPad. "Seriously, these eyes," Lizzie pointed to Addison and Darcie.

"I know." Ryan laughed, signing to Addison, who smiled at Lizzie and signed back. Lizzie looked worriedly between Ryan and Darcie. "Don't worry, she understands. She's just asking if you sign."

"How do I say, 'not yet?'" Lizzie asked.

Ryan showed her, looked at Darcie, and winked. Addison turned on her stomach to lay next to Lizzie, put her iPad between them, and communicated the cartoon she was watching.

Chapter Forty-One

Lizzie stepped out of the shower, hearing a gentle knock at the door.

"Can I come in?"

Lizzie allowed the towel to drop a little as she went to the door and peaked through. "Can I help you?" she raised an eyebrow.

Darcie pushed the door. "Let me in, tease."

"I'm not so sure I can." She giggled.

"Please?" she pleaded.

"No puppy dog eyes," she warned, opening the door a little.

"Can't promise anything. All bets are off when you're opening the door with a towel halfway down your body. You look super hot. My god, you do things to me that I don't think I've ever experienced," she muttered, grabbing the towel and pulling her closer. She sat at the edge of the bath, moving the tips of her fingers to the back of Lizzie's thighs. She slowly raised her fingers until she reached the curve between her thigh and bottom. "I'm not even lying, I can't get enough of your butt. Seriously, it's awesome."

"Is that the wine talking?"

"Maybe, does it bother you?"

"That you've been drinking? Are you kidding? We've drank lots together."

"No, goofball. Are you bothered by my comments about your butt?"

"Gosh, no. You make it sound like I think you're being discourteous to me. Do you have any idea how amazing it feels to hear someone talk that way? And more so to see it in your eyes. It's incredible, and sexy as hell" Lizzie dropped her towel, watching Darcie's breath go still. She ran her tongue over her lips, exploring Lizzie's naked body. Lizzie stepped forward and lifted Darcie's top over her head. "Want some help getting cleaned up?" Lizzie asked.

Darcie looked up shocked, standing face to face with Lizzie. "You ever hear the song 'Yeah' by Usher?" she asked.

"Yes." She smirked, thinking she knew where this was going.

"Why are you smirking?"

Lizzie put her arms around Darcie's neck, pushing her naked body against her. "Just thinking of the song. Are you referring to the part where it says, 'a lady in the streets and a freak in the bed?'"

"That'll be the one. I'm thinking it was written about you," Darcie said, moving in to kiss her fiercely. Lizzie moved her head back a little as Darcie cried out, "I hate your teasing."

Lizzie leaned down to Darcie's neck, kissing softly at her shoulder bone. She placed soft, slow kisses up her shoulder and neck. She felt Darcie's head move, accepting the embrace. Reaching her ear, she breathed slightly into it, feeling Darcie's chest movement increase against her own. "I don't believe you," Lizzie finally answered. She pulled back a little, biting her bottom lip, and looked intently at Darcie. She lifted her hand, and gently caressed her cheek before moving her thumb over her bottom lip. She stroked it softly, noticing Darcie shiver slightly. Lizzie leaned in this time and replaced her lips where her thumb had been.

S.L. Gape

Lizzie loved taking the lead with Darcie, how she seemed to melt into her arms when she did. Slightly grazing her thumb over Darcie's cheek, Lizzie deepened the kiss. Entering her mouth, she found Darcie's tongue, and they each entered a further journey of thrill and excitement.

Chapter Forty-Two

Lizzie woke early the following morning, adjusting her eyes and allowing her tiredness to subside. She turned over, smiling at Darcie's beauty as she slept next to her. Her sun-kissed blonde hair carried tiny curls from their late night love-making in and out of the shower. Darcie was still heavily sleeping, and she couldn't blame her; they were up until after three am. Slipping out of bed, she pulled her shorts and vest on, and quietly left the guest house. Lizzie made her way over to the kitchen to make them both coffee. She quietly opened the door, and instantly heard a small, "good morning."

"Hi Nate, hello Addison." She smiled and waved over to them.

"Addison wants to know where Aunt Darcie is," Nate asked.

Lizzie walked over to the table and sat down with them. "Would you tell her that she's still sleeping?"

"Sure," he responded, telling his sister. "Everyone here is too. We were going to watch a movie or make some breakfast. What you doing?"

"*Movie*? Excellent choice. I was going to make Darcie and me some breakfast."

Nate instantly told Addison everything she'd said. It was the cutest thing she'd ever seen. They kept Lizzie involved so naturally that she didn't feel left out. "Addison and I could help," he said excitably.

"Well, um, when I said breakfast, I was only going to make some coffee. I didn't want to wake anybody."

"We could be extra quiet?" he asked sincerely, and then began laughing at his sister's signs. Lizzie looked over at them, confused. "My sister's so funny. She just said you don't need to worry about her because she couldn't hear anything anyway," He laughed.

Lizzie couldn't help but smile at their laughing faces. "Okay, so we need to be extra quiet. I don't even know what Darcie would like."

"Eggs and bacon. Everyone loves eggs and bacon. Oh, and Addison says sunny side up. If Aunt Darcie doesn't like it, we can eat it. Or what about pancakes?" he asked his sister, who shook her head vehemently.

"You don't like pancakes?" Lizzie asked Addison.

"She likes them for dinner. You're weird." He laughed, signing to Addison. "You like cereal and pancakes at night." He giggled as his older sister playfully slapped him.

"Okay, I have a great idea. I saw something on TV once; it was very cool," Lizzie said excitably, rifling through the cupboards. "First, shut that door so we don't wake your family."

Addison watched her brother's signs and walked over to the door to shut it before coming to stand on the other side of Lizzie.

"Okay, so first, let me cut up some bread for all of us. Are you guys going to come and have breakfast in the guest house with us?" Nate was already signing to Addison, and they nodded excitably.

"Addison wants to know what you're doing."

"Well, tell her we're going to do bacon and eggs, but a cooler version." She smiled. "First, we need breadsticks and bacon." She grabbed the bacon strips and parted them in the middle. "Okay, you both ready?" Lizzie asked, taking the tray over to the table. "Right, so you take the bread like this." She held one end of the long, thin, pencil-like bread, and picked up a strip of bacon. "Then, you take the bacon, and wrap it around all the way to the bottom. You got that?"

Nate turned to Addison who was already half way through. "She doesn't waste no time, huh?" He laughed, rushing to finish his own pieces. "Like this, Lizzie?" he asked, wrapping it around.

"Yes, very good. Maybe you need to space it out just a little more, otherwise, you may end up having all the bacon at the top."

"I bet it would taste better that way," Nate mused. "It'd be like bacon popsicles."

"Maybe." She laughed, looking up at Addison, who held up her first one, and smiled expectantly.

"Excellent!" Lizzie clapped, holding up two thumbs to the little girl, who smiled widely and took another. When they finished wrapping all the bacon around the bread, Lizzie switched the oven on and placed the tray inside.

"What next?" Nate asked. "Addison thinks we should have OJ with it. She wants to know if you like OJ?"

"I sure do. That would be lovely. Next, we need to spray the cake tins. Do you know if you have some spray oil?" she asked, unsure if they even did that over here.

"Addison doesn't think so. She says when grandma and us bake, she uses butter in the tin."

"No problem, we can use that. We won't butter the bread, so a little won't hurt." She buttered four of the cake tins and got out four slices of bread. "Right, now we each have a piece of bread to push in here. Like this," she pushed the bread into the muffin holes so that it made a small holder.

Nate signed to Addison again, and they both giggled. "Sorry, it's rude to leave anybody out. My mom tells us that a lot. Ya know, not to leave Addison out. Addison says it looks like a bread bag." They both giggled loudly.

"That's what it's supposed to look like," Lizzie said.

"*It is*?"

"Okay, so I'll do Darcie's too, and then you guys each have one to do." She pushed another slice of bread into the space. "Your turn," she smiled, pushing it towards Addison and nodding.

"What now?" Nate asked excitably.

"First, we need it to harden. You know, like toast. So, we'll put it in the oven for a few minutes." She smiled and put the muffin tin into the oven. "Right, what can we do while we wait?" she asked. "I know, how about you teach me some sign language?"

Nate smiled to Lizzie as he told his sister, who nodded excessively. "Great, come on then."

Lizzie watched Addison mime what looked like knocking on an imaginary door. "What's that mean?" Lizzie asked Nate, copying the knocking gesture.

"It means yes," he answered. "Addison is saying 'yes' to teaching you sign language."

Lizzie said thank you to the little girl. Addison signed to Nate. "That means 'you're beautiful,'" he smiled to Lizzie.

Lizzie smiled sheepishly. "Oh, thank you. How do I do it, Nate?"

"Just put your hand to your chin and push it away." Lizzie copied the movement and thanked Addison. "What else?" she asked quizzically.

"'Please,' is this," he confirmed, rubbing his hand against his chest. Also, you can use your head if you want, but the actual way to say, 'yes' and 'no' is like this." He nodded to Addison, who used her hand as though she was knocking.

"It's like I'm knocking at the door?"

"Yup, that's for 'yes.'"

"Oh, great. And no?" Lizzie asked.

Addison pressed two fingers against her thumb.

Lizzie copied her actions. "Like I'm making a crocodile mouth?" she asked, and Nate laughed once more, signing Lizzie's interpretation to his sister.

Lizzie looked at the time. "Right, one last thing. How do I say, 'I love you,' before we finish the last part of breakfast?"

"You can do it quick, like this," he advised, holding up his pinkie, thumb, and index fingers.

Lizzie copied it, smiling. "Really? It looks like I'm going to a heavy metal concert." She watched him explain this to his sister, and they both laughed hysterically again.

"Or this way," he confirmed. "I..." He pointed to himself. "Love..." He made two fists and crossed them over his heart. "You," he finished, pointing to Lizzie. "I love you," he said, reconfirming the action quicker this time.

"Like this?" She copied his actions.

Addison nodded, and made the knocking gesture again, telling Lizzie "yes."

Lizzie smiled at the little girl, put her hand to her chin, and brought it down to say thank you.

Addison copied the movement, and Nate explained that it also means, "you're welcome."

"Great. Thanks for my lesson. Okay, let's go back to making breakfast," she questioned, taking the muffin tray out of the oven.

"What now?" Nate asked expectantly.

"Ah ha, here's the best part." Lizzie walked over to the large box of eggs and took out four. "Have you ever cracked eggs before?"

"Sure, we have," he said simply.

"Great. Okay, so now we make the dippy eggs." She smiled.

"The dippy eggs?" Nate asked confused.

"Yes, so we can dip our bacon toast in it." Lizzie cracked an egg on the side of the bowl and pulled it apart, dropping the egg into the makeshift toasted bag.

"Woahhhh, coooool!" he shouted. She watched Nate and Addison both hold their hands out and wiggle their fingers.

Lizzie used the knife to crack another egg and handed it carefully to Nate. "Be careful here now. The pan is hot, remember?" She protected his elbows as he pulled the egg apart and dropped it into the toast. Lizzie gave the next one to Addison, making sure she didn't burn herself. They cracked the last egg and sprinkled a small amount of salt, putting the tray in the oven, and pulling the other one out. Lizzie turned over the bacon toasts, asking the children to get the cutlery and plates ready for their food. "Okay, so I just very quickly need to run to the room. Please, please, don't go near the oven, okay? I'll be right back," she requested nervously.

"That's fine. We'll play on our iPad's," Nate stated, signing to his sister as they both returned to the table and their electronics.

*

Lizzie rushed back to the guest house, avoiding the grass where she could for fear of interacting with some ghastly creature or other. She opened the door and grabbed the t-shirt from the floor, kneeling next to Darcie's side of the bed. She watched her for a moment before gently brushing the hair out of her face. "Hey, baby. Darce?" she whispered, watching her come around.

"Hey, gorgeous," she murmured, stroking Lizzie's face. "You wanna finish where we left off?" She smirked sleepily.

"I'd love to, but you need to put this on," Lizzie threw her the t-shirt.

"What? *Why?*" She whined.

"Just do it, I'll be back shortly. Don't be naked, we have small visitors," she giggled, walking off. "Oh, and Darce?"

"Huh?" she yawned.

"I'm pretty sure we didn't leave off anywhere last night, but we can definitely have a repeat later." She winked and left the room.

Lizzie rushed back over to the house. "Sorry about that guys. Okay, so I think maybe it's been enough time. Let's check," she opened the oven door. "Ohhh, they look suitably yummy" Lizzie held the hot tray far enough away from the children to not burn them, but close enough that they could see.

"*Wow,*" Nate reacted, clutching Addison's arm excitably.

"Come on, breakfast is served," she said, switching the oven off and plating up the food. She put the plates on a tray, and gave Nate and Addison an OJ for each hand as they made their way to the guest house.

"Good morning!" Nate yelled, charging into the room and spilling a little OJ. "Oops, sorry." He pulled a face. "Hey, Aunt Darce. We made the awesomest breakfast, you gotta see it."

"*You did?* Cool, I'm so hungry you guys," she winked to Lizzie and sat up. "Wow, you made this? You cook? What a creation."

"Yes, I do cook." Lizzie nodded.

Darcie communicated with Addison, smiling and giggling with her easily. She pulled her in and kissed her temple as they lay side by side with the plates on their laps. Addison picked up one of her bacon toasties and dipped it in Darcie's egg. It split and she watched her, wide-eyed, playfully punching her niece. "Dude, this is incredible. God, I can't wait to get our own place, and come home to this every night," she smirked.

"Are you guys moving back home, Aunt Darcie?" Nate asked between mouthfuls. "Can we come stay on the weekends? We could cook with Lizzie." He signed to Addison who nodded desperately.

"Um, I don't know, kiddo. That's a long way off yet." She smiled to him, unsure what to say about his hypothetical comment.

Lizzie looked over at Addison eating her food, and held up her thumbs, hoping she might understand the communication. She wished she'd found out how to say "good" earlier. Addison nodded her head quickly, making the knocking symbol again. Lizzie smiled and stroked the little girl's arm. She raised her fingers to her chin and put them down to thank her. Addison copied the movement and returned to her food.

"You learned to sign? How long was I asleep for? Cause I thought it was only like a couple hours." She arched her brow.

Lizzie rolled her eyes at Darcie's sarcasm. "No," she responded. "We had a bit of spare time, and they taught me a couple of things."

Darcie winked, and mouthed "thank you" to Lizzie, feeling a swell in her heart at the kind gesture. *This woman was just... perfection,* she thought.

Lizzie cleared the plates away after they'd finished and put them to one side. "That was the best breakfast ever," Darcie confirmed, pulling her niece closer in to her, and noticed a sadness in her eyes. Darcie was concerned and communicated with her as Lizzie whispered to Nate to see if everything was okay.

"Yeah, Addison's just sad," he said nonchalantly, drinking his OJ.

"Yes, I see. Do you know why?"

He nodded solemnly, looking down at his feet.

"What's wrong?"

"I think I made her sad."

"Are you sure? I'm sure you didn't mean it if you did." She knelt down next to him.

"I didn't mean it. I just... forgot."

"Why, what happened, sweetie?"

"I said I liked your accent, and she got sad because she doesn't know you got a accent," he told them sadly.

"Ahh, I see. I'm sure Addison doesn't think bad of you. She'll know you just forgot." She stroked his blonde hair.

"I hope so. I didn't mean it."

"I know that," Lizzie offered carefully, pulling him in closer as they watched Darcie and Addison. Darcie smiled at the connection between her nephew and her girlfriend.

She turned back to Addison, finishing their conversation. Darcie did the shortened version of "I love you" to her niece, and watched the little girl follow suit. Lizzie blew her a kiss and a wink.

"It means—" Darcie started.

"Excuse me." Lizzie interrupted, holding up her finger. "I'm aware of what it means. They taught me." She copied the action as Nate signed to Addison and they both laughed. Addison made the hand gesture back to Lizzie.

"Wait, who do you love?" Darcie asked both aloud and in sign language, making Addison giggle again.

Lizzie's heart melted. The little girl was adorable. She had white hair, tanned skin, and eyes identical to her auntie's and grandma's. Paired with that cute smile, Addison literally pulled at her heart. Lizzie pointed her finger between the beautiful woman and the little girl, unsure which one to pick, before finally stopping at Addison and making the "I love you" gesture.

Darcie gasped, holding her mouth to a giggling Addison and Nate, and feigned sadness.

Lizzie stroked Darcie's bare leg that hung out of the duvet. She pointed her hand to herself, making a cross with her arms across her heart before pointing her finger back to Darcie, who watched her, speechless.

"We taught her the other 'I love you' too," Nate said nonchalantly.

"Yeah, I see that," Darcie nodded shocked, searching Lizzie's face for some sort of clarity.

Lizzie watched the surprised look on her face, and this time mouthed "I love you" to Darcie, enforcing the statement.

Chapter Forty-Three

"Have a wonderful time, honey, and look after each other," Darcie's mother stated, hugging Lizzie and Darcie individually. "And we'll see you tomorrow."

"I'll get you a gift." Darcie waved back to them.

"Ohhh, we're going somewhere that you can get gifts!" Lizzie squealed to Darcie's parents who both laughed at her.

"Get in the car, goofball."

"Drive safe, sweetie," Darcie's mother called after them.

"So… you better make yourself at home. I got snacks, water, and magazines for you," she advised.

"You're the sweetest," Lizzie leaned over and kissed her cheek. "How long will it be until we get there?"

"A while actually, but it's a nice journey. It'll be like four hours, maybe a little less," she confirmed.

"Okay, guess I best get comfortable then." She smiled, resting her hand on Darcie's thigh.

*

Darcie pulled into the parking lot, gently nudging Lizzie. "Hey baby, we're here."

"I'm so sorry," she apologized. "I'm a rubbish driving companion."

"Don't be silly." She took her hand. "It's fine, I enjoyed watching you sleep. You okay, or do you need to—"

349

"Hell no!" Lizzie blurted, hearing Darcie laugh. "So, you brought me to Four Corners Monument?" She smiled at the sign.

"I did. Have you been here before?"

"No, but I've always wanted to." She crinkled her nose. "Thank you for knowing me, and knowing what I want and like. Thank you for being the amazing woman you are. Te quiero," she whispered, leaning in and kissing Darcie.

"You're going all out with this 'wowing' me in all languages, huh?"

"Are you impressed?"

"You betcha. I'll make sure tonight is as special as what you learning different languages makes me feel." She smiled. "Come on, let's get going."

"You know, you really need to start thinking before you speak." Lizzie laughed.

"How so?" she asked, confused.

"Well, you've just told me you're going to make tonight a special evening, then you're just like 'okay, yeah, we need to go now, but you have to wait.' That's like telling a child there's a whole box of chocolates and sweets, but they aren't allowed to eat them yet."

"Are you always this whiney?"

"Affirmative. Hurry up," she laughed getting out of the car.

*

Darcie loved how relaxed Lizzie was becoming. More so with the tactility. It seemed Darcie couldn't keep her hands or her lips off of her, and Lizzie was happy to just go with it. She didn't want to push her too far, especially given

Lizzie's completely valid point; the anticipation when they didn't act on their temptation was through the roof.

"Are you okay?" Lizzie asked, squeezing her hand.

"Honestly, I've never been better. I'm just waiting for… I don't know, like, for it to not be so perfect, I guess."

"The honeymoon period will someday be over, when we're arguing over who's turn it is to wash up, or whose fault it was that a pair of red knickers ended up in the white wash and turned everything pink." She winked.

"You're amazing, Lizzie, honestly. I love you. And I want all of that, with you. I love the thought that I could spend the rest of my life waking up next to you, and going to sleep wrapped in each other's arms. I'd happily dish wash every night, and if there's red panties in the house, I won't care if they go in the white wash as long as I get plenty viewing time of them on you." She raised her eyebrows comedically.

"Oh, you like red underwear, huh?" Lizzie smirked.

"I do. *Oh my god, I do.*"

"Lace?"

"Cut it out, or I may just end up getting us arrested," she said.

"Why? Are you intending on making love to me in four different states in one go?" She laughed.

"Dude, do not say stuff like that. I'll get ideas." She giggled, pulling Lizzie toward her. "You want a picture on it?"

"Not alone. I want you in it. Here, give it to me. Hi, excuse me, would you mind taking a photograph for us?" Lizzie asked a man standing close by. He took the photo, and they thanked him, moving out of the way for others to have a turn.

"Are we staying here this evening?" Lizzie asked.

"No, but stupidly, I think I planned a bit too much for us. There may be no romance tonight. We may just fall right to sleep," she advised concerned.

"I'm sure that won't be the case, but if it is, then I'm happy with naked snuggles." She nudged her shoulder. "Where to now?"

"Sorry, it was kind of short lived here."

"It's fine. There's, erm, not really anything to see, bar that." She giggled, looking around at the emptiness.

"True. I was going to suggest stopping for a bite to eat as we have another few hours in the car."

"Really?" Lizzie asked.

"Yeah. We don't have a great deal of time in the states, so I wanted to make the best of our road trip."

"Well, personally, I'm loving it so far. Are we doing another activity this afternoon, then?"

"Later, like more evening time."

"Oh, great. Will we get a chance to check into the hotel before we go?"

"Why, you that desperate to get in my panties?"

"Oh my gosh, I can't believe you just said that out loud!" she said, looking around. "And no, I'm not. I was merely wondering if we'd have a chance to freshen up before we go to the next thing."

"Oh, I was gonna suggest we stop by a motel if you were that desperate."

"I am not that desperate. I can wait until we get to the hotel this evening. Or worst case, we can find a quiet road to pull over on." She smirked.

"You would not," Darcie asked wide eyed.

"Why ever not? You just suggested pulling over to a 'pay by the hour' motel. *Ever the romantic.*" She rolled her eyes. "That's potentially our second date, and you're trying to pay by the hour." She laughed.

"Sheesh, don't say it like that." She giggled. "And second date only? I was thinking like eighth or ninth? Geez, I'm such a dyke, if that's correct. I literally brought you home to meet my family," she stated, slapping her hand to her head and laughing goofily.

"I'm kidding," Lizzie giggled at Darcie's silliness. "Now, get your head out of the gutter and let's get out of here."

"You're right, it is kind of slutty. I just thought, it's not like anyone would know, and I wouldn't have paid by the hour; I would've paid overnight."

"I can't quite tell if it's slutty or spontaneous." She laughed, getting back into the car. "Anyway, all this talk and we aren't going to get anywhere. Where's our next stop?"

"You'll find out when we get there," Darcie leaned in to kiss her. "You wanna crash for a while? I'll wake you when we get there."

"No, I've already left you lots. I want to enjoy it together. I'll get comfortable," she confirmed, kicking off her flip flops and lifting her feet up on the dash. "Thanks for today, it was awesome. I thoroughly enjoyed it." Lizzie smiled sincerely.

"I'm glad. And if you loved that so much, then good, because that was only a small part of our road trip. I just always thought it was kind of cool. I thought I'd… well, I can't really say swing by—it wasn't really en route."

"Oh really? Why do it then? I hope you didn't feel obliged."

"No way. I wanted to show you some more of me. You know, where I came from, grew up and stuff."

"Well, just so you know, I love every part I've seen already." She raised her eyebrows animatedly.

"You do, huh?" Darcie turned to face her.

"In your words, 'yup, I do.'" She smiled. "You know what I'd really like to see? If we have time?"

"Sure, what? We may need to leave it until tomorrow though, unless it's like New York or the White House." She laughed.

"No, but the White House is definitely on my bucket list. If we have time, I'd really like to see your school."

"My school?" she asked confused.

"Yeah, like your high school. Where you had your first kiss, your first date. Where you spent the weekends with your friends. Your childhood. That kind of thing."

"You're super cute. Well, I didn't factor in those places for our road trip, so when we get back, I'll take you. You can think about it and decide where you want to go. My weekends were mostly spent at games with my dad, though."

Lizzie looked at her quietly.

"Are you okay?"

"Yeah, I'm fine."

"Have you ever been to a basketball or baseball game before?"

"Erm, no," she said awkwardly.

"Would you like me to take you to one? We could take pops. He'd love that. He doesn't get much time to go these days, but only if you want."

Lizzie watched her, wondering if she was just trying to make her feel like a part of the family or if she genuinely wanted to go. "If we have time, that'd be nice," she muttered.

*

They spent the next couple of hours talking about themselves. It started with their childhoods before Darcie soon realized that it was very much one sided and felt guilty from the lack of love and adoration in Lizzie's adolescence. She diverted the conversation as they enjoyed finding out more about each other, from favorite foods, songs, movies, and colors.

"Okay, so we're here..."

"Oh... my... gosh..." Lizzie threw her book to the floor. "You brought me to the Grand Canyon?!" she shouted.

Darcie looked at her surprised. "Um, is that okay?"

"*Is that okay*? Are you kidding me right now? Oh my gosh, Darce, you've done way too much. I can't believe you've done all this."

"It really isn't much, but before you cut me off, we literally have 20 minutes if you want to very quickly check into our hotel room and freshen up."

"20 minutes until what? Are we going down there tonight?"

"Cut it out. Just get out and hurry up."

*

"I still can't believe you brought me here."

"I still can't believe that you're *still* going on about it. It's fine. I said I wanted to, and you can thank me later," she stated, handing the printed paper ticket to the guy.

"Oh, believe me, I will. We may just need to book another night here because I think you deserve at least a full 24 hours of gratitude." She winked, allowing her fingers to close around Darcie's hand.

"Wow, if I knew all I needed to do was take you out someplace special for you to become a woman all consumed by sex, I would've asked you out on a date sooner into your family vacation." She winked. "Come on, sexy, let's get this over with so I can get my repayment." Lizzie playfully hit her shoulder. "Ouch," Darcie yelled, rubbing her arm. "I was *kidding.*"

Lizzie stepped up onto the helicopter, still completely at a loss for words. She smiled to the couple already in their seats as she slipped in beside Darcie and put the seatbelt and headset on. Moments later, the engines roared, and they soared up and out into the sunset.

Lizzie was mesmerized by the beauty. As they gently drifted along the Colorado River, she watched the evening and the expanse of the Canyon draw in. She felt Darcie's hand cover her thigh as she stroked her thumb across her leg. Lizzie looked up, and saw Darcie mouth, "you okay?" She nodded slowly, motioning for Darcie to come closer to the window to watch with her.

Darcie couldn't believe that someone so highly traveled could be so captivated by it all. The all-encompassing view was incredible, but she never expected anything so perfect—the tranquility, the gentle thrumming, the overall beauty surrounding them. The scene and the company were complete perfection.

Chapter Forty-Four

"I'm longing to kiss you," Lizzie advised, searching Darcie's light pink lips slightly aglow by the sunset illuminating the canyon.

"So, do it then."

"I don't want to. Not here, around people. I want it to be engulfed with my feelings, my emotions. I want it to be personal, private to you and me. Alone. I want it to be everything. I want to give you everything you've given me today in a single kiss. A kiss... you'll remember forever.

Darcie could barely catch her breath at Lizzie's words. She lifted the champagne to touch Lizzie's glass. "I can't wait for that kiss. The explanation alone will stay with me forever," she stated with meaning and purpose.

They were taken out of the moment as the pilot rounded them up to re-enter the helicopter. They finished the last of their champagne, taking a few more pictures before getting back in. "Thank you for today. Seriously, you have no idea," Lizzie spoke shyly, putting the headset back on.

Darcie lifted one side to uncover her ear. "It isn't over just yet." She smiled.

*

Darcie felt butterflies in her tummy. She couldn't wait for Lizzie to take it in. She was so besotted by the grains of pink on her side of the helicopter that she was completely oblivious to the opposite and frontal views outside. She waited until Lizzie finished taking the photo before diverting her attention elsewhere. Even over all the noise in the helicopter, she was certain she'd heard her gasps. Darcie watched her eyes illuminate from the bright lights of Las Vegas as the helicopter glided above the strip. Darcie missed every second of the memorable flight and scenes, instead opting for the meaningful vision of Lizzie consumed by the beauty around her.

Lizzie couldn't believe it; she was in Vegas. It was exactly as she'd always pictured it. *Bright, big... amazing. It was like a make-pretend film set. Like Legos*, she thought. It was incredible. Her heart stopped as the flight continued. "Oh my gosh," she said aloud as they flew past the Bellagio hotel, the water fountains springing to life. She grabbed Darcie's leg and pointed it out. She'd read about them, seen them in TV shows and movies, but never experienced the fountains in real life. They were incredible. This was incredible. Darcie created perfection for her. It was the most romantic, and best date she'd ever been on in her entire life.

*

"You okay?"

"What part of me couldn't be?" Lizzie responded seriously. "Every part of today has been just perfect. Are you okay?"

"Like you said, how could I not be? I don't think I've ever felt more connected to anyone more than I have with you," she said sincerely. "And I don't mean on a sexual level. I mean, yes, obviously, but everything you said before at the Canyon, I don't think I've ever experienced anything like that. It's the weirdest thing. I thought back to

Iconica when you were saying all that stuff about teasing, and foreplay, and anticipation. I was so like, 'this girl is cray cray.'" She laughed, moving her hand to Lizzie's bare shoulder. "Maybe I'm not making much sense, but I—"

"I think you are. I know you thought it was weird, but I honestly do believe it just creates this intensity. And for me, what I was trying to construe today... I wanted to say so much with that kiss, and given the opportunity, I think you'd have known what I was striving to achieve."

"You know, nothing could have portrayed that more than when we got home and the interactions we've had since, Lizzie. I've never been ashamed, or afraid to show my love for another, and I would've loved to kiss you in that moment. But after seeing and hearing your explanation, and as you say..." she rolled her eyes, "...the temptation and anticipation, the build-up, and then seeing your face in Vegas, I was glad we waited. When we got to the hotel, I felt like everything was in slow motion. You made me feel like the world stopped for everyone but us, and I felt everything in that one kiss alone. Truth be told, I've felt it in every kiss and every touch since. There's no place I'd rather be than here with you right now," she said seriously.

"That's lovely to hear because your gestures today have also made me feel like everything I think you feel is what you hoped to convey."

"How do you think I feel?"

"Ohhh." Lizzie covered her face shyly. "Don't ask me that."

"I don't want to make you feel bad. I just wondered. You make me feel on top of the world. You make me feel like I'm the luckiest woman alive. You make me feel *alive*, and I just want to be wherever you are. Because if I'm with you,

I know I'll be complete," Darcie answered seriously, watching Lizzie's eyes water.

Lizzie wasn't sure what she felt first—the pull in her chest, a tear begin to fall, or Darcie's sleek finger wipe it away. "Nobody has ever made me feel the way you do. I love you," she said softly.

"It's the truth. You have no idea how much you mean to me, Lizzie."

"I think I do, and I hope you know it's entirely reciprocated. You have no idea how perfect everything felt on holiday, but that's a fraction of what I've felt since then. Thank you for today."

"Thank you for tonight." Darcie leaned in, touching her lips with her own. "I can't quite work out if we're that much in tune, or if you're just that damn good."

"Uh… offensive." She laughed. "Note to self, impress harder. I wasn't aware you were already questioning how 'good' I am."

Darcie scooted closer to Lizzie's naked body. "Baby, I've never doubted how good you are." She smirked. "In fact, you frequently amplify my judgement of how 'good' you are. I should've made it clear I was referring to your intelligence."

Lizzie gave a snorted laugh. "Charming. I'm one of the top specialists in the world, I'll have you know." She giggled. "FYI, I personally think we're just that in tune. At least I hope."

"Yeah, me too," Darcie agreed. She leveled herself on the pillow opposite Lizzie. "Hi." She smiled.

"Hi." Lizzie laughed.

"*So…*"

"*So?*"

"Watcha gonna do about your job?"

"What job? I have no job."

"You know what I mean. Like you say, you're one of the top specialists in the UK. You can't just give that up."

"I'm afraid I already have."

"What do you mean? What are you intending to do?"

"I asked a good friend and mentor if I was able to take a sabbatical. I said it would be for research purposes, so they're aware I'm out of surgery."

"And they bought that?" she asked, lifting her hand out from under the cover, and stroking Lizzie's face gently.

"Seemingly so."

"Do you want to go back to it eventually?"

"No," she responded simply.

"No?" she asked, surprised. "What do you want to do instead?"

"Be with you. That's as far as I got."

"Well, do you want to stay on the boat? Work? Not work? Go to Haiti and help Miss Lovelie? Do you have any idea? I'm concerned. We need to decide. I don't want to leave Jose Luis screwed."

"I'd never do that. And honestly, I don't know. I don't know what to say. I've never had a choice like this," she answered sadly.

"Well, I guess a good place to start is why you don't want to practice medicine here. You'd easily get a job."

"Darce, I've never wanted to do medicine. I was raised for medicine, not the other way around. I don't know what I want because I've never had an option. I guess it makes more sense to have a two year vacation from my life and do what I want. Unfortunately, I have no idea what that is."

"And what happens after two years?" Darcie asked.

Lizzie looked at her seriously, lifting her fingers to stroke her bottom lip. "All I know now is that I want to stay like this forever."

"Me too."

"What about you?" Lizzie changed the focus.

"What?"

"Well, what would you like to do? Where would you like to go?"

"I don't want to say," she said sheepishly.

"Why not? If you want to stay yachting, we'll do that. I'm not—"

"It isn't that."

"Well, what then?"

"I don't care where we are, or what we do. I just want to be with you," Darcie admitted humbly.

"That sounds like perfection. Would you go back to law?"

"There's only one way I'd do that."

"Which is?".

"If it was the only way to be with you."

Lizzie smiled. "I love this. I love you," she confirmed. "You're really going to get bored soon of listening to that." She giggled.

"Are you kidding me? I want to hear that every day. Almost as much as I want to go to bed like this every night and wake up with you every morning," she added.

"Why would you want to go back into law for me if you hated it so much?"

"Well that's the difference, I guess," she pushed Lizzie's honey blonde locks behind her ear. "I do love law. I always did. I saw what my dad achieved, and I wanted that. I loved it, but I got obsessed. I overlooked life, and everything else. And as a result, I lost my passion for it. The thing is, I *did* love it. That thrill… that rush. I don't want to go back because I worry I'd get embroiled in it again, but if it was my only way to be with you, then screw it. I wouldn't care. The difference is that there's no way I'd choose work over you, so maybe you're all I really needed." She smiled.

"Would you like to go back into it?"

"Nope. I love the Caribbean. I love the relaxed pace."

"Yes, me too. I loved the day at the Bahamas, the normality of it. Just being, and doing what we did as if it was natural. And the bars. I loved that, and the people we met. It was bloody good fun."

"So, let's do that."

"What do you mean?"

"Well, let's find a place in the Caribbean. Of course, it'd have to be where they had regular cruises, like The Bahamas, so we get plenty of customers. We'll get someplace with a pool, and have a party bar."

"You make it sound so easy."

"It is. We're both fortunate enough to have money behind us. The difficulty is deciding where to set up home…"

Lizzie watched the seriousness of her statement, like it really was that simple. "You wanna set up home?"

"If I could, of course."

"Really?"

"Yeah, you don't?"

"No. Yes," she corrected herself. "Yes, of course. If I can ensure a way, then I promise you, I'll find a way." She smiled.

"You would, huh? What, are you planning on proposing?" Darcie laughed.

"Why should I propose?"

"Elizabeth, Elizabeth, Elizabeth. Are you looking for *me* to propose?" she asked menacingly.

"Be quiet."

"Okay, serious question. If I asked you to marry me, would you say yes?"

"Why ask such questions? This could potentially ruin our day."

"Nothing would ever ruin this day," Darcie responded seriously. "I guess for me, it's affirmation. If I'd have thought you'd say yes, especially after seeing your reaction to my surprise, I'd do today all over again, but pay extra for a private ride. When we flew over the strip, I'd propose, and you'd never be able to say no. It's beautiful, you gotta admit." She laughed.

"10 out of 10 for effort." Lizzie laughed with her.

"Only 10 out of 10? I'm offended." Darcie winked. "You reckon you got better?"

"Lots better actually," Lizzie confirmed, moving in, and laying on her chest.

"Really? So, we're getting married, huh?"

Lizzie laughed at their simple idiocy and kissed her again.

"Okay, seriously, nothing bad will come of this question. Would you do it?" Darcie asked.

"What?"

"Marriage."

Lizzie sighed. "Please, let's not fall out."

"Lizzie, even if you told me you'd never ever marry me, yeah, I'd be sad—"

"Don't you dare even finish that sentence," Lizzie warned, leaning up in bed and looking seriously at Darcie. "Don't. There's no part of me that wouldn't marry you someday, but no, of course I wouldn't right now. Not until we decipher what the hell we're going to do."

"So... you're saying you *do* wanna marry me? That's what I got," Darcie winked, with a twinkle in her eye.

"In your words, 'cut it out.'" She smirked. "Come on, it's late. We've got a long drive tomorrow. We should sleep."

"*Sleep*? Are you for real? You just told me you're gonna marry me. Baby girl, I've got other plans for you tonight," Darcie laughed, diving under the covers and hearing Lizzie squeal.

Chapter Forty-Five

"Hey, sweetie, you okay?" Darcie's mom asked Lizzie.

"Yes, I'm fine. Did you have a good day today? I was sorry you didn't make it."

"Oh, sports aren't my thing. I hear you had a good time, though," Linda questioned, sitting in the patio chair next to her.

"Yes, it was incredible."

"You all packed?"

"Yes," she said sadly.

"So, what's with the sadness?"

"Oh, I'm fine," she answered seriously. "I was just thinking."

"Others may buy that, but I don't. Look, Lizzie, Darcie told me everything…"

"Everything!?" she spat.

"Yes, and I know it's difficult for you, but—"

"OH my god… she told you she slept with my sister?"

"She *slept* with your sister!?" her mother cried.

"Shit, you didn't know?"

"What? *No!*" her mother said incredulously.

"You said she told you everything."

"I thought she did," she said confused. "Look, Lizzie, I don't know what's happened here, but that isn't like Darcie."

"Linda, don't worry. That's not what I'm thinking about. Seriously, it wasn't that; I've gotten over the whole sister thing. I just thought that's what you were talking about."

"No, not at all. I was referring to your family situation, love. I meant that Darcie told me about the way your family is with you, and the way they behaved when you were on vacation. How they treat you, and what you've had to deal with throughout your life. You looked sad and I assumed it might have something to do with us?"

"Oh, right. I see. Yes, you're right, but I don't need pity," she stated sadly.

"I'm not pitying you, sweetie. I feel hurt and pained because you're one of the most beautiful people I've ever met, and it troubles me you've had to deal with that all your life. I hate that I can't take that away, but I'll say this much. I've never seen Darcie like this before, and I think you guys are meant to be. Like truly meant to be. I think you're her 'forever' and I'd make sure that you're loved and treated as wonderfully as you should be, by Robert and me. You've become part of our family this week, Lizzie, and I couldn't be happier of the new daughter we've gained. Holidays, vacations, family parties—you're here for the long haul now, love, and we'll ensure that you never have to feel anything, but love, kinship, adoration, and everything else you truly deserve." Linda placed her hand over Lizzie's.

"You're too kind. It's no wonder Darcie is as beautiful as she is, considering the direction you've both given her. You truly have a wonderful family, and instilled such incredible values in both of your daughters.

"You too have a wonderful family now, Lizzie. Don't be sad, this is just the beginning." She smiled, and the door opened.

"Hey, here you both are," Darcie announced.

"I'll leave you girls to it. Remember, just the beginning," Linda stroked Lizzie's cheek and kissed her on the forehead. "She's a keeper, Darce. Treat her well," her mother squeezed Lizzie's knee and kissed her daughter as she left.

"What was that about? Are you okay?" Darcie asked, taking her mom's seat.

"Yes, I'm fine. Although, I may have just disclosed to your mother that you slept with my sister," she said awkwardly.

"You did what!?" Darcie shrieked.

"I'm afraid so. I'm sorry."

"How the hell did that happen? What did... why..."

"Shush baby, it's fine. Let's just forget about it. Your mom and dad are amazing. Thanks for today. I had the best time ever at the game." She smiled widely.

"Well, in that case, you may wanna open this," Darcie offered, leaving her questions for later. For a time when Lizzie was less upset.

"What is it?" Lizzie asked quietly.

"Open it and find out." Lizzie opened the paper slowly, feeling Darcie's eyes on her. She could see the white material as she pulled out the top. "I figured now that you've been to your first game, you should probably become an honorary Suns fan." She smiled. "I hope you like it."

"I do. I really do. Why are you so amazing?" Lizzie asked.

"I'm not, baby. I'm just in love, and this is what you do when you're in love," she confirmed, stroking her face softly. "You okay about leaving tomorrow?"

"Yes. I'll be sad to leave your family, but I'm looking forward to going back home. Well, not home, but somewhere… umm…"

"It's okay, I know what you mean. Thank you for coming home with me. My folks love you. I knew they would, but it's been far better than what I could've wished for. I love you more than anything else in this world. I truly do."

"You do, huh?" She smiled shyly.

"I really do. I don't care what it takes, Lizzie, but I swear, I'm never losing you again. You're my life, my future. You're all I've ever wanted and all I'll ever need. I loved you before I met you, Lizzie, and I'll continue to love you a little more each day for the rest of my life. You're my one, Lizzie. You're *my one,*" she whispered, kissing her lips softly.

Epilogue

Are you sure about this? Lizzie texted her brother-in-law.

How much more are we going to discuss this? It's today, yes?
P.S. send me a pic.
P.P.S. I know things have always been a little strained between us, but I hope, given our newfound friendship this past year, you may be happy for me. Say hello to your new niece or nephew. x

Lizzie finished reading the message and took a deep breath. Bella and Ollie were pregnant. The first grandchild in the family. Maybe it would make up from her being AWOL.

Oliver, that's incredible. Ok, I'm doing it. Eeeekkk.

Lizzie checked the time and breathed in deeply. She pulled the silicone balls out and melted the chocolate in the pan. She filled two of them with the melted chocolate and placed them in the fridge. After showering she threw a t-shirt on, allowing her blonde waves to fall wet on her shoulders, and dry naturally. Something her mother hated. But that was irrelevant. Her mother didn't matter in her life now. Her life was with Darcie.

Lizzie looked at the clock, cursing at how little time she had left. She lit the burner onto the highest heat and placed the pan on top. Pulling the silicones from the fridge, happy they'd already set, she grabbed the diamond international bag and retrieved its contents. She took the two-chocolate bowls from the casings and turned the heated pan upside down. Carefully taking the first chocolate bowl, she rubbed it on the bottom of the heat, watching it melt the edges a little. She left it a few seconds, copying the process with the second bowl, and slipped the contents inside the chocolate. She switched off the gas and slowly stuck the two melted components together. She waited until she was confident of the results and placed the chocolate back into the fridge.

Lizzie grabbed her phone, and sent a message to Darcie, telling her to come straight upstairs when she arrived home. She turned on the AC, got changed, and tried to ignore her racing heart upon hearing the door open.

*

"*Jesus!*" Darcie shouted as she rushed through their bedroom door. "Wha... um... what?" She shook her head, trying to string a sentence together. "You look amazing," she confirmed, looking at her girlfriend laid across their bed in nothing but a red lace underwear set. It was cold in the room from the air conditioning, and that showed through her bra. Darcie moved to the opposite side of the bed, carefully sidestepping the plate of chocolate.

"Charming. I get you dessert, and you ignore it," Lizzie complained.

"I thought you *were* dessert." Darcie was unable to take her eyes off Lizzie. "You look freaking awesome."

"Thank you, I believe you once told me that you liked it."

"You remembered?" Darcie questioned.

"I did, and that you love chocolate," she confirmed, pushing it towards her.

"I love it. Hmmm, where'd you get it from?" she asked, smelling the chocolate. "What is it?" Darcie shook the chocolate egg, feeling and hearing something inside. She watched Lizzie suspiciously as she put the egg to her mouth and slowly and seductively began sucking the chocolate. Lizzie watched her, unable to contain the sexual desperation taking over her mind and body from Darcie softly and delicately sucking the home-made egg. The fine chocolate took minimal time to melt as Darcie sucked her way through it. Finally, she considered the large gape, and let out a deep gasp, her eyes widening as she looked erratically from the egg to her girlfriend.

Lizzie moved over, straddling Darcie. She watched her examine her partially naked body and grabbed Darcie's hand, opening her finger tips and taking the egg. She emptied the contents into her hand. Darcie gasped again, about to speak, but Lizzie covered her lips with her finger. "It's not quite marriage, but I figured it's the next best thing. An eternity ring. I'd like to be committed to you for eternity, and I was kind of hoping you'd want the same," Lizzie said, holding up two black bands, each embedded with a simple heart diamond. "Sorry if they're too manly."

"They're perfect." She allowed a tear to fall as Lizzie pushed the band on her wedding finger. "I love it. I love you, Elizabeth Barrington."

"And I love you, my Darcie. My beautiful, Darcie. So, is that a yes to eternity?" Lizzie asked shyly.

"It is. I do and always will choose you."

"I can't wait for an eternity together," she whispered, giving her the first kiss of many.

THE END

S.L. Gape

About the Author

S.L. Gape enjoys writing, cooking, travelling and photography. She lives in Cheshire with her partner Jen, and currently splits her time between writing and her day job as a Regional HR advisor.

She gets a lot of inspiration from travelling and her experience as a holiday rep for seven years, where she was lucky enough to have lived and worked in Spain, Greece, Bahamas, Egypt and Lapland. She finds writing as a tremendous stress release for her job, and loves to live through the escapism. *Worlds Apart* is her third novel.

Follow her on
Twitter: @louise_7uk
Facebook: S.L. Gape

Other Titles Available From
Triplicity Publishing

Whispers of the Heart by KA Moll. Days after completing her fellowship in pediatric ophthalmology, thirty-five-year-old Aki Williams travels from her home in Los Angeles to a small town in Illinois, interviewing for a job that she doesn't want. What she does want is to meet her biological sister, Jack Camdon, a sister whom she didn't know existed until she dreamt of her. Three years ago on Sunday, forty-three-year-old professor of archaeology, Carsyn Lyndon, lost her parents and her wife in a tragic accident. Since then, she's suffered from PTSD and loneliness. She's kind-hearted and handsome but dates no one. When she meets Aki at her four-year-old Godson's birthday party, they're incredibly attracted to one another, and those feelings intensify during a family camping trip— a particularly interesting development for Aki since prior to that she'd never considered that she might be a lesbian.

Worlds Apart by S.L. Gape. Hollywood A-lister Heidi Spencer-Brady is everything you'd expect of an Idol. Loved by all, the British Beauty is graceful, talented, humble and so far removed from the 'typical' LA scene. When her husband's infidelity with his new 'leading lady' is leaked, Dawn, Heidi's best friend and manager, goes all out to protect her. She arranges for Heidi to go back to the UK and stay on her cousins farm they had visited as children, much to the disappointment of the animal fearing Heidi.

Castor Valley (Law & Order Series Book 2) by Graysen Morgen. Jessie Henry is torn when she reads about the capture of the Doyle brothers, two young men who were part of her old gang. Unable to let them hang for a crime she's sure they didn't commit, Jessie leaves her wife and the Town of Boone Creek behind, and sets out on a journey back to the one place she thought she'd never see again, *Castor Valley*. Ellie Henry watches the love of her life leave, not knowing if she will ever return. When she gets an odd telegram, nearly a week later, she fears Jessie is in trouble. With no other choice, she goes to the one person who can help her.

Close Enough to Touch by Cade Brogan. Joanna Grey injects the deadly poison into the chamber of the syringe—time after time. She's murdered before and she'll do it again. She's intelligent, educated, and beautiful. Rylee Hayes is a respected homicide detective. Her best friends are her grandparents, her coonhound, and her partner—in that order. Kenzie Bigham is the single mom of a thirteen-year-old, a church secretary, and a woman who's struggled much of her adult life with her own sexuality. Their paths will cross when Rylee's new investigation involves members of Kenzie's congregation. Will Rylee have what it takes to meet the challenge of a serial killer who's proven herself to be a more than worthy opponent?

Fight to the Top by S. L. Gape. Georgia is a forty year old, single, Area Director from Manchester, UK who is all work and definitely no play. Having no time to socialise or spend time with her family she prides herself on being fit and well-polished. Erika is an Area Director for the same company, but in the United States. Whilst she is concentrating so heavily on the promotion she has been fighting for, she's starting to feel like her life outside of work is falling apart. The two women are exceptionally different, and worlds apart. Both of their lives are turned upside down when their jobs are snatched from under their noses, and they are suddenly faced with being thrown together by their bosses for one last major project...in Texas.

Boone Creek (Law & Order Series book 1) by Graysen Morgen. Jessie Henry is looking for a new life. She's unknown in the town of Boone Creek when she arrives, and wants to keep it that way. When she's offered the job of Town Marshal, she takes it, believing that protecting others and upholding the law is the penance for her past. Ellie Fray is a widowed, shopkeeper. She generally keeps to herself, but the mysterious new Town Marshal both intrigues and infuriates her. She believes the last thing the town needs is someone stirring up trouble with the outlaws who have taken over.

Witness by Joan L. Anderson. Becca and Kate have lived together for eight years, and have always spent their vacation in a tropical paradise, lying on a beach. This year, Becca wanted to try something different: a seven day, 65-mile hike in the beautiful Cascade Mountains of Washington state. Their peaceful vacation turns to horror when they stumble upon a brutal murder taking place in the back country.

Too Soon by S.L. Gape. Brooke is a twenty-nine year old detective from Oxford, who has her life pretty much planned out until her boss and partner of nine years, Maria, tells her their relationship is over. When Brooke finds out the truth, that Maria cheated on her with their best friend Paula, she decides to get her life back on track by getting away for six weeks in Anglesey, North Wales. Chloe, a thirty three year old artist and art director, owns a log cabin on Anglesey where she spends each weekend painting and surfing. After returning from a surf, she stumbles upon the somewhat uptight and enigmatic Brooke.

Blue Ice Landing by KA Moll. Coy is a beautiful blonde with a southern accent and a successful practice as a physician assistant. She has a comfortable home, good friends, and a loving family. She's also a widow, carrying a burden of responsibility for her wife's untimely death. Coby is a woman with secrets. She's estranged from her family, a recovering alcoholic, and alone because she's convinced that she's unlovable. When she loses her job as a heavy equipment operator, she'll accept one that'll force her to step way outside her comfort zone. When Coy quits her job to accept a position in Antarctica, her path will cross with Coby's. Their attraction to one another will be immediate, and despite their differences, it won't be long before they fall in love. But for these two, with all their baggage, will love be enough?

Never Quit (Never Series book 2) by Graysen Morgen. Two years after stepping away from the action as a Coast Guard Rescue Swimmer to become an instructor, Finley finds herself in charge of the most difficult class of cadets she's ever faced, while also juggling the taxing demands of having a home life with her partner Nicole, and their fifteen year old daughter. Jordy Ross gave up everything, dropping out of college, and leaving her family behind, to join the Coast Guard and become a rescue swimmer cadet. The extreme training tests her fitness level, pushing her mentally and physically further than she's ever been in her life, but it's the aggressive competition between her and another female cadet that proves to be the most challenging.

For a Moment's Indiscretion by KA Moll. With ten years of marriage under their belt, Zane and Jaina are coasting. The little things they used to do for one another have fallen by the wayside. They've gotten busy with life. They've forgotten to nurture their love and relationship. Even soul mates can stumble on hard times and have marital difficulties. Enter Amelia, a new faculty member in Jaina's building. She's new in town, young, and very pretty. When an argument with Zane causes Jaina to storm out angry, she reaches out to Amelia. Of course, she seizes the opportunity. And for a moment of indiscretion, Jaina could lose everything.

Never Let Go (Never Series book 1) by Graysen Morgen. For Coast Guard Rescue Swimmer, Finley Morris, life is good. She loves her job, is well respected by her peers, and has been given an opportunity to take her career to the next level. The only thing missing is the love of her life, who walked out, taking their daughter with her, seven years earlier. When Finley gets a call from her ex, saying their teenage daughter is coming to spend the summer with her, she's floored. While spending more time with her daughter, whom she doesn't get to see often, and learning to be a full-time parent, Finley quickly realizes she has not, and will never, let go of what is important.

Pursuit by Joan L. Anderson. Claire is a workaholic attorney who flies to Paris to lick her wounds after being dumped by her girlfriend of seventeen years. On the plane she chats with the young woman sitting next to her, and when they land the woman is inexplicably detained in Customs. Claire is surprised when she later runs into the woman in the city. They agree to meet for breakfast the next morning, but when the woman doesn't show up Claire goes to her hotel and makes a horrifying discovery. She soon finds herself ensnared in a web of intrigue and international terrorism, becoming the target of a high stakes game of cat and mouse through the streets of Paris.

Wrecked by Sydney Canyon. To most people, the *Duchess* is a myth formed by old pirates tales, but to Reid Cavanaugh, a Caribbean island bum and one of the best divers and treasure hunters in the world, it's a real, seventeenth century pirate ship—the holy grail of underwater treasure hunting. Reid uses the same cunning tactics she always has before setting out to find the lost ship. However, she is forced to bring her business partner's daughter along as collateral this time because he doesn't trust her. Neither woman is thrilled, but being cooped up on a small dive boat for days, forces them to get know each other quickly.

Arson by Austen Thorne. Madison Drake is a detective for the Stetson Beach Police Department. The last thing she wants to do is show a new detective the ropes, especially when a fire investigation becomes arson to cover up a murder. Madison butts heads with Tara, her trainee, deals with sarcasm from Nic, her ex-girlfriend who is a patrol officer, and finds calm in the chaos of police work with Jamie, her best friend who is the county medical examiner. Arson is the first of many in a series of novella episodes surrounding the fictional Stetson Beach Police Department and Detective Madison Drake.

Change of Heart by KA Moll. Courtney Holloman is a woman at the top of her game. She's successful, wealthy, and a highly sought after Washington lobbyist. She has money, her job, booze, and nothing else. In quiet moments, against her will, her mind drifts back to her days in high school and to all that she gave up. Jack Camdon is a complex woman, and yet not at all. She is also a woman who has never moved beyond the sudden and unexplained departure of her high school sweetheart, her lover, and her soul mate. When circumstances bring Courtney back to town two decades later, their paths will cross. Will it be too late?

Mommies (Bridal Series book 3) by Graysen Morgen. Britton and her wife Daphne have been married for a year and a half and are happy with their life, until Britton's mother hounds her to find out why her sister Bridget hasn't decided to have children yet. This prompts Daphne to bring up the big subject of having kids of their own with Britton. Britton hadn't really thought much about having kids, but her love for Daphne makes her see life and their future together in a whole new way when they decide to become mommies.

Haunting Love by K.A. Moll. Anna Crestwood was raised in the strict beliefs of a religious sect nestled in the foothills of the Smoky Mountains. She's a lesbian with a ton of baggage—fearful, guilty, and alone. Very few things would compel her to leave the familiar. The job offer of a lifetime is one of them. Gabe Garst is a police officer. She's also a powerful medium. Her work with juvenile delinquents and ghosts is all that keeps her going. Inside she's dead, certain that her capacity to love is buried six feet under. Anna and Gabe's paths cross. Their attraction is immediate, but they hold back until all hope seems lost.

Rapture & Rogue by Sydney Canyon. Taren Rauley is happy and in a good relationship, until the one person she thought she'd never see again comes back into her life. She struggles to keep the past from colliding with the present as old feelings she thought were dead and gone, begin to haunt her. In college, Gianna Revisi was a mastermind, ring-leading, crime boss. Now, she has a great life and spends her time running Rapture and Rogue, the two establishments she built from the ground up. The last person she ever expects to see walk into one of them, is the girl who walked out on her, breaking her heart five years ago.

Second Chance by Sydney Canyon. After an attack on her convoy, Marine Corps Staff Sergeant, Darien Hollister, must learn to live without her sight. When an experimental procedure allows her to see again, Darien is torn, knowing someone had to die in order for this to happen.

She embarks on a journey to personally thank the donor's family, but is too stunned to tell them the truth. Mixed emotions stir inside of her as she slowly gets to the know the people that feel like so much more than strangers to her. When the truth finally comes out, Darien walks away, taking the second chance that she's been given to go back to the only life she's ever known, but she's not the only one with a second chance at life.

Meant to Be by Graysen Morgen. Brandt is about to walk down the aisle with her girlfriend, when an unexpected chain of events turns her world upside down, causing her to question the last three years of her life. A chance encounter sparks a mix of rage and excitement that she has never felt before. Summer is living life and following her dreams, all the while, harboring a huge secret that could ruin her career. She believes that some things are better kept in the dark, until she has her third run-in with a woman she had hoped to never see again, and gives into temptation. Brandt and Summer start believing everything happens for a reason as they learn the true meaning of meant to be.

Coming Home by Graysen Morgen. After tragedy derails TJ Abernathy's life, she packs up her three year old son and heads back to Pennsylvania to live with her grandmother on the family farm. TJ picks back up where she left off eight years earlier, tending to the fruit and nut tree orchard, while learning her grandmother's secret trade. Soon, TJ's high school sweetheart and the same girl who broke her heart, comes back into her life, threatening to steal it away once again. As the weeks turn into months and tragedy strikes again, TJ realizes coming home was the best thing she could've ever done.

Special Assignment by Austen Thorne. Secret Service Agent Parker Meeks has her hands full when she gets her new assignment, protecting a Congressman's teenage daughter, who has had threats made on her life and been whisked away to a Christian boarding school under an alias to finish out her senior year. Parker is fine with the assignment, until she finds out she has to go undercover as a Canon Priest. The last thing Parker expects to find is a beautiful, art history teacher, who is intrigued by her in more ways than one.

Miracle at Christmas by Sydney Canyon. A Modern Twist on the Classic Scrooge Story. Dylan is a power-hungry lawyer who pushed away everything good in her life to become the best defense attorney in the, often winning the worst cases and keeping anyone with enough money out of jail. She's visited on Christmas Eve by her deceased law partner, who threatens her with a life in hell like his own, if she doesn't change her path. During the course of the night, she is taken on a journey through her past, present, and future with three very different spirits.

Bella Vita by Sydney Canyon. Brady is the First Officer of the crew on the Bella Vita, a luxury charter yacht in the Caribbean. She enjoys the laidback island lifestyle, and is accustomed to high profile guests, but when a U.S. Senator charters the yacht as a gift to his beautiful twin daughters who have just graduated from college and a few of their friends, she literally has her hands full.

Brides (Bridal Series book 2) by Graysen Morgen. Britton Prescott is dating the love of her life, Daphne Attwood, after a few tumultuous events that happened to unravel at her sister's wedding reception, seven months earlier. She's happy with the way things are, but immense pressure from her family and friends to take the next step, nearly sends her back to the single life. The idea of a long engagement and simple wedding are thrown out the window, as both families take over, rushing Britton and Daphne to the altar in a matter of weeks.

Cypress Lake by Graysen Morgen. The small town of Cypress Lake is rocked when one murder after another happens. Dani Ricketts, the Chief Deputy for the Cypress Lake Sheriff's Office, realizes the murders are linked. She's surprised when the girl that broke her heart in high school has not only returned home, but she's also Dani's only suspect. Kristen Malone has come back to Cypress Lake to put the past behind her so that she can move on with her life. Seeing Dani Ricketts again throws her off-guard, nearly derailing her plans to finally rid herself and her family of Cypress Lake.

Crashing Waves by Graysen Morgen. After a tragic accident, Pro Surfer, Rory Eden, spends her days hiding in the surf and snowboard manufacturing company that she built from the ground up, while living her life as a shell of the person that she once was. Rory's world is turned upside when a young surfer pursues her, asking for the one thing she can't do. Adler Troy and Dr. Cason Macauley from Graysen Morgen's bestselling novel: *Falling Snow*, make an appearance in this romantic adventure about life, love, and letting go.

Bridesmaid of Honor (Bridal Series book 1) by Graysen Morgen. Britton Prescott's best friend is getting married and she's the maid of honor. As if that isn't enough to deal with, Britton's sister announces she's getting married in the same month and her maid of honor is her best friend Daphne, the same woman who has tormented Britton for years. Britton has to suck it up and play nice, instead of scratching her eyes out, because she and Daphne are in both weddings. Everyone is counting on them to behave like adults.

Falling Snow by Graysen Morgen. Dr. Cason Macauley, a high-speed trauma surgeon from Denver meets Adler Troy, a professional snowboarder and sparks fly. The last thing Cason wants is a relationship and Adler doesn't realize what's right in front of her until it's gone, but will it be too late?

Fate vs. Destiny by Graysen Morgen. Logan Greer devotes her life to investigating plane crashes for the National Transportation Safety Board. Brooke McCabe is an investigator with the Federal Aviation Association who literally flies by the seat of her pants. When Logan gets tangled in head games with both women will she choose fate or destiny?

Just Me by Graysen Morgen. Wild child Ian Wiley has to grow up and take the reins of the hundred year old family business when tragedy strikes. Cassidy Harland is a little surprised that she came within an inch of picking up a gorgeous stranger in a bar and is shocked to find out that stranger is the new head of her company.

Love Loss Revenge by Graysen Morgen. Rian Casey is an FBI Agent working the biggest case of her career and madly in love with her girlfriend. Her world is turned upside when tragedy strikes. Heartbroken, she tries to rebuild her life. When she discovers the truth behind what really happened that awful night she decides justice isn't good enough, and vows revenge on everyone involved.

Natural Instinct by Graysen Morgen. Chandler Scott is a Marine Biologist who keeps her private life private. Corey Joslen is intrigued by Chandler from the moment she meets her. Chandler is forced to finally open her life up to Corey. It backfires in Corey's face and sends her running. Will either woman learn to trust her natural instinct?

Secluded Heart by Graysen Morgen. Chase Leery is an overworked cardiac surgeon with a group of best friends that have an opinion and a reason for everything. When she meets a new artist named Remy Sheridan at her best friend's art gallery she is captivated by the reclusive woman. When Chase finds out why Remy is so sheltered will she put her career on the line to help her or is it too difficult to love someone with a secluded heart?

In Love, at War by Graysen Morgen. Charley Hayes is in the Army Air Force and stationed at Ford Island in Pearl Harbor. She is the commanding officer of her own female-only service squadron and doing the one thing she loves most, repairing airplanes. Life is good for Charley, until the day she finds herself falling in love while fighting for her life as her country is thrown haphazardly into World War II. Can she survive being in love and at war?

Fast Pitch by Graysen Morgen. Graham Cahill is a senior in college and the catcher and captain of the softball team. Despite being an all-star pitcher, Bailey Michaels is young and arrogant. Graham and Bailey are forced to get to know each other off the field in order to learn to work together on the field. Will the extra time pay off or will it drive a nail through the team?

S.L. Gape

Submerged by Graysen Morgen. Assistant District Attorney Layne Carmichael had no idea that the sexy woman she took home from a local bar for a one night stand would turn out to be someone she would be prosecuting months later. Scooter is a Naval Officer on a submarine who changes women like she changes uniforms. When she is accused of a heinous crime she is shocked to see her latest conquest sitting across from her as the prosecuting attorney.

Vow of Solitude by Austen Thorne. Detective Jordan Denali is in a fight for her life against the ghosts from her past and a Serial Killer taunting her with his every move. She lives a life of solitude and plans to keep it that way. When Callie Marceau, a curious Medical Examiner, decides she wants in on the biggest case of her career, as well as, Jordan's life, Jordan is powerless to stop her.

Igniting Temptation by Sydney Canyon. Mackenzie Trotter is the Head of Pediatrics at the local hospital. Her life takes a rather unexpected turn when she meets a flirtatious, beautiful fire fighter. Both women soon discover it doesn't take much to ignite temptation.

One Night by Sydney Canyon. While on a business trip, Caylen Jarrett spends an amazing night with a beautiful stripper. Months later, she is shocked and confused when that same woman re-enters her life. The fact that this stranger could destroy her career doesn't bother her. C.J. is more terrified of the feelings this woman stirs in her. Could she have fallen in love in one night and not even known it?

Nautical Delights

Fine by Sydney Canyon. Collin Anderson hides behind a façade, pretending everything is fine. Her workaholic wife and best friend are both oblivious as she goes on an emotional journey, battling a potentially hereditary disease that her mother has been diagnosed with. The only person who knows what is really going on, is Collin's doctor. The same doctor, who is an acquaintance that she's always been attracted to, and who has a partner of her own.

Shadow's Eyes by Sydney Canyon. Tyler McCain is the owner of a large ranch that breeds and sells different types of horses. She isn't exactly thrilled when a Hollywood movie producer shows up wanting to film his latest movie on her property. Reegan Delsol is an up and coming actress who has everything going for her when she lands the lead role in a new film, but there one small problem that could blow the entire picture.

Light Reading: A Collection of Novellas by Sydney Canyon. Four of Sydney Canyon's novellas together in one book, including the bestsellers Shadow's Eyes and One Night.

Visit us at www.tri-pub.com